KEEPING SCORE

Playing for Keeps Duet

SAMANTHA BARRETT

PART

ONE

For Leah,
I hope this retelling of your epic could have been fairytale is what you
hoped it would be.
Thank you for the amazing story, covers, graphics and friendship.
This is for you babe xxx

This is your warning!

If domestic violence, bullying, drug use, date rape and
degrading is a trigger for you then close the book and move on
to another amazing read.
If you are into some dark shit and get off on possessive as fuck
asshole alpha males, turn the page babe and wrap your heart in
a condom because these boys are about to fuck your feelings, *real
hard*!

Playlist

G-Eazy ft Chris Brown – Provide
Chris Brown – Under The Influence (Body Language)
Jennifer Hudson – Spotlight
Bow Wow ft Chris Brown – Ain't Thinkin' Bout You
Jennifer Lopez and Maluma - Marry Me (Kat & Bastian Duet)
Ella Mai ft Chris Brown - Watchamacallit
Ella Mai - Trip

CHAPTER ONE

Darius

I'm back in the halls of CHU. Crestview Heights University is a dreary fun-sucking cesspit of horny teenagers wanting to fuck their way through the cheer squad or the football team. You would think that after leaving high school these idiots would have sorted their lives out but no, all they want to do is pick an easy major so they can breeze through their classes and party all weekend.

"Senior year, motherfucker!" Saint shouts, so Corvin and I head toward where he, Crue and Beckett wait in line at the coffee cart. I shake my head when Saint begins to twerk in the busy line garnering the attention of all the girls nearby. Every guy here hates us but they also would suck a dick to be us for a day. Corvin, Beckett, Saint, Crue and me, we run this fucking school and have done so since we became the first freshmen to ever make the starting team. Girls throw themselves at us, and unlike the others, I don't fuck the same pussy twice. I have a hit and quit it rule as I don't want any of them catching feelings. I don't have time for that shit.

"Smile, asshole, it won't break your face!" I ignore Crue's jibe as I say what's up to Saint and Beckett. Saint has filled out a lot in the off season. The guys and me have been hitting the gym every day and making sure that we stay in shape and don't slack off. I don't want no fucking newbie coming in here thinking they can take our spots! Beckett stands silently next to Saint and Crue, his green eyes scan the area taking everything in. He runs a hand through his Ivy league styled black hair. Beckett is the quiet one out of the five of us. He may not say much but he hears everything. The guy is like a vault and loyal as fuck.

"You coming to Shayla's party?" Corvin asks as he nudges me with his shoulder. I look over at my best friend and give him my best *are you fucked in the head* look. Corvin is a pretty boy, tanned skin, brown hair cut into a pompadour style haircut, light brown eyes and a smile and body that can melt the panties off any girl. We've been best friends since the third grade and are polar opposites. Corvin lives to party whereas I hate crowds and people touching me. "Come on, it will be fun," he tries to plead.

I fight the eye roll that wants to break free. "You said that last time and then you, Saint and Crue rocked up to practice hungover and coach made us all run laps and do drills until you threw up! I am not fucking doing that again." I cut a glare to Saint and Crue when they begin to laugh. Saint is a prankster, always making jokes about everything. He's a fucking player and loves the ladies as much as they love him. With his blond hair, pale green eyes that almost look yellow and the tapper rich boy haircut just adds to the boy next door look he has going on. Crue is the baby of our group. He's a year younger but super smart and skipped a grade in high school. He's got a baby face that all the girls fall for—if it isn't that they melt at the sight of his blue eyes, the fucker is so vain, he spends at least an hour every morning fixing his blond quiff just to make it look the right kind of messy.

"Dude, this is our last weekend before practice starts. Let lose for once. Shit, even Beck is coming and not fighting us." I shoot Beckett a look, he just shrugs and says,

"YOLO and all that shit." Hearing the big fucker say *YOLO* has the four of us laughing and a rare grin making an appearance on his stoic face. Beck is a closed book, Corv and I met him when we were freshmen in high school. He was a transfer and we know he hasn't had an easy life from little things he has said but he never goes into details about his life. When these three hit the parties Beck and I normally kick back at the house. Only the five of us live there and that's how we like it. We never allow anyone into our house or throw parties there, that was my one rule.

"Yeah, alright. I'm in." The three whore's all high-five each other at my agreement. I stand here regretting my decision already. It's not that I hate people, I just don't like them. There's a difference. I hate the fake fuckers who make small talk or the ones who talk too much, I don't even talk to the girls I fuck. I nod, they squeal and follow me to wherever. I *never* kiss them or fuck from the front—doggy style only. The last girl I ever kissed is someone I should never have touched. She was forbidden to me and still I broke the first rule of bro code, *never fuck your best friend's little sister.*

I push through the front door of our two-story ex frat house. The house is fucking dope and it's all thanks to Saint's dad who owns some tech company that he wants Saint to takeover. The front of the house has four large pillars and a little porch with a love seat that swings out front. Inside, it's all hardwood floors, windows and top of the line appliances—our five bedrooms all have their own bathrooms. The basement is set up like an underground club fit with its own bar. We even have a pool in the backyard. When Saint's dad heard we were all going to CHU and found out they were going to tear this old frat house down, he bought and remodeled the whole thing for the five of us. Saint and his dad may not get on and I can't blame Saint for hating the prick, he wants him to give up football and work for his tech company. Saint can't outright refuse or he will be forced to pay back every cent his father has spent on him, he'll get his revenge soon enough.

I dump my bag on the couch and follow the sounds of laughter toward the theater room that is just off the side of the kitchen. I pause in the doorway frowning when the sound of a girl's laughter hits my ears. I grit my teeth, pissed that these fuckers broke another rule, no hoes are allowed anywhere except our rooms. I never bring girls here, nor does Beck. I barge into the room interrupting whatever conversation they were having. My gaze lands on Corvin and I pin him with a look that he knows all too well. He raises his hands in defeat and cuts a glance to the recliner in front of me, I narrow my eyes as I march around to see who the girl is and kick her ass out.

"Oh, he's mad," Crue fake whispers.

"Big mad you mean," Saint joins in, laughing. I don't see Beckett so he mustn't be home.

"Who's mad?" That voice! The moment I come face to face with the owner of said voice my mood sours even further. I stand in front of her, glaring, my nostrils flare at seeing her so relaxed and comfortable in *my* fucking house! The fact that this dirty little liar can sit before me and look annoyed at the sight of me grates on my fucking nerves. The moment her green eyes lock onto mine, my blood begins to boil as memories flash through my mind. Her blonde hair is longer now but I can see some brown tints through it like she has dyed it to look that two-tone color. She darts her tongue out to wet her lips and swallows audibly.

"I thought we said no *hos* in the house?" I grit out, her eyes widening in outrage. I lift my chin in triumph, knowing that my insult hit its mark. Corvin leaps out of his seat pulling my attention to him, his face a mask of anger.

"That's my fucking sister you're calling a whore, asshole. She can go anywhere she fucking likes in this house, the rules don't apply to her," he snaps. I turn back to face the two-faced bitch who turned my heart to stone as I answer my best friend.

"The rules never applied to her because like the snake she is, she would slither around them anyway." Leah gasps clearly upset at my words. I don't stick around after that, heading straight back out of the house, I jump on my Ducati and peel out of the driveway needing to get the fuck away from her and clear my head. It's all her fault everything went to shit! I have no destination in mind as I fly down the coastal road letting the sea breeze wash over me. Seeing her again has brought all the anger that I fought to keep buried inside me back to the surface. I thought Leah was different. When we were together, she never treated me differently, their family took me in and gave me a home. I gave their daughter my heart and she broke into a million fucking pieces.

It's in this moment a thought hits me, Leah fucked me over so badly I didn't even see it coming. It's my turn for revenge, I'm going to make sure Leah Williams knows just how much I fucking hate her. Her time here at CHU is going to be hell. I'll make sure of it.

CHAPTER TWO

After Darius stormed out, Corvin, Saint and Crue took me out to a local Mexican restaurant where we sat and laughed for hours before the guys dropped me back at my dorm. Settling into my new school has gone smoother than I thought. I expected to have trouble with my roommate but Cody is actually really freaking cool and loves to hang at the beach like me, is on the dance team I just tried out for and doesn't give a shit what anyone thinks of her! The best part though, Cody doesn't push for answers. When she asked me why I transferred, I clammed up, so she dropped the subject straight away and took me to Starbucks. The week has been a cluster of days with me trying to navigate my way around the new school and finding my place among the hordes of people here.

"What have you got after lunch?" Katie asks from her spot next to me on the picnic table, she is beautiful, legs for days, blue eyes, incredible body and has the blonde poofy *Dolly Parton* hair going on. Oh, did I mention she is from the south and has that crazy, sexy twang to her voice?

"Calculus." I groan, making the girls around me pull sour faces. Cody introduced me to her friends on my first day and we all hit it off. It helps that they are on the dance team and has made getting adjusted easier.

"Girl, you are gonna hate it because Mr. Thompson is an ass," Becca supplies, making me feel even more defeated. I suck at all things numbers unless it's the counts for a routine.

"He fails everyone!" Cody interjects. I peer across the table at her, trying to gauge if she is joking. When she doesn't crack a smile, I drop my head to the table and sigh.

"I'm so fucked," I mumble into the wood, causing the girls to laugh.

"Oh shit, three o'clock. We got incoming!" At the excited tone of Chelsea's voice I perk up and look toward where she said, then scrunch my face. Turning back to the girls, I find them all sitting straighter and pushing their chests out. Well not all the girls, Cody and Katie seem annoyed that we have incoming.

"There's my pretty blonde!" I turn to the side and straddle the bench seat as I look up at my brother and his friends. I learnt on my first day that Corv and the others run this place, they are gods amongst us lowly humans. "Gonna introduce us?" Saint teases as he waggles his brows at me, so I throw him a bone.

"Girls meet the guys, guys meet the girls." Saint narrows his eyes playfully at me before walking around the table and straddling the bench seat behind me and rests his chin on my shoulder. Instead of looking at my brother, my gaze snaps to Darius waiting to see his reaction. It's stoic as usual. Him and Beck never allow you to know more than they want you to.

"Get the fuck away from my sister, asshole!" Corvin snarls as he grips Saint over my shoulder and hauls him away from me by his shirt. The girls, gasp gaining my attention. When I look at them, I find their shocked, almost gleeful gaze on me. I look to Cody for an answer but she just rolls her eyes. Unhelpful much?

"You never told us Corvin was your brother?" Becca says in the most high-pitched tone, that I'm sure she thinks is sultry and alluring. My face contorts and this is the part that I hate and the reason I chose to go to a different college. Whenever any of the girls find out that Corv and I are siblings they flock to my feet and pretend to be my friend just to use me to get close to my brother.

"Must have slipped my mind," I mutter as I turn back toward my brother and his friends, shooting him a look that I hope conveys *fuck off*.

"Don't look at me like that!" Corv growls. All that earns him is a raised brow from me, prompting him to get to the point of his unwanted visit. "Fine. I came to see if you wanted to come to a party with us tonight?" The moment the words fly from my brother's mouth, I feel *his* gaze on me, burning a path down my body and bringing it to life like no other can.

"I do–"

Before I can finish declining his offer, Becca, Chelsea, Molly and Zara all agree on my behalf. It grates on my nerves but I don't want to cause trouble on my first week here and alienate myself from the friends I've just made, all because they have the hots for my brother and his friends.

"Cool, well come round about eight and we'll leave from ours," Corvin states. I flick my gaze to Darius as I answer my brother.

"I thought no *hoes* were allowed at your house?" Darius's eyes spark with vexation telling me I just poked the bear. I feel the stares of the others on me but my focus is on the tall, dark, handsome man before me. It should scare the hell out of me but it doesn't, all that look does is excite me.

"He didn–" Before Corv can finish speaking, Darius cuts in.

"It seems this hoe is exempt," he snaps before storming off toward the gym. Beckett follows after him without saying a word. Corv sighs and shoots me a sad smile before racing off after his best friend. He has no idea what happened between me and Darius. Corvin just thinks Darius and I hate each other, that wasn't always the case though.

"Don't mind him, babe. He's just pissed because he has blue balls," Crue says as he shoots me a wink, then he and Saint follow after the others calling out that they'll see me later. I can't pull my eyes off Darius until he disappears inside the gym. How can somebody who used to make you feel like the center of their world change in an instant and make you feel like shit beneath their boots?

"Guurrrlll, we need the goss…" I tune out Becca and the others as they all harp on about what they are going to wear and who they plan to suck and fuck. I don't plan on taking them with me. Katie and Cody are more than welcome because unlike the others, they aren't panting like bitches in heat ready to get some meat between their legs.

When will women learn that desperation isn't attractive?

The girls weren't kidding. Mr. Thompson is an ass!

The asshole chewed me out because I wasn't up to *his* level of where he says I should be. He didn't even cut me some slack when Garrett, a friend of Katie's that she introduced me to on my second day, tried to defend me. Instead of him listening to what Garrett and I were trying to tell him he ordered that Garrett be my tutor! Which is why I am now sitting in the library at five p.m. on a Friday night instead of being in my dorm getting ready to hang with my brother and friends.

"I know this must not be how you envisioned your Friday night." I shake my head to clear my thoughts and smile sheepishly at Garrett. He has been nothing but helpful and I would even go as far as to say kind to me, when I have done nothing but be in a sour mood.

"I'm sorry," I say. "I guess I just didn't expect my first Friday night here at CHU to be spent–"

"With me?" Guilt washes over me.

"That's not what I meant." He begins to pack up his books as he speaks.

"It's okay, I get it. You probably have a boyfriend you have a date with and the last thing you want to be doing is staring at my ugly mug." I balk at him, Garrett may be a lot of things but ugly sure as hell isn't one of them. He has this whole football player cross surfer guy look going on. With blond hair with tinges of brown through it, shorter on the sides and long enough on the top for you to run your fingers through, and eyes that are filled with life and laughter. They are an odd color of blue, but with flecks of green throughout them. It doesn't hurt that even through his shirt you can see he has a killer body. Reaching across the table I place my hand on top of his, halting his movements, his gaze cutting to mine immediately.

"I'm sorry if I made you feel that way." Some of the tension in his shoulders eases at my words. "No, I don't have a boyfriend but I do have a brother and I promised him I would hang out with him and his friends tonight." His face lights up and I cringe internally at the hopeful look in his eyes. I may be single but that doesn't mean I am emotionally available. I haven't been available to anyone in a really long time.

"Well in that case, let's save studying for tomorrow?" A smile breaks out on my face as I eagerly nod and start to pack my things away. "We can do this test Mr. Thompson gave you tomorrow as well so then we can chill on Sunday and not have to worry until Tuesday." I beam across the table at him.

"I knew I liked you!" I declare, a tinge of pink hits his cheeks and I have to duck my gaze, not wanting to see the look I know will be in his eyes. I don't want to give him the wrong impression but I also don't want to be presumptuous so I decide to leave things as they are and wave goodbye to him as I make my way back to my dorm to meet Katie and Cody. No sooner do I walk through the door and the girls are on me to hurry my ass up and shower so we can get ready, have some pre-drinks and head over to my brother's place. We may be underage but this is college and who the hell doesn't have a fake ID these days?

After showering and changing into a pair of denim cut offs, I pull on a camo, thin-strapped singlet that is longer in the back and short in the front, short enough to show off the bottom of my toned stomach. Years of dance have been so good to my body and that is the only reason I'm excited for tonight. I can't wait to feel the music and dance to the beat. I slip my feet into my low cut Chucks, dab a bit of lip gloss on my full lips and apply a tiny bit of mascara that I know will make my green eyes pop. I give myself one last once-over in the mirror before deeming myself ready. One thought lingers in my head as I follow the girls out of our room and head for the lifts.

I wonder if Darius will be there?

CHAPTER THREE

Darius

Leaning against the counter, I watch as Leah shows her friends around *my* fucking house like she has the right to! I have to bite my cheek to keep from lashing out at her. Corv lost his shit at me today in the gym. He went on a rant about how I have to let this *grudge* I have against his sister go. Corvin thinks Leah and I stopped being friendly because she told her friends about my mom. That was a lie and the only one I could think of to throw him off track that his sister rocked my fucking world and then blew it apart. Aside from Corv and the guys, Leah was the best thing in my life until she fucking betrayed me!

I didn't give her a reason why I ended things, I just ghosted her.

When Corv and me came back for Thanksgiving one year and she walked through the door with Gary Hayes, my hatred for her only intensified. She knew better than anyone that Gary is and always has been my arch enemy on and off the field. The bastard plays for the dolphins and we are set to play them for the first game of the season. We are the two top teams and they beat us last year in the finals.

"Glare any harder and your face will crack." I turn to see Beck leaning against the wall opposite me. He has this look whenever he knows something he shouldn't, and right now, he has that fucking look. "How long?"

"How long what?" I snap, He crosses his arms over his large chest and gives me a dry stare.

"How long have you and Corvin's little sister been sleeping together?" I keep my face blank but inside I am a fucking mess. If Corvin ever found out about me and Leah he would kick my ass and I'd let him.

"No idea what you're talking about," I say as I pour myself another drink. I don't like drinking but Leah being around is fucking with my head, so I need something to take the edge off.

"Hm, see, the thing is even when we were in high school you would always pick her out of the crowd. You were always the first to check on her when we got in late to make sure she was sleeping and whenever she needed a ride anywhere you gave it to her." I keep my gaze facing out the window and try to act unaffected by his observations. "Then the last week before we left for college, you changed. You went from being the over-bearing big brother to the jealous ex." I spin toward him as that last word exits his mouth. I didn't realize he had moved until we are standing chest to chest. Beck is a few inches taller than us all and he uses that height difference to his advantage.

"You don't know shit," I seethe.

"See, your answer should have been to laugh off my claim or tell me I was seeing things and talking out my ass. You confirmed what I already knew, without *confirming* it." Before I can rip into him, Corvin enters the room. Beck and I take a step back from each other as we face our friend.

Either Corvin is already tipsy and didn't notice the tension in the room, or he just doesn't give a fuck as he saunters over to us, steals the beer from my hand and shouts. "Let's get drunk bitches!"

This is going to be a long fucking night!

Living where we do everything is within walking distance. Corv, Saint, Crue and the three girls all walk in front of us, while Beck and I take up the rear. Ever since shit with Leah went down, Corv and I have drifted apart. It isn't his fault and he constantly asks what happened to us... why we aren't as close as we used to be. How do I tell my best friend I stopped confiding in him and going to his place for holidays because his sister turned my world upside down?

"I can't wait to dance the night away!" Leah's excitement pulls me from my thoughts. I grit my teeth to keep from lashing out at her and saying something dumb like, *you can dance right the fuck out of my life again.*

"Shayla always throws the best parties," Saint cuts in. "All the cheer squad will be there and those girls can ride a dick like no other." At Saint's words Crue slows his steps until he is walking on my other side, shoves his hands in his pockets and keeps his gaze down. I don't know what the hell is going on with him but I have my suspicions. I just don't want to be the one to voice them until he is ready to admit it.

"Our team could beat the cheer squad," Katie says in a matter-of-fact manner, causing her two friends to cheer and whoop.

"What's the difference between your crew and cheer squad?" Leah balks at Saint like he just said the most insensitive thing in the world. The three girls slam to a stop forcing me to stop walking or risk bumping into Leah. Her back is to me as she stares ahead at her brother and Saint with her hands on her hips. Her perfume assaults me and I fight the urge to not lean in closer and take a whiff—she's always smelt like strawberries and the ocean. A scent I know too well and have grown to hate!

"For one, cheerleaders are there to entertain and hype up the crowd and team through acrobatics, stunts and tumbling. Dancers, our art form is pure, as we tell you a story through the movement of our bodies and make you feel something each and every time we perform." The conviction in her tone as she explains her craft would be awe inspiring if she wasn't such a conniving bitch.

"So, what you're saying, is you can role play?" Saint says as he wiggles his brows suggestively. I shoot him a glare right as Corvin smacks the back of his head.

"You're a real fucking dick!" Corv grits out before continuing on to the party with the rest of us tailing after him. I can feel her peeking over her shoulder at me every few seconds but I ignore it. I've barely spoken two words to her since I left for college. Every time I look at her all I see is her in that bed with *him*! I shake my head to rid myself of those fucking memories, I can't deal with that shit tonight.

Yesterday is history!

I repeat over and over again in my head until we get to Shayla's. The front yard is littered with students drinking from red Solo cups, and at the sight of us, they all come stumbling over to try to gain our attention. The girls flirt while the guys try to appear interesting enough to hold our attention in the hopes of joining our crew, but they will never be one of us. The five of us built something for ourselves that no one can ever take from us —none of our families, except for Saint's, are wealthy, so we built our own wealth and have enough money to live three lifetimes over. I look around the packed lawn and that's when I notice Leah and her friends have slinked off. I dart my gaze around and that's when I spot her on the porch talking to… Garrett-fucking- Jones, her brother's enemy. The guy is vying for Corvin's start position and hasn't been shy about making it known to everyone but *us*.

I'm gonna fucking ruin you, Goldielocks, is my last thought before I sling my arm around some random girl and lead her inside to get me a drink. The moment we pass Leah, I feel her gaze on me, so I turn my head, quirk a condescending brow and shoot her a wicked smirk before pulling the girl under my arm even closer and stalking away from her, relishing in the hurt look in her eyes.

CHAPTER FOUR

Seeing Chelsea cuddled into Darius's side staring up at him with stars in her eyes and him looking at her like he is mentally undressing her feels like someone poked a red-hot branding iron over my heart. I knew coming here would be hard, but I didn't think after all this time he would still hate me. For months after he ghosted me I had no idea what happened or what I did wrong. When I left for college at BVU, I had no idea *he* would be there. It wasn't a problem at first, we even became friends, until one night, when I was training late at the gym, I heard him and his team talking about my team and who is the most *bangable*. He laughed and told a story about *me* I never fucking knew happened! From that night, everything changed. I was dropped from the team and weeks later I lost my scholarship and had no choice but to transfer.

"You okay?" I pull myself from my spiraling thoughts and focus back on Garrett. I try to plaster on a smile for his sake but I can see I fail miserably when his shoulders slump.

"Yeah, sorry just…yeah," I say.

"Look, Darius and his friends are a pack of jumped-up juice heads who think they are holier than God himself." I can't help it, laughter bubbles out of me at his words because he isn't half wrong. The five of them do prance around with an air of superiority surrounding them. When my laughter dies off, I find Garrett grinning wide at me. He seems more at ease now than he did a moment ago. "Want a drink?" I nod eagerly and allow him to lead me through the hordes of people that are clustered inside the house. Garrett reaches back and grips my hand, pulling me along. I try to spot Katie and Cody but I can't see them among the mass of bodies, Garrett doesn't seem to have any issues finding his way around the place.

As we round the corner and come into the kitchen, my breath hitches at the sight of Darius sitting on the counter with people surrounding him. It's not his popularity that has me short of breath, it's the sight of Chelsea between his legs, running her hands all over him. As if he can sense my gaze on him he shoots me a scathing look that makes me feel like I am discarded trash. Garrett handing me a cup has me tearing my gaze from Darius.

"Do you have anything in a bottle?" He frowns which prompts me to explain further. "A girl can never be too careful, ya know?" Realization dawns on him at my words. He leads me to the other side of the kitchen where there are bottles lined up along the counter.

"No sealed bottles but you can pour your own?" I reach for one of the bottles only for it to be snatched from my hand, I snap my gaze over to an angry looking Beckett.

"Beck, what the hell?" I snap angrily. He pulls his heated stare from Garrett to peer down at me. He reaches into the back pocket of his jeans and pulls out a hip flask, making quick work of pouring some into a cup and handing it to me. "Thanks?" I say, slightly confused.

"Next time you need a drink, you find one of us and don't touch any of this shit. Most of it is spiked." My eyes widen in horror as I look from him to the bottles. Beck shakes his head and leans down to whisper in my ear. "Don't trust anyone here,

Leah. Word will spread about who you are to Corvin and the wolves will come hunting. You need anything, you come find me." When he pulls back, I stare up at Beckett Dawson in a whole new light. He and I have never been *close* per se but him saving my ass tonight means more than he will ever fucking know!

I'm starting to feel pretty drunk but the atmosphere here is amazing and I feel safe enough to allow myself to let loose a little, knowing my brother and the guys are here keeping an eye on me. Corvin would never allow anyone like *him* to come near me. Knowing that I never have to cross paths with that piece of shit ever again has me feeling lighter than I have in a long time. My mom and dad are so angry at me. They had to take out a second mortgage on the house to pay for me to go to CHU. I hate that they had to do that. I also hate lying to them but I also can't tell them the truth as they would never look at me like I'm their perfect little girl anymore.

"Oh my God! Leah, this is my favorite song. We need to dance!" Katie shouts as she grips my hand and hauls me away from my spot next to Garrett, dragging me over to the makeshift dance floor in the center of the living room. Cody, who was already dancing with some others, squeals at the sight of us and rushes over to give us each a hug. When the beat of *G-Eazy and Chris Brown's* song *"Provide"* flows through me, my body takes on a life of its own as my hips begin to sway side to side. I raise my arms above my head as I let my body roll to the beat. Katie and Cody mimic me for a beat before they let loose and begin dropping down low and slowly working their way back up, pushing their asses out as they go.

The three of us have gathered a crowd, which isn't new to dancers like us. Guys think just because we can twerk and pop our asses the way we do that we are some horny available women that are begging for their dicks inside us. When a guy I don't know reaches for me, I pull back only to smack into a wall of steel. When my body hums to life, I know who it is without even having to look over my shoulder.

"Shit, sorry, D. I didn't know she was yours." I want to bristle at the way he speaks about me like I am some possession, but the moment Darius's hands land on my waist and I feel him plaster himself against my back, my retort dies on my tongue. His lips brush the shell of my ear and an involuntary shiver races down my spine. Having him this close to me again feels so fucking right. I don't even care if Corvin catches us right now, I want him to know so then nothing has to be a secret anymore!

"Move for me, Goldie." Like a slave to its master, my body obeys. The beat of *Pia Mia's* song *"Do It Again"* pulses and my body moves. I push my ass back against him, and when a hiss escapes his lips, I am filled with a sense of need to have him closer. I reach up and lock my arm around his neck, holding him there while I move against him in time to the beat. Honestly, all I am doing is grinding against his dick but I turn slightly to see a fire burning in the depths of his dark brown eyes. You would swear I'm giving him a competition piece that I have trained months to perfect. His black hair flops forward onto his forehead. I itch to push it back like I have so many times before. He still cuts his hair in that crew-cut style, the five o'clock shadow he now sports only adds to his bad boy vibes. Darius is the epitome of tall, dark and handsome. Unlike other guys here, he doesn't dress to impress. In true Darius Lockhart fashion, he wears his signature white tee, dark wash jeans, shit-kicker boots and his black, yellow and white letterman jacket. "You like that?" I stifle a gasp when he pushes forward and I feel his hard cock poke into me from behind.

"Darius–" I breath out, but he cuts me off smiling and looking at me like he used to. Hope spurs to life inside me at that look—maybe, just maybe he might give me five minutes to talk to him.

"Can you feel how fucking hard I am right now?" I swallow, suddenly so parched and dart my tongue out to moisten my lips and nod. He tsks and shakes his head, scraping that stubble along my cheek again, causing me to shudder. "You know I need the words, Goldie." It takes everything inside me not to moan at the sound of that husky rasp in his voice that I know all too well.

"Yes," I say in a breathy voice.

"Do you want me, baby?"

"Yes." He darts his tongue out and licks my ear lobe before sucking it into his mouth. This time I can't stop the moan from breaking free.

"How badly do you need me, Goldie?" he says before clamping his teeth down lightly on my lobe.

"So fucking bad," I say in a sultry tone I don't even recognize.

"Good." His grip on my waist turns punishing and forces me to stop moving to the beat. "Because you will never know what it feels like for me to fuck you again." I stiffen in his hold as he presses his cock into my ass. "Just knowing how much you want it is gonna make fucking your friend so much sweeter," he snarls before shoving me away from him and pushing his way through the crowd. I'm left standing here, staring at his back until he disappears into the crowd. Shame, guilt, anger and most of all heartache courses through me at his cruel actions and hateful words.

I'm such a fucking fool!

I stand here berating myself as I stare down at my feet until a pair of Air Forces come into view. I slowly raise my gaze to see Garrett standing in front of me with a sad smile on his face. I try to muster a smile for his sake but I can't. Once again Darius Lockhart has proven he has the power to destroy me. Garrett offers me his hand. I stare at it for a beat, unsure what he is asking. He shrugs his shoulders and starts bobbing his head to the beat of Ella Mai's song "Whatchamacallit". When a boyish smile breaks free on his face as he sways off beat I can't help but laugh. He doesn't stop making a fool of himself until I place my hand in his and that is how I spend the rest of the night, dancing with Garrett. He doesn't say anything but I know the only reason he came to dance with me is because he saw what happened with Darius. I decide in this moment, Garrett and I are going to be good friends.

CHAPTER FIVE

Darius

Walking away from her was bitter sweet. She's always known how to move in a way that makes me putty in her hands, but not this time. The moment I saw Corv disappear out the back with Lana, I had to shoot my shot to get under her skin and it fucking worked. I knew she still wanted me, but I needed the proof and last night I got it. Breaking Leah is going to be a lot easier than I thought—seeing her fucking crumble to a million pieces at my feet is going to be fucking amazing.

I wake with a smile on my face as I replay the memories of last night over and over again on repeat in my mind, until I roll over and see my drunken mistake. I wake Carey or is it Chloe? Who the fuck knows and who cares. I chuck her clothes at her to get dressed and usher her from my room as fast as I can. When she speaks and the smell of whatever she drank last night hits me in the face, I fight the urge to gag. The girl looks like a fucking panda with make-up smudged everywhere. I open the door and have to literally push her out it. She spins around with her mouth open to say something, but before her words can make it to my ears I slam the door and rest my forehead against it. I can already tell that girl is going to be a stage five fucking clinger!

"Well that went well." I spin around at the sound for Corv's voice, to find him standing at the base of the stairs with his hair looking like a birds nest, shirtless and in a pair of black sweats.

"Yeah," I say as I head for the kitchen to get some coffee. I'm not hung over but I'm not one hundred percent either. Corvin follows after me and perches his ass on one of the stools at the bench calling for me to make him a cup as well. Silence stretches between us as I wait with my back to him for the coffee machine to do its thing.

"Did you see my sister last night?" I tense at the mention of Leah, and the annoyed tone of his voice has me worried someone told him about me dancing with her. I keep my back to him as I answer.

"Nah, why?" I ask in a bored tone.

"Don't get mad." At the sound of uncertainty in his tone I spin around and pin him with a look that has him throwing his hands in the air. "I said don't get mad!" he pleads.

"I didn't say shit," I defend.

"Your mouth didn't but your face did!" I roll my eyes.

"You fucked Lana, didn't you?" He flinches and gives me an all-teeth guilty smile that has me shaking my head.

"When will you learn?" I say tiredly.

"Dude, the girl can suck better than a hoover and is always down to fuck," he says that like it makes her fucking with his head last year okay. Lana is the captain of the cheer team and a royal bitch. She fucked with Corv's head so bad last year it had him in a dark place. That girl is a fucking basket case and needs to be put into a padded room with the fucking key thrown away.

"No pussy is worth the shit she put you through," I say in a firm tone that I hope conveys my dislike of him going anywhere near that bitch. I turn back to the coffee machine so he doesn't see the look on my face. I know he really cared about Lana and I hate that she fucked him over. When I tried to be there for him last year, he said I couldn't relate because I didn't know what it's like. I wanted to tell him I did but I couldn't without outing myself.

"Enough about her. We aren't getting back together." I snort which he ignores and carries on. "Leah was dancing with fucking Garrett!" That has me spinning back to him. I have to remind myself not to give anything away, so I lean against the counter and clench the granite in a death grip.

"What do you mean?" I push as I try to hold onto my composure.

"Saint and Crue said something happened that upset her and then Garrett showed up and acted like a *gentleman*." He spits the word out like it hurt him to say it. "Then they danced the night away until Beck cut in and walked the girls back to their dorm." I send up a silent thank you to Beckett and remind myself to be on the watch whenever he is around.

"What a dick," I rush to say as I turn back to the coffee maker to fill our cups.

"Yeah. Hey, Leah didn't happen to mention anything to you about why she changed schools, did she?" I hand him his cup of coffee before taking a sip of mine and shaking my head.

"Have you asked your parents?" He sighs and nods.

"Yeah, they just said she lost her scholarship but I know there is more that they aren't telling me, you know?" I nod. His parents are good people. They work hard and have always tried to give their kids everything they need. What they don't know is Corvin is the one who has been paying their bills while stashing the money they think they are paying the bank into a retirement fund he started for them.

"Have you asked Leah?"

"Ask me what?" My gaze snaps to the entryway to see the little devil stroll in like she owns the place. I narrow my eyes when I see what she is wearing—black yoga pants that stick to her body like a second skin, white sneakers and a black sports bra that shows off her perfect tits. Her long blonde hair is piled on top of her head in some messy-looking bun thing, her face is free of make-up. That was one thing I always loved about her, she never wore much make-up because she said if people couldn't accept her the way she was then why should she have to alter her appearance to appear prettier just to make them happy.

"Why you changed schools."

"How did you get in here?" Corvin and I both ask at the same time. When her gaze lands on me, I narrow my eyes. Her green eyes spark with defiance and I know all too well what that look means, she is up to something.

"Corv gave me a key," she says, then saunters over to the coffee pot to make herself a cup. I pin Corvin with a glare.

"Dude, she's my sister!" My upper lip twitches in anger. Rather than be subjected to the torture of being in the same room as her, I dump my cup in the sink before storming out.

"Darius?" Her melodic voice has me stopping in the entryway and tensing when I hear her move toward me. She moves until she stands in front of me, her eyes shining with a cunning look that has me tensing even further. She runs her gaze down my bare torso. When she reaches my shorts, she quirks a brow and smiles. "I hope you don't snore too loud and I promise not to take up too much space in *our* bathroom." My brows jump to my hairline when her words register. I spin around to face a guilty looking Corvin.

"Her dorm block has to be repaired. They have an asbestos problem. It will only be for a few weeks and then you're back to having your own space again," he rushes out, and my nostrils flare in outrage.

"Corv said since you were the only one with a shared bathroom and it is next to the spare room and that it would be fine." The triumphant tone of her voice grates on every fucking nerve in my body. I slowly turn back to face her with a smile on my face that has the one on hers dropping right off.

"I don't snore." Her shoulders relax but I'm not done. "Just FYI though, get some ear plugs because I'd hate to keep you up at night with the screaming coming from my room." Her eyes widen and blaze with anger. I push past her, making my way up to my room. Before I can reach my bedroom, her shout has me grinding my teeth in annoyance.

"Don't call your a hand a girl, Darius, because we all know you *never* fuck the same girl twice!" Fucking little shit! I slam my door closed so hard the pictures on the wall rattle and threaten to tumble to the floor. I pace my room, trying to calm the anger thrumming inside me when an idea hits. Having her next door could work in my favor. A slow smile spreads across my face as a plan formulates in my mind.

Let the games begin, Goldie.

I don't help the others move her shit in as I want them to all know I don't want her here without saying the words. I decide to distract myself by diving into my homework and running over plays for the upcoming season. With our first game being against the Dolphins, coach is going to be riding us hard. We need to win this game to set the bar for the rest of the season. There is nothing worse than losing the first game, it brings the morale of whole team down and once that is gone, it is fucking hard to pick back up.

My vision turns hazy from staring at the plays from last season for hours. I rub my tired eyes and peer over at the clock on my bedside drawer and see it's seven. Fuck, I've been at this all fucking day and well into the night! Pushing back from my desk in the corner of the room, I stroll into the bathroom and turn the shower on. The best part about this bathroom, the mirror never fogs up because both doors on either side always stay open. I strip off and dump my shorts in the hamper in the corner before stepping under the spray, the scalding water burns but it relaxes my taut muscles. I stay under the spray for a few minutes before washing myself and my hair.

Turning the shower off, I grip my towel that hangs over the side of the glass door and wrap it around my waist before stepping out. I shake the water from my hair then run my hand through it to push it out of my face, the moment I do I freeze at the sight in front of me, or should I say the blonde in front of me, leaning against the vanity while shamelessly running her gaze over me. For a split second I forgot about her moving in and being in the adjoining room!

"Take a picture, it will last longer," I growl. Her body may show that she isn't into me but her eyes, they never lie. I see the longing in her green eyes.

"I got plenty of those," she grits out. I step up beside her effectively dismissing her as I grab my toothbrush and start to brush hoping she'll take the hint she isn't wanted here. "You can't ignore me forever, Darius." I rinse my mouth out and take my time about doing it before turning to her and letting my gaze lazily trail over her body. I make sure when I meet her gaze again that all she can see is disgust.

"I don't want to ignore you." Her features soften, I reach out and cup her cheek loving that she pushes into my touch, almost like she needs it. "I want to fucking destroy you and act like you never existed." Her mouth drops open in shock as I yank my hand back and retreat into my room, this time I close and lock the adjoining door.

CHAPTER SIX

If I thought living with five guys was going to be easy, I was fucking wrong!

I've been here for nearly two weeks and my dorm won't be ready for at least another two to three weeks. Saint has a different girl over every night, Corvin is sloppy and doesn't pick up after himself. Crue is forever brooding and hiding out in his room, blaring music whenever Saint gets home. Beck and Darius are actually okay, well beside the fact that Darius hates me and makes it known whenever we cross paths. The bastard has even resorted to childish pranks like switching the sugar for salt, using all the hot water or dumping my stuff in the toilet in our bathroom. He swears it wasn't him but the laughter that follows proves he's guilty.

Which is why I am currently sitting here in the kitchen on a Friday afternoon waiting for him to come back from the gym. They left about twenty minutes ago and I know it won't be long before he comes running through that door heading straight for the bathroom, that he will find locked. As if the thought of him summons him, he crashes through the door with the shouts of the others following him as he races up the stairs toward his room.

3...2...1...

"Leah!" he shouts my name so loud I cringe, and bite down on my bottom lip to tamper my laughter. I hop off my stool and wait at the base of the stairs ignoring the stares of my brother and the other three at the front door as I stare up at a red faced Darius who is clutching his stomach. "Unlock the fucking doors, now!"

I feign shock. "What do you mean? Is something wrong, darling?"

"Darling?" I hear Corvin spit but ignore him. Darius's eyes are blazing with anger then within a split second his face contorts and he hunches over in pain.

"You fucking did this!" he accuses me. I place a hand over my heart and shake my head.

"I have no idea what you are talking about boo boo." The sweet sultry tone of my voice grates on his nerves.

"Fuck!" he screams, before dashing down the hall to Corvin's room and slamming the door behind him. I roll my lips over my teeth to keep my smile at bay as I turn to Corv and the others, then smile sweetly before dashing up the stairs to my room.

Leah – 1

Darius – 0

Since I didn't know we were having a prank war until yesterday, his previous points don't count. I skip into my room and fish the keys for the bathroom doors out of my dresser before going about unlocking them. I decide to take a shower now while Darius is...*busy*. At the thought of him shitting himself I crack up, unable to contain my laughter any longer, tears streaming down my cheeks from laughing so hard.

◉

I wrap my wet hair in a towel before stepping out and wrapping another around my body, the mirror is fogged up thanks to this bathroom having no ceiling fan and the doors being shut. I slide the door to my room open and freeze at the sight of Darius sitting on the edge of my bed with an angry look on his face. I bite my lip as I make my way over to my dresser, if I look at him I know I will laugh and that will just piss him off further,

"Clever, Goldie, real fucking clever." I peer over my shoulder at him and bat my lashes.

"No idea what you are talking about, *Halfback*." At the use of my old nickname for him, he stiffens. We stand here staring at each other for what seems like hours, but in reality is more like mere seconds before he stands and comes toward me. I turn to face him and back up until my back hits the dresser. He crowds my space, the scent of him invades my senses and it takes more control than I want to admit to not close my eyes and bask in his scent. He cages me in, placing his arms on either side of me as he white-knuckles my dresser.

"You know what this means, right?" His voice is barely above a whisper. I shake my head causing him to narrow his eyes. "I need the words, Goldie."

"No?" It comes out more like a question but I can't help it. Whenever he is this close to me, my brain short-circuits and all rational thought flees. He leans down until his lips ghost over mine causing my heart to thump so hard in my chest, I fear he can hear it.

"You just started a fucking war that you will never win!" he spits before exiting my room without a word, leaving me standing here, strung out and needy. I really need to give myself a orgasm tonight or I risk doing something stupid like throwing myself at Darius and begging him to help get me off like only he can.

⬤

"Oh my God!" I cringe at the shriek that comes from Cody and the shouted words from Katie. "You fucking put laxatives in Darius Lockhart's protein powder?" I give her a toothy smile and nod. Katie howls with laughter, Cody joins a second later. I knew he would never suspect me of tampering with his shakes so I thought it would be the perfect prank and it was. I heard him all night groaning and rushing to the bathroom, it was fucking glorious.

"Okay, okay. So now what?" I finally caved and told Katie and Cody about me and Darius and swore them to secrecy— they both agreed. I may have only known them for a short time but I trust them. A measure of time has no say on when you can trust someone so I went with my gut, which told me these girls are trustworthy.

"Now, I guess we wait and see if he softens toward me." Cody and Katie have spent the whole day trying to help me figure out what could have gone wrong between Darius and me, but we came up blank.

"Well until then, get ready," Katie says.

"For what?" I ask.

"We're going to a beach party!" Excitement thrums through me at the prospect of swimming in the ocean.

"I didn't bring anything with me," I say. Cody rolls her eyes and leaps off the bed in their makeshift dorm room that they are staying in until ours is fixed. She reaches into her drawer and pulls out a bathing suit for me and chucks it at me. I hold it up and can't keep the shock from my face.

"I'm just full of surprises, right?" Both Katie and I chuckle. I never thought I would ever see Cody wearing a suit like this but hey, YOLO and all that. After we all change into our bathing suits, I slip my cut-offs back on and slide my feet into my flip flops. Katie clambers over and yanks the elastic from my hair saying I need to leave it out because it adds to the *look*. I don't know what that means, but I also don't argue either as I follow them out of the dorm building. The sun beats down on me and I smile wide, what a perfect way to spend a Sunday. Hanging with my girls and going to my favorite place. I love dancing more than anything but I love the beach just as much. Something about the ocean calls to me. When I'm sad or going through something, like Darius breaking my heart, I would escape to the beach and dance in the sand for hours until my body was so exhausted that my mind couldn't focus on anything else except sleep.

The beach is only a short minute walk from campus. On the way the girls and I chat, they ask me questions and I do the same. They are shocked to learn that Corvin and I are only eleven months apart and are the same age for two weeks out of the year. When we hit the sand I take my flip flops off and carry them in my hand. The moment we hit the shoreline, music can be heard and students can be seen on the bank, the water and some even play volleyball! I squeal in excitement, I love playing beach volleyball.

"Let's enjoy this last day today before our training really kicks in next week." Both Cody and I agree, Katie is right. Come next week, we will be training hard for nationals. CHU has one of the best hip hop programs and has won the state champi-onship two years in a row, our coach, Mrs. Telford, wants to make it three years in a row and has threatened to cut anyone who slacks off from the team. When we reach the party, some of the girls I know from the team greet us but when Chelsea saun-ters over I can't help the anger that sparks inside me at the sight of her. As she reaches us, her smile appears so fake when she looks at me and before I can call her on it, a shadow falls over me. Turning around and seeing who it is I beam at him before wrapping my arms his waist, hugging him tight.

"Well hello to you to, beautiful." I blush as I pull back. "Ladies," Garrett says to the girls around me. Unlike my brother and his friends, he doesn't preen at the attention the others shoot him, his focus is on me. I know Garrett likes me and I feel bad for him. I've made it clear since we started hanging out that I'm not looking for anything right now. He assured me he under-stood and hasn't asked me out again since. We still meet up three times a week so he can tutor me. I know he and my brother don't get along but as far as I am concerned that is not my business. "Wanna go play some volleyball?"

"Ye–"

"No, she doesn't." I look to my side to see Corvin and Darius standing there with scowls on their faces. I sigh as I face my brother.

"Corv, we talked about this. Garrett is my friend and you're just going to have to deal," I say with a shrug.

"You fucking him?" My eyes widen at Darius's crass words, while Garrett splutters beside me. Corvin's eye twitches telling me he is pissed Darius asked that but he won't go off at him because he wants to know the answer as well. I look to Darius and my anger soars when I find his glare trained on me. I straighten my shoulders and hold my head high as I say,

"Wouldn't you like to know."

CHAPTER SEVEN

Darius

I grind my teeth so fucking hard I think they may snap when she shimmies out of her shorts and kicks them at my feet before leading Garrett toward the game of volleyball. Corvin is brimming with rage at the sight of his sister in a red, two-piece bathing suit that barely contains her tits, and the bottoms are cut like a G-string and fits into her perfect pert ass with ease. I'll admit, at the sight of her running and seeing her tits and ass bounce, my cock is rock fucking hard in my board shorts.

"Get the guys, we're about to beat this prick at his own game!" Corvin growls. I nod but it takes me a full five seconds before I can peel my eyes off the blonde bombshell who is currently bent over waiting for the other team to serve the ball. Garrett stands behind her with his eyes glued to her ass like he has a fucking right! I head off to find Saint and the others. He's sitting near the keg with his Hawaiian shirt unbuttoned and his abs on display for all the girls to drool over. Crue sits next to him with a sour look on his face, something is up with him and I plan to find out what it is once I've dealt with a certain blonde.

"D-man, what up?" Saint says when I stop in front of him. I spy Courtney or whatever the fuck her name is out of the corner of my eye, pushing her nonexistent tits out at me.

"Corv wants a game, let's go." At the serious tone of my voice, the smile vanishes from his face and he and Crue are on their feet and shedding their shirts before following after me. I hunt for Beckett on our way to the court but can't find him. The fuckers height would come in handy but no matter, we got this. That's one thing that I love about these guys, we can shoot the shit and fuck around but when one of us needs something, we're all there at the drop of a hat, no questions asked.

"Oh snap," Crue says when we reach the edge of the court where Corv stands with his arms folded over his chest. We step up beside him and I can feel the anger wafting off him in waves as he watches Leah jump around the court. When she spikes the ball over the net and scores a point, Saint has to hold Corv back when Garrett grabs Leah and swings her around. I don't even realize I've moved until a large hand clamps down on my shoulder halting my movements. I look over my shoulder to see it's Beck who stopped me from making an ass of myself. He nods once, asking me if I'm good. I return his gesture and resume my spot next to Corv seething fucking mad.

"Who's sitting out?" Beck asks.

"I'll sit out, Crue is better than me at this shit, plus I'll make sure to cause a distraction." I quirk a questioning brow at Saint, who has a shit-eating grin spread over his face. "Corvin, do you promise not to get mad?" Just then Leah lands another point and Garrett is there to sweep her up into his arms. Corv is clenching his fists so tight that his knuckles turn white. He cuts a glance to Saint as we get ready to hit the court and play Leah's team.

"Do whatever it takes, that fucker isn't winning!" Saint beams and nods like a child who just got his favorite candy. The twinkle in his eye tells me that what he has planned is going to piss me the fuck off. Corvin and I both take the outside hitter positions while Beck takes the setter spot and Crue slips into the spot of blocker. Crue may be the baby of us but the little shit can keep up and he is fucking quick, the competitive streak he has rivals mine.

"Ready?" Nate shouts from the other side as he sets himself to serve. Beck calls back that we're ready. Nate throws the ball and hits it into the air.

"Mine," I shout as I take a step and leap into the air before spiking it down near Leah. She dives for it and misses, letting the ball hit the ground. The guys cheer behind me while I crouch down and meet her angry gaze and smirk. "Losers weepers and all that, Goldie." Her eyes blaze with contempt.

"You haven't won yet, asshole!" she snaps. Our verbal sparring war is over the moment Garrett, the greasy looking fuck ambles over and helps her to her feet. The sight of his hands on her bare hips has me gritting my teeth.

"Set me up. I'm gonna teach that cunt a lesson." I look to the side to see Corvin standing there shooting a death glare at his enemy. I nod and get into position as Beck serves. Corey hits it up for Nate to try a spike but Crue dives for it, hitting it up. I'm under the ball and following Corv's cues as I get close to the net and tap the ball up enough for him. He takes two steps before leaping into the air. I expect him to spike it down and take the easy point but he doesn't, instead he hits it right into Garrett's face. Before his feet can even hit the sand again, he is pissing himself laughing, Crue, Beck and I are powerless to stop our own laughter from slipping free.

"What the hell, Corv?" Leah snaps angrily at her brother. Corv shrugs.

"My bad, your serve. Come on, no time to argue we're burning daylight here!" Corvin sounds like a complete dick but I'm also here for it. "If the pussy can't hack the heat, then get the fuck off the court!" Garrett's eyes blaze with fury but we all know he is too much of a little bitch to ever go head to head with Corv—he'll run away and talk shit about us behind our backs and deny it when we hit him up. The guy is weak as horse piss. Leah shoots me a scathing look which I return with one of my own. When she turns her back to me, my anger spikes as she bends over to help bitch face to his feet. Her perfect perky ass is on display for all to see and I fucking snap.

Marching toward her I duck under the net. Garrett reaches out to grab her hand but I smack it away before he can touch her. She snaps her gaze up to me in shock. I feel Corv and the others at my back which snaps me out of my possessive as fuck mood. What the fuck was I thinking doing this with him here?

"What the hell is your problem?" Leah snaps, placing her hands on her hips.

"You are my problem! Go home and change and stop acting like a fucking hoe!" Gasps sound out around me but it's too late, the words hang in the air between us. I didn't mean to say that but I'm not mad that I did.

"I think the game is over–" I turn my glare at Garrett, who the fuck does this weasel-looking motherfucker think he is butting his nose in to my business? Too far gone to stop myself, I step into him. The shocked look on his face lasts a split second before it's replaced by a smug fake-ass look that I know is for Leah's benefit.

"Stay the fuck out of our shit or you're done here." I may have crossed a line calling his sister a hoe but Corvin tables his anger as he and Beck flank either side of me. Garrett knows we can end him and have him thrown from the school, CHU is nothing without us. We own it. I'm not talking shit either, we actually own the fucking school but no one knows that. We may be gutter rats, well, Beck, me and Crue are. Corv didn't grow up poor but he wasn't rich either. The only one of us who is loaded is Saint. We all made a pact in high school that before we made it out of college we would never struggle again and we kept our fucking word. The five of us are set for life!

"Fuck you, Darius!" Leah seethes as she pushes between me and Garrett. When her back is plastered to his front the cunt smirks sending me into a tailspin. The growl coming from my right tells me Corvin sees what I do, which is why I know I will get away with my next move. I grab her waist and hoist her off her feet. She squeals in surprise but muscle memory is a bitch, so like she has done so many times before, she wraps herself around me. I don't stop moving even when we are off the court and passing her friends, who stare at us like we are a circus act. I feel the guy's eyes on me but I don't stop, not even when I hit the boardwalk, I keep going until I find myself on the road home. "Put me down," she says quietly, neither of us have said a word for the at least ten minutes. I know it's been that long because my house comes into view right at that second.

"Shut the fuck up, Leah." She stiffens in my hold. I don't give a shit if she's uncomfortable. Having her this close to me makes me remember that she is a filthy little liar and can't be trusted! When I reach the front door, I shove it open—we don't lock our door unless we all go out of town as no one here would be dumb enough to ever try to rob us. As soon as I kick the door shut I strut into the living room and drop her. She screams as she hits the couch and glares up at me. "You ever pull a stunt like that again–" She pushes to her feet and gets right in my face.

"You'll what, Darius? Ghost me, shun me, act like I don't exist?" She snorts and shakes her head. "You are fucking pathetic," she snarls as she shoves past me. Like fuck is she getting the last word. I chase after her and shove her against the front door, she has just enough time to stop her face from smacking into the wood by placing her hands out in front of her before I'm plastered to her back, using my weight to pin her there. "Get the fuck off me!" she shouts.

"Or what? What are you gonna do, Leah? You can't fucking get away." I expect her to fight back, scream and curse me out but what I don't fucking expect is for her to burst into tears.

"Please, get off me!" she cries. Hearing the fear and anguish in her voice, I leap away from her and stare like a fool as she drops to the ground. She wraps her arms around her legs and buries her face in them as sobs wrack her body. I scrub a hand down my face, frustrated at myself for caring about her reaction when I should be happy that I finally got her to break.

"Fuck!" I snarl as I bend down and lift her into my arms and head for her room. I carry her bride style up the stairs as she wraps her arms around my neck and buries her face into my naked chest. I fight the urge to tighten my hold on her and demand that she tell me what the fuck has freaked her out. It isn't my business and she isn't my problem anymore, I tell myself as I place her on top of her bed and leave. It takes every ounce of strength I have to not hop on the bed next to her and hold her close as I promise to kill whoever or whatever has her so upset.

"What the fuck was that?" I look over my shoulder to see Corv storming down the stairs toward me. If he wants to punch me then he's gonna have to jump in the pool because I'm not going to let him. Beck, Saint and Crue strut toward us. Saint jumps in followed by Crue but Beck drops into one of the loungers. "Answer me!" Luckily I'm wearing sunglasses so he can't see me roll my eyes at his macho-man display.

"What the fuck do you want me to say? You should have said something the moment we got there instead of letting her parade around like that," I say, motioning with my hands. My excuse is weak but Corvin doesn't care.

"You call my sister a fucking hoe again and I'll break your fucking jaw, Darius, best friend or not, she is my little fucking sister!" My nostrils flare at his claim on her. I want to yell that she isn't his to defend but she isn't mine either… not anymore.

"Got it," I grit out. He shoots me one last look before storming back into the house to go in search of her royal *holiness*.

"You know he means it, right?" I lull my head to the side to look at Crue as Saint hops on the other floaty and nods his agreement to what Crue just said.

"Yeah, well maybe if she dressed properly, Garrett wouldn't be sniffing her like she's a bitch in heat." Saint clucks his tongue, warning me to watch myself. Beck sits up and rests his forearms on his thighs as he stares at me with an unreadable look on his face.

"You sort your shit." I cock my head to the side. "I won't let you break us because you're too fucking stubborn to say what you want out loud. Find a way to deal and tell him." My face tightens in anger as I stare at the fucker, daring him to push me because he knows out of everyone here I am the only one who isn't fucking scared to throw down with him.

"You gonna snitch on me, Becky boy?" He slowly pushes to his feet and moves to the edge of the pool looking down at me, his pale eyes burn with unbridled rage.

"Nah, *D-bag*. With how you are handling having her around and acting like a fucking prick whenever she is near, he'll figure it out on his own." I'm seething with fucking anger when he turns to head back inside. The fucker pauses at the steps of the porch and peers over his shoulder pinning me with a smug look. "Better get that rage under control because Garrett will be here to pick her up in two hours." My eyes widen behind my glasses, muscles coiling tight in anticipation at the prospect of seeing that cunt again today. His face won't survive this encounter! "Better jump on that bike and run away now or risk Corvin seeing that look on your face when she leaves with *his* enemy. Last I recall, you didn't have a problem with the back-up QB until a certain blonde arrived."

Motherfucker!

"You fucked baby sis, didn't you?" I snap my gaze to my side. Fuck, I forgot Saint and Crue were here! "You know what, don't answer that because I don't want to know." I grit my teeth and slip off the floaty, letting the water wash over me hoping it will calm me down enough to stomach the sight of her leaving with another guy. When I break the surface I look at Saint, then lift my glasses off my face so he can see the serious look in my eyes.

"You keep your fucking mouth shut." Crue edges himself

forward almost like he is ready to fight for Saint if I were to do something.

"You keep your cock out of her and we have a deal." My grip on my glasses is so tight I fear I'll snap them. "She isn't just a random girl, D. She is Corvin's little sister and has always been off-limits to us. I won't let you destroy this family." Saint's words hit me square in the chest. I can't even form a reply to defend myself because he is right. I never should have acted on my feelings for Leah. I knew if we ever got caught that Corv would lose his shit and it would rock the dynamic of the five of us. That is something I would never forgive myself for doing. These four are the only family I have left and I can't lose them. There was a time I would have taken the risk for the girl because I thought she was worth it, until she ripped my fucking heart out of my chest and spat on it!

CHAPTER EIGHT

Leah

I shift into a sitting position and wipe my tears with the backs of my hands at the sound of a knock on my door. I'm sitting here in an oversize sweatshirt and sweats as I showered and changed after Darius left me. I call out to whoever it is to come in. I'm not surprised to see it's my brother. He takes one look at me and all his anger drains away, his face softens as he makes his way over to me and sits on the edge of my bed.

"I'm sorry about D, he can be a real–"

"Dick?" I supply, he chuckles and nods.

"Yeah. He can be, but he means well." I scoff, which just earns me a stiff look from Corvin. "He shouldn't have called you a hoe." I balk at him.

"Out of everything from today that is all you picked up?" His brow furrows.

"Uh, what else was there?" I throw my hands up exasperated at how dense he is being.

"He carried me off the court and home like I am some errant child! Do you know how embarrassing that is?"

"Well, no." I scowl at the idiot. "In his defense he only did it because he views you as a sister." I fight the cringe that wants to break free. "Seeing you with Garrett and how you were…

dressed." I pin him with a look daring him to continue down that path, he wisely doesn't. "Look, Garrett is a dick and is only using you to get at me."

I roll my eyes; men are so stupid. "Garrett had no idea I was your sister when we first started hanging out." That revelation seems to shock him. "Not everything is about you, Corv. I know the five of you are the kings of CHU, but that doesn't mean everyone wants to use me to get to you." His features harden.

"If only you knew," he mutters beneath his breath, which piques my intrigue. We sit here silently for a few minutes lost in our own thoughts until he breaks the silence. "Why did you transfer, Leah?" My heart stops.

"I… uh, I got kicked out of the dance program," I lie. He rolls his lips over his teeth, he knows I'm lying and wants to call me on but I know Corvin, he won't do it.

"Yeah… that's what Mom said." I flinch at the mention of my parents. They are struggling now because of me. They wanted to retire and live their best life but now they can't because paying for my tuition is eating all of their savings and I fucking hate myself for that, but they wouldn't let me drop out of school all together.

I spent the rest of the night holed up in my room, I felt bad blowing Garrett off but he said he understood. I got up extra early to leave the house so I didn't risk bumping into any of the guys. I make my way across campus and head toward the coffee cart to grab me, Cody and Katie a latte. With coffees in hand, I head toward their temporary dorm room. I take a deep breath and steel my spine, ready for them to lash out at me for ditching them yesterday. I knock twice and wait a minute before the door swings open and reveals Cody standing there. I expect to see annoyance at the sight of me in her eyes but when she breaks out into a full blown smile it throws me off kilter.

"Girl, get your ass in here and fill us in!" She drags me into the room and places a kiss to my cheek as she steals her coffee and drops into the desk chair in the corner. Katie sits on her bed and motions with her hands like a child for her coffee.

"Gimme, gimme, I need a caffeine hit pronto for this!" I smile and hand her the cup as I sit on the edge of Cody's bed.

"Girl, spill now!" Cody prompts. I fill them in on everything that happened after Darius carried me off the court and all the way home.

"He is so into you." I pin Katie with a look that I hope conveys that she is nuts!

"Darius hates me," I huff out and drop back on the bed dramatically.

"Babe, if that is what hate looks like then I'mma need him and Beckett to hate me." I turn my head and shoot Cody a playful glare, she puts her hands up as if surrendering. "On the real though, Garrett looked pissed when Darius went all caveman on your ass." I rest up on my elbows and look to both my friends. Katie nods her agreement to Cody's statement which pulls a groan from me.

"I told him I wasn't looking for anything or even interested in dating right now." Katie shoots me a smug look.

"You may not be looking but it sure as hell found you, baby cakes." When they both begin to laugh, I drop back against the bed and groan. Fuck my life. The one guy I want more than anything won't give me the time of day. When we were together, Darius treated me like I was his world, He taught me to view myself in a way no one ever had before. He was the first person to believe in me, that I could make it in dance. I'm eighteen and all I have ever wanted was to dance on stage.

✪

"You okay?" I lift my head from my book and peer over at Garrett. We have taken to sitting next to each other in class now.

I'll admit, I have been a bit awkward today, with what the girls said earlier playing on my mind. Garrett is a really nice guy but he isn't the guy for me.

"Yeah, just tired," I lie.

"Want to meet up after school and grab a coffee?" I furrow my brow confused.

"Aren't you meant to be at training?" He shrugs.

"You're worth blowing it off for." Oh God, there it is. I need to distance myself from him or risk him getting the wrong idea. I'm not the type of girl who leads a guy on.

"I have dance practice after school." His face falls, and I feel like shit when he nods and turns back to face our professor. I try to tell myself that I'm doing the right thing but guilt is a bitch and that is why I tack on. "Raincheck?" He snaps his gaze back to me and beams.

"Yeah, of course, I shouldn't miss our first training anyway." How he can go from sad puppy to happy in a split second stuns me but I don't comment. I wave bye to Garrett as I head across campus to meet with the team, excitement thrumming through me and my body starts to vibrate with the need to move. Dance has always been an escape for me. It helped me deal with the darkest time of my life. I round the science building and smack into a wall–correction, not a wall, just Darius. He glares down his nose at me like I purposely ran into him. Not wanting to ruin my good mood, I try to step around him but he blocks my path.

"What's your rush?" Taking a deep breath I crane my neck back and look at him, I hate that his eyes can still hold me captive, they're like a vortex that can suck you right in.

"I have class," I mumble.

"Hm, going to shake your ass, why am I not surprised?" I bite down on my tongue and count to three to try to calm myself but it doesn't work.

"Coming from the guy who loved it when I shook it for him?" I scoff to drive my point home. Darius strikes out so quickly I have no time to prepare. He grips my arms, then spins us until my back is against the building and he is crowding my space.

"*Used* to like it, now all I can picture is the amount of cocks you've had inside your loose cunt." My eyes widen and my jaw unhinges at his crass words. I shove at his chest but he doesn't freaking budge and that causes my ire to grow.

"Leave me the hell alone, Darius!" I snarl.

"Transfer the fuck out of my school and I will. How trash like you got in here, I'll never fucking know. Open your legs for the dean and he may just put in a good word for you at your new school." I don't know what comes over me but one second my hand is at my side and then in the next, it's cracking across Darius Lockhart's cheek. We both stand here with wide eyes, shocked that I would ever dare lay my hand on him—I've never hit anyone in my life! He bends down until he is right in my face, he is so close his lips ghosts over mine, his brown eyes are so dark they look almost black. "You're gonna pay for that, you washed up has been!" He pushes off me, causing me to smack against the wall harder, turns and storms away, leaving me standing here swarming in my own anger.

Fine, he wants to play this game, then I'll play it better. I'll show him what it's like to play *offside* before I score the final *touchdown*. I decide here and now to put a plan into motion that ensures Darius will be the one stunned the next time we encounter each other. I'm going to make him eat out of the palm of my hand. I just need to keep my heart out of it because it won't survive being broken by him a second time.

I manage to keep up with the team for our first official practice but I would be lying if I said I wasn't beat. My body is aching and my calves are burning from the workout they were put through. I look over at Chelsea and it grates on my frail nerves to see her smiling and standing at attention ready to go another round, the girl is a fucking robot.

"Into positions," Coach Telford shouts. Cody and I groan as we drag our sorry asses over to the others and prepare to run through the routine one final time. Coach told us that the school is considering allowing us to headline the halftime show for the finals of the football game if we make the finals. This would be the first time in CHU history that the cheer squad wouldn't be headlining the event.

CHAPTER NINE

Darius

Coach rode us harder than he ever has before. We're all sweaty fucking messes and my muscles burn in the most delicious way, but I know for the rest of the week I'm going to be fucking sore. We clamber into the locker room breathing like overweight pieces of shit. I ignore the banter of the team and head straight for the ice baths, knowing that is exactly what I need after a training like today. I strip off my clothes and leave them in a heap beside the metal, oval-shaped tub as I climb in. I suck in a sharp breath the moment I hit the water. Gripping the sides, I take deep breaths preparing myself as I slowly slip into the tub. The water is so cold it burns. I slink back and rest my head on the edge of the tub as I settle myself to stay in here for fifteen minutes. Not two minutes after closing my eyes do I hear the guys amble over. I peek one eye open to see Beck, Saint and Crue undressing. Corvin hates ice baths and refuses to willingly get in one. Coach normally has to make his ass and he whines the whole fucking time!

"Dudes, coach is on a warpath," Saint says as he climbs into his bath. Crue hisses like a pussy but not Beck, he gets in the tub on my other side and doesn't need any time to prepare himself, just sliding in like it's a fucking spa bath.

"He has no choice, we have to be ready for the game against the Dolphins in four weeks," Crue supplies. At the mention of the Dolphins, my grip on the edge of the tub tightens.

"They won't win, we got the best QB in the fucking state and Darius is the best halfback out and Beck won't let any of them through. We're solid. That fucker Hayes will be taken down a peg or ten." The guys are the only ones who know what started my hatred for Hayes. I didn't have any reason to hate the cunt, considering he's the QB and not my rival but Corv's. That bastard has had it out for me since we started playing in little leagues and it just grew to the fucking point the cunt fucked my girl at a party. Seeing my arch enemy in the same bed as Leah tore my fucking world apart—that one night changed everything.

"That fucker isn't taking the W, I don't care what we have to do but we are scoring every fucking touchdown!" I growl. The guys nod and grunt their agreement. The bath is no longer cold thanks to the anger thrumming through my veins, if I see her near him at the game I am going to go nuclear on their asses and I don't give a shit if Corvin sees. I'll make sure the whole fucking school knows Leah Williams is a slut and will give it up to anyone.

I kick the stand on my bike down and kill the ignition as I climb off. I peel my helmet off and rest it on the seat as I make my way to the house. I push the door open and freeze at the sound of girlish laughter. I slam the door shut and storm into the living room to find Leah and her two friends Cody and Katie sitting on the couches. At the sound of my arrival they all turn to face me. The two girls look scared—good, they should be. Not Leah though, the dirty little minx sits there with an angry look on her face.

"No hoes in the fucking house," I snarl. Leah's eyes narrow to angry slits.

"They aren't hoes. Believe it or not, not every girl is a hoe, Darius!" she spits.

"Nah they may not be but *you* are!" I snap. Her friend's faces pale while hers slackens with shock. "Have them out of here within an hour... Actually, just fuck off with them. I have company coming over and I would hate for you to finger that used-up cunt at the sounds coming from my room." A hurt look crosses her face but I don't stick around, storming out of the room and heading up the stairs to my room. I kick my door shut once I'm inside and shuck my bag off my back and dump it on the bed before dropping down beside it. I'm full of shit, I didn't have plans for anyone to come over but now, I need to find someone. I pull my phone out of my pocket and scroll through my messages when I spot the unopened ones from Courtney I think her name is. I click on it.

Shit, her name is Chelsea and she is Leah's friend. I don't remember fucking her but I do remember the betrayed look on Goldie's face when she saw me with her at Shayla's party, so I decide she is the perfect person to help me out tonight. I could use a good fuck as I'm too tense and need a release, and it's all the fucking blonde downstairs fault.

Up to tonight?

I don't have to wait a full minute before her reply comes.
Too fucking easy.

My cock isn't even hard at the thought of her. No girl makes us work for it and that right there is the problem. They think fucking one of us will boost their reputation. It may be but the truth is it just shows how fucking easy they are to give it up to us.

CHELSEA

Coming to yours?

Get here at 8, don't make me wait.

CHELSEA

ohh, I love a man that is demanding. Rawr!

A shudder rolls through me, this girl is going to be another hole I fill for the night and then I'll never think about her again. I look down at my dick and shake my head.

"You better perform tonight and not go soft at the sight of her!" I don't have any fucking trouble getting hard when Leah is around or even thinking about her but the thought of plowing some other pussy has my cock flaccid and uninterested. Not tonight though. I'm going to make Carey scream so fucking loud she won't be able to hide anywhere in this house without hearing her screams.

My phone pings with a message at 7:45.

CHELSEA

I'm here babe X

Babe?

Who the fuck does she think she is? I make my way downstairs and eye Crue and Saint in the kitchen. I pass the living room and see Beck and Leah kicking back watching a movie. At the sound of my footsteps her gaze snaps to me. I shoot her a dark smirk and wink as I head for the front door. I swing the door open and it isn't the sight of her that hits me first it's the stench of the perfume she has drowned herself in. I fight the gag from breaking free and plaster on the most fake seductive smile I can. She stands here wearing a tight one-shoulder crop top and skin tight black bike shorts that hug her like a second skin. Her face is plastered with make-up so thick if you pushed on her face you would leave a dent. Her hair is up in a high pony tail which makes me think she did that on purpose for something to hold onto while I fuck her from the back.

"Hey, sexy," she purrs in what I'm sure she thinks is a sexy tone. I keep the fake smile on my face and step aside for her to walk in. Rather than walk past me she stops in front of me, reaches up on her tiptoes and plants a wet kiss to my cheek. I keep my smile in place and nod, my lack of conversation doesn't seem to deter her. She runs her manicured fingers down my shirt-covered chest and doesn't stop until she reaches the waistband of my shorts.

Only then do I step back.

"Let's take this upstairs." She fakes a shiver, bites her lip. I close the door and turn away to head upstairs but she lurches forward and grips my hand. The only reason I don't yank it free is that Leah is sitting on the couch and staring right at us.

"Oh, hey girl, I didn't know you would be here." Chelsea tries to act surprised but everyone on campus knows who Leah is to Corvin and that her dorm building is being renovated. Leah wipes the look of shock from her face and tries to smile but it doesn't reach her eyes.

"I live here," she deadpans. Enjoying the fact I'm getting under her skin, I pull my hand free and wrap my arm around Chelsea's shoulders and pull her into my side. She molds herself into me, loving this display of ownership she *thinks* she has over me. Leah may not see it but her *friend* views her as a threat.

"Oh ya, kay. Well catch you later." Chelsea flutters her lashes up at me, trying to appear all sexy and shit. It's not working but I play along as I bend down and run my nose along the column of her neck and moan.

"Take that shit upstairs, Leah and I have plans that don't involve an audience who can't fake sexual tension to save their asses." I pull back from Chelsea and snap my gaze to Beckett. Shocked that my best friend would try to rile me up and use the situation between Leah and I against me. I may not have confirmed it, but Beckett knows very well that there is something between Leah and me. He shoots me a condescending look, egging me on to deny his claims and say something but I can't. "Leah *babe*, come sit with me and we'll watch the 365 days movie on Netflix." My grip on Chelsea tightens to the point she lets out a small shriek. I quickly relax myself as I watch Leah stand. She shoots me a look that tells me she is ready to play hard ball even if it means using Beckett to get a reaction from me.

"I'd love to," she says. I harden my features, warning her not to do it but when she looks to the girl tucked into my side and smiles brightly I brace for impact. "Don't fake an orgasm to make him feel better, the poor boy couldn't find a G-spot even if he had a map."

Before I can stop them, words spew from my mouth that never should have.

"Managed to find yours every time!"

CHAPTER TEN

My eyes are as wide as dinner plates as I stare at Darius, who is mirroring my expression. I tear my gaze from his to see both Saint and Crue standing in the entryway to the kitchen looking between the pair of us. I have no idea what to say or do. Thank God the tension is broken when Beck stands, wraps an arm around my shoulders and speaks.

"Change of plans. Saint, Crue you in for pizza?" Beck asks as he leads me toward the door. I can feel Darius's gaze on me the whole time.

"Hell yeah, we are!" Crue shouts before racing after us. The moment we step out the front door, I'm able to breathe again. As if Beck knows I'm too stunned by that encounter, he doesn't release his hold on me until we reach his car. He opens the passenger door for me and ushers me inside. Working on autopilot, I clip my belt in and wait for him, Saint and Crue to get in. My mind is reeling over what just happened. If Corvin had been home, Darius and I would both be dead!

The guys slide into Beckett's Audi and the tension from earlier returns. In a weird way Darius just outed us to the guys and I have no idea how we are going to keep this *secret* from Corvin.

Beck reverses the car out of the driveway. We're all silent as he drives us away from the house. As the silence stretches my nerves begin to get the better of me but that's not the only thing, my mind keeps wandering back to Darius and Chelsea and what they could be doing right now. I close my eyes and take a deep breath as I try to rid myself of all the nasty images flashing through my mind of the two of them fucking all over the house. My chest aches thinking about him sleeping with her. I never expected him to be celibate or anything but I did expect that the next time we saw each other that he would at least give me a reason as to why he ghosted me for *years*!

"Well this is awkward," Saint mumbles. I cringe knowing that he's right. The ride isn't exactly filled with easy conversation and laughter.

"Yeah, I'm sorry," I say quietly, feeling like shit for dragging the three of them into mine and Darius's...I don't even know what we are doing right now. When my phone rings, I stiffen at the sound of *his* ringtone. I don't even move to pull it out of my pocket, there is no way I am answering that call in the car where the guys will be able to overhear. I'm not a saint but I'm also in a pickle and I don't know how to get out of it without bringing my deepest darkest secret to life.

"You gonna get that?" Crue asks when my phone begins to ring again.

"Uh, no, I'll call Cody back later," I lie, hating that I have to do this to these guys when I've known them most of my life, but I don't have a choice. I don't have the money to pay him, not that he needs it. If I did, I wouldn't be in this position right now! Crue's phone rings and I'm so grateful for the interruption.

"Yo," he answers. "We're just getting some grub then we'll be back so an hour or so tops." He pauses for a beat listening to whoever is on the other end of the call. "Sweet, see you soon." He ends the call and then says, "Corv says we need to have a meeting about... work." His cryptic words have me turning to peer over the seat at him and Saint, neither of them will meet my gaze, I slump back in my chair and look to Beck.

"What do you guys do for work?" I hedge.

"We help out at Saint's dad's company," Beck answers. Call me crazy but I feel like he's lying to me.

"Why don't I believe you?" I retort. Beck flicks his gaze to me for a second before turning back to the road.

"You need to ask Corvin," is all he says, then pulls into the carpark of the local pizza shop. It's run by a beautiful Italian couple that must be in their sixties. All the students come here to eat as they make the best pizza in town, that is for damn sure! Beck parks the car and we all clamber out to head in to fill our faces with some yummy pie!

I've been sitting on the porch steps since we got home twenty minutes ago. I'm a coward and don't want to go inside and see Darius with her. I'm not a jealous person but when it comes to Darius Lockhart, I become this possessive woman who would throw hands if some woman thought they could touch my man.

Worst part?

He isn't my man, not anymore. I grab my phone and unlock it, four missed calls and three texts, I ignore the calls as I bring up the messages.

PIECE OF SHIT

You're running out of time!

PIECE OF SHIT

Don't ignore me, you either pay up or I go public with this.

PIECE OF SHIT

Out for a bite to eat are you?

A shiver runs down my spine, he was watching me and I had no fucking idea. Fuck. How the hell did I get myself into this mess? I didn't do anything wrong, but because of the fucking tape I have no choice. He knows he can do this to me and there isn't a fucking thing I can do about it. I should have gone to the police but I didn't out of fear. When a guy like him takes the stand against a middle class girl like me, who the hell would you believe?

"Hey." I snap my gaze up to see Garrett standing there on the sidewalk. I smile wide, thankful to see a friendly face that isn't team Darius. I hop to my feet and rush over to him. He hugs me and sue me, I return the friendly embrace before pulling back and smiling up at him.

"What are you doing here?" I ask.

"I was out for a run." I run my gaze over him and sure enough, he's decked out in runners, loose basketball shorts and a white tank.

"Of course, sorry," I mutter. He bends down so we are eye level and smiles kindly.

"You look like you need to get out of here, want to hang out?" I don't even hesitate to answer.

"Yes!" He beams, then we walk side by side back toward campus, talking about nothing and anything all at the same time, which is nice. Don't get me wrong, Cody and Katie are great but right now they aren't the people I need to be around because they are team *Da-Leah* and right now, I'm not. Garrett heads toward the coffee cart and orders us a couple coffees before telling me to grab a seat at one of the tables. I do as he says and look around the quad. During school it's bustling with students but after hours it's empty and quiet.

"Here you go." I smile my thanks as I grab my coffee from Garrett. He slips around to his side and sits down taking a sip of his coffee. "Why the long face, beautiful?" I deflate and drop my gaze to the tabletop unsure how to answer or even if I should. The need to talk to someone wins over rational thought, knowing I shouldn't be telling him, but he's my friend and the opinions of the guys shouldn't matter.

"Darius and I had a fight. Corvin and I are drifting apart because I keep pulling away from him. My mom and dad won't speak to me." It rushes out of me so fast that I have to take a deep breath. Garrett doesn't look put out by my verbal diarrhea.

"Okay, one thing at a time. Why aren't your parents talking to you?" Now that I've started I can't seem to keep my mouth closed.

"I lied to them. I told them I got kicked out of my last school but the truth is I dropped out and transferred here which caused them to have to put off their retirement so they could pay for me to go here." Saying it out loud makes me feel even worse than I do already. I don't blame them for being angry with me. I wanted to tell my mom the truth so many times but I couldn't bring myself to do it. If they knew, they would go to the police and I can't relive that shit, I just can't!

"Okay, I'm guessing the reason you haven't told them why you dropped out is that it's something that is embarrassing for you?"

"Yeah, something like that," I mumble.

"Okay, next thing on our list. Why are you pulling away from your brother?" I narrow my eyes.

"You don't even like my brother," I point out, and he shrugs.

"No, I don't, but you're my friend and I care about you so therefore, if being close to my enemy is what makes you happy then I'm here to help." His words shouldn't make me happy but they do. Garrett isn't at all what the guys say he is. He's kind, caring and even... sweet.

"Corv still thinks I was kicked out of school. He has no idea about Mom and Dad not talking to me. I hate myself but I have to do something to my brother that I don't want to and it is going to kill him, but I have to and I hate myself because of that." I'm rambling but fuck, it feels good to finally say that out loud.

"Does arguing with Darius have anything to do with not telling him the reason for the change in schools as well?" I shake my head. I'm willing to talk to him about my parents and Corvin but not Darius, that is one thing I can't trust him with. "The way I see it is you need to give your parents time to come around and realize that their little girl isn't willing to share everything with them. Corvin, well the guy is such a guy, so give him a couple weeks and he'll forget about it." I snort at his reference to my brother.

"You don't know Corvin, he fixates on things and can't let anything go until he has solved it." That's when I remember I need to talk to my brother about this *work* thing Crue and the others mentioned. I know they don't have a job after school. I also know that the things they have in their house aren't from Walmart, they are expensive, so how the hell are they affording it?

"How about we talk about something else to get your mind off all that?" I nod eagerly. "Good, tell me about your new dance routine I saw you and the team practicing in the gym." A smile spreads across my face. I love talking about dance, but finding someone who isn't on the team, who finds what you are saying interesting is hard. All they want to see is you shaking your ass but not how you learned to pop your hip or how you can rotate your body at a certain angle. We spend hours sitting here talking about dance, football and classes. Garrett hangs onto every word I say and I love that.

"We should head back, it's getting late." I peek down at my watch and that's when my eyes widen, it's nearly midnight!

"Shit, I lost track of time!" I rush to say as I jump to my feet.

"It's cool. Come on, I'll walk you home." I'll admit, I swoon like a high schooler. I bite my lip and nod. We fall into step and continue our conversation the whole way home. The walk ends too quickly and I find myself wanting to hang out with him again. We come to a stop on the walkway out front of the house. He doesn't walk me to the door and truthfully I don't blame him, it's not like he's welcome here. "Leah?" I peek up at him through my lashes.

"Yeah?"

"Um, do you think maybe I could take you to the movies on Friday?" My stomach sinks.

"Garrett, I—"

"Just as friends," he rushes to say. I stare at him for a minute trying to see if he's sincere and when I don't see any change in his demeanor, I agree. He gives me a toothy grin before leaning down and placing a quick peek to my cheek that has me standing stiff and stunned. "See ya tomorrow," he calls out as he turns and heads back toward where we came from. When he disappears around the corner, I finally snap out of my shock and head into the house. I climb the porch steps with a goofy smile on my face, grip the door handle but before I can push it open I'm shoved to the side, then pinned against the wall of the house with a hand clamped over my mouth. Fear skyrockets through my body until he moves his face in, his nose touching the tip of mine, but it's his eyes, they are filled with disgust and anger that I almost want to shrink away from him.

"You enjoy your little *date*?" he spits the word date like it burns his tongue. I try to push him off me but Darius doesn't budge. He pushes in closer until his front is plastered to mine. My treacherous body pushes into him loving his close proximity. His eyes blaze with something other than disgust, lust flares to life to life in his eyes. He yanks his hand away. I drag a full breath before his lips crash against mine. I gasp, and he uses that to his advantage, slipping his tongue inside my mouth. The taste of him has me snapping out of my stupor, and I wrap my arms around his neck, pulling him in closer.

The kiss isn't slow and sensual, it's a fight for power.

Teeth clashing, but there is a hunger to it, like we both have been starved of each other for so long that we need this in order to survive. It's then that I remember why I was sitting on the steps and hanging out with Garrett and my anger peaks. I bite down on his bottom lip so hard that I taste blood. He shoves me back until I smack my head against the wall. I release my hold on his lip, and he takes a step back, giving me the much needed space that I'll need to think clearly after that kiss.

"What the fuck, Goldie?" he snarls, while cupping his lip. I scowl at the asshole.

"You think you can kiss me after you've been doing God only knows what with that skank?" He drops his hand to his side and smirks, it isn't a sexy smirk it's one that promises pain.

"And I thought that the perfect Goldie liked an open relationship." His words have me frowning.

"What?" He closes the space between us but this time he pushes his leg between mine as he places his hands on either side of my head, caging me in. He lifts his leg a fraction higher and a gasp tears from me when he presses it right against my pussy.

"See." He moves his leg rhythmically back and forward as he speaks. "You think I don't know that seeing her with me pisses you off." A moan tumbles from my lips when he presses his leg harder against me, then he shifts slightly and the moment his leg connects with my clit, I moan.

CHAPTER ELEVEN

Darius

Bingo!

I keep moving my leg back and forward, loving how her eyes glaze over. She may *think* she hates me but her body sure as fuck doesn't. She begins to rock her hips trying to chase the high she knows only I can give her. I bend down and lick a trail from the side of her neck to her ear and nibble on her lobe. She moans and reaches out to grip my waist. I hate that her hands on me have a shiver rolling down my spine.

"You want to come, Goldie?" I whisper in her ear before licking it, causing her to moan again.

"Yes," she pants, her thrusts are growing erratic telling me without words that she's close. "Oh God, Darius. I'm so close," she breathes, my mind is in a lust filled haze, and I drop my leg. She opens her mouth to protest but clamps it closed when I push my hand inside her pants. I don't fuck around, pushing her panties to the side and swiping a single finger through her folds, moaning when I feel how fucking drenched she is. I slip a finger inside her tight wet pussy, relishing in the cry that tears from her lips. I wrap my other arm around her waist to hold her up. I feel her clenching my finger. I insert a second one and love the cry that tears from her throat.

"Ride my fingers and fucking come for me, Goldie!" Like the good little girl she is, she comes on command like always.

"Darius!" she screams so fucking loud I fear she'll wake the whole house and the neighbors. I bring her down from her high gently as she slumps forward and rests her head against my chest. At the contact my mind clears. I yank my hand free and jump back. She stumbles forward a step, then shoots me a questioning look. I keep my face blank of all emotions. "What's wrong?"

I lift my head and harden my features as I say. "Just wanted to prove a point that you really are fucking easy and will let anyone in your pants," I snarl before turning and making my way inside. Before I am out of ear shot I hear her quiet words.

"But you're not just anyone." Hearing those five words come from her mouth has a pang hitting me right in the chest. I would have believed those words a few years ago, but not now. I storm up the stairs intending to go straight to my room but pause at the top of the landing when I see Beckett leaning against the wall shooting me a dark look.

"Don't start your shit," I growl as I stalk past him and head for my room. I can't even slam the fucking door because the fucker follows after me. I spin around and pin him with a look that I hope conveys I am not in the fucking mood.

"You hurt her and you ruin us all," he says in a low even tone. I don't know why but him butting his nose into what I do with Leah grates on my fucking nerves!

"Stay the fuck out of this, Beckett!" I growl as I clench my hands into fists at my sides. The big bastard doesn't heed my warning and stalks toward me until we are chest to chest.

"Everything we have, everything we own is tied into the five of us and I won't let you fucking ruin this for me." I detect a hint of fear in his voice and that is the only reason I back down and step back looking at him in a different light. "Corvin will never allow that to happen—"

"Too bad, Beck, because it's already happened." There is no point in lying, he put it all together himself.

"Darius, we have too much to lose this year with the companies merging, and we need to ace these midterms. If Corv finds out about you and his little sister, it is going to derail everything. Find someone else to fuck and torment but not our best friend's little sister." A whoosh of air escapes me, knowing that he is right. We have all worked too fucking hard to get this merger between BCD'S and Sullivan Global. This merger is everything we have worked so fucking hard to achieve—if we get this deal then that means we finally win!

"Okay," I say on an exhale.

"Don't lie to me, D." I meet his stare with a firm look as I say.

"I won't fuck this up. I need this as much you, Crue and Corv." I don't bother mentioning Saint because his dad is loaded and he'll land on his feet either way this deal goes but for the four of us, this deal is our ticket out of here. I didn't have a dad, the useless fucker skipped town as soon as he knocked my mom up. She was weak and went back to jabbing needles in her arm and forgot she had a kid. I didn't know what it was like to go to bed warm and with a full belly until I met Corvin. He and his family took me in, gave me a safe place to rest my head plus, my mom didn't put up a fucking fight when Mrs. Williams asked if I could live with them. The useless bitch packed my bags herself and I haven't seen or heard from her since.

Beck eyes me warily for a second before nodding stiffly. "Stay away from Leah." is all he says before he turns and walks out of my room. Staying away from the she-devil would be a lot fucking easier if she didn't live here!

I manage to avoid Leah for the next three days, in doing so that means I've had to avoid the guys and most importantly, Corvin. I can't stand there and look at him when all I can think about is how making his sister come on my hand is the hottest sexual encounter I've had in years!

I fucking hate it. I hate her and how the sounds that come out of her mouth as she comes has me burning up inside. My cock is rock fucking hard at the thought of her and how her pussy clenched the fuck out of my fingers like she was milking my cock for all it was worth.

"Where the hell have you been?" I spin around at the sound of Corvin's voice. He marches toward me with his helmet under his arm, his boots sounding like high heels as he moves. The locker room is practically empty except for a few guys. I've been staying out later training each night so I wouldn't run into him in the locker room but I guess my luck has run out. He doesn't stop until there is a foot of space between us, his stare burning into me but I give nothing away. "Out!" he shouts, and like good little dogs the remaining guys clear out at the order of one of their kings. Our word is law and no one wants to fuck with us.

When the locker room is finally empty, I step back and lean against the lockers crossing my arms over my chest. Corvin has a look in his eyes that I know all too well, that look means he knows something is up and will do whatever it takes to find out.

"Why the fuck are you avoiding me?" he growls.

"I'm not," I say in an even tone.

"Bullshit!" he shouts. He's my best friend and has been for fucking years, I hate lying to him but I'm also fucking petrified that if he finds out about me and Leah, I'll lose him and I can't have that. "What the hell is going on, D. Something has been up with you and I want to know what it is."

"Nothing is wrong. I just had shit to do!" I snap. I push off the locker and try to pass him but he shoves me back until I slam against the metal. I shove him back only for him to regain his stance quicker than I expected and get right in my face.

"Fucking tell me!" he yells.

"I want Leah out of the house!" I shout back. His eyes widen and his fury is replaced with surprise.

"Your pissy and avoiding me because my sister is living with us?" The confusion can be heard in his voice, I don't blame him for being shocked.

"She… she just needs to move because I don't like living with her."

"Newsflash, asshole, she isn't moving back to the dorms."

Now I get in his face. "The fuck do you mean?" I grit out. The fucker smiles and it's filled with self-satisfaction.

"Until I find out the truth about why the fuck she *dropped* out of her school and came here, I need her close so I can watch her." I pull back and stare at him.

"What do you mean?"

He sighs then drops his helmet on the bench seat behind us, before running a hand through his sweaty hair. "Mom and Dad are giving her the cold shoulder because she won't tell them why she dropped out. They are stressing because they found out that the Flanders from next door are having to sell because the banks upped their repayments and they think theirs will go up. How the fuck do I tell them I paid off their mortgage and everything they think they pay the bank weekly has been going into a savings for them to retire?" My frustration about the Leah situation flees me when Corv drops on the bench seat and cups his face between his hands. I follow his lead and sit next to him, placing my hand on his shoulder in support.

"As soon as this merger goes through none of us have to hide, but right now with the non-disclosure in place, we can't say shit. BCD'S is going to go global. We dominate the stock market and closing this deal with Sullivan Global will grant us the financial freedom we have busted our asses to achieve from the start." From the moment the five of us decided to start BCD'S we have always pushed to go global with the stock market. This merger means we can own the biggest stock company and hotel chains, shit even the resorts, which in turn means we'll have thousands of employees beneath us and never have to worry about finances again.

"I know. It's just keeping all this a secret is fucking hard when I know I can take their stress away." He turns to look over his shoulder at me. "I can't kick her out, D. I need to know what the hell is going on with my sister. My mom said she went home for a few weeks before coming here. She said something wasn't right with Leah and she was really worried about her." A pit forms in my stomach. Leah and her mom have always been close, so for her to not confide in her mom is so out of character.

"What the fuck happened?" He sits up straight and shakes his head.

"I have no fucking idea. Mom said she wouldn't say a word about what happened and apparently she has cut all contact with her friends at DCU." Davidson Crest University is a really good school. CHU is better of course, but DCU does have the best dance team in the country, so for Leah to drop out and move schools means something happened. Now that my interest is piqued, she isn't going anywhere.

"We need to get her to talk to–" He snaps his gaze to me and raises his brows.

"Don't want to kick her out now?" he says with sarcasm thick in his tone earning him a glare from me.

"Shut up, asshole. Like I was saying, we need to get her to talk and tell us what happened." He throws his hands up in the air in frustration.

"That's the thing, she has pulled away from me. It's not like you and her get along, so she won't talk to either of us." I hate that he's right and it fucking grates on my nerves to hear this out loud.

"She'll talk to Beckett." Corv scrunches his face in confusion so I elaborate. "They have become… friendly and I think she will open up to him if Beck pushes her." Corvin shakes his head.

"Nah, dude, she's my sister," he says as he climbs to his feet. I mimic him and get in his face so he has no choice but to listen to me.

"If you want to know why Leah is running away, then

Beckett is your best option." He sighs as his shoulders slump forward.

"Except, Crue, Saint and me have that fucking training camp this weekend and we leave tomorrow night." Fuck, I forgot about that! I don't have to attend because coach said I don't need the extra fitness, but those lazy fuckers do. Serves them right for getting lit every weekend. Beck and I spent more time training than the three of them, which means, we get the perks of *not* spending our weekend spewing our guts out.

"Sucks to be you," I tease. He shoves me back, causing me to laugh.

"You're such a dick."

"I know." He rolls his eyes as he brushes past me, heading to his locker.

"I'll talk to Beck and see if he can talk to Leah," he calls out over his shoulder. I nod and tell him he's making a wise choice but in truth, I don't plan to let Beckett anywhere near her. If anyone is going to find out what the fuck happened, it's going to be me!

CHAPTER TWELVE

"That's it for the day. There will be a pop quiz on Monday, so make sure you study!" Miss Moss shouts as we all scramble to pack our things and get the hell out of the class to start the weekend. This week has dragged on. Cody and I walk out of our English class exhausted. We have been training before and after school, my body is sore and bruised but Coach said we either train twice a day or drop out. On top of training, I meet with Garrett twice a week now to be tutored for calculus, which I still don't fucking understand. All my other classes have been going great and my professors are so chill compared to Mr. Thompson.

"I need an energy drink or a shot." I laugh and shake my head. Cody is addicted to energy drinks. The girl can go through a six pack of Red Bull in a day and still sleep like a baby at night!

"You need to give that stuff up," I say as we exit the building and make our way to the quad to wait for Katie and Garrett. We have dance practice in an hour and Garrett is going away on some football trip with my brother, Crue and Saint, which means, I'm stuck at home with Darius and Beckett.

Beck is great but without my brother around and Beck knowing about Darius and me, I'm worried he'll try something.

We haven't seen each other since he gave me the best orgasm I've had in years!

But of course, he had to go and ruin the moment by talking. To have him bring me to such a high after what happened and not freaking out was a huge thing for me, then his words cut me deeper than he will ever know. I wish more than anything I was able to scrub him from my life so I could finally let him go, except you never really get over or let a guy like Darius go. Not wen he's your first love.

"Grab us a spot and I'll get us some coffees instead." I clear my thoughts and nod as I look around for a vacant table. I spot one near one of the old oak trees and beeline for it. I'm four feet away when I'm gripped by the elbow and spun around so fast, I nearly trip until an arm wraps around my waist to steady me. I look up and still in his hold, when a pair of dark brown eyes stare down at me with an intensity only Darius can master.

"We need to talk," he says in a clipped tone, and releases his hold on me then steps back. I didn't feel cold a minute ago but now without his touch I'm chilled to the bone. It's almost like his touch can set me on fire from the inside in the most delicious way. When he clicks his fingers in my face, I realize I must have been standing here just staring at him. I feel a blush creeping its way up my neck to my cheeks. I shouldn't be embarrassed because he's seen me naked, but with him, butterflies still come alive inside me when he walks in the room.

"About what? If you want to yell about what happened the other night, then I'll pass," I say in a clipped tone as I turn and nab the picnic table before someone else does and honestly, to give Darius a hint that I don't want to talk to him. After he left me on the porch, utterly confused and hurt by his blatant hate, I cried myself to sleep that night and the next. I have no idea what I have done to deserve this type of behavior from him. I should be the one that is angry since he fucking ghosted me!

I feel him slide up behind me and tense. He places his hands on either side of me on the table. I shiver when I feel his warm breath caresses the shell of my ear, he's so close that I feel his body heat radiating off of him.

"Thing is, all I can think about is making you come again but this time, on my cock." My eyes snap wide and I gasp. I'm woman enough to admit that his close proximity and the thought of his cock slipping inside me has me clenching my thighs beneath the table. "Your brother's away for the weekend and I think I need to apologize."

I swallow and dart my tongue out to moisten my lips. "Apologize for what?" My voice waivers and even I can hear how breathy I sound.

"For being an ass. You know I'm always good at making it up to you." I try to fight it, I really do, but a shiver works its way down my spine at his filthy promise. "You remember how long it takes me to say sorry, right?" I slam my eyes closed as memories of how Darius *apologizes* runs through my head. They always end with me naked and spent.

"Uh, hey?" I blink my eyes open to see a confused looking Cody standing in front of me holding two coffees. She isn't looking at me though, she stands there glaring at Darius. I caved and told her about what happened between Darius and me yesterday. She threatened to chop off his balls and burn his eyes out with a hot poker.

"Hey," Darius says in a smooth tone. When Cody looks at me, I shoot her a look, pleading with my eyes to not say anything to him.

"Well nice to see you and all that. Come on, Leah, we have practice and need to meet–" Before I can cut in and stop her from mentioning him, the man himself appears at the other end of the table.

"Hey." I feel Darius tense behind me at the sound of Garrett's voice. Rather than pull back or storm off like he normally does, he whispers low enough for only me to hear.

"If I find out that he has touched you, I'll break his fucking throwing hand and he'll never touch another football, got it?" I gulp and nod, unable to speak and embarrassed as all hell that my two friends are standing here while Darius is plastered to my back, and to top it all off, I now have to go to practice with soaked panties! Darius finally takes pity on me and steps back. I sigh in relief when he heads toward the gym, but calls over his shoulder, "See you tonight, Goldie."

After saying an awkward as hell goodbye to Garrett, thanks to Darius's macho man display, Cody and I headed to practice only for it to run an hour longer because Chelsea and Nikki couldn't keep up with the counts. I'm pissed as hell and fucking aching by the time coach tells us we can leave. She said we could have the weekend off to train on our own time, when we all know it's because she has a weekend away planned with her boyfriend. I grab my bag and sling it over my shoulder as I wait for Katie and Cody. Once they gather their things, the three of us head out. We have barely taken two steps outside before Chelsea is calling out for us to wait. We turn back to see her, Nikki and Becca coming at us. The three of us exchange looks of confusion as we wait to see what they want.

"Hey, babes." I scrunch my face and quirk a brow at Chelsea's fake-ass enthusiasm. She has stopped hanging around us ever since her and Darius *hung out*. "So, what are the plans for this weekend?"

"Nothing," Katie says, sounding just as confused as I feel. Nikki and Becca giggle. Do they realize they look like idiots standing there fake laughing?

"Well, we thought we should totes train, so we were thinking we'll come over around nine?" I reel back in shock at the blatant audacity of this girl. If she thinks she is going to use me to get closer to Darius she has another fucking thing coming.

"Yeah, no." Their fake smiles drop like I knew they would. "If the three of you want to score with the *dream* team find another way, because I'm not helping you bone my brother!" I snarl. Chelsea's eyes narrow.

"Who said I was after your brother?" I grind my teeth in anger. "If I recall, Darius blew his hit and quit it rule for *me!*" I have heard from Katie that apparently that is a thing with Darius, he only sleeps with a girl once and never kisses them.

"Did you want a round of applause for being a slut?" Cody snaps in my defense. My heart soars at her for sticking up for me. I never had any real friends at DCU, they were fake as shit, leaving me to spend most of my time alone and with someone I thought was my only friend. How dumb was I?

"You're just jealous that your bestie's brother isn't interested in your plain ass." I snap my gaze to Cody, her eyes are wide, mouth ajar in shock.

Holy fuck!

Cody has a crush on Corvin and I never fucking knew. She cuts her gaze to me, the guilty look in her eyes spears me.

"Leah, I had no idea he was your brother and I've never done anything with him, I swear. I would never do anything with him now because of girl code and you're my girl." Call me stupid, but I believe her. I can't be friends with girls who are going after my brother because it's just icky!

I shrug and smile as I say, "I know you wouldn't." A whoosh of air escapes her. "I have to go, but you and Katie come round tomorrow and we'll practice and swim, it's only Beck–" I turn back to Chelsea as I finish speaking, "and Darius home." Katie and Cody agree, giving me a hug each as I head home.

I'm just around the corner from the house when my phone rings. At the sound of *his* ringtone, I tense up. I pull my phone out and answer it before I chicken out, knowing I can't keep ignoring him forever.

"What?" I snap.

"Now, now, is that any way to greet me?" I grit my teeth and breath through my nose as I try to calm the fury spurring to life inside me at the sound of his nasally voice.

"What can I do for you?" I say in a sickly-sweet voice.

"You can start by doing what I fucking told you to do! You're running out of time. The game is in three weeks and they won't be taking the field!" Guilt and shame war inside me. If I do what he is asking, I'll ruin them and they will never forgive me! I've tried for weeks to build up the courage to tell Corvin but I can never get the words out.

"Why are you doing this?"

"Because I fucking can! Those five are going to learn a fucking lesson that they aren't untouchable!"

"I… I'll go to the cops and tell them everything," I threaten.

"Go tell them. We all know they won't do shit because of who I am and where I come from. You're the poor kid whose parents own the local hardware store. You can't afford the legal fees and everyone knows you'd let the team run a fucking train to save your brother." I cringe at his reference. "You have till game night, get it done or this shit goes public and it will give me great satisfaction to send it to your brother and daddy myself." The line goes dead. I stand here gripping my phone in a vice-like grip, tears building at the back of my eyes. I will them away not wanting to go home with tear-stained cheeks and red-rimmed eyes. I take deep breaths and try to convince myself I'm doing this to save my family, Corvin and myself the shame of this going public. If it did, people from back home would boycott my parents' business and Corvin would be shunned from his peers. He would no longer be the king of CHU, he would be the *whore's* brother.

I give myself another minute to wallow in self-pity before I pull it together. Straightening my shoulders, I try as hard as I can to plaster on a smile. The fake charade lasts a whole second before it falls away and the first tear falls. Once they start they don't stop. I run the rest of the way home, making it in a few minutes. I take the porch steps two at a time, push the front door open and slam it closed before racing for the stairs.

Beck and Darius both jump to their feet as I pass the living room, but I don't stop when they call my name. I run to my room where I can break down without anyone seeing me fall apart. I'm a horrible person! I slam my door closed and lock it, drop my bag and head straight for the shower. I lock Darius's side of the bathroom and strip off, then turn the water to scalding hot as a form of punishment for myself. I let the sobs tear out of me now, knowing the sound of the shower will mask them and stop the guys from hearing me fall apart. I slide down the wall and wrap my arms around my legs as I bury my face in the top and cry.

I've never let myself feel the full weight of what happened—the demand placed upon me by the person who I trusted and he fucking used me!

I let myself feel everything—all the pain, anger, shame and self-loathing. I thought running away would fix everything but it didn't. I was just a tool for him to use to get back at my brother and the guys, and the worst fucking part is I had no idea it happened until years fucking later!

Two years ago my whole fucking world stopped when Darius left me. I thought I was slowly healing from the loss of him, until three months ago when I overheard a conversation that changed my whole freaking life. I climb to my feet, grab my loofah and begin to scrub my skin, feeling so dirty and used!

CHAPTER THIRTEEN

Darius

"What the fuck?" I say aloud, confused as hell why Leah just ran through the house crying.

"Someone is going to pay for this!' Beck growls, and I nod my agreement. "What do we do, Corv isn't here?" I exhale loudly and turn to face him. His face is a mask of pure fury, fists clenched at his sides, while he stands there vibrating with anger.

"Beck?" He pulls his angry stare from the stairs Leah just ran up to look at me.

"What?"

"I need to make sure she's okay." His eyes narrow as he says, "No, I told you—"

"Something fucking happened, Beckett. Leah doesn't cry, so whatever happened is fucking big. She needs me," I shout. His gaze hardens the longer he stands there staring at me, it takes an age before he gives me a curt nod. I'm racing out of the living room and taking the steps two at a time as I go in search of the girl that I planned to destroy, only by the looks of things, some other motherfucker beat me to it!

I grip her door handle and try to open it, but it's locked. I pound on the door for a minute but when she doesn't answer, I growl, turn and storm into my room to find the bathroom door closed. I try to open it but it's locked. Fuck this. I storm over to my desk, yank the draw open and grab my pocketknife out. I use it to twist the lock on the sliding door open. When it clicks, I chuck the knife onto my bed and open the door. Steam hits me right in the face, and the second it clears, I see her and my chest caves in.

"Fuck!" I growl as I storm into the room, and yank the glass door open. She's too focused or in a trance to even notice me thanks to her rabidly scrubbing her body. Her skin is bright red and raw from the hot water and her frantic need to scrub the skin from her body. Reaching in to turn the water off, I curse when the water splashes onto my arm—the fucking shower is hot as fuck.

I turn it off and it's only then she snaps out of it and snaps her gaze to me. Her green eyes are wide but not from fright, it's… guilt. "Goldie?" She shakes her head and takes a step back from me.

"Stay away from me, you need to get far away from me." Her voice is devoid of all emotion and that scares the shit out of me.

I raise my hands in surrender, keeping my eyes on hers as I ask, "What happened, baby?" Her bottom lip trembles and her eyes fill with tears.

"Leave, Darius!" she screams.

"Never," I growl out as I reach for her and pull her against me. She tries to fight me off but I'm too strong. I wrap my arms around her wet body as she tries to pound her little fists against my chest.

"I hate you! I fucking hate you, Darius. Let me go." I weather her words and fists for a full minute before she finally crumbles in my hold and tears pour from her eyes as she breaks down in my arms. I lift her out of the shower. She wraps her legs and arms around me as she buries her face in the crook of my neck. I snag a towel on my way out of the bathroom and head for my room. I try to place her on her feet to dry her but she won't let go. Sighing I drop down on the edge of my bed and try to dry her as best as I can before wrapping the towel around her back so she doesn't catch a chill. After a moment of hearing her sniffle and cling to me like I'm her lifeline, I give in. I wrap my arms around her and hold her tight allowing myself this moment to get lost in the feeling of being this close to her.

"I'm right here, Goldie. Whatever happened you can tell me about it," I say in a calm tone. She shakes her head against my neck and burrows in deeper, her legs locking around my waist as she tightens her grip with her arms. I've never seen Leah like this before. She is usually so fucking strong and resilient, nothing can keep this girl down. A shiver works its way through her body. I curse before I stand, her hold on me is so tight I don't even need to hold her, then pull the covers on my bed back, ready to place her underneath them but the sound of Beckett's voice has me pausing. I'm fucking glad I have my back to him or I'd have to knock my best friend out for seeing my girl naked.

My girl?

"Is she okay?" I can't even turn my head to look over my shoulder at him, thanks to the head currently buried into the side of my neck.

"She will be, now fuck off," I say in a hurried tone.

"Why is there a towel… oh fucking hell, Darius!" he snarls, and I cut in before he continues down the path of his wayward thoughts.

"I had to help her out of the shower. That's it, nothing more. Now get the fuck out so I can put her to bed," I snarl, getting annoyed at his constant intrusion into everything I do with Leah.

"Her room is next door!" he adds smugly.

"Not tonight it isn't. She stays with me, so unless you want to see our best friend's sister naked and me strip down to get in behind her, you'll get the fuck out now!" He mumbles beneath his breath but it's too quiet for me to make out. The sound of my bedroom door closing has me snapping back into action and trying to place her under the covers. Even when I lay her in the bed she refuses to let go. "You need to get under the covers, Goldie."

"Don't leave me, Darius, please." The broken tone of her voice fucking spears me. I close my eyes, trying not to war within myself. After everything she has done and put me through, can I give her one night of the old me and hold her through this? A small whimper escapes her and that makes the decision for me.

"I won't leave but I need you to let go so I can get out of these wet clothes, then I'll jump in with you."

"Pinky swear?" Despite my torment I smile at her antics— she would always make me pinky swear if she didn't think I would follow through.

"Pinky swear, Goldie, now let go and hop under the covers." My words seem to put her at ease. She releases her hold on me and slips under the covers. I make quick work of stripping off my pants and shirt, then shut off the light and climb in behind her. I keep an inch of space between us. She isn't having that, she snuggles into my side. Her leg is thrown over mine and her arm lays across my stomach. I can feel her bare fucking pussy against my side and it's taking every ounce of power I have not to roll us over and sink my hardening cock inside her tight wet heat.

Silence stretches but it isn't uncomfortable, her tears have stopped and she isn't shivering anymore. I don't know if it's from being under the covers or the fact that she is plastered to my side and absorbing my body heat. She traces lazy patterns across my abs, the feeling of her hands on me is the worst form of fucking torture but I am powerless to stop her.

Girls at CHU think they need to appear easy to capture my attention. Leah never had to do anything to capture it because she had it from the moment I saw her. I may sound like a little bitch but Leah Williams was my childhood crush and my first love. I really thought she was it for me but I was so fucking wrong. A tired sigh escapes me and she tenses.

"You're going to kick me out now, aren't you?" she whispers, her breath fans across my chest causing gooseflesh to erupt all over my body. How this girl holds so much power over me still I'll never know. I open my mouth to answer but snap it closed the moment her fingers trail lower. When she reaches the waist-band of my boxers, she tilts her head back and stares up at me. The only light source is the moonlight streaming in through the windows. I can see the need in her eyes. "Please." That one whispered fucking word seals my fate. I reach out, grip her chin in my hand pulling her to me. She hovers above me searching my gaze for a sign that I'm going to back out and leave her high and dry like the other night, when she doesn't see it, she smashes her lips against mine. I groan at the taste of her when she slips her tongue inside my mouth—she tastes like *home*.

She deepens the kiss as she pushes her dainty little hand inside my boxers gripping my length. I break the kiss and hiss at the feeling of having her hand wrapped around my cock. All my carefully crafted rules fly out the window. I blew my no kissing rule with her twice. Leah has never been shy when it comes to taking what she wants or telling me what she needs. She isn't like most girls, they get shy and look away while they suck your cock but not her, she holds my gaze as she strokes me. Her strokes are slow and measured but the moment her little fingers feel the pre-cum leaking from my dick, her eyes widen and gasp slips free.

"Fuck," she grits out before yanking her hand free and moving away, I rest up on my elbows about to lose my shit at her but she throws the covers back, grips the waistband of my briefs and yanks them down, so I keep my mouth shut.

She moans at the sight of my cock. I settle back against the pillows as I wait for her to get into position to suck me off but what she does next surprises the fuck out of me. She spins around and straddles my face between her legs. I don't have time to ponder the fact she just 69'd me because she bends down and sucks my cock into the back of her throat drawing a groan of pleasure from me.

"Shit, Goldie!" I growl a second before she pushes her pussy down onto my face. I reach around and grip the globes of her ass in my hands and squeeze at the same time I push her down onto my waiting tongue. She moans around me, the vibrations from that travel up my body drawing a shudder of pleasure out. The second she deepthroats me and cups my balls in her hand, I kick up the pace and suck her enlarged clit into my mouth. If she keeps sucking me like that I'm going to be coming down her throat and not in her pussy. I lick my way down to her opening and push my tongue inside her wet hole. Her taste assaults me and fuck if it isn't the best thing I have tasted in fucking years.

She releases my cock with a wet pop. "Oh my God, just like that." She moans as she begins to grind back and forward along my tongue, chasing her release. She grips my dick in her hand and strokes it in sync with her thrusts. After a minute, her moans begin to grow louder, her strokes become jerky and erratic. As she gets closer to her release, she drops my cock and leaps off me. Before a protest can form in my mind, she turns around and straddles me but this time, facing me. Her eyes hold mine as I suck her clit into my mouth, she throws her head back moaning my name.

"Play with my nipples," she breathes out. I do as she commands and relish in the sounds that come from her. "Oh God, hold your tongue out like that and let me ride it." I do as she demands and let her ride my fucking face loving that she is taking exactly what she wants from me. Looking up her flushed cheeks and watching her tits bounce as she fucks my face is one of the hottest sights I have ever seen. "Yes, Halfback, like that, baby, just like that," she cries out. I grip her waist and hold her in place as I quicken my pace and eat her fucking cunt like it's the last thing I will ever do. She grips my hair in her hand and pulls my face in closer. "I'm coming, don't stop." She moans, in the next second her head is thrown back as she screams my name loud enough for Beckett to hear and know what we are up to.

Shudders wrack her body, my cock is so fucking hard it's painful.

I don't bring her down gently, I push her off me and climb on top. She grips my cheeks and pulls me down to her so she can kiss me. When she tastes herself on my tongue she moans. I pull back and reach into the drawer of my side table, grab a foil packet out, then tear it open with my teeth. I slide the condom on, hissing, I'm so fucking horny and ready to fuck the shit out of her.

I grip my cock and slide it through her folds relishing the sounds that come from her, she looks so beautiful beneath me. Hair wild and splayed over the bed, cheeks flushed and eyes glassy from her climax.

"I need you," she says, that's all it takes for my restraint to snap and I line my cock up with her opening. She tenses when I push the head of my cock inside her. I grit my teeth, fuck she is so tight!

"When was the last time you had sex?" I grit out through clenched teeth, she shakes her head.

"I don't want to talk about it," she says breathless. A sheen of sweat dots my forehead as I push inside her slowly not wanting to hurt her but also putting myself through fucking pain going this slow. "Fuck," she moans out when I'm halfway inside her. "I forgot how big you were." Those words have a smile breaking free on my face.

"I need to be all the way inside you, can you take it?" The strain in my voice can be heard.

"Do it, I want all of you," she says. We both cry out in pleasure and pain, I drop to my elbows on either side of her head as I wait for her to adjust to me. She breathes through her nose trying to calm herself.

"Kiss me, baby," I say in the hopes it will distract her from the pain. She obliges me and within seconds she begins to relax enough for me to move inside her.

"Oh shit," she moans against my mouth. I slowly move in

and out of her, loving how she fucking fits me like a glove. I push up to rest on my haunches, grab each of her ankles and place them on either of my shoulders, as I push forward until her knees are against her chest. Leah being a dancer has always benefited me when it came to the bedroom—the girl is so flexible and willing to allow me to bend her any way I like. I draw my cock out, leaving only the head inside her before slamming back in. We both cry out as pleasure ripples through our body. I can't draw this out, I have wanted this for too fucking long. I'll make it up to her later.

"I can't go slow, I need to fuck you and come so badly," I say in a clipped tone.

"Fuck me and make me scream your name." I do as commanded, and fuck her so hard her legs wind up being flat against her chest. When her cries become too loud, I slam my lips against hers to quiet her down. She tries to break the kiss but I don't let her as I continue to pound inside her fucking pussy chasing my own release. She bites down on my bottom lip, making my eyes blaze with desire as I stare down at the little minx. She releases my lip, reaches around her legs and cups my face. "I'm gonna come," she whispers. Her brows dip and then she is arching off the bed screaming my name. I feel my balls tightening and know I'm a second away from joining her in ecstasy. Three more pumps inside her and my head is thrown back as I roar out my release.

I've never fucked anyone but Leah front on and I sure as shit have never tasted another pussy on my tongue except hers. We were each other's firsts and in a lot of ways I may have cut her from my life but I still couldn't allow myself to tarnish what we shared by giving that part of myself to someone else.

CHAPTER FOURTEEN

Leah

Darius and I are panting, breathless from the best sex of my life and grateful Corvin wasn't here to hear me screaming his best friend's name as he made come all over his glorious cock.

"I need to pull out." I nod and bite down on my bottom to brace myself for the pain that will follow. I whimper when he pulls out and I feel the sting. "Shit, I'm sorry." He slips off the bed and my heart sinks, he's going to kick me out. I watch his retreating form head into the bathroom, then I gather what pride I have left and slide off the bed. I snag a black shirt off the floor and try to pull it on, but freeze when I get it over my head at the sound of his angry tone.

"What the fuck are you doing?" I stare at him confused. He stands naked and proud. My gaze drops to his cock and my mouth waters, wanting to taste him again. Sucking Darius off is one of my favorite things to do. "Leah!" he snaps. I shake my head to clear my thoughts.

"I thought you would want me to leave because… well… I mean you need to—"

"Get in the fucking bed, Leah. You're not going anywhere," he snaps as he makes his way back to me. I turn and frown at him as he slips beneath the covers and pulls the other side back for me. I move toward him ready to hold him while I sleep. "Lose the fucking shirt. You know the rules, no clothes when you sleep with me." I can't stop the goofy grin from stretching across my face. I do as he says and yank the shirt off before slipping in beside him. His arms encircle me, while I lay my head against his naked chest and breathe him in. I miss this.

I miss him.

I want to ask him what happened between us and why he left me but I'm also scared as hell to hear his answer. What if it was because I wasn't good enough. Was I shit in bed? Too clingy? Memories of the last time we were together run through my mind. We had a fight before his game. I was tired of sneaking around and being his little secret. I wanted him to tell Corvin about us. He said my brother wouldn't understand because he was eighteen and I was sixteen at the time. I didn't care about age, I just wanted Darius to tell Corv that I was his and there wasn't a thing my brother could do about it.

Except he didn't.

He said it wasn't the right time and to go home and wait for him to get there. I didn't listen. Saint told me they had a party to go to after the game. I decided if he wouldn't tell Corvin, then I would at the party, except I never saw him again after that night. Something worse happened and I wish every day for the past three months that I had listened and went straight home like I was told.

"Darius–" I try to speak but he cuts me off.

"Not tonight, Leah. If we go down that path we won't be sleeping in the same bed or talking to each other again. Leave the past alone for the night." I take a deep breath and try to shoot my shot, the worst he could do is turn me down so I decide to go for it.

"Can we forget the past until Monday night, when Corvin gets home, then we can go back to normal?" I can hear the pleading tone in my own voice but I don't care. If four days is all he'll give me then I'll take them.

Fuck, who am I kidding?

I'll take anything Darius gives me because I'm still in love with the boy who stole my heart years ago.

"That's not a good idea," he rushes out but I know Darius, the tone of his voice and how he went rigid tells me he wants this too.

"It's four days. After that you can go back to acting like you hate me when I know you don't."

"I do hate you!" he growls, and I roll my eyes, even though he can't see me.

"I'll pretend like I believe you and we can also pretend that your cock isn't getting hard right now at the thought of being able to fuck me whenever and wherever you like because my brother isn't here." My words are his undoing, in a split second I'm on my back with my tall, dark and handsome bad boy looming above me. I reach up to touch him but he grips my wrists in each of his hands and pins them on either side of my head. Not one to go down without a fight, I open my legs wider and thrust my hips upward, then smile triumphantly when I feel his hard cock brush against my pussy. "Who's the liar now?" I taunt. His eyes darken but in the most delicious way. I know that look and it means Darius is going to fuck me into submission until I tell him I was wrong and he was right, even when he wasn't.

"You know I'm gonna make you take that back, right?" The husky tone of his voice has my fucking pussy fluttering! I lock my legs around his waist and pull him down to me, gasping when I feel the tip of his cock push against my entrance, his eyes blaze with need.

"Give me these four days and I'll let you do whatever you want to me. I'll take them back right now if you give in." I can't keep the desperation out of my voice even if I tried. I need this and I know he does too. We can work everything else out on Tuesday but for now, I just want to let our bodies do the talking and fool myself into thinking that Darius could somehow be mine one day. That will never happen after I do what I have to do, but four days with him means I'll finally be able to let him go and in my own weird way, say goodbye.

"Four days," he says as he slowly pushes inside me, drawing a moan from deep within my chest. "Wherever and whenever I want. You deny me once and the deal is off, got it?"

"Yes," I moan.

"I want to fuck in the living room while Beckett is next to us, you gonna say no?" he asks just as he buries himself fully inside me, I moan. "Answer me," he snaps as he begins to thrust in and out of me lazily.

"No, I'll fuck you in front of him whatever you want, just don't stop moving, please!" He places a quick kiss to the tip of my nose before saying,

"Good girl." His thrust grows harder and deeper—fuck he feels so good inside me! He releases his hold on my wrists, rests back on his haunches then pulls me up so I'm sitting on top of him. I look at him and my heart lurches to life at the sight of this God beneath me. I wrap my arms around his shoulders and capture his lips in a kiss that I hope conveys everything I feel for him. "Move for me, Goldie," he rasps out, and I do just that. I glide up and down on his cock. He feels so much deeper from this angle and fuck, it feels so good. He captures my nipple in his mouth and swipes his tongue over my enlarged bud pulling a moan from me.

"Bite it!" I demand. He clamps his teeth on my nipple and that's it, I cry out as my pussy clenches his cock trying to milk it of its cum as I come all over his cock.

"That's it baby, ride me while you come." Shudders wrack my body as I come down from my high. He places a soft kiss to my lips before maneuvering us so he is once again on top of me. Unlike last time, he doesn't rush. He takes his time sliding in and out of me, making sure I can feel every glorious inch of him. His hands cup either side of my face as he bends down, I expect him to kiss me but he doesn't, he holds my stare as he makes… love to me.

Moisture gathers in the corners of my eyes. Darius may not be able to say it with words but he is saying it with his body, he loves me but something from our past still haunts him to the point he can't let me in.

My emotions get the better of me, before I can stop them the words fly out of my mouth. "I love you." My eyes widen but I don't regret saying them because they are true. He doesn't miss a beat, his pace remains the same and his expression doesn't change as he speaks.

"I know you do, Goldie," is all he says before he kisses me. Questions swirl through my mind and I feel hurt but what did I expect? For him to say it back? All thought flees my body when he pushes deeper inside me, drawing a long deep moan from me, he breaks the kiss and buries his face in the side of my neck. He sucks my flesh into his mouth while he fucks me, and his pace begins to quicken.

"Oh God, like that," I say, he keeps the same pace and intensity, a minute goes by and my pussy clamps down on his cock.

"Fuck yes, come with me, baby," he growls out, gives two more pumps and then we are both flying over the edge into euphoric bliss. My pussy is greedy and clamping down on him, not wanting him to ever leave. I have to agree with her. But the moment he pulls out of me he rests his hands on the tops of my knees, pushes my legs open wider and smiles possessively. "Fuck, do you know how good you look with my cum dripping out of you?" My eyes open so wide they begin to hurt.

"What the fuck! You didn't put a condom on?" He shoots me a condescending look.

"You were the one who pulled my cock into *you!*" I roll my eyes.

"How do I know you didn't catch anything from that ratty bitch you had over?" His brows hit his hairline and it pisses me off when I see him trying to fight his smile from breaking free. "I'm serious, this isn't funny!" I snap.

"So, you're more worried you caught herpes than you are that you might be pregnant?" I glare up at him, also fully aware I am naked and have his cum currently dripping out of me. I feel it sliding into my ass and fight the shudder that wants to break free. Darius doesn't miss a beat, running his finger through my folds, capturing his cum and pushing it back inside me. I can't help the moan that breaks free. "My cum belongs inside you," he says as he pulls his finger out and smears it over my stomach. "And on you." His words shouldn't turn me on but they fucking do. As if he has a direct link to my pussy, it clamps down trying to hold his cum inside me.

To distract myself from thoughts of him fucking me again and coming in my mouth I answer his question. "I'm on the pill and have been since I was fourteen, remember? It helps control the flow of my periods." He smirks and nods, motherfucker. "You remembered?" He quirks a brow at me.

"I've never fucked a girl without a condom, Leah, and I also never fucked Chelsea. You are the only one and of course I remembered. I would never take an uncalculated risk like that." Embarrassment washes over me, his features soften at the sight. "Come on, we need to clean you up so I can fill you up again." I frown at him in confusion and he rolls his eyes playfully. "We're going to wash my cum out of your beautiful cunt then I'm going to fuck you in the shower and fill you up. Tonight, you will wear panties to bed so I know my cum will stay right where it belongs."

I fucking moan at his dirty depraved words. I can't lie to myself though, it has always been a turn on for me seeing Darius get all possessive and alpha male. Some women hate it but I'm not one of them. When he slips off the bed and offers me his hand, I take it without hesitation, excited for him to ruin me over the next four days before *I* ruin him.

CHAPTER FIFTEEN

Darius

I sip my protein shake and lean over the railing on the back porch as I watch Leah, Katie and Cody practice their dance. I don't know what the fuck any of the moves are called but I do know Leah looks fucking good doing them. The three girls are standing around in a makeshift circle having a water break. Leah throws her head back and laughs at something Katie says. I watch her body tense and her laughter die off as she peers over shoulder at me. I smirk, I knew she would feel me watching her. She always said that she could pick me out in a room full of people blindfolded. What she doesn't know is the same goes for me. Her eyes twinkle in delight at the sight of me shirtless and wearing low-slung basketball shorts.

She's going to pay for letting me wake up to an empty bed. I'll admit, the moment I woke up and felt her side empty I panicked until I heard laughter and peeked out the window to see her outside with her friends. I decided to work out in the basement while she trained. We didn't get much sleep last night but fuck, I've never felt so alive. She shoots me a wink before turning back to her friends who both shoot her a knowing look. She shrugs and the three of them laugh before dropping their drinks and getting ready to go another round.

"You're playing with fire." My shoulders slump and my good mood sours at the sound of Beckett's voice. I know he is only trying to watch out for Corvin and me in his own way but I'm a big boy and know what I'm doing. He slides up beside me and mimics my position, but instead of a protein shake, he sips a coffee. When I see him in a pair of sweats and shirtless, I quirk a brow.

"I know you didn't work out, which means your lack of dress is because you just walked your pussy out the front door." He pins me with a dirty look, I return it.

"At least she wasn't one of our best friend's sisters." I grimace, then turn back to watch the girls as they slowly lower themselves to the ground and then push their hips up and down while punching the ground, it looks fucking hot. "Stay away from her." I look back to Beckett and shake my head.

"We agreed, her and I have until Monday night when Corv gets back. Give me this, Beckett, Corvin will never know," I plead.

"She isn't some random girl, Darius. She is part of our... family."

"You don't think I know that?" I snap. "I wish she wasn't his sister but I can't help that I lo..." I clamp my mouth closed and curse as I turn away from him, drop my glass on the table and march over to the girls. They don't hear me coming, thanks to the music blasting from the JBL speaker. I creep up behind Leah and wrap my arms around her waist. She screams in surprise but I don't allow her to recover as I spin and rush toward the pool.

"Darius, no!" she shouts but it's too late, we're already soaring through the air then crash through the surface of the water. She pushes away from me as she swims to the surface. I break the surface and laugh at the angry look on her face. "You are such a dick!" Her words pack no heat, so I swim over to her and push the loose strands of hair from her face, grip her waist and lift her. She wraps her arms and legs around me as she melts into my hold.

"You looked hot, I thought I would help you cool off." She throws her head back and laughs.

"You are such a dork," she says with a smile. I press a chaste kiss to her lips and shoot her a wink.

"Throwing you in the pool was my form of revenge for letting me wake up alone!" Her features soften and now she is the one placing a kiss to my lips. She pulls back and ghosts her lips over mine.

"I'll make it up to you tonight." I growl my approval, but before I can kiss her again, she turns to her friends and waves them over.

"Leah, I think I just got pregnant from watching that display of raw sexual need." Leah and Cody both break out into a full-on belly laugh at their friend's crazy ass. At the sound of pounding footfalls. I snap my gaze to the other side, but I'm too late to cover my face from the splash as Beck leaps through the air yelling.

"Toron Amo!"

"Motherfucker!" I snarl as water drips down my face. Leah laughs and wipes the water off my face, kisses me once more before wigging free of my hold to go hang with her friends. I've decided at this moment, I don't like her friends, they are taking up too much of *my* time. All her time should be spent with me, not them.

"Glare any harder and your face will crack." The sarcasm is thick in Beck's voice, which just grates on my fucking nerves.

"Shut up," I snap as I swim to the other side of the pool. Beck follows and we lean against the edge and watch the girls laugh and splash each other. Seeing Leah happy brings a smile to my face. The longer I look at her, the more I wonder, how am I going to let her go?

"You need to end whatever this is before it goes too far." I lull my head to the side and stare at Beck. His gaze is on the girls. I study him for a moment and watch as a small smile twitches at the corner of his mouth when Leah begins to laugh at something Cody said. My eyes widen as I push off the wall to block his line of sight. He frowns when he sees the look on my face, I can't fucking believe this. "What?"

I shake my head annoyed at myself for not seeing this earlier, how the fuck could I have missed it? "You noticed everything about what I was up to with Leah years ago because *you* were watching her too! You care so much about what I do to her because *you* want to be the one doing it to her as well." Beckett's face hardens, his upper lip pulls back in snarl. "Now, how long have you been in love with *my* girl?" He pushes off the wall of the pool and gets right in my face, pushing his forehead into mine. The conversation behind us stops as the girls focus their attention on us.

"You don't know what the fuck you are talking about," he seethes.

"Why the fuck do you care so much if you don't have feelings for her, big man?" I taunt, his gaze searches mine for a second.

"Fuck you, Darius, you stay the hell out of my business!"

"I'll stay out of yours if you stay the fuck out of mine and Leah's. You think you can get her to notice you?" I scoff like an arrogant son of a bitch before continuing. "I've always been the center of her world and her attention will always be on me. You will never have a chance where she is concerned."

"You are such an asshole!" I spin away from Beck to see Leah and the other two girls looking at us with looks of disgust, anger and the one that cuts me deep is the look of betrayal on Leah's face. I push away from Beck to go to her but the three of them scramble to get out of the pool and away from me. I reach the edge of the pool, grip the side ready to jump out but the look she pins me with has me pausing. "I don't know what is worse, the fact that I can let a guy who ghosted me for years back into my bed without thought, or the fact that I was stupid enough to ever believe that you would ever see me as anything more than your dirty little secret." I grind my teeth so hard they begin to ache. She thinks she can stand there and look down her nose at me after what she fucking did!

I push out of the pool, move into her space until my chest is against her. She cranes her neck back to meet my angry stare. My fists clench and unclench at my sides as I battle within myself to try calm the anger that is coursing through my body like wild-fire. The sound of Beckett getting out of the pool and heading around to us makes the decision for me, my anger wins out.

"You stand there like you're the perfect fucking Virgin Mary and yet you're the whole fucking reason I do what I do now!" I scream in her face. She stumbles back a step with wide eyes, fear flashes through them. "Miss fucking perfect thinks she can come *here* to *my* house and have a right to be pissy with me?" I laugh but there is no humor to it. I close the space between us again, grip the back of her neck, bending down so we are eye level, then deliver the final blow that I know will break her. "I knew fucking you again would be easy because a girl like you spreads her legs for anyone." Her hand strikes out so fast I don't have time to block the hit. My cheek stings from her hit but I don't try to soothe the ache. Her gaze spears me, her green eyes burn with hatred.

"You love to call me a slut and whore but let's not forget who is the one with the track record here, *halfback*." Hearing my old pet name from her roll off her tongue with such venom has me stilling. "I never left you for anyone, you left me, remember?" I push in closer until the tips of our noses are touching. I can feel her breath fanning across my lips.

"Nah, you just like to get fucked at a party by my worst enemy because you're a deceitful bitch like that and like to play offside, don't you, Goldie?" Her eyes are so wide they remind me of dinner plates. I pull back and stare down at her pale face and shake my head in disgust when tears fill her eyes as her body begins to tremble. "Oh, baby, don't act so shocked. You didn't really think you were different, did you?" I tsk like an asshole. "Goldie, you were a phase, the forbidden fruit if you will and fuck, did I love destroying your innocence," I say as I bite my lip and run my gaze up and down her body. "But now, you're nothing but a used up, cum dumpster for the team to hit when they feel the need."

I expect her to fight back, scream, shout, or even hit me but what I don't expect is for a gut-wrenching sob to tear from her as tears pour down her cheeks before she takes off... running. I watch as she runs through the gate around the side of the house, soaking wet with her two friends chasing after her and shouting her name, for her to come back. My breaths are coming in short rapid pants as my anger continues to ride me. She fucking had it coming! I repeat that over and over in my mind until a pissed off looking Beckett comes into view.

"Go," I snap and do a shooing motion with my hand. "Go chase after her and be her savior. Now's your chance to finally nail her, Beck. Believe me, bro, the girl can suck dick better than *Jesse James*." The words have barely left my mouth before his fist connects with my jaw, sending me sailing through the air and crashing through the surface of the pool water. I push off the bottom of the pool and swim to the top, the moment I break the surface his angry shouts await me.

"I don't like her like that. Leah reminds me of someone I fucking lost, you dumb fuck!" My brows raise, I've never heard Beck talk about someone from his past before. "You think she cheated on you, is that it?"

"Stay out of it," I growl.

"You're a fucking pussy, Darius. Leah is everything you aren't. That girl has loved you since she was a child. Anyone with fucking eyes can see it. How Corvin hasn't noticed beats me. You are a fucking idiot. Just to clarify shit for you because you're a fucking dumbass, I am going after Leah, but it isn't to get in her pants. It is to make sure our best friend's little sister is okay!" Before I can think of a witty retort he is running toward the house. I punch the water and growl out in frustration, fucking Leah! The girl is like a poison I can't seem to get out of my fucking system. Truth is, I don't know if I want her out of my system.

CHAPTER SIXTEEN

I don't know where I'm running to, Cody and Katie gave up chasing me a while ago and I'm grateful for that. I couldn't face them after knowing they heard what Darius just said to me, his words cutting me deeper than he will ever know.

He knew.

He knew this whole fucking time and never once said a thing. After all these years I finally found out why he disappeared from my life. I slipped into the worst depression after I found out what happened to me. I couldn't claw my fucking way out of that dark hole. I can feel the claws of my depression trying to drag me under again, only this time, I don't think I have the strength to pull myself out knowing that Darius thinks I wanted what happened.

I slam to a stop when I realize I've found my way to the beach. I trek out to the bank and drop down allowing the sobs to claw their way out of me. The sea breeze sends a chill down my spine thanks to my soaked clothes. I try with all my might to stay out of my head and soak in the beauty around me. The beach is empty and the only sounds that can be heard are the waves crashing against the shore, the ocean is so beautiful and yet equal parts deadly. The beauty of the ocean can lull anyone into thinking that they can master it and control it but the truth is, the ocean is like a heart. No matter how hard you tell the organ to stop feeling what it does, it never listens because love is the same as the sea—equal parts beautiful and deadly.

When I feel arms lift me, I snap my eyes open ready to scream until I look up and see his face. My heart breaks at the sight of him. I dart my gaze around and that's when I realize night has fallen, I must have fallen asleep! A shiver works its way through my body, making me realize that I'm freezing. He curses beneath his breath and quickens his pace.

"I got her!" Darius shouts. I lull my head to the side to see headlights in the parking lot. "Turn up the heat, she's freezing." I close my eyes not wanting to see his face, how can he come find me asleep on the beach, act like he cares when he and I both know he hates me. "I don't hate you, Leah." His clipped tone has me snapping my gaze open and cursing under my breath for speaking my thoughts out loud. When we reach the car, I see Beck standing there with a sad smile on his face holding the passenger door open for me. Instead of putting me in the seat like I thought he would, he slips in with me still in his hold. I try to wiggle free but his hold around my waist tightens. I maneuver myself so I'm sitting on his lap rather than being held bride style. Beck closes the door and moves to the other side. I hold my hands out in front of the vent and sigh when I feel the heat starting to thaw my frozen fingers.

Beck slips into the driver seat of his car, puts it in drive and peels out of the lot. The tension in the car is palpable but I refuse to speak, I already feel uncomfortable at the fact I'm sitting on Darius's lap rather than on the actual seat. I sigh in relief when I see the two-story I have now come to call home until my dorm building is ready. The moment Beck puts the car in park, I grab the handle and push the door open. I nearly fall flat on my face trying to escape Darius but I don't care. I steady myself and hold my head high as I march toward the house ready to take the longest, hottest shower in the history of showers.

"Unless you're hiding a key in that sports bra, the doors locked." I freeze on the second step, then inhale a deep breath as I turn back toward the two assholes who are leaning against the car with smug looks on their faces. Darius holds his keys out to me. "Give me a kiss and I'll unlock it for you." I keep my face blank and I make my way down the stairs, the self-satisfied smirk on his face makes what I'm about to do so much sweeter. I stop two steps away from him, bend down and grab a rock. Beck and Darius's eyes are wide. I spin on my heel, march up the stairs and peg the rock through one of the windows on one side of the door. "What the fuck."

"Leah!"

They both shout at the same time, I turn my head to the side and shoot them both a wink as I carefully go through the *new* front door I made and make my way upstairs, ignoring the pair of them calling for me. They can sort out the fucking window. It's the least Darius can do after the shit he put me through today! I don't even bother to lock his side of the bathroom knowing he'll just break in again like he did last night. I kick off my sneakers and cringe at the feeling of having soggy socks on, knowing my feet will look like prunes. My clothes are next to go. Dumping them into the hamper in the corner, I step into the shower stall and switch the faucet to hot. I step back and give it time to heat up before I'm stepping under the spray and allowing it to wash away the pain and aches of the worst fucking day.

How I went from waking smiling with Darius beside me, to him flipping out and saying such horrid things to me is confusing as fuck. I need to learn that Darius and I are doomed, we will never be more than shared kisses in the dark corner of the room. We will never be a couple and happily in love. We are destined to be apart. If I could just find the courage to tell him, then maybe he would understand but in order to tell him the truth that means I expose myself to my stupidity and the fact that I should have listened to him and just stayed the fuck home!

After shaving and washing my hair and body, I flick the shower off and step out onto the bath mat only to realize I forgot to grab my towel. Shit! I wring my hair out as best I can as I make my way into my bedroom, I just want to hop into my *Oodie* and snuggle up in bed for the rest of the night.

"Jesus Christ!"

"Close your fucking eyes!" I snap my wide-eyed gaze to my bedroom door, to see both Beckett and Darius standing there. When Becks gaze lands on me, he slams his eyes closed like Darius commanded. I ignore the heated look in Darius's eyes as I roll mine in return. "Put some fucking clothes on!" I keep my back to them and fight the smile from breaking free when I bend over and grab my towel off the ground next to my bed. The sharp intake of breath tells me Darius got a good eyeful of my pussy. "I'm not fucking with you, Leah!"

I snort as I wrap the towel around my head, turn back to them both—still naked—then place my hands on my hips. I dart my gaze between them both. I can see from the strain on Beck's forehead he is trying so hard not to let his gaze drop lower. I shoot him a wink before looking back to a seething Darius, his face taut with tension, fists clenched at his sides.

"For someone who continues to call me a slut daily, you are mighty concerned about who happens to see me naked." My voice is breathy and sounds sexy to my own ears. Darius's eyes blaze with heat but there in the depths of his brown eyes I can see fury lurking. Beck, on the other hand, just looks stunned. Fuck it, I'm gonna play this out. Knowing both their gazes are on me, I move toward the dresser and pull open my panty drawer. I keep my back to them as I fish out my black lace thong, then bend and relish in the hisses that I hear coming from behind me.

"Close your fucking eyes!" Darius shouts. "Better yet, fuck off, Beckett!" I pull my thong up and just to drive my point home, I stretch out the pencil-thin elastic on the sides and let it snap into place. I grab the matching bra and spin around to face both guys as I slowly put my bra on. I cock my head to the side, loving how my body can have both these guys' attention so captivated.

"I never picked either of you two for being voyeurs." Darius growls, warning me not to push this. Fuck him. I clip my bra into place, remove the towel from my head and shake out my long blonde hair before sauntering over to them. I can feel Darius's heated stare drinking in every exposed inch of my nakedness. He smirks, thinking I'm going for him, but at the last second I turn to Beck. He gulps as a gleeful feeling erupts inside me knowing I have the both of them eating out of the palm of my hand. Good, because Darius is going to see what it feels like to be hurt!

"Darius and I have had sex in *a lot* of places but my favorites are the places where there is a chance we could get caught, you know the whole thrill of it." I dart my tongue out and suck my bottom lip into my mouth to drive my point home, knowing they are both watching my every move. "It really turns me on!" I barely get the last word out before Darius has me swung over his shoulder caveman style and landing a swift slap to my ass that has me squealing.

"Your fucking show is done! Beckett get the fuck out!"

I cut the arrogant bastard off. "No, Beck, stay! If Darius wants to fuck me like the whore I am why not watch, shit I might even let you run a fucking train!" I scream in anger. Darius throws me off his shoulder. I squeak in surprise when I land on my bed, and two seconds later he is on top of me, pinning my arms on either side of my head as he glares down at me. I return his angry look with one of my own.

"You think this is fucking funny?" he snarls bending so we are nose to nose.

"I thought this is what you wanted?" The confused look that mars his beautiful face pisses me off. "Let me spell it the fuck out for you, Halfback. I never let a team run a fucking train. I never let anyone touch me—" I feel the lump start to form in my throat, tears build in the back of my eyes but I fight through it. "The only person I ever wanted or let touch me was you. Now, get the fuck off me so I can pack my shit because I'm done." The stunned look on his face would be comical if I wasn't fighting with everything I had to not cry in front of him and Beck. I try to push him off me but he's too lost in his own head, trying to decipher my words.

"Show him." I stop fighting and turn my head to the side to see Beck now stands a foot away from my bed with a look of... lust in his eyes. Lust? There is no freaking way Beckett Dawson finds me attractive, is there? He drops his gaze to me and the intensity in his pale green eyes has my breath hitching. "Show him you only want him, with me standing right here." I hold his stare for a second before slowly looking back at Darius, who is frowning down at me. I don't know what the hell is going on and I am so confused.

"Do you want him?" The husky tone of Darius's voice has need building inside me. What the fuck is wrong with me, he was cruel and mean today and here I am beneath him getting wet just from the tone of his voice. Unsure on how to answer him, I turn away. He grips my chin and forces my gaze back to him, the intensity in it has my body warming and my chest feeling tight. "Answer me, Goldie."

"I... I don't..." I can't even form a coherent sentence. I only want Darius but the thought of living out a fantasy with Darius and Beck is hard to deny. I trust both of these men to care for me and keep me safe, which is why it's hard to say *no*. Darius bends down and runs his nose along the column of my neck to my lobe before clamping his teeth gently. Despite me trying not to, a moan still slips free. His hot breath fans across my ear, sending a shiver down my spine and my eyes rolling back. Darius has always had a way of making me forgive him just from the way he can play my body like an instrument.

"I want you, Goldie." His whispered words are my undoing, all thoughts of Beckett fly out the window when I cup Darius's face and pull his lips to mine. The moment my tongue pushes through his lips, he groans at the taste of me. I know this is so fucked up and isn't healthy, I just don't care. He may never be mine publicly but a huge part of me will always belong to him and I came to terms with that a long time ago. He deepens the kiss as he grinds his growing erection into me. I gasp into his mouth granting him full access that he takes advantage of. He becomes my oxygen, he has the ability to suck the life out of me only to breathe it back into my lungs.

CHAPTER SEVENTEEN

Darius

The anger I felt toward her earlier has vanished as I lose myself in the kiss. Beck and I had searched for her for hours. Cody and Katie had no idea where she went and it was then I remembered her love of the ocean. The sight of her tucked into a ball asleep on the beach killed me—I hate that I can't hate her!

Seeing her parade around her room naked with Beckett watching had a rage I never felt before come to life inside me. I wanted to tear his eyes out for seeing *my* girl naked but watching the way her eyes blazed at having both of us staring at her, wanting her had my cock hardening. I break the kiss and stare down at her, both of us are panting and gasping for air. Her cheeks are flushed, eyes bright and glassy unlike earlier when they were devoid of all emotion except heartbreak.

If I'm to give her the four days like she asked then I need to let the past go for now. The only bonus is, come Monday night when Corv gets back, I know I will be able to let her walk away. All I have to think about is what she did and the anger makes all the want, need and… love I feel for her evaporate in an instant. I search her gaze for a second before flicking my eyes to Beck to see him standing there stiff and struggling with what to do next.

Can I share her with him?

I find her trying so hard not to allow her eyes to stray toward him. I know they care about each other but she doesn't feel for him what she does for me, and having both Beck and I would be an experience she could check off her bucket list. Yes, that is a thing. She has a list and told me about it when we were together, one of those things was having a threesome with me and another guy. I never thought I would ever consider it until *now*.

"If we do this," I say drawing her attention to me, "I call the shots, you don't argue and do everything I say, got it?" She bites her bottom lip as her little nose scrunches up, uncertainty clouds her features.

"Will you hold this against me?" Her quietly asked question has a smile tugging at the corner of my lips.

"No. But this will be a one-time thing," I say as I look from her to him. She swallows loudly as she slowly lifts her gaze to Beck. Whether she notices or not, her hands grip my forearms in a way that has me filled with pride that she knows even if I'm angry, I'll always protect her.

"D-do you want this?" she asks Beck hesitantly. Rather than use words, the big fucker sits on the edge of the bed next to us. He reaches out and brushes his knuckles over her cheek, a blush begins to form where his knuckles touch. The thought of someone else touching her has always sent me spiraling, but watching Beckett touch her, it has a whole new sensation of feelings soaring to life inside me.

"Yes." His quietly spoken word has her eyes darkening and her chest rising and falling faster. Her bed is too small for what the three of us are planning to do. I slide off her, feeling her gaze on me the whole time. I shoot her a smile trying to ease her nerves as I offer her my hand. She hesitantly takes it, allowing me to help her to her feet. Fuck she looks gorgeous in this black lace pantie set, hair out and wild with no make-up on, she is effortlessly beautiful.

"Your beds too small, mine is bigger." A whoosh of air escapes her as I lead the three of us through the joining bathroom into my room. I release her hand and step aside allowing her to call the shots. She may think I have fucked my way through the school and had plenty of threesomes but the truth is, I have only ever had one and it was with some random girl Beck and I picked up at a party over a year ago. She takes a step forward, then another and pauses. Beckett and I stand here shoulder to shoulder shamelessly checking out her ass. Fuck, I want to smack the shit out of it and then kiss it better before pushing my cock into her tight ass.

I snap out of my thoughts when the sound of her sharp intake of breath can be heard. She reaches around her back and pops the clasp of her bra. Beck and I share a side glance before we watch silently for her next move. She chucks her bra to the side pulling a small smile from me, is it wrong that I'm proud of her for going after what she wants unlike most girls who would be too scared to admit that they want to be fucked by two guys?

She grips the sides of her thong and pushes them down her long-ass legs. A groan escapes the both of us at the sight of her bent over and her bare pussy on display. She steps free of her panties and slowly turns back to face us. I expected to see hesitation in her eyes but no trace can be found, all I see when she looks at me is trust and excitement.

"Don't hold back." Those three little words from her mouth have the both of us snapping into action. Our shirts are first to go, then the shoes and lastly, the pants. We both stand here in our briefs, hard and ready to give her the best time of her life. She runs her eyes over Beck, then she nibbles her bottom lip at the sight of his body. Before I even have the chance to feel insecure, her gaze cuts to me. When her eyes glaze over and her chest begins to rise in quick succession, all the worrying flees my body. She wants Beck but only in a physical way, when she looks at me, she wants everything I can give her physical but she also wants my fucking soul. Stupid girl, doesn't understand the meaning of soulmate.

She's my soul which is why every time I'm inside her I feel

whole again. Being near her makes me feel like I'm not lost anymore, that I finally found my way home.

"Get on the bed," I order. She does as she is told but in a sexy as fuck way. She crawls up the bed offering the both of us a view of her glistening pussy that has my cock twitching at the thought of slipping inside her tight wet fucking cunt. She rests against the pillows with one leg straight and the other bent at the knee. I cock my head to the side as I watch her slowly lift her other leg, and before I can even grasp what the hell she is doing, she opens her legs at the knees giving us a front row seat to the show she is putting on. She runs her hand up the middle of her chest in a slow measured move, I swallow to try to moisten my throat when she reaches the top of her pussy. I hear Becks sharp intake of breath when she swipes a single finger through her folds. I expect her to start playing with her pussy to torture us a bit, I should know by now she doesn't ever do what I expect.

"Want a taste?" she asks in the sexiest voice I have ever heard as she holds her finger out to us. The both of us move in unison. I want to lick her finger clean but I decide to leave that taste to Beckett and go for the real thing. We stalk over to her, side by side; Beckett branches off to the side of the bed while I crawl up the bottom. The bed dips when he climbs on, and I watch with rapt attention as he reaches out, grips her tiny wrist in his hand and sucks her finger into his mouth, drawing a gasp from her. He moans at the taste before slowly releasing her finger with a wet pop, her eyes wide and filled with lust.

He doesn't take his eyes off her as he asks, "What's the boundaries, D?" Her eyes look to me. I search them for a second wondering how far I can let him go. The truth is, this is supposed to be about her but in reality, this is about me and what I am willing to allow her to do with someone else under my guidance.

I grip her thighs in a tight hold that has her squirming from the pressure of it. "Give her everything she wants until I say no." That's all he needed to hear before he bends down, gripping her face and smashing his lips against hers. I stare at them for a minute. How can I be okay with seeing her kiss my best friend, but not okay with walking in on her naked in bed with Gary?

I push those dark thoughts from my head, I won't ruin the time we have left. I slide my hands up her inner thighs, relishing in the shiver that rolls though her body at my touch. I part her pussy with my fingers before I bend down and swipe my tongue through her slick folds. A moan sounds from her but Beckett won't allow her to break the kiss. He moves one of his hands to her nipple and rolls the hardened bud between his fingers as I continue to lap at her, savoring the taste.

"You like that?" I hear Beck ask before he shifts on the bed and captures her other nipple in his mouth whilst tweaking the other with his hand, she throws her head back.

"Fuck yes," she says on a moan. I push a finger inside her tight pussy, loving the whimper that tumbles from her lips. "Oh fuck!" she cries out as I push it in and out of her while sucking her clit into my mouth at the same time. Beckett releases her nipple with a wet pop, shifts and maneuvers himself so he is sitting behind her. He reaches around her and cups both her tits in each of his hands growling his approval. I keep my gaze on them as I continue to eat her. My cock is so fucking hard just from seeing them together and how she responds to his touch.

"Watch him eat your pussy." She nods and does as he says, her eyes hooded and glazed over. "You keep your eyes open and on him when you come all over his face, do you understand?"

"Yes," she cries out, doing exactly as he says. Beckett is a dominant fucker when it comes to sex, he likes control but he knows he won't get that here tonight. Leah is mine and I call the fucking shots where she is concerned. Right now, I'll let him have his control because I want exactly what he is demanding of her. "Darius, don't stop," she cries as she arches off Beck's chest. I keep to the same pace doing *exactly* what I have been doing. Women don't want a guy to go harder or change up exactly what they are doing when they say *don't stop* or *I'm coming*. "Fuck!"

she cries out a second before the walls of her pussy are clenching my finger and spasms begin to wrack her body. I gently slide my tongue up and down her slit easing her down from her high.

As the shudders roll through her, I lean back on my haunches, pull my finger free and hold it out to her. Her eyes burn with desire as she shifts forward, opens her mouth and sucks my finger clean whilst holding my gaze. When she swirls her tongue around the digit, a small moan tumbles from my lips as I envision her doing the same to my cock. Beckett brushes her hair to the side and kisses a trail down the side of her neck.

"You think you can take both of us, at once?" Beckett's whispered words have her eyes shooting wide and looking to me for reassurance. I keep my face neutral letting her dictate whether she wants this or not. I slip my finger from her mouth and wait. Her green eyes bore into mine searching for what, I have no idea.

"Yes." Desire spurs to life inside Beck's eyes. She reaches out and grips the waistband of my boxers pulling them down just enough for my cock to spring free. "But we do this my way," she says as she begins to stroke, pulling a long-drawn hiss from me. "Get on your back, I'm gonna fuck you while I suck Beck off." Her words have both of us scrambling to do as she commands. I don't take orders in the bedroom but when they are delivered by Leah, in that tone and looking at me the way she is, I'll do anything she wants.

CHAPTER EIGHTEEN

Darius lays naked on his back with his cock out, I straddle his lap and watch as Beck stands at the edge of the bed pushing his boxers down to reveal his *huge* cock. It's about the same length as Darius's but the girth on his is fucking wide to the point I would most likely need two hands just to jerk him off. Darius's grip on my waist has me focusing back on him. He smiles reassuringly at me and it eases some of the tension inside me. I lift up and line him up with my opening but before I sink down onto his waiting cock, he holds me steady as he looks to Beck and says.

"Only I get to fuck her bare, not you, got it?" Beckett raises his brow in a condescending way as he flicks his gaze to the side drawer to reveal foil packets waiting. Now that he got his answer, I push his hands away and slowly lower myself onto his glorious cock, I've only got half of him in me and already my pussy is clamping down on his shaft. I don't get to draw this out, he thrusts the rest of the way inside me, causing me to scream out in the best type of way. Beckett uses that moment to his advantage. He shoves his cock in my open mouth. I don't have a gag reflex but I do have a fucking jaw that cannot dislocate to accommodate his size. He stands on the bed with his hand fisted in my hair, fucking my face while I try to find my rhythm so I can fuck Darius.

"Fuck, Leah, swirl your tongue just like that." Tired of him dictating the way I suck his dick, I take over. I continue to rock my hips and bounce on Darius's cock as I grip the base of Beckett's and stroke as I bob my head up and down loving the moans that tear from his throat.

"Told you she could suck dick like a pro," Darius smugly says. To shut him and his smugness up I lift up and drop down hard twice. "Fuck, yeah, baby, like that." I follow his orders and keep doing that until Beckett yanks his cock from my mouth. Spit drips down my chin, I reach up to brush it away but Beck drops to his knees and shocks the fuck out of me when he pulls me to him and kisses the breath out of me, when he pulls back I'm a panting mess. I can feel an orgasm cresting and try to latch onto it, needing to come all over Darius's cock and marking him as mine.

"Don't come!" The command in Beckett's tone has me stopping, I watch as he grabs a foil packet from the drawer, making quick work of tearing it open with his teeth and sliding the condom on. He jumps back on the bed but this time he moves so that he is behind me. Darius's eyes blaze with a look I can't decipher. I bend down and place a chaste kiss to his lips and say.

"All you have to do is say stop and everything stops." His eyes search mine for a beat before he shakes his head.

"This is the one and only time, cross it off your bucket list and burn the fucker." My heart soars at the fact he remembers my list. He smashes his lips against mine in a kiss of ownership. I tear away from him when I feel liquid sliding down the crack of my ass, I peer over my shoulder to see Beck squirting some KY on me and his cock. Darius wraps his arms around me keeping me plastered to his chest, without permission my pussy flutters drawing a satisfied smirk from the arrogant bastard whose cock is currently buried deep inside it.

"Try not to tense and try not to come." I frown at Beckett's words.

"Why can't I come?" I ask.

"You can but only when I'm inside you. If you come before, your body's natural reaction is to repel me from you. Darius is going to work you up and keep you focused on him while I slip in." The excitement of knowing I'm about to have two cocks inside me at the same time has me grinding my pussy down on Darius. He kisses me as I continue to ride him. I feel Beck circling my ass and slowly pushing using his finger to push the lube inside me. I moan into Darius's mouth. He and I have done anal a few times previously—it wasn't a favorite of mine but I also didn't hate it. When Beck uses his finger to fuck my ass and stretch me open a sheen of sweat begins to coat my body. "That's it, just keep doing that," he says as he pulls his finger free. I feel him lining the head of his cock up with my ass, not warning me when he pushes the tip inside.

"Fuck!" I cry out as I break the kiss. Beck snakes his arm around my front grips my throat and pulls my back flush against his chest before leaning around and kissing me. He uses my moment of surprise to sink deeper inside me, I moan into his mouth. Darius reaches up and cups my heavy boobs, brushing his thumbs over my hardened nipples. I slowly begin to rock into Beck only to feel Darius shift inside my pussy but in the best fucking way.

"Fuck you feel so tight!" Darius growls. I pull away from Beck to lean down on Darius to give him better access into my ass. Beck grips my ass cheeks and pushes them apart, he rocks back and forward easing into me as moans continue to tumble from me. It feels like torture—Darius is hard and ready in my greedy cunt while Beck is taking his sweet ass time pushing into me. The need to come is overwhelming which is why I shout.

"Just fucking do it!" He obeys my order and fuck me seven ways sideways. The pain that accompanies the feeling of plea-sure is only drowned out when Darius thrusts his hips into me continuously as if knowing an orgasm is the only way to get me over the urge to scream at Beck to get the fuck out of me. He is too big. The harder Darius fucks me the more the urge to get Beck to match his pace wars inside me. "Beckett, fuck me," I moan as I lay my hands flat on Darius's chest and attempt to hold on. If you have ever had two men inside you at the same time, you will know that when the orgasm crashes into you it is like nothing you have ever experienced before. It feels like your body is being ripped apart and sewed back together while having your pussy eaten exactly like you dreamed of. "Fuck yes, fuck me like that," I scream as I ride out my orgasm and come all over Darius's cock.

I slump forward onto Darius's chest, spent and wrung out in the best possible way. Beck pulls out of me and suddenly I feel empty. That feeling doesn't last long when his hands grip my waist and I'm lifted off of Darius, and spun around. I wrap my legs around his waist and rest my hands on the tops of his shoulders staring at him in surprise. Beck lines his cock up with my opening and slowly pushes inside me, my gaze holds his the entire time. Something about looking him in the eye as his cock eases inside my pussy is erotic.

"Fuck, you feel so good," he grits out before slamming his lips to mine. His grip on my ass tightens as his pace begins to quicken. I moan, loving the feeling of him inside me, stretching me. I gasp and break the kiss to look over my shoulder when I feel Darius at my back. He places a kiss to my cheek as he runs his hand down my back and slaps my ass causing me to shriek in surprise.

"My turn, baby," he says. Beckett moves his hands to my waist as Darius parts my cheeks and pushes the head of his cock inside my ass. Heat begins to spread throughout my body, he's pushing inside at the same time Beck lazily thrusts inside me. I lean back against Darius, the move allows me to sink onto his cock and gives Beckett better access to pound into my greedy pussy. Like the both of them are mind readers they give me exactly what I want. Beckett's thrusts begin to grow harder, surer while Darius slips all the way inside me. Darius grips my thighs and pulls them open so I'm practically doing the splits in the air. I cry out, at this angle the both of them feel so fucking deep and fuck me, it feels amazing!

"Jesus, hold her like that," Beck demands, a fine sheen of sweat dots his forehead. "Fuck yes, I'm gonna come like this."

I shake my head. "No. I want the both of you to come at the same time." The pair of them eye each other over my shoulder for a second before they come to some kind of agreement and start pounding into both my holes. It takes a solid minute before I'm screaming at them not to fucking stop, I feel my orgasm cresting ready to rip through me like a welcome tidal wave.

"Get there, D, I'm about to come," Beckett growls. Darius's grip on my thighs turns punishing, his fingerprints will be marked into my flesh for the next few days.

"Fuck!" Darius shouts from behind me as he comes. I scream his name at the top of my lungs as I shatter on their cocks. Beck roars out his own release. Tonight has been the most euphoric night of my life and the best sex I have ever had. I gave up on the idea of ever crossing this off my bucket list because there was only one person I wanted to experience it with. Thanks to a twist of fate and my brother being out of town, my beautiful dream became a reality. The only sounds that can be heard are our heavy breaths. Beck's green eyes bore into me and I frown when he shoots me a grateful smile.

"Swear to God, if you say thank you, I'll head butt you," I say. Beck and Darius both laugh, I don't because I am 100% serious. Beck shakes his head and smiles kindly at me. Something about the way he is looking at me tells me that what just happened between us wasn't just for my benefit.

"I'm gonna pull out, you ready?" I nod as Beck slowly eases out of me, then grips my waist and helps me to my feet. An involuntary shudder rolls through me when I feel the cum dripping out of my ass.

"Come on, let's get you in the shower." I nod and let Darius lead me to the bathroom. He flicks the shower on and holds his hand under the running water. When the water reaches the temperature he likes he steps back and ushers me into the stall. I turn to close the glass door but pause when I see him stepping in behind me. I shoot him a questioning look, he just shrugs and says, "There's a drought somewhere so we should conserve water and all that shit."

"A drought, really?" I laugh as I turn around and step under the spray, keen to wash off the cum currently leaking out of my ass. It's an odd feeling having something leak from your ass, no matter how much I try to clench it continues to leak out of me.

"Turn around." I do as he says and my heart melts when I see him holding my loofah. He proceeds to wash me thoroughly, making sure there is no surface of my body left unwashed. When he finally deems me clean, I snatch the loofah from him and return the favor, except unlike him when I drop to my knees to wash his legs, I have ulterior motives. I drop the loofah and grip the base of his cock, he's already growing hard. I peer up at him through my lashes and love the way his eyes darken as I slowly suck him into my mouth. I relish in the sounds he makes as I pleasure him. There is no greater feeling in the world then knowing that I may be on my knees, but I am the one who holds all the power.

CHAPTER NINETEEN

Darius

Her mouth feels like heaven.

I stretch my arms out wide to stabilize myself, then widen my stance to give her better access to my dick. She uses her hand to pump the base as she sucks the head swirling her tongue around the tip, then a low moan from her sends vibrations straight to my balls. As good as her mouth feels wrapped around me, I need to be inside her. I need to wash away Beck's touch by fucking her again and coming inside her tight cunt. I grip her hair and yank her head back, a small hiss escapes her mouth as she darts her stunned gaze to me.

"Get up," I growl, using my hold on her hair to help her to her feet. "Did you like Beck fucking your pussy?" Confusion colors her features. I slip my free hand between us and cup her sex. The confused look on her face vanishes and is instantly replaced by one of desire.

"Yes." I narrow my eyes as I push two fingers inside her, her mouth drops open to form a perfect O. I lean down and lick her bottom lip before sucking it into my mouth. I release her lip when a small whimper breaks free. She pushes down onto my fingers making me smirk.

"You just had two cocks inside you and yet your cunt is still hungry for more?"

"No. I'm just hungry for more of *you*." Her words shouldn't have my ego bolstering but they do. I yank her forward and mold my mouth to hers. I release my hold on her hair as I lift her, then back her up against the tiled wall. She arches forward to try escape the coldness of the tiles but I'm not allowing it, I use my weight to push her flat as I slowly lower her onto my shaft.

"This," I growl as I thrust inside her drawing a loud cry from her lips. "Is." Thrust. "Mine." I repeat those three words to her over and over again until we are both screaming the other's name like it's a Hail Mary play in the last quarter.

I wake to the sound of my alarm blaring. I reach out and grip my phone to snooze it. I sit up straight when I realize it's not the alarm but Corvin calling me. I slip out from beside Leah, careful not to wake her as I grab some shorts and leave the room, closing the door quietly. The call ends and starts again, I answer it on the second ring as I hold the phone between my shoulder and cheek while I pull on my shorts.

"What up?" I say.

"Dude I have been calling you for ages!" I roll my eyes and make my way downstairs as I answer him.

"You rang me once, don't be dramatic."

"Whatever, asshole," he says. I hear a door close and then some rustling before he speaks again. "Did you know Coach is ordering drug tests for the team?" I frown as I enter the kitchen, not sure why this news warrants a call at five in the fucking morning.

"So? Why do you care? It's not like any of us use drugs." When a sigh escapes him I tense. "Right?" His silence stretches and I curse under my breath as Beck walks into the kitchen shooting me a worried look. "Hold on Beck's here, I'm gonna put you on speaker." I put him on speaker and place the phone on the counter and I gather what I need for a protein shake.

"What's going on?" Beck asks as he begins to make his own shake.

"Coach wants us to take weekly drug tests. Apparently, someone made a complaint and said that CHU players are doping up on roids," Corvin grits out, Beck and I share a look of concern before I ask.

"Why are you acting so cagey, Corvin. What the fuck is going on?" A tired sigh comes through the phone and I brace myself for the worst.

"Dude, Kyle, Lance, Rick and Spencer have been kicked from the team already." My eyes shoot wide at that bit of news. "They swore black and blue that they never touched any drugs at the party they went to but the test doesn't lie." The anger in Corvin's voice matches how I'm feeling.

"Kyle and Spencer wouldn't risk their scholarships," Beck adds.

"I know. Something isn't right and given the test was administered here and not at school makes me think it's one of the other teams setting us up." At least six other colleges are at the camp Corv and the others are at which means, Gary and his team will be there and I'd put money on the fact it was that son of bitch that set up our guys.

"We need to get on top of this. We can't afford a scandal right now," I say.

"I know, why do you think I'm calling, dumbass?"

"Let me call Troy and see if there is any way we can push the merge up to next week. If we are all thinking it's the same person targeting our team then we need to be smart about it. Gary has the money to get people to do his bidding. Parties are out until after the merger and the season." Beck is right, we need to keep our heads on straight.

"Yeah, okay. I'll tell Saint and Crue but they won't like being on house arrest."

"I don't care, Corvin, we can't risk it. If you, Saint and Crue want to go pro then the three of you need to suck it up until we find out who the fuck is doing this," I growl.

"Yeah, okay. You and Beck call Troy and see if we can bring the merger forward. If we get that done, then we should be okay to take our time and figure this shit out." Beck and I agree before ending the call. The silence stretches between us and begins to grow uncomfortable, so I decide to leave him and hit the makeshift gym in the basement to get in a workout.

Ten minutes go by before the door opens and Beck walks in as I'm lifting weights. He goes for the treadmill to warm up. The only sound that can be heard is the music coming from the Bluetooth speaker. The both of us continue to work out in silence until it begins to get on my nerves that we have tension between us.

I know last night was a lot but, coupled with the news from Corvin, we can't afford to be divided right now when we have some fucker gunning for us. Unlike the other three, Beck and I know we don't have the skill set to go pro. We love the game and would kill to go pro but that isn't in the cards for us. We decided a long time ago that Beck and I would run the company and manage everything while the three of them worked their asses off to get drafted and play in the NFL. Saint needs this, if he doesn't get drafted his father has ordered him to take over his tech company, the company Saint hates.

"Are we good?" I place the dumbbell on the mat and turn to see Beck leaning against the treadmill with a towel draped around his neck. The uncertainty in his eyes vanishes the moment I shoot him a smile.

"Yeah, bro, we're always going to be good." The tension in his shoulders eases a bit.

"So, you gonna be good with me and Leah living under the same roof?" The smile vanishes from my face in an instant as old feelings resurface. I slam my eyes closed and try to block them out but it's fucking hard! "What happened, D?" I cover my face with my hands debating if I should tell him or not. "Darius, whatever happened between the two of you has been eating at you for years. I'm not prying or trying to be nosey, I am just genuinely worried about you."

The words spew out of me before I can stop them. "I told her not to go to the party after we won the final in high school as she wanted me to tell Corvin about us. I was going to, that night." I feel him drop down onto the weight bench beside me. I drop my hands and rest my forearms on the tops of my thighs as I hunch forward. "I knew she was serious this time when she said I either tell him or we're done. I weighed up the options and I fucking love Corvin but the truth is…"

"You love his sister more," Beck adds. A whoosh of air escapes me and I nod. "So what happened?"

"We got into a fight when I told her to stay home and that I would tell him at the party. She didn't listen. When I got to the party, Jeff told me Gary was there and upstairs with Corvin's sister. I raced up the stairs and what I saw… broke me man. She was naked and crashed on the bed while Gary was getting dressed. The bastard smiled and winked at me as he shouldered past. I stood there for like five minutes just staring at her naked ass until I heard Corvin yelling out for shots downstairs, I closed the door and left her there." Bitterness coats each of my words. I fucking hate Gary Hayes because that son of bitch knew exactly who Leah was to me and threatened to out me to Corv if I didn't shave points on the game. That motherfucker got his ass beat on the field and as payback, he slept with my girl and ruined the only good thing I had in my life aside from the guys.

"Jesus!" Beck says on an exhale. "I had no idea. I mean I knew something bad happened because you went from over protective to just… not giving a fuck where she was concerned."

"Yeah," I say in a dejected tone.

"Fuck and she went to DCU with him!"

"She sure fucking did, brother," I grit out. "Corv and I went home one year for Thanksgiving and guess who she brought to fucking dinner?" Beck's eyes widen as he shakes his head trying to deny my claim.

"No way."

"Yes, fucking way. I had to sit across the table from the motherfucker that fucked my girl and play nice because of Corvin and his parents. Want to know the worst fucking part?" I don't give him a chance to answer. "Leah acted like nothing happened and kept shooting me hurt looks like I was in the fucking wrong! I was about to lose my best friend that night by telling him I was in love with his sister. Thank God I found her first or else I would have lost Corv for nothing."

"Fuck. I had no idea man. I'm really fucking sorry that happened. I really didn't think Leah was like that."

"Yeah. Neither did I." I can hear the hurt that laces my own voice.

CHAPTER TWENTY

Leah

I wake with the biggest smile on my face. I reach out for Darius and frown when I can't find him next to me. I blink my eyes open only to find the space next to me vacant. I climb out of bed and grab one of his shirts from the floor and pull it on as I check the bathroom for him. Finding the space empty, I quickly relieve myself and brush my teeth before going in search of him. Before I can exit the room my phone rings and cringe at the ringtone. I rush into my room and grab it off my dresser and answer the dreadful call.

"What?" I snap.

"Good work, little mouse, four players down." I slam my eyes closed as guilt eats away at me.

"What the hell do you want?" I grit out. He is the last person I want to be hearing from first thing in the morning. I check the time on my phone and stifle a groan when I see it's only six-thirty in the freaking morning.

"The four players that are out aren't the ones I told you to take out! Fix this fucking shit now or–"

"Or what? You're gonna share the video? What proof do I have that you will even hand it over?"

His dark laughter fills the phone. "You don't. Now be a good bitch and do as you're told, the game is in three weeks and they better not take the fucking field." He ends the call. I growl as I toss the fucking phone onto my bed and storm out of my room. I head downstairs in search of Darius only to find the space empty. I frown but then I hear the music playing and follow the sound to the basement, but at the sound of voices, I pause.

"Jesus!" Beck sound appalled. "I had no idea, I mean I knew something bad happened because you went from over protective to just… not giving a fuck where she was concerned."

"Yeah." Darius sounds so sad and it breaks my heart. I'm about to make my presence known until Beck speaks again.

"Fuck and she went to DCU with him!" They're talking about me!

"She sure fucking did brother. Corv and I went home one year for Thanksgiving and guess who she brought to fucking dinner?" Shame washes over me knowing which Thanksgiving he is talking about.

"No way."

"Yes, fucking way, I had to sit across the table from the moth-erfucker that fucked my girl and play nice because of Corvin and his parents. Want to know the worst fucking part?" Tears prick the backs of my eyes knowing how that must have looked to him. "Leah acted like nothing happened and kept shooting me hurt looks like I was in the fucking wrong! I was about to lose my best friend that night by telling him I was in love with his sister. Thank God I found her first or else I would have lost Corv for nothing." He thinks he knows what he saw but he has no fucking idea and that has my stomach churning.

"Fuck. I had no idea man. I'm really fucking sorry that happened. I really didn't think Leah was like that."

"Yeah. Neither did I." I slam my eyes closed and lean my head back against the wall as the first tear falls. I hate that he thinks of me like this but if I tell him, he will never look at me the same again! "I fucking loved her man. She was the first person I ever let in and now I'm so fucked up because of it. I can't even look at another girl or kiss them while I fuck them because it hurts to know they aren't her. Fuck." The devastation in his voice is killing me! "She is the only girl I have ever kissed, how fucked is that?" He laughs but there's no humor to it. "Want to know something else that is so fucked up?" He doesn't give Beckett a chance to answer. "I still fucking love her and that is what fucks with my head daily!"

That's it, I can't listen to any more of this shit!

I round the corner with tears trailing down my cheeks, both their heads snapping up at the sound of my arrival. Darius looks devastatingly beautiful, even with the angry look on his face. I hate that I am the one who hurt him so badly. I will never forgive myself for that but I made the mistake of not coming clean when I found out months ago. If I'm going down I refuse to take any of these guys with me.

"Eavesdropping?" Darius snarls, his eyes shine with hatred and I can't blame him for that. Beck stands to leave to give us some privacy but I shoot him a look and shake my head. "Oh, you gonna fuck my best friend as well, Goldie?"

I look back to Darius and plead with my eyes that he can see I didn't hurt him purposely. I didn't mean for any of this to happen. "I'm sorry," I sob. He climbs to his feet and runs his gaze up and down my body in disgust, the way he looks at me is like I'm shit beneath his shoe and it kills me.

"I thought I could give you the four days, I really did," he says, shaking his head. "Seems I can't do it," is all he says before storming from the room and yanking my heart out of my chest again. Sobs tear from me, they steal the breath from my lungs as I crumple to the floor crying for the boy who was meant to be mine. I bury my face in my hands and cry, if I thought losing him the first time was bad, this time it feels like I won't survive. Strong arms wrap around me and lift me into his lap. I cling to Beck as I bury my face in his shirt and soak it with my tears.

"Why do I feel like there is more to this story and that you never cheated on him?" he quietly asks after my sobs finally subside enough for me to breathe a bit easier. I sniff and burrow into him, he rests his chin atop my head.

"There is more but I can't tell you," I whisper. I feel him exhale and know he is disappointed in the fact I won't just come clean.

"If you really love him like I think you do, you need to fix this, Leah, because Darius can't handle another person letting him down."

"What do you mean?" I ask.

"If he finds out I told you this he is going to kick my ass."

"I won't say anything, I swear," I rush out.

"His dad… he left and that fucked D up more than you will ever know." I knew about this, his dad skipped town or something when his mom got pregnant and Darius has no idea who he is. "His mom is a fucking junkie and will sell her body for her next hit. All he had was you, Corv and your parents, until Saint, Crue and me came along. Darius doesn't have anyone, only me, Saint, Crue and your brother. For him to have trusted you was a huge thing. He let you in, Leah, and he doesn't let anyone in."

"I don't understand," I say confused.

"Leah?" He pushes me back until we are staring each other in the eyes, his face is serious. "He has never let any of us in, only you. We all know what Darius wants us to know but none of us can read him or know what his next move is. I saw it years ago. You can read him and that's because he let you in. If whatever happened years ago isn't what he thinks it was, you need to tell him because I won't watch him fuck up his life again."

"Again?" I hedge, he takes a shuddering breath and nods.

"Darius was wild and angry when we first got here. None of us knew why and he wouldn't let us help him. He threw himself into training. He trains harder than anyone on the team and applies himself to everything he does even when we started the comp… He is crazy smart and buries himself in work because he thinks hiding from his feelings will make them go away. You coming back brought everything he thought he had worked through back to the surface and it is scaring the hell out of him."

"It scares me too. I love him, Beck, and I hate that I hurt him but I don't have a choice," I defend, his eyes soften as he runs his knuckles along my cheek, not in a sexual way but in a comforting way.

"We all have a choice, Leah. You just need to decide if the choice you are making is benefiting you or not. Whatever you are hiding from and keeping from him is hurting him. Darius isn't the type of guy to play games. If you push him too far, he will snap and you will never get him back. Make your choice, babe, but make sure it's one you can live with." I smile sadly up at him.

"How did you get so wise about relationship advice?" I ask teasingly, not expecting him to answer.

"I fucked up a long time ago with someone who meant everything to me, so I can relate to how Darius is feeling."

After leaving Beck in the basement, I decided it was best for me to move out. Cody and Katie said they would make room for me in their dorm room. I took the offer and packed my shit. As soon as Beck and Darius left to hit the gym at school, I texted Cody. She drove over and helped me load my things and brought me back to their dorm. I have a futon on the floor and the room is jam packed with all our things but it beats living next door to Darius. I just need some space from him, need to think about what I'm going to do next.

I know if I go through with this plan, I will definitely lose him. Me telling him about what happened is one thing but him seeing it is another. I feel sick every time I think about it.

"Want to tell us why *Da-Leah* is a no go anymore?" Katie's softly asked question pulls me from my inner thoughts. I sigh and sit cross legged on my futon as each of them lays on their beds on their stomachs facing me, waiting for an answer.

"Everything was great until it wasn't," I answer.

"Well what happened yesterday after you took off?" Cody asks. I fill them in on how Darius and Beck found me but I don't share details about how the rest of our night went. What happened between the three of us is private and no one else's business. "So, if everything was good, why are you here? I mean we're glad to have you here but I'm just trying to piece it together."

"My past came back to bite me in the ass and Darius can't let it go, and I can't explain it to him."

"Why not?" Katie's question is innocent but if she knew the truth she would understand that I can't.

"Because I can't. I wish more than anything I could give him what he wants but I'm too much of a coward." I wrap my arms around my middle and drop my chin to my chest ashamed and disgusted in myself for the choices I have made.

CHAPTER TWENTY-ONE

Darius

"What up, fuckers?" Saint shouts as he, Crue and Corv burst through the front door. I smile wide as each of them waltz into the living room and give me a hug hello. Beck walks in and greets each of the guys, the four of them drop down onto the couches. They looked fucking wrecked.

"Where's Leah?" Corvin asks. Beck and I share a quick look before I answer.

"She moved out." When we got home yesterday, Beck went to check on her and found her room empty. I spent the rest of the night in the gym working out my anger that she just left. In hindsight it was a good thing because with her not being here it's going to be a lot easier to keep my dick out of her.

"What the fuck do you mean?" Corv growls as he shifts forward in his seat pinning me with a look. I throw my hands up in the air and roll my eyes frustrated.

"What the fuck are you looking at me like that for? I didn't do shit." I'm lying through my teeth but I don't care.

"I'm not blaming you for shit. I'm asking *you* why she left and didn't tell me?"

"I don't know, she's your sister so maybe call the impulsive little shit and find out," I grit out through clenched teeth.

"Someone must be on their bitchy time of the month," Crue jokes, earning a glare from me. "Oh, calm down, we just got back and don't even get a day off tomorrow before we have to train. So, how about we order in some pizza and go over this merger and read the fine print because we all know that fucker will try and stiff us in the fine print." Each of us voices our agreement as we head off to shower and leave Crue to order the pizza. I make quick work of showering, step out and wrap a towel around my waist before going to my room. I freeze when I see Corvin sitting on the end of my bed with a black thong dangling from his finger, shit!

He wiggles his brows suggestively at me as he says, "Been busy plowing through pussy while I was away. Anyone I know?" I swallow the retort that is on the tip of my tongue as I turn and head for my dresser as I answer him.

"I think you've seen her around." If only he knew that the thong currently dangling from his finger belonged to his sister.

"Just wanted to check in and see if Leah said anything to you or Beck about why she transferred?" I drop my towel and laugh when Corvin begins to curse me out for having my ass on display.

"Nah, man," I say as I pull on a pair of sweats and turn to face him. His face falls and I hate that I keep lying to him but it's just the way it has to be.

"Yeah, okay. Come on, we need to sort out this merger before we get fucked." I nod and follow after him. Crue, Saint and Beck are sitting in the living room with boxes of Pizzas set out on the coffee table. Corv and I snag a box each. As we drop into the vacant two-seater, Beck hands out a folder to each of us.

"These have the contracts in them. I spoke with Troy and we are set on our end. Sullivan Global management is willing to stay and keep things running, as well as show us each the day to day operations. I'm happy to do that once we finish school, are you all okay with that?" The four of us agree, Beck will be the perfect man for the job. He's a fast learner and takes pride in everything he does. "I think we make Darius the face of the company when the merger is complete."

"No!" I snap.

"You are the one who will be based out of the office in the city. You will fill the position as CFO until I can grasp the day-to-day shit with the hotels and resorts." We may own the stock market and dominate in that field, but acquiring Sullivan Global means we are branching out into foreign waters. They don't just fuck with the stock market, they also own hotel chains worldwide and resorts in Alaska, Hawaii, Australia, Japan and New Zealand. "It was your idea to bring them down and that shit you leaked to the papers is the only reason we are in the position to afford to buy them out. We need this, D." I scrub a hand down my face. If this is the sacrifice I need to make for my brothers, then so be it.

"Fine, but any board meetings the four of you have to sit in on them because I'm not making decisions on my own." I look to each of them letting know how serious I am about this point. Honestly, I'm nervous as fuck to be doing this on my own. I've always had them with me, so the thought of us all parting ways when school is over has me feeling scared. Crue, Saint and Corv have their football shit lined up, but Beck will head off to Alaska to learn the ropes and then I'll be here on my own.

"Deal, if we can't be there in person we'll be on video," Saint suggests and I agree.

"Man, if someone asked me what I would be doing at twenty I would never think this would be it." I grunt my agreement, Corv is right.

"We built this whole company from the ground up at sixteen and now look at us. We are about to be Forbes richest." We all laugh at Crue. we won't be the richest but we will live without worry for the rest of our lives.

"I don't think I have ever said it before, but thank you guys." The serious tone of Saint's voice has me sitting straighter. "You all knew that I hated the thought of ever running my dad's company and I fucking hate him, but I didn't have a way out until now. So, thank you all for helping me." Crue wraps an arm around his shoulders and gives him a side hug. Saint's dad is a piece of shit. He may have bought us this house but it wasn't from the kindness of his heart. If Saint doesn't take over for his father, he has to pay him back every cent for his tuition, living costs and this house. He thinks Saint doesn't have his own money, but thanks to this merger, Saint can buy his freedom and in turn take his fucking father down.

"We all helped each other," I say. "Without all of you I would have been under a bridge somewhere so the feeling is mutual, brother." Corvin slaps me on the shoulder and pins me with a look that says over his dead body that would have happened.

"Okay, we officially settle on SG next Tuesday and once that is final and underway, we focus on taking down Lexington Corp." The four of us nod our agreement. "Once we finally finish this, what next?" Beck's question has stumped me. I have no idea how to answer that. For years all we have focused on is this end goal and nothing else. What do I want to do with my life? A picture flashes through my mind of a house on the beach and a gorgeous blonde on a surfboard, but I shake that away.

"I plan to play in the NFL for as long as I can then retire, buy a yacht and drown in pussy for the rest of my days." We all groan and mutter about Saint being a dick.

"Once I hang my boots up for the last time, I'm gonna travel and see the fucking world." I could really see Crue being a tourist.

"Mine starts now." I furrow my brow at Corv. "When this is done, I'm coming out to my parents and buying them a house in the mountains like they have always wanted and never let them work again. I'll get Leah set up somewhere before I leave and hire guards so no fucker can get near my baby sister. Best part is, with us being the majority shareholders in the school, Leah will never have to pay for her schooling." I turn away from him, not able to look at him knowing I'm the one who took his sister's innocence. We spend the rest of the night talking shit and allowing ourselves to finally breathe a bit easier knowing that this is all going to work out. We fucking did it. Excitement thrums through me at the thought of seeing the looks on their faces when they find out it was me that ruined their lives and they had no fucking idea. He thought he fucked me over. That dumb fuck was playing a quick game while I was playing the long game from the start. Touchdown, motherfucker, I'm coming for you.

CHAPTER TWENTY-TWO

Leah

The week goes by in a blur, I've managed to avoid my brother and only speak to him on the phone, but I know it won't last. I've managed to avoid all five of them. I hate hearing how they are worshiped and looked up to as kings. It fucking grates on my nerves more when I have practice every day and have to hear Chelsea talk about how her and Darius are meant to be. Nikki thinks Beck is going to whisk her away and treat her like the queen she thinks she is. Both these bitches are bat shit crazy. We've run the same counts six times because Donald can't get the steps and it is grating on my nerves. I just want to get the hell out of here!

"Okay, listen up." Thankful for the reprieve I place my hands on my knees and take some deep breaths as we wait for coach to speak. "I have some bad news, we won't be dancing at the championship." Shouts and boos erupt from around me. "Quiet!" Coach yells, then blows her whistle. "I know you are all pissed off but there isn't a thing we can do. The school board tried but the other schools vetoed the idea and said no." I deflate, this is like a kick in the gut. This was our one chance to showcase our skills and show everyone we are more than some dance team that teaches girls how to shake their assess.

"Why the hell are we training so hard then?" Donald calls out, a devilish smirk graces coach's face.

"I said the school said no, I never said I agreed." Gasps ring out. "I mean I could never condone you all going against the school as a faculty member but I mean, if I taught you a kick ass routine and you all happen to rush onto the field at halftime and do said dance, who am I to stop you?" Everyone screams in excitement. Cody, Katie and I all scream and do an awkward three way hug. This is exactly the type of news I needed. After everything with Darius, I really needed a pick me up!

"Seriously, pineapple on a pizza?" I glare across the table at Garrett, who raises his hands in surrender. The girls and I ran into him after practice. We didn't tell him why we were happy, just that we got good news, so he insisted on taking us for pizza to celebrate. After the workout we just did, who are we to turn down free carbs?

"What's wrong with it?" I say around a mouthful of food, causing him to laugh and a blush to raise to my cheeks.

"What's right with it? It doesn't belong on a pizza, it shouldn't even be classed as a topping!" Cody and Katie both chime in with their agreement, which just earns them an eye roll from me.

"It's great, try it," I say as I pick up another slice and hold it out to him. His face scrunches in disgust, making me laugh. The girls join in when he recoils back into his seat as I lean over the table and hold it practically in front of his face.

"Well, what do we have here?" The smile vanishes from my face. At the sound of his voice, all the muscles in my body go rigid. Garrett sits up straighter as I slowly lower back into my seat and drop the pizza on my plate, keeping my gaze focused on it. I can feel Katie and Cody staring at me but I can't move, what the hell is he doing here? "Don't get all shy on me, little mouse, I drove all the way here just to see you." When his meaty hand lands on my shoulder I flinch away. At the sound of Garrett's chair scraping back, I snap my gaze to him and watch him stand up.

Shit!

"What the fuck are you doing here, Hayes?" I frown confused as to how he knows Gary but then it hits me, he's on the same team as the guys, so of course he would know him.

"Just came to visit an old friend," he says as he grips my shoulder again. This time he squeezes it so hard a whimper escapes me.

"Get your fucking hands off her now!" Garrett snarls. I peek over my shoulder to see Gary didn't come alone. There are at least six guys with him and they look like they are ready to throw down.

"Or what? You think you can take us, on your own?" he mocks. Garrett darts his gaze to me and I plead with my eyes not to do anything stupid.

"He won't, but I fucking will." It's been five days since I have heard his voice and it's a welcome balm to my tattered nerves. Gary's grip on my shoulder tightens the moment he feels me relax, a whimper escapes again. I hear him move toward us and tense in preparation for what is to come. He comes to a stop in front of us. I look up and find his brown eyes laser focused on Gary's hand that is gripping my shoulder in a punishing hold. He snaps his hand out, grips Gary's wrist and shoves him back a step. Gary rights himself quickly and gets in Darius's face. D has a few inches on Gary and you can tell from his posture that he hates it.

"You think you stand a chance alone? There are seven of us, you piece of shit!" Gary spits right in Darius's face. Instead of backing down or rethinking his move, Darius smiles cockily.

"Who said anything about him being alone?" I look past the

two guys to see Saint, Corvin, Crue and Beckett marching toward us like gods with fury written over each of their faces. They come to a stop behind Darius, the bond each of these guys shares is awe inspiring. I can kind of see why everyone worships them. "Now, unless you want us to leave tread marks all over you and your band of cheerleaders' faces, I suggest you get the fuck out of our town." I've never heard Crue sound… so serious or aggressive before.

"Take the warning and fuck off," Darius says in a tone so low and deadly it sends a shudder through me. Gary pulls back, smiles and brushes the nonexistent wrinkles from Darius's shoulders then turns to me. The look in his soulless blue eyes has my breath hitching. He tilts his head forward causing his brown hair to flop onto his forehead. The guy thinks he can pull off the *Jax Teller* hairstyle but he really can't. His teeth are crooked and the fact he has a tongue ring with a dice on it makes me ill.

"Don't worry, mouse, I'll be seeing you again real, *real* soon." I say nothing as he and his band of misfits push their way through Corvin and the others. The moment the restaurant door closes, I sag into my seat, ecstatic that my nightmare is gone.

My reprieve is short lived.

"What the fuck was that, Goldie?" I slowly lift my gaze to Darius's and a whirl of emotions war in his eyes—anger, confusion, hatred but the worst of all it's when I see betrayal that it burns me.

"I don't know," I say as I stand, grab my jacket and bag. The girls follow my lead and quickly gather their things, while Garrett drops some bills on the tables. I try to move past Darius and the others but they form a wall, a hulking fucking wall full of glares and accusations. "Excuse me," I grit out.

"Answer him, Leah. What the fuck was Gary doing here?" Corvin sounds pissed and I can't blame him, I decide to go with the truth.

"I have no idea, we came here to celebrate after practice and then he just showed up." I hold my brother's gaze so he can see the truth in my eyes. "I swear, Corv, we were just hanging out and then he... ruined it." I whisper the last part. Corvin reaches out and places his hands on the top of my shoulders. I hiss and flinch away. Before I can take a full step back, Darius is in front of me ripping the sleeve of my shirt down to expose my shoulder, which I know will already be bruising. His eyes darken at the sight of it, he grips the back of my neck and pulls me into him until his forehead rests against mine.

"You are going to tell me everything, but right now, I have a quarterback's arm to break." He releases me and races from the restaurant with the other four following him. I take a second to gather myself before I'm following after them. I break through the door in time to see Gary and his friends peeling out of the car park in their cars, hollering out the window. "Fucking pussy ass bitches!" Darius roars as he watches their cars driveaway. When he turns back to face us, his gaze finds mine immediately. "Say goodbye to your friends, your ass is coming with us!" My mouth unhinges. I look to Corvin expecting him to stop him but the bastard just crosses his arms over his chest and quirks a brow at me, daring me to defy king broody beside him.

"I can take you back." I turn my head to the side to see Garrett, standing there with his hands in his jeans pockets. I smile kindly, ready to accept his offer but the king asshole cuts me off.

"Accept his offer, Goldie, and see what happens." I cut a glare to Darius, narrowing my eyes in warning as I grit out,

"You gonna tell my brother..." his eyes shoot wide, "on me?" I smirk when his face becomes a picture of annoyance. "Just so we are clear, I don't live with you lot anymore and newsflash, assholes, I'm eighteen!" I shout. The smirk that crosses Darius's face has the triumphant feeling inside me dwindling rapidly.

"Either Corvin throws you over his shoulder and puts your ass in the car or I do. Those are your only choices!" I look to the girls and shoot them a look that has them grinning like fools before turning to Garrett who just looks pissed off.

"Thanks for tonight," I say.

"Don't even think about–"

I cut Darius off before he can finish his threat. "Run!"

CHAPTER TWENTY-THREE

Darius

She screams she's eighteen and then runs off like a fucking child!

"Beck, Corv, get the cars, You two with me," I bark out as I race after the pain in my ass. Crue and Saint are right with me as we chase down the girls. I see them dart across the road heading for the park. It's fucking dark out and these idiots are running into a park surrounded by woodlands? Fucking morons. We race across the road. Gaining on them, the moment we hit the grass of the park, Leah looks over her shoulder and shouts.

"Split up!" I growl. She is going to pay for this. Her friends do as she ordered and break away in separate directions.

"Saint get Cody. Crue get Katie. I got the little shit," I snarl as I sprint after her. I'm only a couple steps behind her when I break through the brush. She chances another look over her shoulder and squeals out a laugh, then darts around a tree and I lose sight of her for a couple seconds. I round the same tree and come to a halt when I don't see her anywhere.

"Boo." I snap my gaze to the side where she leans against the tree, huffing. I crowd her space and place my arms on either side of her head, caging her in. Our breaths are coming in rapid pants thanks to her impromptu race. The smile that is plastered on her face pisses me off.

"You think this is funny?" I snap.

"Yeah, I do actually." Her sarcastic reply grates on my already frayed nerves. "You act all big and tough, and pretend to hate me but look where you are, Darius. You had a choice to chase three girls and from what I heard back there you didn't even have to think about which one you were gunning for!" She steps into me so our chests brush against each other, then grips the sides of my shirt keeping me anchored in place as she slowly cranes her neck back to meet my gaze. "You either want me or you let me fucking go because I can't keep playing this game with you."

"Game?" I snarl as I yank free of her hold, putting a couple feet of space between us. "You think this is a fucking game?" I roar. She shrinks back into the tree but my temper is too far gone to be controlled. "None of this was ever a fucking game to me. This is my life you are destroying just by being near me! I fucking hate you, Leah." She flinches and drops her gaze to her shoes as her shoulders hunch forward. "I'll never fucking forgive you for what you did to me, I can't," I grit out before storming away from her. I break the tree line to find Beck standing there with a pitying look on his face. Before I can say anything, he holds out the keys to his car and flicks his head toward where it is parked at the curb.

"Saint and Crue have the girls in there, drop them at their dorm and grab her a bag. I'll get her and bring her back with me and Corvin." I nod my thanks and begin to move away but his words have me halting. "She's right, though. You either want her or you don't, you need to decide." The only response he gets is a grunt before I'm storming off toward his car.

I made Cody pack her bag and smacked Saint across the back of the head when he offered to pick out her panties. After leaving the girls, we headed straight home and have been sitting in the car for five minutes. I know we have to go in but I don't want to. Beckett's words keep replaying over and over in my mind. They may be true but it's fucking hard to let go of your first love. What makes the whole situation more fucked up is I can't even escape my first and only girlfriend because she is my best friend's little fucking sister!

"You know if we don't go in we'll never find out why Gary was here." Crue's attempt to get me out of the car works, my curiosity is peaked and I need answers. We storm through the door only to find Beck and Corv sitting in the living room, *alone*. At the sound of our entry Corvin slowly turns his head toward us and pins me with an angry fucking look that promises pain.

"Gary fucking Hayes doesn't walk off the field. That mother-fucker goes out in a box!" I dart my gaze between Beck and Corvin utterly fucking confused.

"What happened?" I hedge. Corv jumps to his feet and flips the coffee table before storming up the stairs. When I hear his bedroom door slam shut, I look to Beck for answers. He shakes his head and stands.

"All I know is, he hurt her and Corvin won't tell me any more than that. Him showing up tonight wasn't because she wanted him there. You need to talk to her, Darius, because Corvin is out for blood." Beck turns and heads up the stairs to check on Corv I presume.

"Dude, what the fuck did we miss?" Saint mumbles as he brushes past me and heads for the kitchen. Crue pats me on the shoulder as he heads for the basement. I stand here stunned and fucking confused as hell as to what happened in the twenty minutes it took us to get here. I'm too angry to go to her, so instead, I drop her bag at the base of the stairs, grab two beers from the fridge and head out the back to kick it by the pool. I kick my shoes off and drop down onto the ledge of the pool not giving a fuck that my jeans are getting wet as I kick my legs back and forward into the water. I grab one of the beers and twist the cap off before downing half the bottle. I don't normally drink but the cluster fuck of events from the past few days has me need-ing it.

Just as I finish the last bottle of beer, I hear the door open behind me. Looking over my shoulder, I see Corv coming toward me with two beers in each hand. He hands me two before dropping down beside and placing his feet in the water. We sit here silently, sipping our beers and looking up at the night sky. The silence isn't tense or uncomfortable. Sometimes, it's actually nice to not be alone with your thoughts and have someone to just sit with you. I never knew what that was like growing up. I was banished to my room to fend for myself while my mom *worked*. Having an addict and a whore as a mother fucking sucked but her being useless led me to Corvin and his family, and for that reason only, I can't hate my childhood. I made a vow to myself the night I moved into the Williams' house, I would never allow myself to become like my mother and still to this day I have never touched a single illegal substance.

"He hurt her," Corvin's whispered words pull me from my inner thoughts, my temper has settled enough for me to talk now.

"What did she say?" I ask in an even tone.

He runs a hand through his hair in frustration. "It wasn't what she said, D, it was in her eyes. I could see the fear. She completely shut down when I asked her if he had ever hurt her at school. She went pale, started screaming that she was so sorry for being a fuck up and if she could change it she would, then ran upstairs to her room."

I mull over his words trying to make sense of what he is saying. Tonight I saw that same look on her face when I walked through the door and saw his hand on her. At the sound of my voice I saw her relax almost like she was grateful that I was there to get him away from her. If that is the case and she is scared of him, what changed from them fucking to her being fearful of him?

"What do you want to do, Corv?" I ask.

"I want to bury the fucker six feet deep for ever hurting her. This is what I have always been scared of, her finding a guy and him being a piece of shit! Why couldn't she end up with one of you guys," he says before he begins to laugh. Meanwhile, I sit here frozen.

"Would that be a bad thing… if she did end up with one of us?" I keep my tone light, trying to act nonchalant when in truth, my heart is beating so fucking fast. He bumps me with his shoulder and snorts.

"Dude, I would fucking rip all of your dicks off if any of you touched my sister. I know what you fuckers get up to behind closed doors and that isn't happening where Leah is concerned." I force out a laugh for his benefit but inside my hope of him ever accepting me and Leah together fizzes out. "We have a couple weeks before the season starts and we play them, I want him carted off the fucking field and out for the whole season. I don't know exactly what he did to her but I know he did *do* something to her and he's going to fucking pay for that!" I grunt out my agreement.

Morning times in this house are fucking chaos. We all fight over the toaster and cereal boxes like pigs. Don't even get me started on what it's like when the five of us make protein shakes at the same time.

"You used all the fucking milk!" Crue shouts. Beck shrugs his shoulders as he scoops another mouthful of his breakfast into his mouth. "You asshole, now I have to have toast!" Crue is always a grumpy bitch first up in the morning.

"Dude, I'll buy you a bagel when we stop to get coffee." Crue beams at Saint.

"You do love me!" Crue sing songs.

"More than anything!" Saint replies in a fake British accent.

"Leah?" The four of us all turn toward the door to see Corv rushing toward his sister who looks like shit. She has dark circles under her eyes, her hair is piled on top of her head in a messy bun. She wears a loose fitting tee that she has knotted in the front and plain black yoga pants. "Are you okay?" She nods in answer to her brother's softly asked question. "Uh, want a lift to school?" Again she doesn't respond verbally, just shakes her head and tries to move around Corvin but he blocks her path. "Talk to me, Leah, what's going on?" he pleads.

"Nothing, I'm fine, everything is fine and dandy. Now can I go or I'll be late for practice." Stunned by her response, he nods and reluctantly steps out of her way, letting her walk right out the door without a fucking fight.

"Why the fuck did you let her leave?" I snap the second the front door clicks closed. Corvin spins around to face me looking utterly lost.

"What did you want me to do?" he growls angrily.

"Chain her ass to the bed if you had to!" I can hear the anger in my own voice. He eyes me warily for a second before asking,

"Since when do you care so much about *my* sister?" The accusation in his tone is clear. I should try to cover my ass but I'm tired of choosing between the Williams siblings. Like Beck said, I need to make a choice and I think I have. I stand, grab my bag off the floor, sling it over my shoulder and close the space between Corvin and me until we are standing an inch apart.

"I've always cared, more than you know or should I say more than you cared to see. I was the one who was worried about her while you were out dipping your dick in whatever had a hole. So don't fucking stand there and question my motives where *she* is concerned." I leave him standing there with a stunned look on his face as I chase after Leah.

CHAPTER TWENTY-FOUR

I don't get more than a few meters from the house before I hear someone running after me. I spin around ready to tell whoever it is to fuck off but clamp my mouth closed when I find it's Garrett.

"Morning, sunshine." I try to smile but from the look on his face I guess I fail. "Not such a good morning then, huh?" A whoosh of air escapes me as I shake my head.

"Not really," I answer honestly.

"How about I walk you to school and we can grab a coffee and chat?" I open my mouth to answer but clamp it closed when Darius appears out of thin air and answers for me.

"She's with me," is all he says. Garrett's eyes blaze with fury.

"She doesn't belong to you!" he snaps. Darius winks at him before shocking the hell out of me when cups my face and smashes his mouth to mine. The kiss isn't deep or anything like that, this kiss is for a purpose and that is to show Garrett that I'm Darius's. I want to fight him off and demand he never touch me but this is the first time he has ever kissed me publicly and in front of someone! He pulls back, smirks at me before wrapping an arm around my shoulders and hauling me away from a wide-eyed Garrett.

"I think he gets the hint now, don't you?" The gleeful sound of his voice snaps me out of my stupor. I pull away from him and quicken my pace to try to escape but of course he isn't having any of that and grips my bag yanking me back into his side.

"Leave me alone!" I hiss as I struggle to get away from him. He spins me around so I am facing him and cups my face.

"I can't," he says softly

"I thought you hated me?" I spit the words at him. He bends until we are eye level and I can see the seriousness in his eyes.

"I'm gonna tell you something before I let you run away to practice." I plaster a bored look on my face. "One, I am going to get to the bottom of why you freaked out on Corv last night." I struggle to keep my face blank when inside fear is threatening to cripple me, when he finds out the truth he is going to hate me. "Two, I do hate you." I suck a sharp intake of breath in as his words spear me right in the heart again. "I hate you because I can't fucking hate you. I keep thinking the more I say it might make it true." My mouth slackens in shock. "I hate that I can't hate you, Goldie. I fucking hate that you can still have me wrapped around your finger and I'm powerless to stop it." Tears cloud my vision, he takes a shuddering breath as he releases me and steps back. "Most of all, I hate that I still fucking love you." I stand here frozen and rooted to the spot as I watch him turn around and head back to the house.

I stand here for so long that my phone ringing is the only thing that snaps me out of my thoughts. Darius loves me, he doesn't hate me! I fish my phone from my bag and curse when I see the time and answer Katie's call.

"Sorry, I'm on my way now!" I say in lieu of a greeting.

"Run bitch run because coach is on a warpath." Shit, I end the call and run as fast I can to get to practice before I get in more shit from coach.

I head to my last class of the day, groaning. I fucking hate calculus and Mr. Thompson has it out for me! The asshole has failed me on the last two pop quizzes. I walk into class and head to my usual seat up the back. I drop into my chair and grab out my pad and pen as I wait for Garrett to show up, only he doesn't and Mr. Thompson spends the whole fucking lesson telling us how he doesn't get paid enough to teach idiots. The moment the bell signals the end of class everyone is flying from their desks and racing for the nearest exit trying to escape this fucking room.

I sling my bag over my shoulder as I make my way to the exit. Before I can round the corner to the door, a hand grips my wrist and yanks me into a classroom. I see who it is before I can yell, and stop struggling the moment his lips find mine. He grips my waist and I melt into him, trying to block out the thoughts that taunt me that this won't last, it can't. He groans into my mouth before leaping away from me like I burnt him.

"What happened?" I ask breathlessly.

"If that had lasted another second I would be fucking you against that wall and be late to practice." I bite my lip to stop my smile from breaking free. Darius narrows his eyes playfully. He grips my hand and drags me from the empty classroom after him, then he drops my hand and wraps his arm around my shoulders, drawing me into his side. I don't miss the snide looks and glares that random girls shoot me as we make our way outside. I tense the second we hit the quad and I see my brother and Saint walking toward us. I expect Darius to drop his hold on me but he doesn't and by the looks of things, Corvin views the gesture as a friendly type of thing.

"Well isn't someone looking... flushed." I shoot Saint a warning look that has him laughing and a frown marrying Corv's face.

"You okay?" he asks me.

"Yeah. I'm good but I have to get to practice," I rush to say, I can't be late again or coach will murder me!

"I'll walk you," Darius says. He doesn't wait for a response from my brother as he leads me away from them. I'm a little taken back by his sudden change in attitude and the way he is acting toward me, but I won't question it and risk him going back to not even looking at me in public. He drops me at practice, kisses me on the cheek before running off to his training. Cody and Katie both shoot me wide-eyed looks and I mouth that I will fill them in later.

After practice Katie, Cody and I were too exhausted to go anywhere for food so we grabbed something from the cafeteria before heading to our room to shower and sleep. I'm too exhausted from not sleeping last night to even think about touching my homework. Katie and Cody were out the second their heads hit the pillows, it's not even seven-thirty at night on a Friday and the three of us are in bed. I smile to myself. My phone pings with a message, my heart lurches into my throat thinking it's from that asshole but when I see the name *Big D* flash across my screen I snort out a laugh as I unlock it and read the message.

BIG D

Miss me?

I bite my lip to keep from smiling as I reply.

New fone, who dis?

BIG D

The guy who had you screaming his name loud enough to wake the dead last weekend.

Now I can't help but laugh at the audacity of him.

Definitely wrong number, I'm not that type of girl!

BIG D

Oh but you are the type of girl to drop to your knees in the shower and suck my cock?

Instantly my thighs clench together as I reread his message.

And are you the type of guy to fuck a girl bare, then push your cum back inside her pussy when it leaks out?

A second passes then my phone begins to vibrate with an incoming call, I bite my lip as I answer it and whisper.

"Hello?"

"You seriously want to send me a fucking message like that and expect me not be rock fucking hard?" The ache between my thighs intensifies knowing that he is rock hard for me.

"You started it," I hiss.

"I didn't think you would reply with that shit!"

"Well, I live to surprise you." He snorts.

"Yeah, you sure fucking do. Where are you?"

"In my dorm?" I don't know why I answered that more like a question.

"Not tonight, get your shit your coming over for the weekend."

"Darius, I can't–"

"I'm out front, you have five minutes before I get someone to let me in and drag your sexy ass out."

"What about Corvin?" There, I addressed the elephant in the room.

"His room is down the hall and he has a party to go to tomorrow so we can fuck in the kitchen while he's gone." I choke on my own spit.

"That's pretty presumptuous," I say before a sigh spills from my lips.

"Spit out whatever is on your mind, Goldie." I take a deep breath and say it.

"Are you gonna kick me out again and hate me when the past creeps up on you?" I hear him exhale and wait with bated breath for his answer. I'm terrified he is going to hang up and end whatever this is between us.

"I'm gonna try. I need you to give me a chance to wrap my head around shit but I also need you to tell me the truth, Leah. After last night I know there is more to the story and when you're… ready to tell me, I'll be here." His words are like a balm to my tattered heart.

"I'll be down in two minutes. Not like I need to pack much since I plan on being naked and under you for the weekend." I end the call before he can reply and smile to myself feeling slightly victorious that I was able to stun him.

CHAPTER TWENTY-FIVE

I stare at the black screen on my phone for a solid minute, lost for fucking words. This girl is fucking killing me. I'll admit, my actions tonight aren't noble. Corvin is worried as fuck about her and after seeing me with her today, he asked me if I could get her to stay at the house. I lied to her, Corvin isn't going to a party, he's meeting with Troy to sign the last contract and then everything is done, the merger is complete and we can finally move onto phase two of our plan. I of course agreed to help my best friend out. What he doesn't know is she only agreed to stay because my dick is on the menu and I think it best if I leave that part of the story out. The front door of the dorm building opens to reveal Leah, grinning at me with a bag swung over her shoulder. I frown when I take in her fucking outfit.

"What the hell is that?" I growl while pointing to her sports bra and tiny as fuck shorts that leave nothing to the imagination. She rolls her eyes.

"This is what I sleep in. You wouldn't know this because I can't seem to keep clothes on when you're around." I tilt my head side to side not agreeing and not denying her claim either. This is what I love and miss, the banter between us and how easy we can just be ourselves. I need her to open up to me if this is ever going to be more than… what it is.

"Come on, I got Corv's car," I say as I grab her bag from her and lead the way to the parking lot where Corvin's car waits idling. We slip into the car and a light laugh leaves her when she sees Beck in the backseat.

"Why am I not surprised he brought you for backup?" Beck shrugs as he says,

"Had to make sure he didn't need help breaking in to get you out." She laughs, but the truth is what he says isn't far from the truth.

We spend the night hanging out with the guys. It was actually nice to just kick back with them and not think about everything. Leah called it a night about twenty minutes ago and I plan to follow her shortly and spend the night getting lost inside her.

"When are we going to go public with everything?" Saint asks, I turn to him and watch as Crue places a hand on his shoulder offering his silent support. Saint tries to put on a brave face but I know this shit must be fucking hard for him. Out of the five of us, when this thing goes public, it's me and Saint that will wear the brunt of it all.

"We keep it under wraps for a few months before we move onto phase two." Saint nods and tries to hide his feelings behind a mask but he forgets we know him too well and can see the anguish in his eyes. "We'll be here for you every step of the way, brother," Corv tacks on. "I'll finalize everything with Troy tomorrow. Beck will finish out the rest of his schooling online and go to Alaska to learn what he needs to help us." A pang hits me in the chest knowing that Beck is leaving soon. We all have skin in the game but he is the one who has to leave while we stay back.

"Don't look so fucking sad, you pussies!" Beck says on a light chuckle. The rest of us force a smile for his benefit but since high school we haven't been apart, so this is going to be hard. "It's only a couple months and then I'll be back." I stay with the guys for another hour before I call it a night. Beck shoots me a knowing look as I leave them but I know he won't say anything. I make my way upstairs and head for my room. I don't feel tired, when I should after the practice we had today but fuck it, that just means I need to fuck Leah until I pass out. I find her cuddled up in *my* bed.

Smart girl.

I lock the door behind me and for good measure, lock the bathroom door just in case. I strip down to my briefs and climb in beside her. She stirs as I pull her into me and spoon her tiny body. I'm rock fucking hard but I also know she must be tired, so instead of waking her with my face between her legs, I just lay here holding her for hours. When her phone keeps pinging with incoming texts, I debate on leaving it but then it rings. It's two in the fucking morning! I reach over to her side of the bed and grab her phone off the side table and frown at the name.

Piece of shit!

It rings out before I can answer it, and I hold the phone, wondering who the fuck she could hate enough to save their contact info under a name like that. I try to unlock it but of course, there is a fucking passcode! Another message pings through and thank fuck for iPhone's displaying messages on the lock screen.

PIECE OF SHIT

You have until game day to end this!

I stare at the message until the screen turns black again, what the fuck did that mean? What the fuck is she up to and what the hell does our game against the Dolphins have to do with it? I'm too fucking wired to sleep now. I lay here until the sun begins to crest the horizon, only then do I give up on the idea of sleep and slip out from beside her. I grab some clothes and head to the basement, needing to work out my frustrations. I fucking hate not knowing what the hell is going on. I know she is keeping shit hidden and that is fucking with my head! I spend the next hour and a half working out, only stopping when my arms feel like lead. I make my way to the kitchen to make a protein shake before taking it out back.

"You're up early." I look over my shoulder to see Crue walking toward me with a coffee in hand. He runs a hand through his bed hair as he drops down into the lounger beside me. The fucker still wears plaid bed pants to bed and no shirt, even though we told him years ago that they went out of fashion.

"Couldn't sleep," I answer in a flat tone.

"Hm, one would think having a hot blonde next door to you would help you sleep better." He wags his brows at me suggestively. "We all know you want to hit that."

I turn the tables on him, tired of them all knowing my business. "Like we all know you want to *hit* Saint?" He chokes on his coffee, sitting forward, spluttering. I lean over and pat his back fighting my smile. When he finally stops coughing, he pins me with a filthy look.

"What the fuck?" He tries to sound angry but he isn't pulling that shit off.

"You know none of us give a fuck, right?"

He shakes his head. "I don't know—"

"Crue, stop," I cut in. He clamps his mouth closed and lowers his gaze. I swing my legs over the side and rest my hand on the top of his knee. "If you want him, tell him. You know Saint, he lives in the moment and never lets shit get to him so you're gonna need to spell it out for him, brother."

"I'll do it when you tell Corvin about Leah." I sigh knowing that he's right but it isn't the right time.

"My shit is complicated but yours isn't. If it bothers you seeing him with all these girls then tell him. Don't watch from afar and live your life wondering *what if*." He nods solemnly.

"I can't tell him." A smile spreads across my face finally hearing him admit it out loud. "He has too much stress on him with this whole business shit and me telling him that I'm in love with him is only going to complicate shit. He needs me and if that means I have to stand by his side and watch him fuck everyone, then so be it because I would rather have him in my life than not at all." I know exactly how he feels and that fucking sucks.

"Just don't wait too long, okay? If he's what you want, then go for it."

"What if… what if he doesn't–"

"Dude, I've seen the way he looks at you. Saint may not know it or even want to acknowledge it but he has feelings for you as well. You're just going to have to give him time to come to terms with the fact that he isn't as straight as he thinks he is." A whoosh of air escapes him.

"You are actually really good at giving advice. You should try taking some of your own." I shove him back and we both laugh.

"I'm the guru, my man. I give advice, not take it."

I spend the day hanging with the guys and Leah in the pool playing volleyball. Her, Crue and Saint against me, Beck and Corv. She gets her shit talking from her brother. The girl can talk so much shit, she has been laying out insults since we started playing. Her and Corvin are so competitive and it's fucking funny to watch them battle it out. I have to admit my attention is constantly pulled to her when she jumps out of the water to hit the ball over the net. Her tits bounce up and down in that yellow bra thing she wears that is tied in so many different fucking knots. Beck spikes the ball over the net and her and Crue dive for it but they crash into each other. The three of us scream and shout that we got a point.

"Shit!" I turn away from Beck and Corv to see her holding

the front of her top, my eyes widen when I realize it's come undone. I don't think as I wade through the water to shield her from Crue and Saint's eyes. I duck under the net, grip her waist and push her back until we are in the corner of the pool. I keep my back to the others shielding her, she smiles her thanks as she begins to retie her top. I watch shamelessly biting my bottom lip to suppress the groan that wants to break free, my cock is hard as fuck inside my board shorts.

"The fuck are you doing?" Both our eyes widen at the sound of Corvin's voice, I didn't even think about him as I covered her.

Fuck!

CHAPTER TWENTY-SIX

Leah

My mouth hangs open in shock, Darius's eyes are wide. When I hear the splashing I quickly finish tying my top and not a second too soon, because Darius is yanked away from me to reveal a pissed off looking Corvin standing there. I reach out to grab my brothers arm but he yanks it away as he gets in Darius's face.

"What the fuck was that?" Corvin shouts in his face. Darius schools his features, keeping his face blank and looking bored.

"Would you have rather me let everyone get an eye of her tits?" I flinch at the harsh tone of his voice. Corvin frowns as he looks over to me. I nod agreeing that what Darius says is true.

"My top came undone when Crue and I were diving for the ball, Darius covered me while I fixed it." My voice trembles and I hope like hell he doesn't notice. He turns back to Darius and eyes him warily for a second.

"You better not have looked, dick!" Darius rolls his eyes and shoves Corv playfully. "I mean it, my sister is off limits to all you fuckers." My heart sinks. Darius shoots me a quick glance before swimming back to his side of the pool where Beck stands waiting. Corvin places his hands on my shoulders and smiles but it doesn't reach his eyes. "Don't get cute with any of these guys because they know touching you would mean the end of the five of us." Unable to speak I just nod and fight to push the feeling of dread out of me.

Corvin left an hour ago to go to some party thing. It's only three in the afternoon so it must not be a good party. The guys and I have been hanging out in the pool all day. I invited Cody and Katie over as well and they have been trying to teach Saint and Crue our routine. Beck and I are laying on the loungers laughing at them while Darius dashed inside to get us some drinks.

"You move like a freaking giraffe!" Cody abolishes as Saint tries to do the *Monestray* dance. "You're so stiff!" She adds, exasperated. Saint stops trying and presses into my friend. Cody doesn't move or even seem affected by his nearness, the reason for that is because I know who she has a crush on.

"I'll show you what's stiff," he says cockily. Cody runs her hand down his naked chest suggestively. Saint smiles triumphantly.

"Oh, baby, if I wanted to prick my vagina with a needle, I'd get a sewing kit." The smile vanishes from Saint's face while the rest of us burst out into fits of laughter.

"What's so funny?" Darius asks as he comes back and hands Beck and I our drinks. I cringe when I see he opted for a protein shake instead of a water.

I'm going straight to hell!

Beck fills him on what happened. Saint shoots us a glare as he pushes Cody in the pool. Not one to be deterred, he moves onto Katie who holds her hand out stopping him before he can get too close.

"I have recently discovered I prefer to eat pussy than suck dick, so unless you're down to have your ass eaten, I'm not the girl for you." Saint throws his head back laughing as he slings his arm around my girl's shoulders and pulls her into his side.

"I think I fucking love you!" Katie rolls her eyes and pushes away from Saint to dive into the pool. I cut a glance to the side to see Crue standing there with a hurt look on his face, my mouth dropping open in shock. I spin to face Darius and Beck. Darius clamps a hand over my mouth and shakes his head.

"Mind ya business, Goldie." My eyes dart between him and Beck, they both knew! "What they get up to behind closed doors does not concern us." I nod and he drops his hand. Feeling like ruffling his feathers, I stand and love the way his eyes travel the length of my body and drink me in.

"Does what we do behind closed doors concern Beckett?" Beck's mouth drops open. Before Darius can reach for me, I take off laughing and jump into the pool laughing so hard I swallow a bit of water before I break the surface.

"So, are you like, living here now?" Cody asks me. Me, Katie and Cody are sitting out on the back deck on the loungers while the guys are inside catching up with Corv. Today has been the best day I have had in months. Hanging out with my brother and the guys, then having the girls come over has made this the best day ever.

"No, I'm just staying here for the weekend," I answer.

"So have you been nailed against the wall yet?" I swat Katie on the arm as the three of us laugh.

Shaking my head, I say, "No, we just slept and it was… nice."

Cody scrunches her face up. "If I was tapping that, the last thing I would be doing is sleeping!" I roll my eyes.

"We all know who you would rather be sleeping with," Katie teases. Cody stiffens, and I place my hand atop hers and smile.

"I would be the world's biggest hypocrite if I told you to stay away from my brother. If you like him then… go for it." Cody stares at me like I have lost my mind. Who knows, maybe I bloody have. We spend the rest of the night laughing and joking around, talking about our dance and if we are really going to do it at the finals. I've never had girlfriends like this before and honestly, it is the most amazing feeling to have friends who don't judge you or want to use you because of who you are related to. Cody and Katie support me and my choices, which is why I would do anything for these girls because friends like this are once in a lifetime type of friends.

Darius and I spend the rest of the night tangled in the sheets. He makes me come so many times that I pass the fuck out, utterly exhausted and spent in the best possible way. When Sunday morning rolls around, the guys decide that we need to pack a picnic and spend the day at the beach. I of course invite my girls who are always down to hang out. I love that they get on with the guys and there is no tension between any of us, just good vibes.

When we sit down to eat, guilt washes over me at the sight of Saint and Darius drinking their pre-made protein shakes they brought from home. I am a shitty fucking person. I spend the rest of the day in a sour mood as the reality of what I'm doing crashes down on me. When it's time to call it a day, I decide to head back with the girls, much to Corvin and Darius's dismay. Truth is, the guilt is eating me alive and won't allow me to be near them any longer.

The girls and I spend the rest of the evening catching up on homework. I ignore the numerous texts and calls from *Big D* and *Piece of shit!* I just need to get through the next few weeks and then everything will be fine. I just hope that they can forgive me when the truth comes out. I just need to finish this and then he will be gone for good and I'll finally be free of this weight on my shoulders.

I manage to avoid Darius and the others for the entire week. With the game coming up they have been training hard and every spare minute they get is spent in the gym, so I've been lucky. When the weekend rolls around, that was more difficult. I had to fake being sick and not wanting to spread my germs to the guys before the big game. Darius blew my phone up nonstop. I've barely been replying to him all week. What the hell do I even say to him, I'm sorry I ruined your life?

He is going to hate me, I can feel it in my heart there is no coming back from what I've done. I'm trying to distance myself from him so when the inevitable happens, I'm hoping the pain won't be as crippling. I'm kidding myself, I know it is going to destroy me but I can't look him in the eyes knowing what I've done.

CHAPTER TWENTY-SEVEN

Darius

She keeps avoiding me!

It's now Wednesday and I am tired of her one or two word replies so I skipped out on training early and wait outside the studio she practices in with her dance team. I check my watch, it's six o'clock so she'll be out any second. The doors open and dancers pile out. I spot her, Cody and Katie laughing as they jog down the stairs. I step out from the shadows right into their path, making them slam to a stop and Leah's eyes widen at the sight of me. We stand here silently for a minute just staring at each other, but then the sound of her nasally voice shatters our moment as she slides up beside me. Leah pulls her gaze from me to glare at Carrie as she clings to my arm.

"Hey handsome, I missed you." I don't take my eyes off Leah, waiting to see what she'll do. Will she finally stake her claim and continue to let her *friend* fawn all over me.

"He didn't miss you," Leah growls. My eyes widen in surprise when she steps forward leaving a sliver of space between us, yanks me free from Courtney's clutches and places my hand on her ass! I stand frozen, waiting to see what she does next. "The next time you think you can touch him, I'll make sure you don't stick the landing on your next turn out." Her mouth gapes open at Leah's threat.

"Have my sloppy seconds then, bitch." Leah grips the back of my neck and pulls my face down to hers and kisses me. I grip her waist with my other hand and grip her ass tighter. I try to deepen the kiss, horny as fuck but she pulls back and smiles at Callie.

"He was never yours, Chelsea." That's her fucking name! "Just so we are clear, we all know he never fucked you no matter how much you sucked his cock. He just couldn't get hard for you." She better have a fucking good point to this because announcing my performance issue to a crowd is not fucking cool! "Want to know why?" She doesn't give her a chance to answer. "He just used you to try and make me jealous." Chelsea burns red with rage.

"You're nothing. He's slept with half the school and he'll be knocking on my door the second he's over you." Leah chuckles.

"Oh, but babes, you never forget your first love." She doesn't wait for a reply as she grips my hand and leads me away. Katie and Cody stay back laughing and cheering for their friend and the smack down she just laid on the bitch. She doesn't stop walking until we're standing out front of her dorm building. She releases my hand and takes a step back. Confused as fuck at her sudden change in attitude I ask.

"You literally just cocked your leg and pissed on me marking your territory not five minutes ago and now you can't get further away from me. What the fuck is going on, Goldie?" She drops her chin to her chest and scuffs the toe of her shoe along the ground. "Look at me, Leah!" I snap. Her gaze lifts to mine and I see anguish in her green eyes.

"I love you, Darius. I have since I was a kid and I probably will for the rest of my life." I open my mouth to speak but she shakes her head forcing me to wait until she is finished. "I'm so sorry for what I have done, I wish I could take it all back and never transfer here and land you in my shit, but I can't and now you are going to pay the price." Tears streak down her cheeks as I stand here confused as fuck. "Please forgive me because I can't stand the thought of you hating me for the rest of our lives. Just know, I didn't have a choice." Too stunned I stand here and watch as she races inside her building sobbing like her fucking heart just got broken.

What the fuck just happened?

"Darius!" I spin around to see Saint and Beck running toward me with angry looks on their faces.

"What the fuck happened?" I demand when they come to a stop in front of me.

"Dude, we have to go. Coach just called an emergency meeting." Fuck, I follow after them deciding to give Leah some time before I break through that fucking door and demand answers. I'm tired of waiting!

◉

"Bullshit!" I shout.

"I'm sorry, son, you tested positive for narcotics." I stand here brimming with rage and shock, there is no fucking way I could test positive.

"Coach, you know Darius has never touched any of that shit!" Corvin jumps to my defense, Beckett, Saint and Crue all voice their agreement. When the guys said *meeting* I thought they meant with the whole team, instead it's just the five of us, Coach and the two assistant coaches in his office.

"I know, Corvin, which is why I have asked for the urine sample to be re tested but–" I slam my eyes knowing what he is going to say next. "We won't have the results back in time for him to take the field. I'm sorry, son, but you're benched for the game against the Dolphins until we can sort this out." I block out everything else as I stand here spiraling. I've never touched any type of drug, not even weed for the fear of becoming an addict like my mom! I've busted my ass to get ready for this final season, what if I never get to take the field again? Corv leads me from the room. I'm too numb to even think of speaking. I get in the car acting on autopilot.

When Corvin pulls into the driveway, no one makes a move to get out. My mind is reeling with possibilities as to how this could have fucking happened. Yeah, I've had a couple beers but I haven't done any fucking thing else!

"We're down a halfback and tight end," I snap my gaze up to meet Corvin's in the rearview mirror.

"What?" I grit out.

"I tested positive as well." I turn to the side and look at Saint who looks fucking crushed.

"How the fuck did this happen?" I roar. I may not be as good as Saint, Corv and Crue but I fucking love the game. When I had nothing I knew I could always count on football and now that has been ripped away from me.

"I don't know, but we'll figure it out, I swear it." Beckett's words don't bring me any comfort. I get out of the car and slam the fucking door as I storm inside the house. I head straight for my room and that's when I let all the anger out. I start smashing shit and throwing it around my room. Why can't I ever have one thing, one fucking good thing in my life? Corvin comes crashing into my room and wraps his arms around me from behind so I'll stop destroying everything.

"I got you, D. We all got you, brother." I'm breathing so fucking hard I can hear the blood rushing in my ears.

"I didn't fucking do it, Corvin."

"I know you didn't, D. Someone fucked with us and we are going to find out who it is and end them."

"I broke my vow," I whisper. He spins me around to face him and wraps me in a hug.

"You didn't break shit, brother," he says in a pained voice. I vowed the night I moved in with Corv that I would never touch any type of drug, it is the one cardinal rule that I live by. I stand here hugging my best friend trying to think of how this happened, when I start to think about how I haven't been able to sleep, can't sit still for long and have been spending more time than usual in the gym just to try and curb the edge off how I have been feeling.

Holy fuck!

I pull back and stare at Corvin, his eyes widen when he sees the look on my face. "I know who drugged us."

"Who?"

"Your sister." He stumbles back a step, shaking his head.

"Nah, man. Leah would never do that, are you out of your mind?" he yells. I spy the other three standing in the doorway but keep my focus on Corvin. Leah's words to me tonight make sense now, she doesn't want me to hate her because she knew what she had fucking done to me!

"It was her, Corvin," I yell.

"Fuck you, I know your angry but–"

I cut him off. "Pull your head out of your ass, Corvin, you even said yourself she's been acting strange and something is up with her. Leah fucking did this to us."

"Where's your proof?" he snaps.

"I'll get your fucking proof for you and when I do, I never want your sister near this house or near me again. As far as I'm concerned, Leah is dead to me."

CHAPTER TWENTY-EIGHT

Darius

It's game day and I am fucking raging.

Corvin and I have been at odds since Wednesday night. I know I'm fucking right and my point was proven when he tried to call her that night and she sent him to voicemail. He has rose-colored glasses on when it concerns his sister. He needs to realize she is a lying, cheating bitch. How I let myself fall into her orbit again I'll never fucking know!

I skipped yesterday and spent the day fixing my room and didn't bother going today as well. I didn't want to run the risk of bumping into her and strangling the fuck out of her. Sitting on the bench with Saint is fucking killing me, the both of us are itching to be out on that field with our team.

"Fuck, man, we're getting slaughtered!" Saint hisses. I grunt my agreement. Corvin may not think it was Leah but Saint, Crue and I do. She is the only one who had access to our house. The thing that is tearing me up inside is not knowing why the fuck she would do this. What does a dancer gain out of getting two football players benched, but what if it isn't about football and this is just her way of getting payback for me ghosting her?

"I'm gonna kill her," I snarl as the buzzer sounds to signal the end of the third quarter. The defensive and offensive teams huddle around our coach as he tears them a new asshole. Saint and I are banished to the end bench, away from the team so we can't hear shit. The stands are packed with people, there isn't an empty seat in sight. I tear my gaze away from the team as streak of blonde in the stands catches my attention. I grind my teeth so fucking hard when I see it's the bitch who tried to ruin me. She races down the bleachers and runs onto the field.

"What the fuck is she doing?" Saint says as we both climb to our feet. I feel my phone vibrate in my pocket with a text. Saint's phone also pings with and incoming text but we're both too focused on watching her storm toward the Dolphins, or more to the point toward Gary fucking Hayes! My fists clench at my sides as I begin to see red.

"Motherfucker!" I snarl as I stalk across the field. I'm too far away to see what she is saying but she shoves her phone in his face. The fucker laughs and shrugs before saying something back, then out of nowhere, she slaps him across the face.

"Shit!" Saint says in awe, my vision blurs when I see him cock his arm back and punch her in the face. "You're fucking dead, cunt!" Saint screams and he and I break out into a sprint as the crowd goes nuts.

"I'll fucking kill you!" I hear shouts from behind us. Fuck, Corvin saw what just happened. Before we can reach him the huge screen behind where the Dolphins are switches from displaying the score to a… video. Leah is sobbing on the ground, Gary's team mates have gathered around him and are shoving him while a few others crowd around Leah. The video comes into focus and I freeze, my blood runs cold at the sight in front of me. Leah lays naked sprawled out on the bed with a guy whose face you can't see pounding into her. Tears roll down her cheeks, her eyes are open but glazed over, her mouth opens and she whimpers out a name.

My fucking name!

The tone of her voice in that video, it's filled with fear and confusion and that is what has me snapping out of it and charging after Gary. I know it's him in that video, I recognize the fucking room as the one I walked in on and found her in that fucking bed! Corvin blitzes past me and tackles Gary to the ground. His arms start swinging as he lands punch after punch. Gary's team mates pull him off their captain but I'm on him next, landing right hook after right hook to his fucking face. I shrug off the fuckers who try to pull me off him. This isn't how I wanted to take the fucker down but it feels fucking marvelous to finally get my pound of flesh.

"You're gonna kill him," someone shouts, the moans coming from the videos around the field fueling my need for his blood. An arm wraps around my throat and waist and yanks me off the bastard. He's groaning on the ground like the fucking piece of shit he is… *Piece of shit.*

I still in Beckett's hold as I turn my head to see Crue holding Leah as she sobs into his chest. It all clicks into place as I dart my gaze between her and Gary. He's the one who was blowing up her phone, he told her she had until game day, she did this for him. I break free of Beckett's hold and march over to her. Crue shoots me a warning look but I ignore it as I look at Leah. Her cheek is red and already starting to bruise, her eyes plead with me to understand.

"You drugged *me* for him?" I shout as she flinches at the harsh tone of my voice. "Why the fuck did you do it?" I yell.

"I… I didn't have a choice!" she cries, assuming she did it is one thing but hearing her admit it out loud cuts me so fucking deep. "He said if I didn't, he would post that video everywhere." Said video is playing on repeat in the background, it's then I realize that the message Saint and I got earlier is probably from an unknown number with a link to the video of him fucking her.

"You could have come to me!" I roar.

"And tell you what, Darius?" she screams. I feel Beckett and Corvin behind me but I keep my focus on her.

"The fucking truth, Leah! You could have told me the fucking truth." She throws her hands in the air.

"Fine. You want the truth here it is. Gary Hayes spiked my drink at that party and raped me to get one up on you." The air whooshes from my lungs. "I found out when I overheard him bragging to his friends at DCU. When I confronted him, he showed me the video and threatened to post it unless I took the five of you out. I didn't even know it had happened until I saw the video!" Crue steps away from her as Corvin comes to my side.

"Why the fuck didn't you say anything?" Corvin shouts. I ignore him as I address her, letting her see all the anger in my eyes.

"You could have come to me the moment you found out, I fucking told you I loved you!"

"You what?" Corvin snaps but I push on.

"I would have fucking ended the son of bitch before this ever got out." I wave my hand around the stadium gesturing to the screens displaying the video. "But no, you wormed your fucking way back into my life like the snake I always knew you were and fucked me over so good. You broke my cardinal vow and I didn't even have a fucking say in the matter!" I scream in her face. "You are done, Leah, there will never be an us again. You know better than anyone what drugs mean to me and still you fucking played me. Well done, baby, that was the one play I didn't see coming."

"You've been fucking my sister?" Corvin pushes in front of me, blocking his sister from my view. I take a shuddering breath as I brace for this shit show to blow up in front of everyone, except I don't get a chance to answer.

"Your sister is a fucking slut and has been fucking your best friend for years!" I whirl around to Gary using the bench seat to try to push himself to his feet. I don't think, I just act. I close the space between us, and hold his hand on the bench with my own as I apply all my weight to stomp down on his elbow relishing in the scream that tears from him when his bones break.

"You'll never throw another fucking ball again, your career is over, you cunt." I'm rushed from all sides, coaches and players step in to break up the fight. Shouts are heard from all around but I can't keep the smile off my face knowing I just ended the fuckers dream of making it big in the NFL.

"You're done!" The sound of his voice has the hairs on the back of my neck rising, I turn my head to the side to see Victor Hayes standing right there. The bastard looks murderous, he stands there in his thousand-dollar suit, brown hair slicked back to try look young but his brown eyes betray him and show his age. I feel Saint and Crue stiffen on either side of me as they let go of my arms, they know what this means for me. "You are going to fucking pay for that, you have no idea what the fuck you have just done!"

PART
TWO

CHAPTER ONE

Leah

I stand tucked into my brother's side as we watch the exchange between Gary's father and Darius. Instead of looking fearful that one of the richest men in the whole state, shit maybe even the whole country, is standing there promising to ruin his life, Darius just smiles wide looking slightly unhinged.

"Oh, so you only care about *that* son?" Victor's upper lip twitches.

"I'm going to make sure you spend the rest of your life rotting in a jail cell," Mr. Hayes seethes. Gary is on his feet again, thanks to the help of his team mates, clutching his arm to his chest. It brings me great joy to see he is in agony—serves the bastard right. I did as he told me to, okay well maybe I got two out of five off the field but how was I to know only Saint and Darius drink that particular protein shake that I put the powder in! Before the end of the last quarter everyone's phones began to ping with incoming messages. The moment I felt eyes on me I just knew what happened before I even opened the link.

"As long as you're in the one next to me," Darius says like he isn't worried.

"You broke my fucking arm!" Gary screams. Darius just shrugs and smiles at both the Hayes men.

"You're lucky that's all I broke, you rapist." Gasps ring out around us and I drop my gaze in shame.

"That's bullshit and that video proves it!" Mr. Hayes tries to defend his son. Darius steps forward until they are chest to chest. Corvin releases me as he and Beck move in closer ready to pull Darius back if he swings at Gary's dad.

"No, that video just proves that you put your son up to it. You tried to use your golden boy to fuck me over and keep me quiet, except now, it won't work." Victor eyes Darius with careful scrutiny.

"You have no idea who you just fucked with," Victor growls.

"I know exactly who I picked a war with and believe me, I'll fucking win this," Darius spits.

"Someone call the cops, Dad I want his ass arrested," Gary yells like a little bitch. Darius tears his gaze from Victor to look at Gary.

"Fuck," Corvin mumbles, almost like he knows what is about to happen.

"Daddy won't let his son get arrested, he was talking out of his ass. He can't afford the publicity right now with the sale of his company being announced in a few days." Victor's eyes widen, Gary frowns and scoffs.

"I'm not getting arrested, you dumb fuck, you are!" Darius shakes his head and tsks. I look around us to see everyone has stopped and are watching this scene instead of stepping in, I guess this just proves that the five of them really are the kings and no one touches them.

"You didn't hear me, dipshit. Daddy won't let his son go to jail right now."

"I am his son!" Gary screams.

"No, you're one of his sons." I suck in a sharp breath as I look between the three of them with wide eyes.

"What the fuck, Dad, what the fuck is he on about?" Gary demands, but Victor is too busy staring at Darius in shock.

"You picked the wrong twin, Victor. I promise you, I will

outshine you and your pick of the litter. When I'm done fucking you over, you won't have two pennies left to scratch together." Gary stares at Darius for a second before snapping his gaze to his father who is grinding his teeth so hard I fear he may snap them. "Watch your back, Hayes, well as best you can because you won't see me coming when I end you." Darius turns and stalks toward me. He doesn't even spare me a glance as he shoulder checks me on his way out. Crue, Beck and Saint shoot me pitying looks before they race after their friend.

I feel sick. Darius and Gary are twins. One raped me and the other one I'm in love with.

Corvin's coach goes to him and whispers something in his ear, Corv nods and marches to me gripping my arm and dragging me from the field. I don't question him when I hear the sounds of sirens in the distance, somebody really did call the cops.

The second we get in the car and Corvin peels out of the lot he starts. "Tell me Gary was full of shit and you haven't been fucking my best friend behind my back for years?" Just as we are about to hit the street, Corv slams on the breaks lurching us both forward but thanks to the seatbelts we both jerk back in our seats. "Fucking hell," he snarls as he winds his window down. I look up and my heart leaps at the sight in front of me. "Either get the fuck in the car or move your asses!" Katie and Cody exchange a quick glace before they both race toward us and climb in the back. I turn in my seat and look to each of them.

They both smile awkwardly and shrug. "We thought you might need some friends to talk to," Cody says. Too choked up by their show of love for me, I turn around and look over at my brother as he white knuckles the steering wheel and speeds down the road. I frown when he doesn't turn down the street that will lead us to his house.

"Where are we going?" I ask hesitantly.

"Unless the next words out of your mouth are to tell me the truth about you and Darius, shut the hell up Leah." I clamp my mouth closed and slink back into my seat. "Call Beckett." The car's Bluetooth system registers his command and dials Beck's number.

"Where are you?" Beckett says in lieu of a hello.

"About to hit the interstate," Corv answers.

"We got the go bags, I'll get Leah's shit." I frown as I peek over at my brother.

"Pack extra, we got two strays in the back." Cody and Katie bristle at being called strays and I don't blame them.

"Is that a good idea?"

Corvin sighs tiredly, he's dressed in his football uniform, pads and all. "I didn't have a choice, they blocked my car."

"We going off grid?" What the hell does that even mean?

"Yeah, brother, for at least a week until we can get out in front of this shit."

"We'll see you in eight hours." Corvin ends the call.

"Where the hell are we going?" Cody asks.

"To the Batcave." I roll my eyes at Corvin's stupid answer. The longer we drive, the more the ache in my cheek begins to grow. I didn't feel it before but now that the adrenaline has worn off, it's fucking painful.

My eyes sting and my cheek continues to ache but I refuse to say anything and risk Corvin going off at me again. I check the time on the dash and stifle a groan. It's after one in the morning, the girls fell asleep a couple hours ago. If the pain in my face wasn't so bad I would be fast asleep as well. Corvin exits the interstate, I look around and see nothing but mountains. Where the hell are we? We continue to drive for another twenty minutes on darkened roads with no street lights. He finally slows the car and pulls into a gravel driveway that is lined by pine trees. Even with the windows up I can still smell the scent of pine. It reminds me of Christmas. Mom always said we could never have a fake tree, it had to be real or it just wasn't Christmas.

I spot a lone light up ahead and gasp when the car's head-lights display the cabin in front of us—it is majestic looking. It's a two-story with a wraparound porch on the second level, and huge A-frame windows, allowing you to see the beautiful moun-tains that surround the property. Downstairs is all windows, allowing the natural sunlight to beam in daily. Shrubs are planted around the house, and a swing seat hangs on the front porch. Corvin parks the car and shuts the lights off, taking away my source of light. I sigh. I guess I'll just have to take in the beauty of this place tomorrow in the daylight.

"We're here!" Corvin says loud enough to wake the girls. They both yawn and stretch before we pile out of the car. My ass is numb and my back is aching from the long drive, I need a hot shower and some Tylenol to numb the pain in my face, then a nice comfy bed would be great. "Come on," Corv says as he leads the way up the paved path to the cabin. The moon is high in the sky and lights the way for us to not trip on our own feet, well the moon and the porch light. I stumble up the stairs thanks to the lack of lighting. My brother doesn't even offer to help, just grunts and continues to the door. I sigh, Corvin has never been this angry at me before. Katie reaches out and squeezes my hand in silent support. Right now, they are the only two people I have on my side and who actually seem to care about what I went through at the hands of Gary.

Corvin reaches behind the porch light and pulls out a key, he unlocks the door, reaches in and flicks some switches before light blinds us. I blink my eyes to adjust before taking a deep breath and following my brother inside. My jaw hits the floor, this place is stunning. High vaulted ceilings with a chandelier that hangs in the entryway. Beautiful pictures of landscapes adorn the walls, I round the corner and gasp, a sunken living room with high ceilings and another chandelier, white suede couches that wrap around the area and a cozy open fireplace. I turn the other way and find an open plan kitchen with wooden bench tops and a stainless steel gas stove—a pot rack hangs above the butcher's block in the center of the room.

I continue through the kitchen to the open door off the back where Corvin disappeared. I marvel at the room. It's a game room with a pool table, air hockey and a projector screen on the other side with recliners. I follow Corvin as he leaves through another door that leads us past the kitchen and living room. We head up the beautiful wooden stairs that lead up to the second floor. I peek over the side and love how you can see the entire downstairs from the landing.

"That's Beck's room." I turn to where Corvin is pointing to a closed door on the other end of us. "Next to his is… Darius's, then a spare room which your friends can sleep in." I get the double meaning, I'm not to be trusted to share a room next to Darius anymore. "There's the bathroom." He points to the open door next to the spare room. "Then that's my room." He points to the last door, I frown.

"Where do Saint and Crue sleep?" I ask.

"We converted the basement for them, they stay down there," he answers in a clipped tone.

"And, where do I sleep?" I ask as I nibble on my bottom lip nervously. His gaze drills into me and I look away unable to meet his angry glare.

"Next to me so I can make sure you don't sneak out for a midnight romp." I cringe and Cody snorts next to me. Corvin swings his gaze to her. "Something funny?" he snaps. I expect her to remain silent but she surprises me when she steps into Corvin, spearing him an angry look of her own.

"Yeah, it is, actually. You stand there and judge her for sleeping with your best friend but not once have any of you selfish sons of bitches acknowledged what happened to her! Your sister was fucking date raped and all you care about is

Darius fucking her?" She doesn't give him a chance to answer. "You're fucking pathetic and she isn't sleeping in your room either." She reaches back, grips my arm and drags me toward the spare room leaving an open-mouthed Corvin standing there on his own.

CHAPTER TWO

Darius

My forehead is numb from leaning against the window for hours, none of us have spoken a word since we left the house. I know Beck, Saint and Crue are pissed at me. I told them that I wouldn't let things with me and Leah come between any of us and I fucking broke that promise. I'm so fucking livid at her for what she has done to me! But, I'm also so fucking angry at myself for not piecing together what happened to her on my own, I didn't even question it when I found her in that bed, I assumed the worse of her.

"You couldn't have known." I turn to look at Beck, he keeps his eyes on the road as he shrugs. "You aired that shit out loud." I shake my head and go back to looking out the window.

"You know Corvin is gonna beat your ass, right?" Irritated by Saint's stupid ass statement I just flip him off. He scoffs and doesn't take the hint to shut the fuck up. "Stay quiet all you want but you brought this on yourself. You should have fucking told him!" he shouts.

"I know!" I yell. "I should have done a lot of fucking things, but I didn't." My breaths are rushing in and out of me as my annoyance grows.

"Yeah you should have! We are all in the shit because we

fucking knew you were fucking his sister and you didn't have the balls to fucking tell him." I fucking hate that Saint is right. I've landed them all in the shit because I didn't come clean. "I won't fucking let this family that we've all created be torn apart. You guys are all I have and sister or not, I won't let pussy come between us." My first reaction is to turn around and punch him in the mouth for speaking about Leah like that. My second, is to feel immense guilt for putting our makeshift family in jeopardy because I fell in love with the wrong girl.

"I'm sorry," I say.

"Not as sorry as Gary is right now," Crue butts in, and within a second the four of us laugh and some of the tension flees from me.

"He's fucking lucky he's still breathing," Beck grits out. I grunt my agreement.

"I really didn't think you were going to drop the twin bomb on him tonight."

"I didn't either, Saint," I answer. I was supposed to save that nugget for the press release on Monday but it just felt like it would cause more damage saying it tonight.

"Hundred bucks says Victor is on the phone to his lawyers now, trying to do damage control." I laugh, Crue is bang on the money. Victor Hayes will be trying to get out in front of the mess I caused tonight, but thing is, he has no power anymore. The reason this merger was so important is because the company we merged with is Victor's. We now own the business that has been in his family for four generations since it was started. Thanks to his gambling problem and shitty investments, we were able to pretty much steal the company out from under him, we just had to make sure he had no idea who was buying it which is why BCD'S didn't buy it per se, we used a shell company to acquire Sullivan Global and all the hotel chains.

"How the fuck are we going to spin you breaking your brothers arm." Hearing Saint refer to Gary as my brother makes my stomach churn. I may share blood with that pussy but he isn't my brother. I have four chosen brothers—well, I hope I still have four.

"Simple, I lost it when I found out my father deserted me and only took my twin instead of the both of us. I was blinded by jealousy that Gary got the life I always wanted while I had to fight to survive because my mother was a junkie and a whore." Saint whistles and shakes his head.

"Fuck me, dude, you're one cold motherfucker but also a genius." I roll my eyes at Saint. We all fall silent. I feel the tension building again and know either Saint or Crue is about to bring the one thing up that I don't want to think about.

"Brother or not, Corvin is going to kill him for what he did to Leah." There it is, Crue just voiced the one thing I was trying to avoid.

"No. If anyone is taking that motherfucker out it's me." My tone is firm and lets them all know I'm not fucking around. Gary won't live to see our twenty-first birthday, I'll make fucking sure of that.

Pulling into the driveway of our cabin, I start to relax. I don't know what it is about this place but being out here in the woods surrounded by nothing but nature always calms me. This cabin was our first big purchase. We wanted something to call our own, a place where we could one day bring our families together and always keep our bond alive. We made a pact, when one of us has a kid, we spend the Christmas holidays here every year no matter what. I see Corvin's car and the tension returns, Beck parks behind him and shuts off the engine. Saint and Crue practically leap out. Beck pops the trunk for them to take all our bags inside while we sit here.

"You have to face him eventually," he says quietly as we watch Saint and Crue lug all the bags inside.

"He's never going to forgive me." A whoosh of air escapes Beck.

"Look, I'm not gonna sugarcoat it for you, okay? Tonight he found out one of his best friends is sleeping with his sister. On top of that, he also just learned said best friend's brother raped his little sister. That is a lot for anybody to fucking digest." Hearing Beck say that shit out loud makes me feel like even more of a piece of shit. I flinch at the thought of those three words. Beck opens his door but before he can get out I grip his arm, halting his escape.

"Don't stop him when he comes at me." Beckett tries to protest but I push on. "He needs this, I've known it's been coming for years, so I'll take it like a man."

"Your funeral, brother," he says as I release my hold on him and get out of the car. I follow Beck up the pathway to the cabin, roll my shoulders and crack my neck side to side, getting myself ready for the beating I'm about to get. The moment I walk through the door I go on high alert expecting Corvin to jump out at me and try to catch me off guard. I keep my wits about me as I follow Beck past the living room and into the kitchen. I freeze at the threshold. Leah stands there with an ice pack against her cheek. I grind my teeth to keep from losing my shit. Saint, Crue and Beckett rally around the lying bitch. She flicks her gaze to me. Her eyes dim as her face morphs into the perfect picture of a guilty person. Unable to stomach the sight of her, I spin on my heels ready to head to my room but instead, I'm met with a fist to the face.

"Fuck!" I snarl as I stumble back a step. I push off the counter and step into Corvin.

"Corvin, stop it!" He and I ignore Leah's plea, his eyes shine with betrayal and guilt courses through me.

"Stay out of this, Leah, and go to your fucking room," Corvin grits out between clenched teeth. We stand staring at each other, chest to chest, for a minute not moving a muscle. "Now!" he shouts. A second later, I hear her moving toward us and tense when she brushes past me. Instead of doing as she was told she stops beside us.

"If you want to be mad at someone, be mad at me," she says tiredly. I fight the urge to roll my eyes and step away from her in case some of her toxicity rubs off on me. "None of this is his fault." Corvin turns to face her and I manage to draw in a full breath now that I know we aren't about to fight, yet.

"Let me guess, you managed to convince him to keep fucking you a secret?" he yells. I flinch and she recoils but doesn't back down. She squares her shoulders, lifts her chin and that's when I see the bruising on her face.

Fuck!

I knew Gary was a piece of shit but I didn't think he would fucking punch a woman! The guy is twice her size and from the look of it, she must be in a shit load of fucking pain. I grit my teeth and push those thoughts from my mind. She fucking drugged me, she doesn't deserve my fucking pity!

"It wasn't like that, Corv. If you would just let me explain—"

"Explain what?" he yells, cutting her off. "How you fucking lied to me, Mom and Dad? Or how you lied about why you transferred schools, or what about how you lied about trying to fucking drug us because your fuck buddies twin told you to!" Her bottom lip begins to tremble and her eyes fill with tears. I fucking hate her right now but even I have to admit, Corvin went too far.

"Yes, I did do all of those things," she says as she fights back her tears. Corvin still doesn't budge, he stands there tense and vibrating with anger. "I did it because I didn't want the whole fucking world to see me getting raped!" she screams. Fuck! I turn away unable to look at her, she sounds fucking broken and I can't handle that shit.

CHAPTER THREE

Tears begin to roll down my cheeks, the anger on Corvin's face from a minute ago has vanished. He stands here looking at me like I'm a fragile doll. When his eyes fill with pity, I shake my head so angry at him, at them all.

"I'm fucking sorry. So sorry for what I did, but you have no fucking idea what it's like to have no memory of some asshole defiling your body and yet he has proof and dangles it over your head. I never wanted you to see that or D–" I cut myself off before I can say his name. He keeps his back to me and that stings so bad. "By noon that video will be everywhere and everyone at school, shit maybe the fucking world will know what I look like naked and because of who Gary is, no one will believe me, they will all say I wanted it." Darius spins around but I can't look at him, I don't want to see the disgusted look in his eyes. "I thought out of everyone, my own brother would actually give a shit enough to even ask if I was okay, but how fucking stupid was I?" I don't wait for a response. I don't even care if they fight anymore as I make my way back upstairs to the spare room where the only two people who actually care about me sleep.

"Leah." I pause at the top of the landing and don't bother to turn around. I'm tired and mentally drained, don't even get me started on being emotionally exhausted and wrung out. I hear him climb the stairs but he doesn't stop behind me, he bypasses me to stand in front. Beck's eyes shine with pity, I turn away unable to look at him. "I'm so fucking sorry for what Gary did to you." Hearing that has me slowly turning back to face him, shocked that out of all of them it wasn't my brother or Darius who cared enough to come to me and say that.

When a sob tears from me he rushes forward and wraps his arms around me as I collapse in his arms. He lowers us to the floor as I cling to him. I cringe when the sounds of screams begin to pierce my ears, taking me another second to realize the screams are coming from me. I've never cried like this before, I don't think I have ever really allowed myself to feel the full weight of what actually happened to me that night. There's a pain inside my chest that feels like it's crushing me from the inside out. Beckett tightens his hold on me as he lifts me into his lap. I clutch his shirt in a vice-like grip, terrified he will let me go, not because I'm scared to be on my own but because I feel like I'll fall apart if he lets go.

"Fuck!" The sound of Darius's anguished shout has me burrowing into Beck further as I cry out the injustice that robbed me of my happiness. I may have only found out about this a few months ago, but the truth is, Gary ruined my life years ago when he drugged me and Darius saw what he did. I lost the boy that I loved but I also lost a part of myself that I will never get back because Gary stole that from me.

I hear the others climbing the stairs. I shake my head against Beck's chest conveying to him without words I don't want to talk to them. "Give her to me!" Corvin snaps, I press myself closer against Beck.

"No." Relief washes over me at Beck's answer.

"She's my fucking sister!" Corvin shouts.

"Exactly, Corvin! This should have been you but it isn't because you and Darius can't pull your fucking heads out of your asses for two seconds and realize it was *her* that was fucked over tonight! She is the one who had her body displayed to the world without consent and I'm the only fucking one who thought to call Troy and have the video shut down and the ball rolling to have Gary charged with child pornography." I tense in his hold unsure what to make of what he is saying, but also grateful that he was willing to do this for me even after he knew what I did. "You selfish sons of bitches both need your faces punched in." His voice drops to an even tone but it holds more weight than if he shouted. "Your sister was drugged and raped, Corvin, and the only thing you cared about was the fact she fell in love with your best friend. You want to be angry at someone, be angry at yourself for not being there for her when she needed you *and* Darius the most."

Beck pushes to his feet. I wrap my arms around his neck and he holds me bride style, then turns and moves toward the end of the hall, where I know his room is.

"I don't fucking think so. She stays with me!" Corvin shouts angrily. Beck pauses but doesn't turn around.

"Do you want to sleep in his room?" he asks me quietly. I shake my head against his chest unable to speak past the sobs that claw their way out of me. "She stays with me!" Beck says. Corvin shouts and rages behind us but then I hear Saint and Crue telling him to chill. They must be holding him back. Beck kicks his door shut behind us and uses his elbow to flick the light switch. He walks us further into the room, then gently begins to lower me but I cling to him. "I'm right here, I'm just putting you on the bed so I can get one of my shirts for you to sleep in." I slowly release my hold on him as he places me on the bed, keeping my chin tucked against my chest lost in my own thoughts.

I cover my face with my hands and cry. The sounds coming from me are foreign and unheard of, I feel so used, dirty and worthless. Seeing that video again broke me, the look on my own face will haunt me forever. The fear and confusion as I stared at the camera has bile rushing up my throat, I leap from the bed ready to race down the hall until Beck wraps an arm around me and ushers me through another door that leads to a bathroom. I race in and drop to my knees in front of the toilet just in time before everything I ate today comes rushing out of me. Beck grips my hair and holds it back as I throw up.

"Get the fuck out!" Beck snaps, I have no idea who's in here and I can't look. I can't stop throwing up.

"She might have a fucking concussion, Beckett!" The sound of his voice has me tensing but I don't look back, I can't as I continue to heave.

"Now you fucking care?" Beck snaps as he brushes a loose strand of hair that slipped free of his hold back. "I got you Lee." I manage to stop myself from heaving and slump back onto my haunches. Beck drops my hair, then turns to the sink as I sit here trying to pull myself together. He returns a second later with a warm washcloth, bends down beside me and gently wipes my face and mouth. I try to smile gratefully but flinch when the pain in my cheek stings—I couldn't feel it while I was breaking apart in his hold, but I can now. "Come on." He chucks the cloth over his shoulder then gently grips my arm and helps me to feet. He wraps an arm around my waist to keep me steady as he turns us toward the door. I tense at the sight of Darius, standing there with a war of emotions on his face. He looks like a dark angel dressed in all black but he isn't an angel and I'm not a saint. I lean into Beck as a wave of dizziness washes over me.

"She can't even stand," Darius grits out. Beck bends down, then scoops me into his arms bride style again.

"Get out of the way," Beck orders, waits a second, before he pushes forward and doesn't give Darius an option but to move. Beck places me on the edge of his bed in a sitting position, grabs the shirt he got for me earlier from the end of the bed, and hands it to me.

"Thank you," I rasp out, my voice is gruff and coarse from all the tears. I can feel how puffy my eyes are already, I'm going to look like a million bucks tomorrow.

"You okay to dress yourself or do you need help?" Beck asks gently.

"Like fuck, you stay the fuck away—"

I cut Darius off, unable to listen to anymore of his fake concern. "It's not like he hasn't seen it all before." That has him clamping his mouth shut. I push to my feet, sway a little and Beck is there gripping my waist to steady me.

"You need help, Lee, you can barely stand." I nod my head accepting that he is right. "Do you want me or… Darius to help you change?"

"I don't care, everyone's already seen me naked so can we just get it over with?"

Truthfully, I'd always choose Darius but I can't stand the thought of his hands on me when I know he can't stand the sight of me. He made it clear he hates me and just thinking that has more tears falling down my cheeks.

CHAPTER FOUR

Darius

Beck reaches for the hem of her shirt and I snap. I shove him out of the way and shoot him a look that promises pain if he pushes this. I may be fucking angry as hell at her and want to ring her fucking neck but I also can't stand here and watch Beck dress her. I grip her shirt, she turns her head away as if she can't stomach the thought of looking at me. Good because I don't want to look at her either, all I see is betrayal. I pull the shirt over her head, leaving her in a pink bra and her pants. I pop the button on her pants and of course it's right at that second the door opens to reveal Corvin, Saint and Crue. Corvin's gaze is laser focused on where my hands currently grip his sister's pants.

The universe fucking hates me today!

"I'm gonna fucking kill you!" he yells as he charges toward me but Beck steps into his path blocking him.

"She has a concussion and just threw up, she can't stand on her own let alone dress herself. Given their history I thought it best he was the one to help her change, I mean unless you want to see your own sister in a thong, then by all means." Beck steps aside, sweeping his arm toward us, taunting Corvin. When Leah stumbles forward into me, I catch her by the waist as she leans her forehead against my shoulder, I shoot Corvin a look.

"Fucking decide, Corvin!" I yell. He takes a look at her, then nods stiffly before turning around. "You two turn the fuck around as well!" I snap. Crue and Saint do as they are told. I make quick work of taking her pants and socks off, reach for the shirt—Beckett's fucking shirt, the thought of her in his clothes grates on my nerves.

"Take the bra off, can't sleep in it," she mumbles.

"Jesus fucking Christ!" Corvin snaps. "I am going to fucking kill you, Darius, but before I end you, I'm going to beat the fucking shit out of you!" I fight the smile that wants to break out at how uncomfortable he sounds. I reach around her and undo her bra, gently pushing the straps down her arms. I ignore the goose bumps that break out across her skin from my touch. I hate that it takes a lot of fucking willpower to not look at her tits, and gently pull the shirt over her head. I help her into the bed and pull the covers up, neither of us will look the other in the eye and I think that's for the best because if we do, I will fucking destroy her for what she did to me. Right now, she is too fragile to handle that. "Now get the hell away from her," he hisses as he shoulders me out of the way to check on his sister. I chance a peek at her, she's already fast asleep, the bruise on her face is fucking dark, her cheek is swollen. "I'm so sorry I wasn't there."

The pain and regret in Corvin's voice spears me. I stalk out of the room unable to be in there any longer. I head straight for my room, needing to be alone so I can sort my thoughts out and to put a plan of revenge into place. The only person who gets to fuck with Leah is me. Gary will get his. I strip off, leaving my clothes on the floor and hop into bed in just my briefs. I can still hear the others next door, that's the one shit part about this place, the walls are paper thin.

"You're not sleeping in here with her!" I roll my eyes, Corvin is being a bitch. Leah is eighteen and old enough to make her own choices. I snort to myself, he's pissed as hell that I was sleeping with her imagine what he would be like if he knew Beck and I both slept with her.

"Get the hell over it, Corvin, and go to fucking bed. Everyone needs to sleep. We'll deal with this shit tomorrow, starting with you and Darius sorting shit." Beckett, always the fixer.

"Fuck him! The bastard betrayed me, he was fucking my sister—"

"Jesus Christ!" Saint snaps. "Are you fucking dumb? They were never just fucking, Corvin. Leah is in love with Darius and whether you like it or not, Darius loves her to." I grind my teeth in frustration, I don't fucking love her.

Liar.

I hate that stupid little voice in my head when it calls me out on my own bullshit.

"Wait a second, how do you know he loves her?" Oh shit, Corvin just figured it out.

"We figured it out a while ago," Crue says hesitantly.

"Man, fuck all of you!" Corvin snaps, then I hear footsteps pounding past my room. A door slams a moment later, Corvin is big fucking mad!

"Well, that went well," Saint says, chuckling lightly. "We're going to get some shut eye, dude. Need anything before we go?"

"I'm good, I'll catch you in the morning." I'm on edge the second I hear Beckett's bedroom door close and Saint and Crue head to bed. I last two minutes before I'm leaping out of my bed and throwing my door open. I stop and glare at the smirking fucker leaning against the wall outside my room. "I wondered how long it would take you."

"Fuck you, you touch her–"

"And you'll do what, D? You made it clear tonight that she is dead to you and you want nothing to do with her." He's right, I do fucking hate her but that doesn't mean I'm ever going to be okay with seeing her with anyone else. "I'm fucking beat and need a solid eight hours of sleep and I can't get that with you glaring holes through my wall." I stare at him confused until the fucker barges past me into *my* room, closes the door and locks it. "Go to bed, Darius," he calls from the other side of the closed door.

"You locked me out of my room!" I seethe.

"I sleep naked, would you rather me sleep next to Leah with my cock out?" The laughter in his tone pisses me off. He thinks this is a joke but none of this is funny to me. I stalk back to Beck's room and close the door. I stand here and stare at her sleeping form in the soft glow of the bedside light. How can someone so evil look innocent? Too tired to deal with this shit I decide to just get this night over with. I slip in on the other side of her and make sure there is plenty of space between our bodies.

"What the fuck!" I bolt upright in bed still groggy from sleep. I look around confused for a second until it all comes rushing back to me—the game, the video, coming to the cabin and Beck locking me out of my room which means, I drop my gaze to my side to see Leah still sleeping then turn back to the doorway where Corvin stands seething. "Get the fuck away from her!" he snaps. I oblige without complaint, wanting to get as far away from her as I can. I throw the covers back ready to climb out of bed but her voice has me stilling.

"Both of you go the hell away!" It's not the anger in her voice that has me tensing, it's the fact she thinks she has the right to be pissed at *me* after what *she* did! I feel her shifting from me and peer over my shoulder to watch her climb out of bed. She stands there with her hair wild and untamed, her eyes are red and swollen from all the tears last night. I slowly climb to my feet and stare her down—I hate the sight of Beckett's shirt on her.

"You're going back to Mom and Dad's today." Leah's eyes widen for a second before she schools her features and nods.

"Fine. I'm also dropping out of school and moving." That has both me and Corvin stumped for a second but he manages to gather himself quicker than me.

"Fuck no! I just paid your tuition so your ass is staying in school!" I scrub a hand down my face as I shake my head. He just let the cat out of the bag and Leah is smart enough to have caught his little slip up. She places her hands on her hips and cocks her head to the side.

"*You* paid for my tuition?" Corv darts his gaze briefly to me before focusing back on the she devil.

"Yes! Now, shower and meet me downstairs." He chucks the bag I didn't notice he was carrying at her. She catches it, then shoots him a glare before rummaging through her bag to grab some clothes. The moment she grabs out a black bra and matching lace thong, I know I'm dead when a gasp sounds from the doorway. That was the thong he had twirling around his finger not long ago in my room asking if he knew the girl it belonged to.

"You son a bitch!" he roars before he flies across the room, a fist landing to the right underside of my jaw, a left hook connecting with my ribs before another right hook has me falling back onto the bed. Leah screams for help and for her brother to stop but I can see the look in his brown eyes. If I fight back, it will destroy any hope I have of ever repairing the damage I have done to our friendship. "Fight back, you fucking pussy!" He leaps on top of me and swings a good fucking right hook that has my head snapping to the side. I see the guys in the doorway, Beck fighting to hold Saint and Crue back from interfering and stopping Corvin. "You fucking bastard," Corvin screams as he lands a hit to my ribs. I groan in pain. "You took advantage of my sister." He rears his arm back, ready to hit me again.

"I was the one who came onto him!" His arm freezes midair as he looks at Leah. "We were at Tyresse's party and you said I wasn't allowed to drink, but I did anyway. Darius found me and took me home. I kissed him that night and told him…" I close my eyes and brace myself for the torment that her words are about to put me through. "I told him I loved him."

Corvin snorts. "It doesn't matter what you did, Leah, he took advantage—"

"Fucking hell, Corvin, while you were away with Mom and Dad at football camp, I walked into his room, stark naked." Corvin cringes in disgust. "He told me to get out. I refused and do you really want to know the rest?" Corvin rests back on my thighs as he looks between the two of us.

"How long?" he asks in an even tone with his gaze on me.

I don't pretend to not know what he is asking. I hold his gaze as I answer. "Pretty much the whole of senior year," I answer. his chin drops to his chest and I feel like a real dick for not coming clean.

"Who else knew?" he asks in a dejected tone.

"No one, Beck only figured it out when Leah moved in and Saint and Crue only know because they overheard us fighting. They never betrayed you, the three of them warned me to stay away and I... didn't." Corvin slowly lifts his gaze to me and I hate that I can see he doesn't trust me.

"She's the reason you pulled away from me and closed me out, isn't she?"

"Yes," I answer honestly. I ignore Leah's sharp intake of breath.

He nods like he can finally understand why I put so much distance between us. "When this is all over, you will stay away from my sister."

"Corvin–" He ignores Leah and continues on.

"You'll pack your shit and move to Chicago and run the daily operations of BCD'S from there, you won't call or ever come back." His words feel like he dropped a boulder directly on top of my chest, the air sucked from my lungs. I knew when the truth did come out that he would be pissed but I didn't expect him to banish me from his life entirely. My worst fear is coming to life, I'm going to be alone again but this time, I won't have either Williams' sibling by my side.

CHAPTER FIVE

I sit on the couch next to Cody, with Saint on my other side. No one has said two words since Corvin told Darius he had to leave. The guys tried to change his mind but Corvin wouldn't budge and what could they really say when Darius agreed to my brother's terms. On top of everything that I am already feeling, I can now add feeling like a homewrecker to the list. I never meant to come between my brother and Darius. I knew he would be angry but I never thought he would throw away years of friendship with D because of me!

"Take these, it will help with the pain." I flick my gaze up to see Crue standing there with a glass of water and two pills in his hand. I eye them skeptically for a moment. "It's just pain relief for your cheek." I take them and the water from his hands, mumbling my thanks before handing the empty glass back to him and flopping back against the couch. Cody rests her head on my shoulder, I lean my head against hers, sighing. Beck and Corvin disappeared to organize some press release thing that I have no idea what for. Darius has been locked in his room all morning while the rest of us hung out downstairs.

"Holy shit!" I snap my gaze across to the other side of the room where Katie sits on the window love seat with her phone in her hand. I frown, how the hell does she get service here? Katie flicks her gaze to Saint and Crue who are both already staring at her with curious looks on their faces. "Gary just released a statement saying that Darius paid him to sleep with Leah and he was the one who drugged her!" Crue and Saint are across the room, peering over Katie's shoulder reading whatever it is she is showing them.

"Fuck!" Saint curses. "Beckett, Corvin, Darius get the fuck in here now!" he shouts. It takes a second before I hear feet pounding the stairs and then another two sets coming from the theater room end of the cabin.

"What?" Corvin snaps. Saint turns to face the three newcomers with a grave look on his face. I peer over the back of the couch to see Corvin and Darius have kept a couple feet of space between them, not wanting to be near each other. It kills me that I can't go to him and wrap my arms around him, promising that he isn't alone. That I'm right here by his side, but there is so much water under the bridge that I can't get past my own hurt feelings.

"There's a warrant out for Darius's arrest for breaking Gary's arm. The Hayes are pressing charges against him and you're wanted for questioning as well." My stomach sinks.

"Fuck, we need to call Troy," Beck grits out.

"Wait, how the fuck do you know that?" Darius asks cautiously. Saint and Crue both step aside to reveal a smug looking Katie who slowly climbs to her feet, takes a deep breath and squares her shoulders as she stands between the guys.

"I found it," she says confidently and a little bit smug.

"How? There is no cell service out here and Corvin had a blocker put in place to stop anyone from tracking us while we are here." Katie doesn't cower under the accusation of Darius's words like I assumed she would. Cody and I both shift so we are looking at them all over the back of the couch.

"I feel like this is the best time to tell you all something you don't know about me." The five guys tense. "I am a dancer and

I love what I do, but my true passion is in computer science. I'm really good at it, which is why I was able to nullify the blocker you have. I was also able to reroute your Wi-Fi that you have disabled and have it re connected so I could get online." Saint and Crue stare at Katie with their mouths opened in shock. Beck, Corv and Darius look stunned. Katie drops her gaze and scuffs her foot along the wooden floorboards.

"You're the one who hacked into Beckett's computer, aren't you?" Katie looks up at Saint nibbling her bottom lip, she nods. I stare at her in shock. I look to Cody who seems just as shocked as the rest of us that our friend slash roommate was able to keep something like this a secret from us!

"Look," she says as she runs her gaze over each of us. "I know your lawyer is good and all but he sucks at computers and is slow as shit. I had the video scrubbed from the web two minutes after I got in Corvin's car. If anyone sends the link to try to keep it circulating their phone is going to download a virus and wipe their entire phone including the cloud."

"Why the secrecy?" Darius asks as he steps forward eyeing my friend warily.

Katie snorts. "Dude, guys don't like it when a chick is smarter than them or able to hold her own. Imagine me being able to tell them on a date that I know what their SAT scores were?" Darius doesn't look convinced. Corvin steps up beside him and I'll admit I'm more shocked that he didn't keep an ocean of space between them. They may be mad at each other but when shit hits the fan, they will always band together. I see that now.

"What did you find on Beck's laptop?" Corvin asks her, his tone is filled with warning. Katie gnaws on her bottom lip nervously. Crue turns to her, reaches out and uses his thumb to pry it free. Her eyes shoot wide as she stares up at him, her cheeks tinge red.

"You gonna answer my friend, doll?" he says in the sexiest

voice that has me waiting with bated breath to see what happens next between them.

"Uh… I… um." Katie shakes her head causing Crue to drop his hand back to his side. "I found contracts and files on there about the Hayes." All five guys turn ridged.

"What else?" Saint asks as he steps into her back, plastering himself flush against her, drawing a gasp from my poor friend who is now sandwiched between him and Crue.

"I know this merger with Sullivan global goes public in two days. I also know you have been trying to find dirt on Saint's dad's company." I see Saint stiffen behind Katie at the mention of his dad. "I didn't find anything at first but the moment Gary released the video and I tracked the IP that granted him web wide access it led me back to Saint's father's company and this video isn't the first he has released to gain him the upper hand."

"What does that mean?" Saint grits out. Katie turns so her back is now to Crue as she faces Saint. She reaches out and places her dainty little hand on his chest.

"Your father uses his company to help blackmail other companies into selling their stocks, assets and many other things because of the back door access he has to their servers. I'm sorry Saint, but your father isn't a good man and he has been trying to find dirt on you and your friends since the contract for Sullivan Global was drafted. I put a firewall in Beck's computer to stop it from being hacked again but he can access your phones and other devices you have that are connected to the internet." My jaw is practically on the floor, not just from the information Katie is sprouting but from the sexual tension that is pulsing between Saint, Crue and Katie.

"How much do you know about what we are doing and why we are doing it?" Darius asks. Katie flicks her gaze to him and then me for a split second before focusing back on Darius.

"From what I could gather off of Beck's laptop, you have had this ball rolling for about four years. I must say, what the five of you have accomplished in that short amount of time is freaking impressive, men twice your age couldn't do half of what you five have done." Corvin and the others puff their chests out with pride. I hate that I'm still confused as hell as to what is going on here. "Except, with the merger going public in two days, you are going to have to do damage control and if I may suggest, you and Darius call your lawyer and discuss the charges so it doesn't look like the youngest billionaires in the United States ran from the police." I choke on my own spit.

"Say what now?" I squeak out as I stare directly at my brother. Corvin doesn't even spare me a glance as he answers.

"Guess you were too busy sleeping with my best friend to notice I was the one paying all the bills at home." I recoil at his harsh tone. I drop my gaze in shame. "You're gonna help us," he demands. Katie shakes her head. "You don't have a choice, you either help us or I have *you* arrested for hacking." I balk at my brother, he is being a complete dick right now.

"Fine, but you all have to sit down and explain to Leah what you have done. She has a right to know that Gary only targeted her because of what you five planned to do to his–excuse me, and Darius's father." I flinch at the reminder of Darius and Gary being twins. My stomach churns just thinking about it. Corvin reluctantly agrees. The guys come round and claim seats on the couches, Beck taking the spot next to Corvin and shoots Darius a smirk. It's then that I realize the only available seat left in the room is beside me. Sighing, I say,

"Just sit down, Darius, don't be a douchebag." He spins around and pins me with a look loaded with disgust. I keep the hurt from my face.

"You're one to talk, Goldie. Sitting there acting all innocent and shit when it's your fault all of this has happened." I climb to my feet pissed off that he would dare stand there and blame me for any of this.

"My fault?" I shout. "How the fuck is it my fault *your* brother drugged and raped me, huh?" He closes the space between us until his chest brushes against me, forcing me to crane my head back to meet his stare.

"I told you to stay home!" he growls.

"I only went because I didn't want you to be on your own when you told Corvin," I snap right back.

"Tell me what?" Corvin asks in an icy tone. Darius slams his eyes closed, I step around him and face my brother.

"Darius planned to tell you about him and me that night. I didn't want him to have to face your wrath on his own, so I snuck out to meet you all at the party, then Gary…" I clamp my mouth shut and drop my gaze to the floor. I try as hard as I can to fight back the tears. It seems that's all I do these days is fucking cry. I'm so over crying! Darius grunts as he is shoved aside by Beck, arms wrap around me pulling me against him. I return his embrace without thought.

"I promise you, sweetheart, Gary Hayes will not get away with this. I swear." Call me crazy but I believe Beck.

CHAPTER SIX

Darius

I have to bite the inside of my cheek to stop myself from snapping at Beck to get the fuck away from her. How can he forgive her so easily after what she did—tried to do to them but only succeeded in getting me and Saint benched. She could have done anything else and I would have forgiven her but not when it concerns drugs. I refuse to end up like my crack whore of a mother.

"Can you tell us what Gary did or said to get you to…" Beck lets his sentence trail off so she has a chance to back out if she doesn't want to answer. She nods. They break apart and sit down leaving the only seat vacant next to Corvin. I grit my teeth and drop down beside him, ignoring how he flinches when my leg brushes his. Beck wraps an arm around her shoulders and pulls her into his side. Cody reaches over and places her hand on the top of Leah's thigh offering her resilient support.

"I was waiting for Darius and you guys to arrive when Gary came to me and offered me a drink." Her tone is flat and void of emotion as she speaks. "I refused the first time, I didn't want Corvin to catch me drinking and piss him off before we could tell him about… us." Corvin is grinding his teeth so hard I can hear it. "But as time dragged on and none of you guys showed up, my nerves got the better of me. When he offered me a drink again, I took it and downed the whole thing." She chokes up and tries to take some deep breaths to calm herself enough to continue, I'm two seconds away from fleeing the room not wanting to hear any of this. "I just remember feeling dizzy and then..." She slowly lifts her gaze to mine and the duplicity in her gaze has me stiffening. I feel Corv burning holes into the side of my head but I'm trapped in the orbit of her green eyes as they hold me captive. "Calling out for *you*." Tears flow faster down her cheeks, my breathing becomes unsteady. "I kept crying out for you, I couldn't move, I didn't even know what was happening."

"I thought you couldn't remember?" Beck asks tentatively. She nods and smiles sadly but never takes her eyes off me.

"I couldn't. It wasn't until Gary showed me the video that memories of that night came flooding back. I don't remember all of it but I do remember him carrying me upstairs and telling him I was waiting for Darius. He laughed." I clench my hands into fists, her eyes beg me to not look away or she'll lose the nerve to continue, so I don't. I hold her gaze the whole time offering her my strength. "He said *'by the time I'm through with you he won't want you again. Breaking you will break him.'* I didn't know what that meant but I knew it wasn't good. I screamed for you!" she growls, the venom in which she says it tells me she blames me for not being there sooner and right now, I blame myself as well. "I woke up feeling sick and confused. I didn't understand what happened or why I was naked but there was..." This time she drops her gaze, I brace myself for her next words to send me free falling over the edge. "So much blood, I never bled when... Darius and I had sex." Corvin groans and scraps a hand down his face.

"What happened next?" Beck gently asks.

"I got changed, walked home expecting to find Darius in his room and ask him why he left me at the party. At that time I thought I had spent the night with him but then I couldn't find him anywhere he just… vanished. Blocked my number and I didn't see him until the following year at Thanksgiving." My eyes narrow at the memory.

"Why the fuck did you bring Gary to thanksgiving then?" Corv grits out.

"I saw him in town when Mom and I went to get the plum sauce. He stopped me out the front of the store and made small talk, then said he was alone as his dad was away. *I* didn't invite him, Mom did! You know what she's like. She never wants anyone to be alone during the holidays, neither of you two gave me a chance to explain. As soon as dinner was done you both took off and I haven't seen you until I transferred."

"You transferred because of him." It's not a question but she nods anyway so I push on. "Did he tell you to drug us before or after you transferred?" She blows out a breath before speaking.

"After. I was still at DCU when he showed me the video. I heard him bragging to a couple of his friends as I was walking past. I stopped when I heard him mention my name. He proceeded to tell his buddies that he ruined Darius and made sure he would never look at me again. I hit him up and he showed me the video. I went into a dark hole. I dropped out of dance and school unable to stomach the thought of ever seeing him again knowing that he had… been inside me." She chokes out a sob, I'm fucking powerless to stop myself. I'm out of my seat in the next second crossing the room, smack Beck's hand away from her and lift her into my arms. She wraps her legs around my waist, wraps her arms around my neck and buries her face in the crook of my neck as she cries. "I'm so sorry," she sobs.

I push all my anger away as I stand here holding her, not giving a fuck that her brother is behind me. Right now she needs me. "None of this is your fault," I say quietly. Beck stands and offers me his seat, I take it with her still in my hold. I meet Corvin's stare over her shoulder. I don't see any of the anger from earlier—his eyes brim with tears as he watches his sister break down and tell her story. Last night none of what she said registered because we were both too angry and caught up in our own shit to process the fact that Leah was hurt by Gary because of *us*.

"I-I never meant to hurt you." She hiccups. I rub my hand up and down her back trying to soothe her.

"Don't worry about it, Goldie," I say. She pulls back and stares down at me with doubt in her eyes.

"I don't know how he found out I was transferring to CHU but he did and started calling me, texting me and telling me if I didn't take you five out of the game, he was going to post the video. I... I couldn't let that video get out. I didn't want you to ever see it." Her face contorts in pain as she cups my face with her hands. "I never wanted you to look at me like I was ruined. I was so scared to come to you or Corvin."

"Why?" Corvin demands. She doesn't take her eyes off me as she answers.

"I was scared neither of you would believe me. Gary told me no one would ever believe me if I went to the police. He said his father would make sure that everyone knew I was the one who wanted it. I never wanted it, Darius, you have to believe me." She cries harder, I shift forward and grip her face between my hands and swipe her tears away with my thumbs.

"I would never have doubted you for a single second, Goldie." My words seem to ease some of the tension in her body.

"I'm going to fucking kill that motherfucker!" Corvin announces. I grunt my agreement and so do the others. Her green eyes shine with an emotion a lot like hope, but if I'm being honest with myself, I don't know if I'm ready to pick up what she's putting down in regard to where we stand.

"We can have him done with the distribution of child pornography and link it back to Saint's father." I peer around Leah to stare at Katie. This girl is a fucking mystery, and by the looks of things, she has gained the attention of both Saint and Crue without even trying.

"How?" Beck asks.

"If I'm calculating things right, Leah was underage and Gary wasn't so we can counter the arrest and charges. As far as Corvin and Darius go with the beating doled out to Gary, Corvin was enraged his sister was hurt and Darius was protecting his girl-friend." I tense at the word *girlfriend*, Leah doesn't miss it.

"How do we do this?" Crue asks, again Katie cuts in.

"Simple, you lay low until the press release tomorrow and explain that no one ran. You both decided to take Leah out of town so she could rest and get help to overcome the tragedy that she went through. You then apologize for your actions and accept any charges thrown at you." The guys begin to protest but she raises her hand halting them. "Hear me out. If you both accept responsibility for your part and explain why you did it, no one is going to side with Gary. The press is going to eat him alive when you announce that your girlfriend slash sister was targeted by the Hayes family because of you being successful without using your rightful name, and them wanting to destroy you by using Leah to do that." I mull over her words for a moment. What she says does ring true but it's a fucking risk.

"If they do this, that means we all have to go public and announce that we are the owners of BCD'S which means everyone at CHU will also know we own the school." Leah and Cody gasp, Crue frowns at them but continues. "You know there is a chance that the school board will vote us out of school, right?"

"Our football career will be over," Saint whispers.

"No, it won't," I say as I lift Leah off my lap and place her on the seat beside me. "Victor is bluffing. At the press release I'm going to announce he is my father and my twin brother found out, in his rage he targeted my ex-girlfriend." I feel Leah bristle next to me. "I'll tell them that I snapped and had a mental break-down, given the circumstances and my positions at CHU, I'll announce I'm dropping out and… moving to Alaska to run our resort." Everyone begins to shout and throw in their piece of how we should do things and I appreciate their efforts but they know this is the only way we can get out on top. If I stay, Victor will find a way to come after us and I can't allow them to take the heat for me.

"What if I come forward and charge Gary?" Leah says quietly. She may have muttered the words but we all heard them loud and clear.

"You don't have to do that," Corvin says.

"If I do it, will it help?" she asks her brother. He cuts a glance at me. I nod, letting him know if Leah does this then it would take some of the heat off us and allow us to continue on the path we have paved.

"Yes, it would," he says in an even tone.

"Okay, I'll do it," she says with conviction that has me feeling proud of her.

CHAPTER SEVEN

Leah

We spent a couple of hours sitting there listening to how my brother and the others began their company and amassed their fortune through the stock market. I'm in awe of how they managed to accomplish all of this while in school and playing football. Proud of the sheer determination they all had to make sure they never struggled to want for anything. I learned Saint hates his family and wants nothing to do with them. Crue only has his aunt who brought him up after his parents abandoned him when he was one. Darius, well everyone knows he has no one except us so it made sense for him to push for this to excel. Corvin, I get it. He has always wanted to make sure our parents were able to retire and never worry about money again—his reasons are noble. Beckett is a closed book, the guys don't even know his whole story and it baffles me why he won't confide in anyone about his past. After that, the guys disappeared to get everything in place for tomorrow. Cody and Katie wanted to practice our routine but I wasn't feeling it. So, I decided to hide out on the balcony of the second floor and stare out at the mountains.

"Can I join you?" I look to the side to see my brother standing there with his hands stuffed in his pant pockets, a remorseful look on his face. It's getting dark now, which means I must have been out here for hours and not known.

"Depends," I say.

"On?"

"Are you going to yell at me again?" His shoulders hunch forward as he shakes his head. "Then sure, you can." He makes his way over to me and drops down into the seat beside me as we stare at the amazing view. We remain silent for a long time lost in our own thoughts until Corvin finally breaks it.

"Why my best friend, Leah?"

"Why not him?" I retort.

"Because he's my best friend and you being with him complicates that." He runs a hand through his hair and slumps back in his chair. "I trusted him with you. He betrayed that trust Leah. I'll never allow you and him to be anything, I can't." I swivel in my seat to face him.

"That isn't your call to make. Darius is a good guy—"

"He was the fucking one who found you in bed with Gary and left you there! Why the fuck are you sitting here defending him?" He's angry and I get it, but I won't allow him to blame Darius for what happened to me.

"What happened with Gary wasn't his fault. He told me not to go to that party, I didn't listen so that is on me, Corv, not Darius."

"Leah, you're eighteen. You have so much time to do whatever you want before you settle down with a good guy who treats you right." I bristle at his dig.

"Darius is a good guy!" I defend. He lulls his head to the side and pins me with a pitying look.

"You need to let him go, Leah."

My stomach sinks. "Why should I?"

"Because he will never forgive you for drugging him." My breath hitches. "Darius swore he would *never* touch a single drug and risk becoming like his mother. He never hooked up with any girl who dabbled in any type of that shit. He barely drinks because he's worried he'll become an addict. You doing what you did to not only him but Saint as well, is unforgivable to him, Leah."

"I'm sorry. I'll tell your coach it was me and not them–"

"You don't get it!" he says with his voice raised. "It's out of coach's hands now, it's with the board. On matters that concern each of us we aren't allowed to vote. They are going to be kicked off the team. Darius will be pissed but he'll get over it. But, Saint, he won't. Unlike Darius and Beck, me, Saint and Crue planned to go pro and if Saint is out, then Crue won't go without him. Your actions have cost us all, Leah. You could have come to me and I would have helped you deal with this but you didn't trust me enough!" I bite the inside of my cheek to focus on something else aside from the pain I feel inside my chest. "You slept with him and fucked with his emotions. What the hell did you think would happen when all of this came out?"

I open my mouth, then snap it closed. I truthfully don't know what I thought was going to happen. "I thought I would figure a way out of it, then Gary showed up at the diner that night and I knew I didn't have a choice," I whisper in a defeated tone.

"Darius broke his arm. He will never play again and despite what they all think, I know Victor Hayes, he is not just going to let Darius off the hook for that one." I flinch.

"What does that mean?" I press.

"It means, tomorrow isn't going to go our way no matter what we do. The press has their story and they don't care about the truth. They just want drama and the headlines don't paint you in a good light, sister." I balk at him.

"What do you mean?" I ask hesitantly.

"They are saying you have been sleeping with the twins the whole time and that what happened yesterday was your fault." I splutter, that is not true. I never even knew about them being related!

"Corvin, I—" He holds his hand up silencing me.

"It doesn't matter what you, me or anyone else thinks or

knows. Ninety percent of the world believes what they read. We'll try to do as much damage control as we can but I can't promise this won't blow back on you."

"I get it," I say in a dejected tone. "I'm going to be the whore who bagged DCU's best QB and the girl who fucked her brother's best friend." Corvin flinches but doesn't say anything, which makes me believe that is exactly what people are going to be saying about me.

🏈

We all sit around the twelve seater dining table not saying a word. I push the food around my plate. I'm not even hungry, the thought of food makes me nauseous. Plus, chewing hurts thanks to fucking Gary's fist. Beck filed a police report pressing charges against Gary for hitting me and started the process with their lawyer to have him charged with rape. Beck said I would have to give a statement and tell the police what I told them today. I wish I could just put this whole ordeal behind me, but that can't happen until after tomorrow. The guys are leaving early tomorrow morning to head into the city, the girls and I are staying back at the cabin.

"I'm out, thanks for dinner Beck," Darius says as he pushes back from the table, loads his plate in the dishwasher and heads upstairs, not sparing me a glance once. Corvin is right, Darius is never going to forgive me for what I did to him and honestly, I can't blame for that. I just wish his dismissal of me didn't hurt as much as it does.

"Ya'll need to talk or something because the tension is killing me!" I ignore Saint, I don't need any of them weighing in on my situation with Darius.

"Shut the fuck up, there is nothing to sort," Corvin snaps, the tension in the room only amplifies, thanks to his outburst.

🏈

Laying here on the couch, I can't stop from tossing and turning. Cody and Katie offered to share a bed so I could have the other but I refused. They have been put through enough thanks to me, so I refused to allow them to be any more uncomfortable then they are already by being locked away in this cabin for a week. Corvin glared as I carried my pillow and blanket downstairs, but I just ignored him. I know it is going to take a long time for him to trust me again.

"He'll forgive you." The sound of Darius's voice has me bolting upright and turning toward the kitchen where he leans against the wall sipping a glass of water. My eyes drink him in. Thanks to the soft glow of the moon I can make out that he is only in a pair of sweats. I fight the groan that wants to break free.

"How did you know that?" I ask to distract myself from ogling his body.

"You talk out loud."

"Hm," is my only response. I don't know what else to say, saying sorry won't fix what I did to him.

"I'm gonna break this down for you, Goldie." I sit up straighter in my seat and watch as he saunters into the sunken living room with a swagger only he can pull off. Rather than sitting on one of the seats he drops down onto the coffee table directly in front of me. I dart my tongue out to wet my lips, his eyes track my every movement causing me to flush red. "I may not be able to see it but I know you're blushing." I snort and quickly clamp my mouth closed. He releases a tired sigh and I slump into the couch.

"Just say whatever it is," I hedge.

"Fine. You and I are done, for good." Getting a white hot branding iron to my heart would have hurt less then hearing those words come from him. "You crossed a line, Leah, and there is no way for you to come back from that. Even when I thought you cheated on me, I still gave you a second chance!" The hurt that laces each of his words feels like a knife to my heart. "What you did… I can't get over that and I'll never forgive you for it.

So, from here on out, you stay away from me and I stay away from you. Don't text or call, better yet, just delete my number." I nod stiffly. "Look, I'm fucking sorry for what happened with Gary and I swear I'll do everything in my power to make him pay. If you had told me, things would have been different but instead you lied and used us."

"I did try to come to you. I called, text and searched for you but *you* left! Who the hell was I supposed to turn to?"

"Your brother," he snaps.

"How the hell was I supposed to explain what happened to Corvin when he had no idea about you and me? Would you have rather I outed you and told my brother that we were together?"

He shakes his head, climbs to his feet and stares down at me with a vacant look in his eyes. "You did the damage, now you live with the fall out of the choices you made." He storms out without another word leaving me alone to deal with this on my own. I know he's right and I did fuck up, but can he not for one second see it from my side? I can't let this go. I race after him, catching him just as he's about to close his door and shove it open. He stumbles back in shock before pinning me with a glare. "Get out!" he snarls.

I ignore him as I push his door closed and move toward him. "You stand here judging me because I made a mistake, a mistake I will forever regret, halfback. I won't keep saying sorry. You want to hate me go for it, but just know the feeling is mutual because *you* left me without a word. You could have come to me and you didn't, you ran like a pussy!" That pushes him over the edge, he gets right in my face breathing heavy.

"Get the fuck out, Leah. I told you we're done. You want to go spread your legs for the fucking team and let them run a train? Do it because I don't fucking care anymore!" he screams. I stare at him in a new light. He's hurt and I get that, but it doesn't mean I have to take his shit.

"Fine. Remember you said that shit, because I'm tired of

waiting for you to man the hell up and admit to my brother you're in love with me." He scoffs then laughs darkly.

"Aww, Goldie, your sweet and innocent act may fool everyone else but not me. You are a lying little cunt who likes to play games. Well, guess what, baby," he reaches out and tucks a stray strand of hair gently behind my ear, which shocks the hell out of me, "I'm going to ruin you for taking the only family I have ever known from me. I'm going to fuck your world right up and relish in seeing you burn in front of my eyes." My mouth drops open in horror. How the hell can he be so cruel, when hours ago he held me while I broke down in front of everyone. The door opens. Darius flicks his gaze toward it and rolls his eyes. "Get the fuck out. Your bodyguard is here to save you from me."

"You're being a fucking dick!" Beck snaps. Darius turns his dark eyes back to me. I don't find any trace of the kind attentive lover anywhere in the depths.

"And still she wants me. Fancy that, Becky boy. The girl you're pining over still wants my cock in her even when I'm a cunt but not yours. That must be a huge blow for the ego." I gasp as his hurtful words, shaking my head in disgust.

"Fuck you, Darius, you are a real piece of shit–"

"Don't fucking call me what you call my brother!" he seethes.

"Then maybe you shouldn't act exactly like him!" I shout before spinning around and storming toward Beck. He steps aside to let me out. I don't fuck around, I head downstairs even though I know I won't be able to sleep a wink after that confrontation.

CHAPTER EIGHT

Darius

The second we walk into the hotel lobby where the press release is being held, cameras are shoved in our faces. Troy calls out to us and tries to fight his way through the paps. We manage to push our way through the cameras and follow after Troy as he leads us into a room off to the side. Beck has to force the door closed and lock it so no one can barge in.

"Fucking hell, that was intense," Crue says as he drops down into one of the vacant chairs around the oval-shaped table.

"We only have twenty minutes before we have to head in, take a seat," Troy says, the rest of us grab a seat and wait for him to stop shuffling through the files he has and tell us what the fuck to do. "Okay," he says as he grabs a stack of papers out. "I received a call last night from Victor's lawyers."

"About?" Saint butts in.

"They wanted to renegotiate the terms of the contract given the events that unfolded on Friday. I said no and that the press release would still go ahead today."

"They're coming, aren't they?"

"Yes, Corvin, they are already waiting for the conference to begin." When we all start shouting Troy raises his hand to silence us. "We can come out on top of this."

"How?" I snap. "I broke his fucking arm and beat the shit out of him. Our stocks are going to drop the moment we go public as the owners of BCD'S."

"They are going to bury us in legal shit and halt all the plans for us to expand the hotel chain," Crue interjects.

"We're fucked," Beck breaths out as he leans back in his chair.

"Boys!" Troy snaps, gaining all our attention. He smiles cunningly as he slaps his hands atop the table and looks to each of us. "I must admit, I thought you were all finished but then this morning I got another call."

"From who?" Corvin asks.

"A witness," he answers.

I frown. "A witness to what exactly?" I ask.

"Gary Hayes telling Victor Hayes that he *did* in fact drug and rape Leah. It was all caught on camera and the witness is here to speak today." I dart my gaze to the guys to see they are just as shocked as I am.

"How does this help us?" Saint asks.

"It would mean that the charges Gary has pressed against Corvin and Darius won't hold much weight now that there is proof their attack was warranted in the defense of Leah Williams. All we need to do is have both Corvin and Darius make a formal apology before anything is mentioned about the merger. When the merger is announced, Darius will then close out the conference by saying he is heading straight to the local precinct and will be out on bail within a couple hours." A whoosh of air escapes me.

"I'll still have to go to court though?" I ask.

"Not if I have anything to do with it. Now, let's get this over with and get the hell out of here because I have a mountain of paperwork to finish and new employee contracts to draft for you boys."

"And this is why we keep you on retainer, Troy," Crue jokes, earning a scowl from the old man.

I stand from my seat and look out at the crowd of reporters, spotting Gary and Victor in the back with smirks on their faces. It brings me great fucking joy to see Gary sporting a cast on his throwing arm. I fucking hate that I have to say sorry to the son of a bitch and act like I mean it. Troy said I have to sell it or I risk fucking up this whole thing up.

"Ladies and gentlemen, firstly we would like to thank you all for being here today. Before we dive into the announcement I would like to address a matter that occurred Friday night at Crestview Heights University involving myself, Corvin and another player from DCU–"

"Is this about the fight?" someone yells. I nod.

"What was the cause of the fight?" a woman shouts.

I recite the speech Troy had told me to. "An explicit video was shared by Gary Hayes involving Corvin's underage sister. Gary drugged and raped her."

"Allegedly!" is shouted from the back. I focus on Gary allowing a small smirk to be seen on my face as I speak.

"No. This is the truth and we have proof." Gary turns to his father who is glaring directly at me.

"Mr. Lockhart, is the rumor true that Gary Hayes is in fact your brother?" I plaster a fake smile on my face and answer the guys question. We have always been in the spotlight because of how well we play football, but recently, since rumors spread that we may be the owners of one of the wealthiest stock companies in the US, the press have been sniffing around a lot more lately.

"It is." Murmurs break out around the room. "Gary is my twin brother and Victor is my father. We were reunited when Victor graciously sold his company to us."

"What company?"

"Who bought it?"

Questions are shouted but I ignore them as I press on. "I apologize for my outlandish actions on Friday night. I know because of the severity of it that I will be barred from taking the field again. But I don't want my actions to overshadow the real reason we are standing here in our newly acquired hotel." If looks could kill, I would be dead and six feet under from the way Victor is looking at me. More gasps ring out and questions are shouted at me. Corvin stands beside me turning the attention to him. He raises his hand and a hush falls over the room, waiting to hear what he has to say next.

"I would also like to extend my sincerest apology to you all for my actions. I have no excuse, except that seeing my sister being hurt and abused by that man sent me spiraling into a fit of rage, which I am not proud of." He points directly at Gary who looks utterly thrown by the turn of events. "My sister was nothing but a means for him to use to get at me and… Darius."

"Why would that affect Mr. Lockhart, your sister being hurt?" A guy calls from the front. I stand beside Corvin wanting to answer for him. Troy warned us someone would ask this question and it had to come from Corvin, not me to show we have no bad blood. But that's a lie, Corvin won't even look at me.

"Because at the time of the… incident, my sister and Darius were dating." Before any more questions can be asked, Corvin raises his voice to be heard over them. "We will be pressing charges against Mr. Hayes and my sister will also be pressing charges for assault as he punched her in the face." Angry shouts erupt as cameras are turned away from us for a moment to snap pictures of Gary and Victor as security leads them from the room as questions are being shouted at them about the *incident*.

"If I could redirect all your attention back to the front, please," Troy calls. "Thank you, now for the actual reason we are all here. I would like to introduce you all the new owners of Sullivan Global, soon to be known as Saint Hart Holdings. As you may all have deduced by now, these five young men are the founders and CFO's of BCD'S, the most profitable stock trading company in the US. These five young men have applied themselves to this business and sunk every cent they had into making sure it excelled and it did. BCD'S will remain as a stock trading company but with the merger of Saint Hart Holdings, the resorts will run as they always have, as will the hotels, but they will also now offer master classes in stock trading. What these five young men have achieved at the tender age of twenty is incredible. Now, are there any questions?"

We have question after question hurled at us for at least an hour before Troy finally calls it. I'm beyond grateful to get the fuck out of here and take off this monkey suit he made us all wear. I don't do a suit and tie, never have and never will. We're ushered straight outside into a waiting limousine that will take us to the police station downtown.

"You boys did great. You all handled yourself well and dealt with Victor and Gary with poise. Now, I must say, I don't think we have seen the last of them." I grunt out my agreement, too nervous to speak. There is so much that could go wrong with me handing myself in like this. There is no guarantee that I will be granted bail and I refuse to spend the next few years in a cell.

⬤

By the time we finish at the station, it's dark out. I'm fucking hungry and pissed off that I've been sitting in a cell for hours. The only reason I was let go Troy said is because Gary dropped the charges against me. Why though? We stand around the empty car park at the back of the station waiting for Troy to get off the phone to whoever the hell it is.

He ends the call then looks to Corvin before looking at me. "Gary dropped the charges because apparently he received a call from a young woman who threatened—excuse me—warned him that she would come forward and press charges for blackmail, rape, assault and a few other things. Gary had no choice but to withdraw the charges or spend the better part of his life behind bars." Surprise courses through me. I look over at Corvin to see he has the same look on his face.

"How did she call when there is no signal at the cabin?" Saint states.

"Clever girls," Beck whispers.

"What does that mean?" Crus asks.

"We took Corvin's car and they clearly took mine into town." That was… actually really smart, but something tells me Beckett left his keys in a place they could find them because he knew Leah wouldn't be able to sit back and do nothing.

"Look, boys, we still need to do a few more press releases now that you five have come out as the owners. You have a Forbes 500 company now. You boys own hotels, resorts and shares in two colleges, you have amassed an empire and I'm proud of you all. But, your work is just beginning, so be ready for the press to be following your every move. Don't do anything dumb." We all agree to Troy's terms and promise to be on our best behavior. The limo takes us back to the hotel so we can get Corvin's car and start the eight hour drive back to the cabin. We're all quiet and lost in our own thoughts as Corv drives us back. It's hard to believe that four years ago this was a pipe dream. We all busted our asses and put every penny we had into investing. The truth is, we were lucky that one of the investments we made took off and allowed us to bring in more income so we could grow quicker than we ever thought.

"My dad is gonna know about this," Saint whispers quietly from the back.

"He can't do shit. Troy has already started the process of taking him down. Once that has begun we'll partition his board and go in for a hostel takeover and push his ass out. The board will be put to a vote and trust me, Saint, they are gonna want you to run that shit." Corvin is right, the plan was to always take Victor out and then go after Saint's dad.

"I know. It's just fucking hard, ya know. I mean, we know he has been dealing in shady shit involving distributing videos of kids but to actually see his work in action with that video of Leah…" He lets his sentence trail off. We all feel the same. This is a lot for anyone to take in.

"You guys know what this means, right?" Crue asks from his seat in the middle of Beck and Saint.

"What does it mean?" Corvin asks tiredly.

"We don't have to hide any more and watch what we spend so no one suspects us. With Victor out of the picture and shit being public, Devon is gonna know he's next." I see Saint deflate out of the corner of my eye at the mention of his father and I feel for him. He didn't always hate his father, but when we brought him the evidence of what his father was really doing, he couldn't deny it. He jumped on board with our plan straight away and hasn't looked back since. His loyalty is awe inspiring but we also know this is fucking hard for him.

CHAPTER NINE

I spot Corvin's headlights through the windows, my nerves go haywire inside me knowing that I probably overstepped and pissed him off more. I thought going to the police would be the right thing, at the time it seemed like a really good idea to do it but now as I sit here in the living room, with my friends on either side of me, I begin to doubt my decision. When the headlights cut off, I take a deep breath and begin to pick at my hangnail. I wish I had trained for another hour with the girls, maybe then I would have been too tired to care. When the sound of car doors close, I begin to pick at my nail harder.

Cody places a hand on top of mine, shooting me an encouraging smile. "We're right here with you, every step of the way."

I melt a little inside. "I don't know what I did to deserve you both but I am so grateful to have met you," I say to them both. We share a quick awkward three-way hug just as the front door opens, then we slowly pull apart. I sit here biting my bottom lip as I slowly lift my gaze to see the guys walking in. I release the breath I didn't know I was holding at the sight of Darius.

He's safe.

He glances at me for a brief second before he turns and heads up the stairs, Cody grips my hand and squeezes while Katie leans her head on my shoulder. Saint and Crue wave out as they head for the basement to have an early night. Beck and Corv drop into the couch opposite us, both looking wrecked. Corvin rests his head back on the couch as he gazes up at the vaulted ceiling.

"I see my car is still in one piece." I cringe and shoot Beck a toothy smile that has him smiling back.

"I swear I didn't scratch it and I even put gas in it." He narrows his eyes at me.

"Leah, I don't give a shit about you using my car. I knew your ass wouldn't be able to stay here and do nothing, so I left the keys out on the counter." That shocks me. I cock my head to the side and study Beck. He may be quiet but he pays attention and listens to everything. It's weird to find a guy who actually does that.

"You saved his ass, you know." I pull my gaze back to Corvin who still won't look at me.

"What do you mean?" I ask hesitantly.

"You going to the cops saved his ass. He would probably still be sitting in a cell right now if it wasn't for you." I flinch at the casual way he says that, like it isn't a big deal that his best friend could have gone to jail because of me! I climb to my feet, glaring at my brother. The girls follow my lead. He lazily lifts his head and looks at me with a bored expression on his face.

"You can be angry all you want but guess what, Corvin, none of this has anything to do with you." He opens his mouth but I push on needing to get this out while I have the nerve. "You're just angry because Darius and I went behind your back. Look how you're acting now. This is the reason we never wanted to tell you because we knew you would act like a damn baby! Grow the hell up and get over it. I'm eighteen and will do whatever the hell I like. Starting tomorrow, the girls and I are going back to school and if you don't like that then you can suck a dick!" I storm out of the room with my head held high, but on the inside I'm screaming because I can't believe I just said that to my brother! I race up the stairs and slam to a halt when I spot Darius leaning over the banister as I reach the landing. He turns his head toward me with a ghost of a smile on his lips. The girls slip past me and head for our room, closing the door quietly.

His eyes spark with mischief as he looks at me. "Corvin can suck a dick, huh?" I snort out a laugh and quickly cover my mouth with my hand and nod. He nods a couple times before he pushes off the banister and moves toward me. My breath hitches when he stops a step away from me. His brown eyes bore into mine, his hair flops forward onto his forehead and I want to reach up and push it back, but I don't. "Thank you for what you did today, you didn't have to."

"Yes, I did," I say quietly, afraid that any loud sound will scare him away.

He shakes his head as a sad smile graces his handsome face. "Nah, you didn't. Enjoy school, Leah, and I hope you and Corvin sort everything out." He tries to walk away but I reach out and grab his arm pulling him to a stop. I stare up at him in fright, panic begins to claw its way up my throat.

"Why did that feel like a goodbye?" I ask, scared that he may actually leave.

"Because it was. I finished what I set out to do." I shake my head rapidly.

"You can't go, you… you can't leave. You have to stay!" My voice rises as hysteria begins to take hold of me.

"Corvin needs space—"

Before he can finish he's cut off. "You run away like a pussy, then don't fucking come back. Be a man and face this shit." I spin around to face my brother and stumble. Darius grips my waist to steady me. Corvin's gaze is laser focused on where his best friend's hands are now gripping me. Darius drops his hold on me and steps back. "That shit," Corvin says as he points between us. "Doesn't happen. Leah, you're moving back to the dorms when we get back. You stay the hell away from Darius. If you don't, his face is going to pay the price." My mouth drops open in shock, I expect Darius to rebuke his claims but he just stands there silently. "Go to bed, Leah. We're all leaving early tomorrow morning to head back." His tone is final. I shoot him a glare before I shoulder past Darius, angry that he didn't say anything and just stood there like a mute. I slam the door closed to my room only to find my friends sitting up in their beds with shit eating grins on their faces.

"We have a plan," Cody says excitedly.

"Operation make him regret letting you go is in operation," Katie says before her and Cody break out into giggles. Whatever their plan is, I'm in!

We've been back at school for two weeks now since leaving the cabin. I barely see any of the guys except for Beck. I know Saint is still mad at me and I honestly don't blame him but when are they going to let this go? I mean for God's sake, they are back on the team. Once they explained everything to their coach and what happened, they were reinstated but I didn't get off as lucky. I was lucky not to be kicked out and I think I have my brother to thank for that, but I was kicked off the dance team and that fucking sucks! Mrs. Telford said I can try out for the team again next year as long as there are no more incidents. She accused me of drugging Kyle and the others, but I truthfully had nothing to do with that. I'm still being monitored by all the staff and all the students here hate me because of what I did to their star players. Most of the students still make lewd remarks about the video—those comments are harder to ignore than I would like to admit.

"Heads up." Katie says from her seat next to me on the picnic table. I look up to see Garrett and a couple of other guys making their way over to us. Aside from Cody and Katie, Garrett is like the only other person who will speak to me in public. I knew people would be pissed but I didn't expect to be the social outcast. I feel like Moses, everyone parts when I walk through the halls.

"Hey, beautiful," Garrett says to me when he reaches us. Cody gags earning a glare from Garrett, Katie blatantly ignores him—neither of the girls trust Garrett. They think he is using my social outcast status to his gain, thinking that I will change my mind and give him a shot. I'm still not even close to thinking about another guy or dating. I've been texting Darius every day since we got back. For the first few days he would leave me on read but now he just won't even open my messages.

"Hey," I reply.

"So what are your plans tonight?" he asks, and I shrug.

"Nothing, movie night I guess."

He tsks me. "Nope. You ladies are coming out with us tonight." I frown and shake my head.

"I don't think that's a good idea—"

"Nonsense!" he says while smiling down at me.

I sigh. "Garrett, I appreciate the offer but no one here wants me at any parties and I don't feel like getting yelled at or mocked by more girls." The guys around here just act like I don't exist, but the girls go out of their way to make sure I know that I am hated and the worst of them all is Chelsea. She likes to throw it in my face that Darius is so over me and blowing up her DM's.

"Well, lucky for you this isn't a party. A friend of mine from back home is the DJ at the local club and I happen to know the bouncer so I can get you ladies in." I look to Cody and Katie who both shoot me looks saying *hell no*. "Come on, I know you must want to dance and let loose. We have a bye game this week, so no one from school will be there, they will be at Shayla's party." I won't lie, the thought of dancing and being able to hang out without having to worry about being glared at does sound appealing.

Fuck it.

"YOLO," I say smiling up at him.

He grins down at me. "Sweet, I'll pick you ladies up at ten

out front of your dorm." I nod and wave as he and his friends head to practice.

"You're playing with fire, Leah." I turn to Katie who is shaking her head.

"How? I can't stay locked in that dorm room for another night. I can't even go anywhere without being harassed. I need this, please say you'll both come," I beg. I can't even practice in the gym or on the quad without being abused and our dorm room is too small for me to dance in. Cody and Katie trade a loaded look before Katie throws her head back and groans. I squeal and clap like an idiot. For the first time in weeks I actually feel excited.

CHAPTER TEN

"Yo!" Saint shouts loud enough to be heard over the pounding bass of the music that plays at Shayla's. He shoves his phone in my face and I frown at the picture of Leah, Cody and Katie all dolled up and wearing scraps of clothing that don't leave much to the imagination, the caption reads.

L_Wills_<3 - YOLO, girls night out on the town, let's dance bish's.

I flick my gaze back to Saint as I hand his phone back to him. He shakes his head, clearly annoyed I'm not picking up what he's putting down.

"Read the fucking comments!" I grab the phone from him again and scroll through the comments. It pisses me off when I see guys commenting on how hot she looks but the one comment that stands out to me has me clenching Saint's phone so tight, I may actually break it.

G-Bizz_69 - See you in 10, gawjus, can't w8 to see you move.

I snap my gaze back to Saint. "Where the fuck are they going?" I snap.

"I asked Dylan, he said Garrett mentioned going to Smart Bar because his buddy is the DJ."

Fuck! I scour the crowd trying to find Corvin. I spot him on the couch with a brunette sitting on his lap. I storm over to him and tell the girl to beat it. She pouts but does as she's told. Corvin drunkenly climbs to his feet trying to scowl at me.

"What the fuck?" he growls right in my face.

"We have to go, your sister is at a club." He scrunches his face in annoyance and waves me off as he drops back into his seat and motions for the girl to come back. "Corvin!" I yell, pissed off he isn't listening.

"You go, you seem to know more about my sister than I do, so you go and save her ass." I grind my teeth in anger as I grit out.

"Garrett took her to a club." Within a second the girl is pushed off his lap and he is on his feet. His eyes are clear now as he looks at me.

"Get the others, we're leaving." I smile and nod as I rush off to find Beck and Crue.

⚜

We managed to find a parking spot a block away. When we get closer, we notice that there is a line half way around the block of people trying to get in. We bypass the line and move straight to the front. The bouncer opens his mouth to tell us to fuck off I'm sure, but I pull out five hundred from my pocket and wave it in his face. He snatches it and opens the red rope for us. People shout and curse us out but we ignore them, money talks and it will gain you entry to anywhere. The second we push through the main doors, the bass of the music hits me, Akon's "Hypnotized" blares thorough the sound system. The place is packed.

"How the hell are we going to find her?" Corvin shouts in my ear. I'm about to say we need to split up when the crowd begins to part as the music begins to quiet down and the DJ speaks.

"I got a surprise for y'all. I need y'all to back up and make some room for my girls, Leah, Cody and Katie to do their thang for y'all." Before he has even finished speaking the five of us are pushing our way through the crowd to get to the center where the patrons have formed a circle to watch the show the girls are about to put on. The moment the DJ blasts Fifth Harmony's – "Work from Home" the crowd on the other side opens to let the girls through.

Fuck me!

Leah looks… like a fucking wet dream. Her hair is straight and out, she wears this tiny little black top where the sleeves are off her shoulders, only big enough to cover her tits. She's wearing denim cut-offs that are so fucking tiny they only just cover her pussy and expose half her ass cheeks. But it's not the clothes that have my cock getting hard, it's the knee-high black come-fuck-me boots that she's wearing. Images of me fucking her in those boots race through my mind—my cock is rock fucking hard now.

"Jesus Christ!" Corv snaps. I look over to him expecting to be focused on his sister. I follow his gaze and my eyes widen in surprise to find he is focused on Cody and not Leah. Cody is dressed in a one-piece purple outfit that has a split from the top to her bellybutton. When they twirl around and bend over all their asses are on full display for all to see. Guys go nuts when they start to thrust their hips and throw their heads back as they run their hands down their body.

"Get it, Katie baby!" Saint shouts from behind me. I peer over my shoulder to find him and Crue both jumping up and down cheering and hollering for Katie. What the fuck is going on with them and the computer geek? I turn back to the girls when the crowd screams louder. I scowl as Leah and the other two lay flat on the floor and begin to pound their fists against the ground as they push their asses up and down like they are fucking. Having had enough of the fucking free porn show she's putting on, I take a step forward but Beck slaps a hand against my chest halting me.

"What the fuck?" I snap.

"She needs to win this, D." I frown confused at what the fuck he is saying until he points across from us and I see Chelsea and two other girls I recognize from Leah's old dance team. Fuck me! They're having a dance battle! I'm proven right when the song ends and the three girls slink back into the crowd as the others take the floor. None of them have the sex appeal or the stage presence like Leah. They move to Little Mix's "Touch" but nothing about the way they move makes me feel anything. To be honest, I have secondhand embarrassment for them. The crowd seems to love it when they all begin to dance all over each other.

"We gonna stop this or what?" I snap, but then zone out when I see Garrett push his way through the crowd and hug Leah from behind. I clench my fists at my side, she looks tense and uncomfortable in his hold.

Tell him to fuck off, Goldie.

It brings a satisfied smirk to my face when I watch her untangle his arms from around her waist, then plasters a fake smile on her face as she turns to talk to him. I hate that I don't know what she is saying. My blood begins to boil when he bends and whispers something in her ear that has her throwing her head back and laughing. It's in that moment Cody turns toward us and her eyes widen. I shake my head and place my index finger against my lips urging her to not say anything. She darts her gaze back to Leah then back to me —no, not me—she looks at Corvin who stands next to me stiff and brimming with anger. I dart my gaze between the two of them, trying to get a read on what the hell is going on between them, but my attention is snagged when the song ends and the DJ speaks.

"Dammmmm, y'all! I can't choose, I think we need a final round." The crowd goes crazy. "I got y'all, how about for the final round we make it interesting." The crowd goes nuts beginning to shout out their suggestions. "Okay, I like that one. What do ladies say to a lap dance?" I turn ridged, grinding my teeth so fucking hard I think I may actually break them. I feel eyes on me and I look to my left to see Chelsea grinning at me as she shouts her agreement. I turn back to Leah and the girls to see them deep in conversation then they nod and Leah steps forward.

"Fuck this!" Corvin snaps, but Beck cuts in before he can end this.

"You storm out there and drag her out, she is never going to make it at CHU. She has to prove herself and winning this will do that." Corvin glares at Beck, his face is turning red with anger.

"I'm not watching her give some douchebag a lap dance!" he grits out.

"Ladies pick your men!" The DJ calls. I spy Chelsea stalking toward me and I know I have a choice to make, I swallow my nerves and turn to Corv pleading with my eyes that he sees I am the better option. "Hell no!" he snaps angrily.

"Corvin, Chelsea is coming to get me to throw her off. Let me do this for *her*." He searches my gaze for a minute. I begin to worry that he is going to deny me and I know seeing Chelsea with me will throw her off her game, making her lose.

"Don't fucking touch her and this doesn't change shit!" I can tell that was painful for him. I nod my agreement just as Chelsea reaches us.

"Come on, good-looking." I allow her to take my hand and lead me out to the center of the dance floor where there are now two chairs waiting. I cut my gaze across the crowd to see Leah standing there with wide eyes, her brows push in, as hurt begins to show on her face. Garrett slides in beside her and leads her out to where I stand with Chelsea. She drops her gaze to the floor unable to look at me.

"What's wrong, Leah? You seem… upset?" Chelsea taunts. Leah shakes her head and slowly lifts her gaze to peer up at me through her lashes.

"I… I can't watch this–" The DJ announces for us to take a seat. Chelsea pushes me down into mine as Garrett slip-drops into his with a shit eating grin on his face as he looks at the beautiful blonde standing in front of him. I know I said I would ruin her but I can't, not with how hurt she looks right now thinking she is about to watch Chelsea grind all over me. I flick my gaze to Corvin who looks like he is ready to throw hands and mouth. *I'm sorry.* If this is what she wants then Leah is gonna have to woman up and come get me. I know she can do it, she just needs to come claim what's hers.

CHAPTER ELEVEN

Leah

I can't look at him.

It hurts too much knowing that Chelsea is about to give the best performance of her life and using *my* man to do it. I shoot Garrett a look ready to tell him that I'm sorry I can't do this, but then the DJ drops the beat and *our* song comes on. I spy Chelsea begin to move out of the corner of my eye and I don't know what it is that comes over me but when Ella Mai begins to sing, a possessive urge to claim him comes over me. Without thinking I dart across the floor until I'm standing directly in front of Darius, his eyes blaze at the sight of me. Chelsea begins to protest behind me but everything begins to fade away except for the music, me and him. I place my hands on the tops of his knees and push them open before slowly dropping down in front of him and then popping my ass out as I slowly rise up.

"We have a switch up, folks!" The DJ shouts. I sweep my leg out wide as I spin around and face Chelsea, then reach behind me and place my hands back on his knees as I hold her gaze and slowly lower to the floor right in front of him, but this time, I go down into a side split. The crowd goes wild. Her eyes blaze with hatred as she scurries over to Garrett to try to salvage this battle. I push up to my feet and take a couple steps away from him before spinning around to face him. I bend my knees and run my hands all over my body as I sway my hips before dropping to my hands and knees. I flick my hair round and round, before thrusting my hips up and down as I slide across the floor, right in front of him. His eyes burn with lust as I grip the tops of his knees and stand right between them. He sits up straighter as I run my hand through his hair, then grip the back before pushing his face forward until it's in line with my pussy.

"Damn, my girl Leah isn't playing," I hear Rex the DJ call out over the mic. I release my hold on his head, then push him back as I spin around and drop down onto his lap, grinding my ass against his… holy shit! Darius is hard as fuck. I continue to swirl my hips as I lean back against his chest and rest my head beside his. Our eyes lock as I reach for his hands and run them all over my body. His eyes burn with raw need and fuck, I'm a slave to that look.

"Move for me, Goldie." Those four words light a fire in my belly as I push off him and spin around so I'm straddling his lap. I grab his hands and place them on my ass—the crowd goes off. I place my hands on his shoulders as I lean forward and begin to bounce up and down on his dick for a few seconds before I smack his hands away and mimic *Jordan's* move that she did to *Chris Brown* and recline back until my hands are on the floor and flip back into a front split right in front of him. He leans down until our faces are a sliver apart. I lean forward and ghost my lips over his just as the song ends. The crowd goes crazy but we stay frozen in this position staring into each other's eyes, my breaths coming out in rapid pants. "Leah–" He's cut off when hands grip my hips and I'm hoisted into the air. I spin around and come face to face with Garrett.

"You fucking nailed that!" he shouts excitedly. I smile my thanks and turn back to Darius, my shoulders hunching forward as I fill with disappointment when I see the chair is now vacant. Cody and Katie are there in the next second screaming in my face.

"We won!"

"You killed it," they shout in unison. I smile and join in on their excitement, deciding to unpack what just happened when I get home to my dorm room. The crowd surrounds us and shouts their approval. The DJ begins to play again and everyone starts to dance but this time, I'm not really feeling it. My mind is too focused on the fact that Darius was here and I gave him a fucking lap dance. I feel my cheeks heat with the memory of feeling how hard he was beneath me. We spend the next hour dancing and having fun. Garrett doesn't seem bothered at all by the fact that I ditched him in front of everyone, and gave Darius the best lap dance of his life–well, I hope it was.

Garrett leads us out of the club with his buddies following behind. They are actually pretty cool guys and so easy to talk to. Nathan is gay and such a freaking vibe, the guy is amazing! I told him I planned to make him my new BFF. He agreed and put his number in my phone. As we all stumble outside, Cody and Katie bust out laughing at something Nathan said.

"I mean it, I would have licked that man like a fucking lollipop!" I smile and quirk a brow at Katie, she rolls her eyes playfully and says.

"Nathan wants to lick Darius like a lollipop." My brows jump into my hairline as I stare at my new BFF.

"Baby cakes, he is too much man for little old you." I snort and shake my head.

"Who cares about Lockhart. Him and his friends are a bunch of dicks." I bristle and pin Garrett with a disapproving look.

"Those *dicks* you are referring to are *my* friends as well and one of them is also my brother! I would appreciate it if you would stop making snide remarks about them," I say in a stern tone. I yelp when an arm wraps around my waist and pulls me back flush against a rock-hard chest. I relax immediately when he rests his chin on top of my head, I don't need to see him to know who it is. The way my body hums to life just from his nearness tells me who it is.

"Yeah. Garrett, stop making snide remarks," Darius mocks. I'm too flustered by the feeling of him pressed against me to chastise him for being rude to Garrett. The latter stands there scowling at Darius, his face is a mask of fury.

"You're like a leech. Why don't you and your band of misfits bugger off, we have plans." I search my brain for a memory of us making plans and come up blank. We had all agreed to call it a night, so I don't know what plans Garrett is referring to.

"A leech she doesn't mind sucking on her." I gasp as my eyes shoot wide.

"God dammit, I knew that was more than a dance," Nathan whines, causing me to laugh. Darius pulls back but keeps his hands on my waist. I look around to find it's only him and Beck here. "Baby cakes, you ever had two men at once?" I choke on my own spit as I hear Beck and Darius cough behind me, trying to mask their laughter. Nathan darts his gaze to the two guys behind me, and when understanding dawns in his eyes, I quickly cut in before he can out my secret to the group.

"Well, I'm beat and going to call it a night," I announce, forcing a yawn out.

"Dorms are locked, it's after curfew so you ladies can crash at our house," Garrett kindly offers. I smile my thanks.

"Nice try, Garrett boy, but they're coming home with us." Garrett's eyes burn with hatred as he stares at Darius. Honestly, I would rather crash at my brother's house than in a house filled with strange guys that I don't know. To stop this from getting out of hand, I pull out of Darius's hold and give Garrett a quick hug and thank him for tonight before I turn to my new BFF, who wraps me in a bear hug.

"Baby cakes, I want all the details, every single one over coffee tomorrow," he whispers. I giggle as I pull back and shoot him a wink. Nathan darts his gaze over my head, he has zero shame as he checks Darius and Beck out. He whistles between his teeth then lets out a dramatic sigh. "I bet they both have huge ass cocks and know how to use them." I splutter, so do Cody and Katie.

"Right, so on that note, deuces," Darius calls out as he grips my hand, and yanks me toward him. He drags me across the road with Beck and the girls following us.

"Scream my name when you come riding his juicy cock, baby girl!" Laughter bursts out of me. I hear the girls laughing hysterically behind us as well at Nathan's remark.

"You need new friends," Darius grumbles as we reach Beck's car. I slip into the backseat with the girls as Beck slips behind the wheel and Darius rides shotgun.

"Oh my God, I love Nathan!" Cody giggles beside me.

"Babes, same!" Katie agrees.

"Hey, he's mine!" I cut in causing the three of us to break out in another round of laughter. The laughter dies in my throat when Darius leans around his seat and pins me with an angry look.

"Who the fuck is Nathan?" he growls.

Cody snorts. "The guy who wants your cock in his ass." Katie and I break out into uncontrollable laughter at Cody's answer. The horrified look on Darius's face is priceless.

"How much have you three had to drink?" The three of us girls share a look before laughing again. "Leah?" Darius snaps.

"We may have had a few or is it a couple, maybe I don't know. Nathan kept bringing us fruity yummy drinks," I answer, which just earns me another look from the broody bastard. "Stop looking at me like that. You're just pissy because I made new friends and you weren't invited tonight. Wait, why were you there tonight?" Rather than answering he turns around and faces forward but I'm not having it. Maybe it is the alcohol but I feel reckless and emboldened suddenly. I climb over the console, ignoring Darius's shouts to sit my ass down. Beck swerves but rights the car.

"Leah, sit the fuck down!" Darius yells. I manage to climb in the front and plant my ass right on his lap, then unclick his seatbelt while he sits there stiff as a board. I pull the belt around both our bodies and clip it back in as I shimmy back against him. I feel his cock twitch in his pants and smirk triumphantly.

"Now that you can't escape me, tell me why you were there tonight. Don't lie either because Cody told me she saw you with Corv, Saint and Crue as well." It takes him a minute to finally relax back into his chair. When he does, he wraps his arms around my waist and pulls me flush against his chest. I rest my head on his shoulder. Suddenly feeling really sleepy, my lids begin to grow heavy, and I feel myself drifting off to sleep.

"Because I didn't want you to choose Garrett." I swear I hear him whisper before sleep claims me.

CHAPTER TWELVE

Darius

Beck kills the engine when we pull into our drive. Saint's jeep is here so they must be home. Corvin refused to hang around the club and wanted to go back to the party. I refused to leave, which pissed him off more. Beck drove the three of them back to get Saint's car before coming back to get me and the girls. We sit here for a moment saying nothing. Beck checks his rearview mirror and sighs.

"They crashed as well?" I ask.

"Yeah, you want to take her in and I'll take Katie then come back for Cody?"

"Yeah," I say tiredly. I unclip my belt ready to get out when Beck's words stop me.

"She needs to go in the spare room." It grates on my nerves that he's telling me what to do with her but I also know he is right.

'Yeah, I know," I answer somberly. I push the door open and maneuver Leah so she is laying bride style in my arms. I carefully climb out of the car, making sure she doesn't hit her head, then turn to see Beck lifting Katie from the car, holding her the same way I hold Leah. We both make our way toward the house, Beck comes to a stop in front of me at the porch steps. I peer around him to see Corv sitting there. He looks to me then drops his gaze to his sister in my arms. He sighs as he runs a hand through his hair.

"Cody in the car?"

"Yeah, she's out cold," I answer, taken back that he isn't yelling at me for holding his sister. He even seems like he's sobered up. Did they even go back to the party?

"You two take them up, I'll get Cody," he says as he climbs to his feet and steps around us to head back to the car. Beck shoots me a look. I just shrug and shake my head.

"Let's go before he comes back and yells at me," I say, causing us both to chuckle quietly as we make our way inside. We pass the living room and come to a stop at the sight of Saint and Crue sitting on the couches watching a movie. "I thought you guys would still be out," I say. They both look over the back of the sofa and the second they spot Katie in Beckett's arms they are launching off the couch and rushing around to grab her off him. Utterly baffled and weirded out at the sight of Crue holding the girl close to his chest, with Saint running fingers down her cheek tentatively, I decide to leave them and their fucking trio issue alone, then head upstairs.

I climb the stairs and head for the spare room. The door is ajar so I use my shoulder to push it open. I walk over to the bed and gently lay her down before reaching for the throw blanket at the foot of the bed. I pause at the sight of her boots. Dropping the blanket, I gently peel the boot off her left foot—how the fuck she can walk in these I will never know, but fuck they make her legs look they go on for days. I reach for her right one and gently pull it off. I drop her boot to the floor when I see a tattoo on the side of her ankle.

My eyes widen to the size of dinner plates as I skim my thumb over the letter. Right there on the side of her ankle is a small *D*. I may be being presumptuous here but I'm 99.9% sure that D stands for Darius. When a shadow fills the doorway, I gently drop her foot and throw the blanket over her before turning around to see Beck standing there. I sigh, not in the mood for another one of his fucking bullshit heart to hearts. I make my way toward him and he steps back as I close the door quietly behind me. I take two steps toward my room before I stop and turn to face him. He stands there with a look on his face I can't decipher.

"Just spit it the fuck out," I snap, too tired and over everyone butting into my shit.

"She made a mistake, D. When are you going to let it go?"

"Stay out of this, Beckett. You and I both know why this shit will never happen," I say angrily.

He shakes his head in a way that makes me think the fucker is mocking me. "Maybe it's time you choose a different Williams sibling. A girl like that doesn't come around often, Darius."

"And how the fuck would you know?" He closes the space between us until we are chest to chest.

"Because I lost the best thing in my life. I was too stupid to realize how good I had it until I fucking lost it. Don't be stupid like me, because you'll spend the rest of your life regretting every choice you ever make because *she* won't be by your side. No amount of success or wealth will ever fill the void she will leave in your life."

🏈

I can't sleep!

I've been laying here for hours mulling over Beck's words. What the fuck happened in his past and who is this girl he speaks of? When I hear the adjoining bathroom door slide open, I close my eyes and feign sleep. I hear her shuffling around my room. I open my eyes to slits as I watch her head for my dresser, open the draw and pull out a shirt before quietly closing it. She turns to leave but then pauses. She slowly swivels back toward me. I keep my breathing even and lay still as she tip toes quietly over to me. I keep my eyes closed fully waiting to see what she does next, when I feel her lips press against mine it takes everything inside me not to move and remain still.

She pulls back and runs the pads of her fingers against my stubble. "I'm so sorry for everything I ever did to you," she whispers brokenly before retreating back into the bathroom and closing the door. When I hear the shower start running, I bolt upright in bed. The thought of her naked and dripping wet mere feet away from me has my restraint taut and ready to snap. If I go in there, I have to let go of the anger I harbor toward her for what she did to me. I'll also be risking my friendship with Corvin. He's warned me to steer clear of her—if I fuck it up he won't give me another chance.

Maybe it's time to choose a different Williams sibling.

Beckett's words play on a loop in my head, taunting me, daring me to take what I want. I'm still mad at her but my need to bury my cock inside her outweighs some of my anger. I throw the covers off and swing my legs over the side of the bed. I scrub my hands down my face as a war of emotions spur to life inside me.

"Fuck it!" I growl as I storm toward the bathroom. I grip the handle ready to slide it open but the sound of a moan has me pausing. I lean my ear against the door and strain my hearing. Another moan slips from her mouth.

"Oh God." A thought hits me, what if she's in there with Beckett? "Darius." The sound of my name slipping from her sinful lips has the worry fleeing my body. I edge the door open just enough for me to see her with her fingers buried inside her pussy. Her other hand is pinching her nipple. She throws her head back as another moan crawls its way out of her. My cock twitches in my boxers from seeing the water dripping down her delectable body and seeing her cheeks heat as she chases her high. Her eyes are closed as she continues to pump her fingers in and out of herself. An irrational sense of jealousy overcomes me.

I'm the only one who gets to make her come. I quietly slide the door open, she's too lost in the pleasure she is inflicting on herself to notice me.

I push my boxers down my legs. My cock springs free and smacks against my stomach as I kick them to the side. I slowly creep forward and open the shower door. Her eyes snap open. Before she can scream in fright I dart into the stall and cover her mouth with my hand as I push her flush against the wall. Her eyes are wide and filled with shock and lust. The showerhead soaks me and has water dripping down my face, forcing my hair to flop against my forehead. She gingerly reaches up and pushes it back, making an involuntary shiver work its way down my spine at the feeling of her touching me.

"This is just me needing to fuck you, nothing more." Her brows bunch into the center of her face. "Can you handle that?" I slowly remove my hand from her mouth and use it to grip her waist. A small gasp slips from her lips. I know I sound like a prick but right now I can't promise her more than this. I'm not ready to jump into trying to work things out with this anger still inside me.

"I'll take you anyway I can," she says with determination. Rather than using words I answer her by slamming my mouth against hers. She opens for me like always, and the moment I push my tongue inside her mouth, a groan tears from me at the taste of her. She reaches out and runs her hands down my chest. The second her fingers skim across my cock, I break the kiss and groan as I lean my forehead against hers.

"Get on your knees and suck it." My voice is raspy and thick with need. She doesn't hesitate to do as she is told. She lowers to her knees and grips the base of my cock. She pumps it a couple times forcing me to reach out and lean my hands against the wall to keep my balance. She darts her tongue and swipes it across the head of my dick. "Fuck," I snarl as a shiver works its way up my spine. The second she wraps her lips around my cock, a strangled moan tears out of me—the girl is a pro at sucking dick.

The way she swirls her tongue around the underside of my cock has my hips thrusting forward of their own accord. Unable to take her teasing, I drop one of my hands into her hair, fisting it as I begin to fuck her face without mercy. I force her to take everything I have to give. She doesn't protest, instead she grips my ass and pulls me forward until my dick is rammed all the way down her throat.

My breathing picks up, my thrusts grow unsteady. When I feel my balls begin to tighten, I rip my cock free of her mouth, grip my shaft and pump it four times, then roar out my release as I watch jets of my cum spurt all over her face and tits. I stare down at her, expecting her to be pissed at what I just did. When she swipes a finger across her cheek, wiping my cum onto the digit, she brings it to her mouth, flicks her eyes to mine and sucks it clean as she moans at the taste.

"Jesus!" I growl as I push off the wall and offer her my hand. She takes it, then steps under the spray of water with her back to me.

"You don't have to stick around," she says before ducking her head under the water. Her dismissal of me pisses me off. If she thinks her sucking my cock was enough, she is so fucking mistaken.

CHAPTER THIRTEEN

His hand grips my hair and yanks my head back drawing a strangled groan of pain from me. He pulls me toward him and gets right in my face. Water drips down his own, making him look like a literal wet dream.

"I'm not done with you," he grits out before his mouth crashes against mine. I kiss him back, pouring everything I feel for him into this kiss. His hold on my hair releases as I wrap my arms around his neck. Then his hands slide down my body to grip the back of my thighs, and hoist me up. My legs lock around his waist instinctively. He turns us so my back is against the tiled wall. The look in his eyes steals the breath from my lungs. I can see the hurt lurking beneath the surface, but the one emotion that pushes to the surface of his eyes is desire. We remain still, staring at each other for a long time. It causes a lump to form in my throat. Before I can call him on it, he plasters his mouth to mine, this time his kiss isn't hurried or angry, it's soft, slow and sensual.

I run my fingers through his hair before allowing my hands to roam his body. I touch everywhere I can. I feel him doing the same but I also know that he is doing it for the same reasons as I am—we're cementing the feeling of each other into our memory because this isn't just him and me wanting to fuck. This is his way of saying goodbye to me and this is my way of trying to convince myself that I just need to feel him one more time inside me so I can let him go. He breaks our kiss and shifts me until I feel the head of his cock at my entrance. I hold his gaze as he slowly lowers me onto him. My mouth opens as a heady moan escapes me at the feeling of having him inside me again.

Once he is buried inside me, we both sigh in contentment. He keeps his eyes on me as he slowly rocks in and out, drawing a strangled whimper from me. The longer I look into his eyes and feel his body pressed against me, it gives me everything but at the same time takes it all away. I bury my face in the crook of his neck, unable to look at him anymore—it hurts too much. Tears cascade down my cheeks. I don't understand how I can feel so heartbroken but in turn feel so fucking alive because of how amazing he is making me feel. When he thrusts inside me with more force then a second ago, I cry out. He does it again. I try to remain quiet but I can't.

"Bite me or you're going to wake your fucking brother." I do as he says and clamp down on the soft skin between his neck and shoulder. He growls at the feeling. His grip on my ass tightens as he continues to thrust inside me at the right speed. I can feel the walls of my pussy clamping down on his cock and he groans his approval. "Fuck you feel so good, Goldie," he grits out. I drag my nails down his back, drawing shudders from him. I tear my mouth off his neck and smash my lips against his, kissing him with everything I have. I feel my orgasm cresting and try to break the kiss but he won't let me. He reaches up with one of his hands, grips the back of my neck and holds me in place as he continues to pound inside me. I scream into his mouth as an orgasm so intense and raw rips through me.

He doesn't slow his pace even as I turn to jelly in his hold, his thrusts turning frantic which tells me he's close. He breaks our kiss and bites down on the tender flesh between my neck and shoulder, the same place I bit him. I cry out at the exquisite feeling that spurs to life inside me. His jaw clamps down harder as he grunts out his release. He unclenches his jaw from my shoulder sending a shiver down my spine when he places a tender kiss to the mark before resting his forehead against it. I wrap my arm around his neck and use my other hand to run my fingers through his hair. I soak in this moment and try to store the memory of what touching him feels like in my mind.

"Our hearts are wild creatures, Darius, that's why our ribs are cages." He slowly leans back so he can look at me. I wall off my emotions from him so he can't see the anguish in my eyes.

"I don't even know what that means."

"It means you can't help who you love." His brows draw in, I cup his face between my hands as I place a soft kiss to his lips then rest my forehead against his, closing my eyes. "I fucked up. I know you hate me… I hate myself for what I did to you." Tears continue to fall down my cheeks. "I'll always love you." He tenses at the sound of my whispered words. He says nothing as he slowly pulls out of me and lowers me to my feet, holding my waist until I'm steady on them. Once he's sure I'm able to stand, he withdraws his hands. I close my eyes when I feel a rush of cold air hit me, knowing he's just left. I cover my mouth with my hand and slowly drop to the shower floor hugging my knees to my chest as I cry. I have no one to blame but myself—I destroyed us.

"Get up, breakfast time!" I bolt upright in bed and scream in fright. "Fuck!" I dart my gaze to the door to see Crue standing there with wide eyes. My breaths come in ragged pants as I try to calm my racing heart. The bathroom door flies open to reveal an angry looking Darius who stands there in nothing but a towel with a shirt clenched in his first. He glares at Crue then swings his gaze to me. Seeing the hickey I left on him last night on display fills me with a sense of smug satisfaction.

"Shit!" he grits out before tossing the shirt in his hand at me. I catch it before it can smack me in the face. I frown. "Cover the fuck up!" he growls. "You, get the fuck out now!" he snaps at Crue as I drop my gaze and squeal. I was hot as fuck when I crawled into bed so I'm only in a pair of panties. I race to tug the shirt over my head before I bury my face in my hands in embarrassment. "If you plan to fuck my friends, at least don't do it in my fucking house!" I snap my gaze to his, my mouth is ajar in shock that he would even think that! He shoots me a disgusted look before turning around and marching back into the bathroom, slamming the door behind himself. I stare at the closed door for so long my neck begins to cramp. I shake it off and tell myself to suck it up. I need to get used to how Darius is going to be. I did this and now I need to live with the consequences.

I sluggishly make my way downstairs, wearing my shorts and Darius's shirt while carrying my boots and top from last night in my hand. I hear conversation coming from the kitchen, so I drop my stuff on the couch before following the sounds of laughter. Crue and Saint sit at the table laughing with Beck. I dart my gaze to the other side and frown when I see Katie and Cody standing there helping Corvin plate up.

"Uh, what are you two doing here?" I ask. My friends snap their gazes to me. Katie's eyes widen and Cody pales at the sight of me. When I hear the guys laughter die off, I look at them and suddenly Crue and Saint both find their plates more interesting and can't stop looking at them. My eyes widen as I snap my gaze back to my girls, realization dawning on me. Cody steps toward me but I hold up my hand, her face falls. I open my mouth to speak when I suddenly feel Darius at my back, Corvin's face morphs into a picture of rage.

"Don't be salty, Sis. You fucked my best friend, so only fair I fucked yours." My eyes pop wide as Cody's face falls. Seeing the hurt in her eyes sends my anger soaring. I meet Corvin's angry stare with one of my own.

"You can be pissed at me all you want but you do not get to hurt Cody to get at me." I'm so proud of myself when my voice doesn't waiver.

"Nice shirt," Corvin grits out as he shoulders past me. I sigh, knowing that he won't believe me even if I told him the truth. I close the couple feet of space between me and Cody and wrap her in a hug. She tenses for a second before relaxing and returning my embrace.

"There are so many better looking guys in the world then that idiot I share DNA with," I say sarcastically. We both break out into a fit of laughter that eases the tension.

"Still better looking than you," Corvin mumbles from his seat at the table.

"That's debatable, Brother. I'd rather stare at her ass than yours." I roll my eyes, Saint is such a dork. Darius mutters something behind me before making his way into the kitchen. He reaches into the pantry to grab his protein powder and freezes, he looks to me and I cringe.

"Did you drug all of it?" I bite my lip and shake my head, suddenly feeling so unwelcome I decide it would be better if I left given Darius's remark has tension filling the room and all eyes on me.

"Thanks for the ride, Beck. I'll catch you guys later," I say as I turn and head into the living room to grab my stuff.

"Leah, wait." I don't listen, grabbing my top and shoes and head for the door. I grip the handle and pull it a quarter of the way open before Corvin reaches above my head and slams it shut. I spin around and glare at him.

"Wait for what, Corv? You want to call me a whore again? Or what is it this time, you gonna call me a junkie now since I doped your buddies?" I'm beginning to get hysterical now and I'm unable to stop myself. "You won, Corvin! I'm the fucking town bike according to the rumors. Your bestie kicked my ass to the curb, so don't worry, I'll only let the basketball team run a fucking train on me this time!" We stand here glaring at each other, not even flinching, when the sound of glass shattering can be heard from the kitchen. I blow out a tired breath and shake my head, tired of the tension and fighting. I decide to add on, "I'm going to take the rest of the semester off and take my classes online." Katie and Cody rush around the corner looking at me with horrified looks on their faces.

"Where are you going to go?" he asks. My shoulders slump. He didn't even try to convince me to stay, he wants me gone just as much as Darius, and that fucking stings.

I shrug my shoulders. "Does it matter?"

"You're my sister," he says solemnly.

"I'm not your problem, Corvin. You got your business, school, football and your friends to worry about. At least with me gone, that will be one less worry for you." When I feel tears begin to build in the backs of my eyes, I know I need to get out of here. I reach up on my tip toes and place a kiss to his cheek. "For what it's worth, Corvin, I am really sorry. I never meant to hurt any of you and I swear, I never meant to cause a rift between you and Darius," I whisper before turning and opening the door. This time, he doesn't stop me.

CHAPTER FOURTEEN

Darius

Three weeks…

"Throw the fucking ball then, you pussy!" I yell. Corvin takes his helmet off and throws it to the ground, then storms toward me. I do the same until we both smack into each other.

"You think you can do better?" he grits out through clenched teeth.

I press my forehead against his. "Yeah, I fucking do!" Corvin and I have been fighting daily over the stupidest things. None of us thought Leah was serious when she said she was leaving three weeks ago. When Corv went over to speak with her the next day, Cody slammed the door in his face after telling him it was his and *my* fault that her best friend left. She hasn't returned his calls or texts. He had no choice but to tell his mom and dad, they are worried sick. He didn't tell them why she ran just that some shit went down and she bolted. He made it seem like she just gave up, when that wasn't the fucking case at all.

"Both of you, get the hell off my field and hit the showers. You are done for the day!" Coach shouts. I shove him back and stalk off the field, heading for the locker rooms. The second I barge through the door, I throw my helmet across the room then punch the locker beside me. I grit my teeth when pain radiates up my arm.

"Hope you're pleased with yourself." I spin around and glare at Corvin. I clench my fists at my sides as he walks toward me, leaving an inch of space between us.

"Fuck you," I snarl.

"Nah, you've fucked enough Williams, I think," he snaps. I punch him right in the jaw. He stumbles back a step before he roars and charges at me, tackling me into the lockers. I grunt then drop an elbow to his back. It doesn't have the desired effect because he's still wearing his pads. He lands a solid punch to my side before I manage to shove him back. I land another hit to his face. His head snaps to the side and he spits blood on the floor. When he slowly turns back to face me, his eyes are filled with hatred as he looks at me. "You and me, we're done." He spits blood at my feet. My anger begins to dissipate, then I curse and stab a hand through my hair.

"Corvin–"

"No, Darius. You've done enough!"

"I didn't do shit!" He charges at me again, this time I don't defend myself when he hooks me in the cheek. I stumble and quickly right myself as I wait for him to come at me again.

"She was doing good… you fucking ruined it!"

"How the fuck did I ruin it?" I shout. He reaches up and tugs on the strands of his hair in frustration.

"You should have left her alone." All the anger flees my body, I decide I need to be open with him.

"I couldn't, Corvin." His gaze bores into me. I push on knowing that I need to tell him so he knows she wasn't just some random girl I was fucking. "I tried to stay away from her, I swear I did. But then after time, I couldn't bear the thought of being away from her."

"Were you fucking my sister the whole time?" I shake my head.

"No. I swear, the first time was on her sixteenth birthday." He scrubs a hand down his face.

"What the fuck happened, Darius?" I blow out a loud exhale as I dive into the story.

"I told her that we could never be more than friends because she is your little sister and was fourteen at the time, she didn't take that well." He snorts knowing how stubborn his sister is. "Then a year went by and we hung out a lot more, she started becoming… more. Then about three months before her sixteenth birthday shit changed and I couldn't deny how I felt for her. Look, shit got real and I had planned to tell you until I got to that party and saw her in bed with Gary. We fought earlier that night and in my head, I thought she assumed I had chickened out and decided to fuck me over by sleeping with him. I had no fucking idea that he had drugged her. If I had, I would have killed the bastard for hurting my girl." He quirks a brow at me.

"*Your* girl?" I don't cower, I hold his gaze as I nod my head stiffly. "How exactly did—do you feel about my sister and don't fucking lie to me?" I mull over his words for a second and decide I need to stop lying to myself.

"I've been in love with Leah since I was seventeen." His face slackens in shock at my honesty. "I thought us going away to college would help me get over her, but it didn't. I could only fuck another chick doggy because I couldn't stand the sight of their face. Shit, Corvin, the only girl I have ever kissed is Leah. I've never kissed another girl." He throws his head back and groans.

"What the fuck happened that night after you and Beck brought them back from the club." I scrunch my face. "Fucking hell, skip the dirty details." I nod.

"I… let her go," I say quietly.

"What the fuck does that mean?"

I throw my hands in the air and scowl at him. "You didn't give me a choice. You told me to stay the fuck away from her," I shout.

"Seems like you didn't listen though, huh?"

"I can't, Corvin. I fucking hate drugs and you know that, but she is a fucking addiction that I can't get rid of. She's under my skin, she's inside me," I say as I pound my fist against my chest.

"Do you still… love her?"

A whoosh of air escapes me. "Yeah, Corv, I still love her and I'm sorry I lied to you. But I have to be honest with myself, if you ask me to choose between you or her…" I hold his gaze so he can see how serious I am. "I choose her, I fucking love her and I know you will hate me for that but it's the truth. I'm done lying to myself and everyone else." He stands there silently staring at me for a long time. I begin to prepare myself for him to tell me to get out and stay away from him. It's gonna suck losing my best friend but she is worth the sacrifice.

"Help me find my sister?" My brows rise to my hairline.

"Seriously?"

He narrows his eyes. "Don't fucking push me. Help me find her and then… we'll deal with this shit but, Darius?"

I swallow audibly. "Yeah?"

"You need to let go of the drug shit. You and I both fucked up. She needed us after that shit with Gary and neither of us were there for her." I hang my head in shame.

"You both might not have been, but I was." I spin around to see Beck leaning against the wall with a smug look on his face.

"How long have you been there?" Corvin demands.

Beck shrugs. "Long enough to know you two have kissed and made up." Both Corv and I snicker while Beck shrugs. Saint and Crue appear, drawing a groan from me. Clearly the three of them have been standing there listening the entire fucking time!

"So, is this the part where we tell you that Leah has been talking to Beck every day?" I snap my gaze to Beck's the second I register what Saint just said. He stands there staring directly at me, daring me to come at him. I refrain from giving into my instincts of wanting to rearrange his face.

"Where is she?" Corvin demands as he slides up beside me.

Beck pushes off the wall and stands a couple feet away from us with his arms crossed over his chest. Saint and Crue stand either side of Beck mimicking his stance.

I roll my eyes over their display of power they think they have. "Spit it the fuck out or I'll beat it out of you." Beck cuts his gaze to me and narrows his eyes.

"What guarantee do I have that you two won't fuck it up again?" I grind my teeth and try to take some deep breaths through my nose to calm my temper.

"I need to apologize for being a right prick and make it up to her, please, Beck." I can tell that was hard for Corvin to say from how tense he is. Beck nods and then flicks his gaze back to me expectantly, I narrow my eyes.

"Her ass needs to get back here so I can remind her who the fuck said ass belongs to. Happy now?" No sooner have I finished speaking, than I am shoved into the lockers. I shoot Corvin a glare.

"Don't ever fucking talk about my sister's ass!" I last a whole two seconds before I laugh. Before long, the five of us are all laughing. It's been a long time since the five of us have been in a room and actually laughing, it's been nothing but tension and dirty looks for weeks.

"Okay." I turn back to Beck and wait. "I suggest you two plan something good for Thanksgiving and be ready to grovel!"

"Fucking tell me where she is!" I snap at Beckett.

He shakes his head and smirks smugly. "I was sworn to secrecy, my dudes, plus it serves you both right to suffer for being fucking assholes." I gape at the motherfucker as he turns and walks out with the cocky duo following after him.

"I'm gonna beat their asses," Corvin growls.

"Fuck, yes!"

"Prank war?" I slowly turn to face my best friend and grin like a kid on Christmas.

"Fuck yes, those bastards are going down!"

Corvin and I wait out back for the three assholes to get back from practice. Excitement thrums through me when they realize what we have done! I stuff my hands into the pocket of my hoodie, the weather is starting to get colder and I couldn't be happier. I fucking love winter.

"You know Saint and Crue are going to take this to the extreme, right?" I lull my head to the side to smirk at Corvin, who is reclined on the lounger beside me.

"They can try." The sound of the front door opening alerts us to their arrival. Corvin wiggles his brows at me as we wait.

"Fuck!" We hear Crue shout, then we are both launching out of seats and racing over to peer through the back door as we watch the three of them slip all over the wooden floor. We poured oil from the front door to the stairs. Corvin and I both burst out laughing at the sight of them skating all over the place. I completely lose it when Beck begins to do the running man and falls flat on his ass.

"I'm gonna fucking kill them!" he roars from his spot on the ground. I open the back door and step inside with Corv right behind me, the three of them swinging their angry glares our way.

"Oh my goodness gracious, what is going on here?" Corvin mocks.

Saint points at the pair of us. "You're going down for this motherfuckers." If they think this is bad, I can't wait for them to see what awaits them in their rooms.

Corvin and I decide to help them out and give them a hand. The fuckers think we are trying to suck up so they won't turn this shit around on us. Truth is, we just want them to go upstairs, which they are doing now leaving us to clean the floor. The moment the three of them turn their backs and head upstairs, Corvin and I shake with silent laughter. Once they reach the landing we move to the base of the stairs, I count to three and then it happens.

"Darius!"

"Corvin!"

"You motherfuckers!"

They all shout in unison. Corvin and I race out the back door laughing our asses off as we race around the side of the house. I push the side gate open and we make a break for Corv's car. We can still hear the three of them shouting inside. I'm laughing so hard, I have tears and my stomach is hurting. I yank the passenger door open and slip inside the car. Corvin is a second behind me, just as he slams the car into reverse I spot Beck running around the side of the house looking furious.

"Go, go, go!" I yell as he plants his foot and peels out of the driveway, with a pissed off Beckett chasing after us until we hit the end of our street.

CHAPTER FIFTEEN

Leah

Two weeks later…

"Thanks, Val, I'm so glad Katie told me about you."

"Leah, it's my pleasure, honestly. Thanks for working with my crazy schedule." I smile at Val. The girl is not only stunning with her red hair, blue eyes, and cheekbones to die for, but she is also crazy freaking smart. Since transferring to online classes my grades have slipped and I'm so behind in English. Val is my tutor. She makes everything so easy and the way she explains it to me I actually understand what it means.

"Of course. Honestly, your son is so cute so I get how you would get distracted," I say. Her son is so freaking cute. He's four, and oh my God, you can tell the boy is going to be a heartbreaker. He has tanned skin, thick black ringlets and her blue eyes—the boy is going to have a line of girls wanting his attention.

"Thanks, You, Cody and Katie seem to be the only ones who are cool with me being a mom and student." I frown.

"Seriously?" She rolls her lips over her teeth and nods.

"Yeah. I don't have friends because I can't go partying every weekend and hit the beach whenever I want." That makes me so sad. I've never met Val in person, we talk every day over video while she tutors me. The school pays her for her time which is freaking amazing.

"Well, you have me, Cody and Katie and we don't care you can't party. You and that gorgeous boy are welcome to hang out with us anytime." Her eyes begin to fill with moisture and my heart breaks for her. Being a mom must be freaking hard, but being a mom with no support must be hell. She mentioned that Dawson's father isn't around and I never pushed for more information. I could see that was a touchy subject for her.

"Thanks, Leah, I better go bathe him and get him ready for bed." We say our goodbyes and agree to video at the same time. I really like Val. She never pushes or tries to pry into the reason why I decided to take my classes online for the rest of the semester. She seems like a genuinely nice person. Katie and Cody both adore her. I speak to my besties every day and even Nathan. He is fast becoming one of us and that makes me so happy because he truly is an amazing guy.

I close my laptop and place it on the bedside table before climbing off my bed and stretching. My shoulders are burning from spending hours sitting there working away on my papers. I peer out the window and marvel at the beautiful view, Alaska is fucking breathtaking. Five weeks ago when I walked out of my brother's house, I had no idea where I was going to go. I just knew I needed to get away and clear my head. Truthfully, I needed space away from Darius. It was killing me to see him and know that I could never have him. Beck came to my dorm that afternoon and told me to pack a bag and meet him at his car. I didn't argue. What I didn't expect was for him to hand me a plane ticket and tell me that I was going to be traveling to their resort in Alaska.

Spending the past five weeks here at this amazingly lavish resort has helped me heal so much. I found a strength within myself I didn't even know existed, which is the only reason I agreed to Beck's request of returning home for Thanksgiving. I even found the courage to call my parents last week and tell them *everything*. Mom cried, Dad lost the plot and vowed to find a way to ruin the Hayes. It took me a while to convince him that Corvin and the others have everything sorted. I told them that I was taking a break from dance and finally chose a major. My dad was happy that I decided to major in business, but mom is worried about me giving up dance. I love to dance, but after seeing what my brother and the others accomplished, it inspired me. I still want to dance but just not full time. I can't find the passion for it anymore and the reason for that is because the last time I danced it was for *him*.

My phone pings with a message. I turn away from the window and grab it off the bed, smiling when I see who it's from.

> BECKY
>
> you set for your flight tomorrow?

> I think so...

> BECKY
>
> what's with the dots, babe?

Beckett has been my constant. He has been there for me daily and never judges me. I never in a million years thought I would ever become close with Beck, but here I am. I am forever indebted to him for what he has done for me. My phone rings with an incoming FaceTime from Beck and I answer without hesitation.

"Hey," I say the moment his face fills my screen. Beckett is gorgeous, there is no doubt about that. I've wondered for weeks why he couldn't be the one I had fallen for.

"Hey, beautiful, what's up?" I sigh.

"I'm nervous." His eyes fill with understanding.

"Don't be, no one knows that you are coming back." I nibble on my bottom lip, debating if I should ask the question that has been burning in the back of my mind all day. "He doesn't know, Leah." I swear Beck is a mind reader, my shoulders slouch and I nod. "I haven't told anyone. If you don't want to see them, then you don't have to but we are doing a bonfire at the beach." This will be the first year I won't be at home for Thanksgiving. Corvin has sent our parents away on a cruise—needless to say our parents jumped at the chance. Dad has sold his business and they are finally retiring and planning to travel like they have always wanted. They wouldn't be able to do that if it wasn't for Corvin.

"Can I get back to you on that one?" I ask nervously.

"Babe, you do what is right for you. He's an idiot for letting you go. You're a diamond and if he can't see past his own pigheadedness, then he doesn't deserve you." Beckett always knows what to say to make me feel better.

"Thanks, Beck. I couldn't have done any of this without you." He smiles sadly.

"Yeah, you could have. You're strong as fuck, Leah, and what you have been through, not a lot of women would have survived it like you have." Feeling choked up, I decide to change the subject.

"How's the prank war?" Beck told me a couple weeks ago about Darius and Corvin finally making up. That same day they poured oil on the floor and then put a dozen chickens in each of the guys' rooms. Beck was furious. He said it took a week to get the smell of shit out of his room and ever since, they have been pulling pranks. It warms my heart to know that Corvin managed to work things out with Darius. I'm glad they are still best friends.

"Saint took it too far when he stole the handle bars off Darius's bike and took the spark plugs from Corvin's car, making them both late to practice. Coach made them run laps the whole time. Saint wound up with a black eye from Darius that day, so now we are at a stalemate and I fucking hope it lasts." I laugh, these boys will never fully grow up. We chat for another twenty minutes. I fill him in about my studies and tell him about the resort. He seems so excited to move here after Christmas, I am going to miss him so fucking much while he is here for six months.

Excitement thrums through me as I wheel my suitcase behind me and head toward the exit. The moment I break through the sliding doors, I spot Beckett leaning against his car. I stop in my tracks as I take in the sight of him. He wears his Ray Ban sunglasses that shield his eyes, his hair a tousled mess but in the most perfect way. He wears a dark green shirt under his leather jacket, his dark wash jeans hug his legs perfectly. I shake myself out of my staring and run toward him. He spots me when I'm a few feet away and a broad smile stretches across his face as he pushes off the car. I drop the handle of my case and launch myself into his waiting arms. I wrap my arms and legs around him as he buries his face in the crook of my neck. To people looking at us we would look like a couple but this is just… us.

"I fucking missed you, babe." His words have me melting. I lean back in his hold and smile down at him.

"I missed you too, Becky." He glares playfully at the use of my nickname for him. He swats my ass causing me to yelp in his hold. He grins up at me, causing me to roll my eyes.

"Put me down, caveman, my girls await my arrival," I say in a horrid accent that has us both laughing. Beck and I spend the drive back to CHU catching up and laughing. It's so easy with him. I would have thought us having sex would have complicated things but it didn't. If anything, it has brought us closer. I admit, Beck is fucking hot, but I don't have that burning sensation in my belly when I'm near him. His touch doesn't set me ablaze or have me squirming. We pull into the carpark of CHU, nerves thrum through me. Beck parks the car and doesn't move to get out, instead he reaches across and clasps my hand in his giving a squeeze.

"They aren't here," he says softly.

"Do they…" I exhale loudly and pluck up the courage to ask him what I really want to know. "Does *he* know I'm back?" Beck reaches over with his free hand and clasps my chin in his hand as he slowly turns my face toward him.

"I told them to plan something good for Thanksgiving and that was it. They have no idea you're here." I nod as I nibble my bottom lip. Beck pries it free with his thumb before brushing the pad of his thumb along my lip.

"Why couldn't it be you." My eyes widen when I realize I said that out loud, and his eyes soften.

"You and me fit too well to work, babe." I frown, not understanding what he's saying. "You need someone who is going to fight you and not cave to your demands when you bat your lashes and shake your ass. I would cave in a second." I giggle which draws a sad smile to his face. "Darius won't. He will fight you and tie your ass down and say fuck it to the repercussions."

"He hates me, Beck," I whisper brokenly.

"He was hurt. He has trust issues because of how he was brought up. Give him a chance to explain it to you and I promise you, it will make things clear. He is going through a lot right now. Gary is trying to sue him." I gasp.

"What the fuck, why?"

"He says that Darius has cost him his future and is suing him for money lost or some shit. Troy's on it now but it's just a lot."

"I bet."

"Look, you have girls waiting for you, so get your cute ass out of my car and enjoy your night with the girls. If you change your mind, we're doing a bonfire and picnic at the beach tomorrow for Thanksgiving. Classes are out for the holidays so there won't be a lot of people there." I nod.

"I'll think about it."

"Perfect, but there is a dress code."

I frown. "What do you mean?"

"Saint made it a dress up party and it's swimwear or lingerie." I roll my eyes, of course Saint would make it a dress up party so he could spend the night checking out every piece of ass.

CHAPTER SIXTEEN

The five of us walk out of our last practice until after the break. I love football but fuck me, I'm glad to be having a break. In two weeks' time we have our next game and I am chomping at the bit to be back on the field under the spotlights running the length of the field.

"Hey, stranger." I grind to a stop when Chelsea darts in front of me, her sickly scent of perfume assaults my nose. I fight the gag that wants to break free.

"Oh look, it's a stray," Crue sing songs beside me. Chelsea cuts him a glare as some of her friends come to stand with her, all standing tall and popping their chests out, trying to garner our attention.

"Hey, Darius." I frown at the brunette behind Chelsea. I have no idea who the girl is but her greeting brings a dark look to the nasally bitch's eyes in front of me.

"Sup," I reply just to fuck with her.

"So, we heard about the party tomorrow and can't wait." I cut Saint a dark look, he shrugs.

"Dude, it was an open invite to whoever is staying behind." I shake my head.

"Cool, see ya then," I grit out as I try to step around her but she blocks my path. A growl of annoyance tears from me as I pin her with a warning look.

"I know Leah being back must upset you, so I can stop by later if you'd like me to make you feel better?" She is misreading the look on my face, she reaches out and rests her hand on my chest in fake support. "She is such a bitch!" she hisses. Corvin saddles up next to me and pushes her hand off me.

"That bitch is my sister, you fucking cunt." Chelsea gasps at Corvin's harsh words. I don't stick around, I use her shock to my advantage and take my leave with the others following after me. My mind is reeling. Leah's back. I head for the carpark, jump on my bike and don't wait for the others as I peel out of the lot heading straight for her dorm building. It takes me less than five minutes before I'm pulling into the carpark of her building. I park my bike and march toward her building, but when the sound of laughter hits my ears, laughter that I know all too well, I follow the sound around the side of the building and freeze. I keep to the shadows as I watch her, Cody and Katie do cartwheels on the quad. A smile breaks free at the sight of her. I'm about to make my presence known, but stop when I hear him.

"Looking good." I pin the motherfucker with a death glare even though he can't see me. Now, I get why the fucker wasn't at practice, he blew us off to hang with my girl.

"Garrett, you are so good for my ego," Leah says as she laughs. I hate the way he looks at her. He thinks he has the right to run his eyes over her body, when he fucking doesn't.

"Well, I'm beat and going to call it a night," Katie announces.

"Same," Cody chimes in. Leah opens her mouth to speak but Garrett beats her to it.

"Have dinner with me." My blood turns to ice inside my body as I implore her with my mind to say no. She looks taken back by his offer. That's a good thing, right?

"Nope, I am not dealing with Beckett pounding down my door the second he hears she went out with you so nope, Leah stays with us!" Leah seems to relax and shoots Cody a grateful look. I'm starting to like Cody more and more now.

"Leah's a big girl, she can make up her own mind," Garrett says. My fist aches to smash his face.

"I'm beat from the long flight back from Alaska." *Alaska?* Beckett, you son of a bitch. "I'll catch up with you tomorrow?" It brings me great joy to see the crestfallen look on his face at her rejection.

"Yeah, okay," he says dejectedly. Leah gives him a quick hug before heading toward me. I turn and race back to the carpark to avoid being seen. I'll give her tonight, but come tomorrow I plan to take back what is mine!

I barge through the front door of my house heading straight for the kitchen ,knowing that's where he will be. Sure enough, there he stands laughing at something Corvin said. They all turn toward me the moment I enter. I march toward him and hit him. He stumbles back into the counter. Corvin jumps in the middle of us and shoves me back a step. I glare at Beckett over his shoulder. Saint and Crue rush over to check on Beckett who is cupping his mouth.

"What the fuck?" Corvin yells in my face. I keep my glare on Beckett as I answer him.

"That fucker sent her to Alaska!" I shout. Corvin spins around to face Beck, who drops his hand and shoots us a bloody smirk. His lip is split and that gives me great satisfaction.

"You sent my sister to *our* resort?" Corvin demands.

"Sure did and it was genius. Neither of you thought to look for her there, did you?" I try to rush him again but Corvin blocks me.

"You are going to pay for that!" I growl. Beckett pushes forward but Saint and Crue hold him back.

"Fuck you. She needed that time away. She healed there,

Darius. She is happy again and darkness doesn't shine in her eyes anymore."

"She will never be yours, Beckett. She's mine!" Corvin growls but remains silent. "You think because I let you fuck her that you have any type of claim over her?" The moment his eyes widen and Saint and Crue snap their horrified stares to me, I realize I just fucked up, badly.

"You did what now?" Corvin asks in a deadly calm tone that has me backing up a step.

"Oh shit," I hear Crue mutter.

"I-we... It's not what it sounds like–" Corvin cuts off my rambling as he turns so he can keep Beck and I both in his sights.

He points to both of us as he says, "You *both* had a fucking threesome with *my* sister?" I flinch, Beckett drops his chin to his chest. "Answer me!" Corv yells.

"Yes," I answer, while Beck nods his head.

"Jesus Christ!" Corvin snaps as he scrubs a hand down his face. We all stand here silently as Corv processes what he just learned. He looks to Saint and Crue and pins them with a harsh look that has them both raising their hands in surrender and taking a step away from Beck.

"Nope. Never touched her," Crue rushes to say.

"I talk shit about doing her but swear to God, never laid a hand on her," Saint rushes to add.

"Oh, that's great so only two out of four of my best friends have fucked my sister." I fight the cringe that wants to break free.

"It isn't how it sounds, Corvin. I would never hurt Leah," Beck says as he stares at Corvin.

"How am I supposed to believe that?" Beck flicks his gaze to me briefly before answering Corvin.

"Who has she been talking to everyday? I'm the one she has been coming to for help, not any of you."

"You both are so fucked," Corvin breaths out as he storms

out of the room, making sure to shoulder check me on his way out.

"Fuck!" I rasp out. I just fucked up again. Beck presses up to me, I hold his stare waiting for him to bust a move.

"Stop trying to find someone to blame for how shit turned out. You want to be pissed, be pissed at yourself because this is on you." His words hit me hard.

"Did you mean it?" I ask cautiously.

"Mean what?" he asks, slightly confused.

"That she's happy?" He sighs and places a hand on my shoulder.

"If you're asking me if she is over you, then just ask." I suck up my pride and hold his stare.

"Has she moved on?" I can hear the sadness in my own voice, my heart is beating so fast as I wait for his reply.

He gives me a dry stare. "Dude, I know she has a tattoo on her leg with the letter D." My eyes widen in surprise that he knows about that. I mean, I assumed it was for me but I never got that confirmed. "A girl doesn't just tattoo a guy's name on her, then move on. She loves you, Darius, but she hates that she can't let you go. If you want her back, then you need to work your ass off because she won't forgive you easily."

"She straight up has his name tattooed on her?" Saint butts in but we ignore him. "Corvin is going to lose his shit!" Beckett's phone begins to ring. When he tenses, I slam my eyes closed and take a step back nodding my head.

"Answer it," I say in a defeated tone. He sucks in a sharp breath as he pulls it out of his pocket and answers.

"Hey, beautiful." I clench my fists at my sides at his endearment. Unable to listen to their conversation, I decide to call it a night and hope like hell she decides to come tomorrow night.

I feel like a pubescent teen with how fucking nervous I am. I'm even drinking to try calm the fucking nerves inside me. We've been sitting at the beach for a couple hours, some of the team is here and other students from CHU crowd around us, but I don't hear a fucking word any of them say, too focused and keeping a look out for my girl. Beck gave me a heads up this morning and told me she is going to come tonight. Ever since then, I have been a fucking wreck. Corvin hasn't killed me yet, so I'm hoping that means he isn't pissed at me for what happened with me, Leah and Beck.

"Looking good, handsome." I roll my eyes heavenward, this girl just won't fucking quit. I look at her and grit my teeth in disgust. She stands before me with a lacy lingerie set on with garters and all. I mean we're at a fucking beach. I look past her to see her skanks have all dressed the same.

"Look…" The words die in my mouth the moment I see her break through the crowd. Her long blonde hair is out and blows in the wind, her eyes bright and vibrant. Her lips are glossy and perfect. I run my gaze down her body, noting she has a black, one-piece swimsuit on with the sides cut out, leaving her hips and ribs on display. When she turns to the side to say something to Katie, I see the back of her swimsuit is open. The wind blows her skirt thing up and I have to bite my lip to keep my groan from breaking free when I see it's one of those G-string swim-ming suits that show off her ass cheeks. She turns around again with a smile that is so infectious I find myself smiling as well, but it drops off my face when I see Garrett step up beside her and wrap an arm around her waist.

"They actually look cute together," the annoying bitch says. I ignore her as I march toward Leah, ready to rip her off Garrett, until Corvin steps in front of me.

"Move," I growl.

"I hate him more than you but believe me, I know my sister and you will just piss her off." I cut my gaze to him. "It's going to take me a minute to adjust to the fact you're into my sister but

I saw the second she arrived you shifted, your eyes told me everything, Darius."

"And what exactly did they tell?" I push.

His eyes darken. "That you really are in love with her and she isn't just some girl to you."

I feel a weight lift off my shoulders, he gets it now. "She never was just some girl to me." He sighs and nods his head.

"Then, let's make a plan to get you *your* girl back, because if you thought I was pissed finding out about you and her, you would hate to see what I would be like if I found out she was dating Garrett." I narrow my eyes.

"I'll break his fucking arm as well if he ever touches her." Corvin smiles wide and smacks me on the shoulder as he says.

"My man."

CHAPTER SEVENTEEN

Leah

We've been here not even five minutes and Garrett has his arm wrapped around me like we're a *thing*. We are so not together and I hate that he does this. I told him earlier when he showed up at the dorm with Nathan to walk us here, that I wasn't looking for more than friendship. He said he got it. Clearly, he doesn't. The second I spot Beck walking toward me with a grin on his face, I yank free of Garrett's hold and race toward Beck. I fling myself at him and he catches me around the waist with ease. He buries his face in the crook of my neck. I feel him smiling.

"You looked like you needed an out," he says as he puts me back on my feet. I shoot him a grateful smile.

"I totally did, you're a lifesaver!" I answer as the girls come up beside me. The girls greet Beck before turning to me.

"Coming for a sunset swim?" I nod eagerly, Cody knows I will never turn down a chance to swim in the ocean. I turn back to Beck.

"Want to come with?" He shakes his head and smiles.

"Nah, you girls go have fun. Come find me when you're done and I'll get you a drink." I reach on my tip toes and plant a kiss on his cheek.

"You're the best, Becky!" I shout as the three of us race off toward the water. I untie my sarong and drop it on the sand before racing after my friends. The feeling of the waves crashing into me and the smell of the sea in the air has me feeling happy. I missed this.

"Touchdown!" I hear shouted behind me before being tackled into the water. I shove the person away from me and break the surface to yell at whoever it is until I'm met with the cheesiest grin. "Baby girl, that ass was begging to be put down." I throw my head back and laugh at Nathan, he is fast becoming one of the girls. I have no idea how he and Garrett became friends considering how different they are, but thanks to Garrett, I now have another friend. I tried to get Val to come tonight but she said Dawson had a cold. She promised to come next time. The four of us stay in the water until long after the sun has set. I didn't know how much I needed this, just to be surrounded by my friend's and be a teenager without the weight of the world on my shoulders.

"Boo boo." I swing around to face Nathan, who has a mischievous look on his face.

"What's up?" I ask hesitantly.

"If you can't feel Mr. Tall Dark and Handsome's gaze on you, then there is something wrong with you, baby." I tense, I've been ignoring the feeling of having his eyes on me the whole time we have been in the water. I know if I turn around I'll find him standing there and I'm not ready, not yet. Nathan wraps his arms around me and pulls me into a hug. I wrap my arms around him and rest my cheek against his naked chest. "I got you. I also know Garrett is trying to bust a move on you."

"I don't like him like that," I say honestly.

"I know which is why I am going to tell you to be careful." I pull back and frown up at him.

"What do you mean?"

"Garrett and I have known each other for a long time. Over the years we have drifted apart, since I got into cheer and him into football. Rumors circulate fast around here and some of the things I have heard aren't good."

"Things like?" I press. I feel Cody and Katie creep in closer to us listening.

"He gets rough with girls."

I gasp. "But you're his friend." Nathan shakes his head.

"The night I met you at the club I came with Alex, not Garrett, and the only reason I came tonight is because of you three. Garrett showed up outside your dorm on his own accord." That throws me, Garrett said earlier that he and Nathan didn't want us walking alone making it seem like they had discussed that plan earlier.

"My nipples are hard and I need a drink," Cody says, causing us all to laugh and agree. We make our way back to shore. I snag my sarong on our way back toward the partygoers. As far as Thanksgivings go, this would have to be one of the best I have had in years. Beck spots us and nods before disappearing to get us drinks, I assume. I'm proven right when he appears carrying four red cups. We all thank him as we each grab a cup and cheers before taking a sip.

"Want me to help you with your wrap?" I close my eyes and pray for patience. I slowly open them and turn to face Garrett who has pushed Nathan out of his spot beside me.

"I'm—"

"She's good, I got her," Beck says in a tone that has me standing straighter. Garrett cuts Beck a dark look before turning back to me with a warm smile on his face, but it doesn't reach his eyes. Before he can say another thing, Cody screams and shoves her cup at Garrett, forcing him to hold it or risk the contents spilling on him.

"This is our jam," she shouts as she drags me and Nathan with Katie following us to the center of the crowd where students are dancing. When I hear the words of the song, I burst out laughing. Little Mix's "Shout Out to My Ex" blares from the speakers that are set up. The four of us form a circle of sorts as we dance. I let loose and allow myself to enjoy this moment with my friends. When the next song plays, I feel giddy. Fifth Harmony's "All in My Head (Flex)" has me feeling the beat and moving my hips. Nathan whistles as he steps up behind me, grips my waist and rocks his hips in time with mine. He's plastered against my back and I feel nothing, I'm not worried he will expect something or want more, we're just two friends dancing. I mean, for goodness sake, I'm rubbing my ass against his dick and the guy is as soft as butter.

I look at my girls and I'm surprised to see a guy dancing with Katie, before I can even get a look at the guy he's shoved out of the way and replaced by Crue. Katie opens her mouth ready to have a go at him no doubt, but then he stuns the fuck out of me when he grips the back of her neck and holds her in place as he smashes his lips to hers. Cody squeals and claps for our girl while I stand here stunned. Katie wraps her arms around Crue's neck, I'm about to turn away and give them a moment but Saint plasters himself against her back, and grips her waist. I expect Crue to pull back but he doesn't. Feeling like I'm intruding on a private moment, I turn back to Cody but falter when I see my brother standing next to her with his gaze on me. We stand here still as statues just staring at each other. My feet move of their own accord and take me toward him. He meets me halfway and wraps me in a bone-crushing hug. I fight back the tears that want to fall as I bury my face in his chest clutching his shirt in my fists.

He drops a kiss to the top of my head resting his chin there. "I missed you, Lee." I inhale a shuddering breath.

"I missed you too," I choke out. I close my eyes and will my tears to not fall. I promised myself I wouldn't cry. I've cried too much these past couple months and I'm not a crier.

"I'm so sorry, Leah." I pull back but keep my grip on his shirt as he holds my arms, I can see the sincerity in his eyes. "I should have been there for you and I wasn't. I was too caught up on the whole you and Darius thing. I was a fucking poor ass excuse for a brother, can you ever forgive me?" The tenderness in which he speaks, I know he means what he says. I pull him to me and hug him tight.

"I love you, Corv, and of course I forgive you." I feel the tension in his body evaporate at my words.

"I love you too." We stand here for a minute just holding each other. "I know we just made up and shit but I have to ask…" I release him and take a step back, cringing when I see his white shirt is soaked thanks to me.

I quirk a brow at him, prompting him. "Just ask whatever it is," I say.

His eyes widen mockingly as he forces a shudder through his body. "What the fuck are you wearing and why in God's good name is your ass out?" I can't help it, I throw my head back and laugh so hard that tears leak from the corner of my eyes. I can hear Cody laughing along with me, our laughter reaches new heights when Nathan says.

"Because her ass is a peach and even gay men want to take a bite." Corvin's face pales.

"Nah, fuck that," he grumbles, grips Cody's hand and begins to lead her away. I stare at their blacks wondering what the hell is going on between them, clearly in the five weeks I have been away my friends have been *busy*.

"Well, I guess you're stuck with me," Nathan says, garnering my attention and snapping me out of my shock. I turn around and smile ready to dance some more but the moment the song switches, the smile drops from my face and my whole body begins to heat. The hairs on the back of my neck stand up alerting me to the fact he is near. The second Nathan's eyes crinkle at the corners and a sly smirk graces his face, I know he's behind me. I close my eyes and will myself to be strong—I can do this.

His hands grips my exposed waist. The feeling of his hands on me, sets my body ablaze. He presses in until his chest is flush against my back, bends down and a shiver trails down my spine when I feel his lips brush against the shell of my ear. "Move for me, Goldie." Those four words have me obeying his command, Ella Mai's voice sounds out around us. This song is becoming ours. I sway my hips side to side, he keeps pace with me. The second I press my ass harder against him, his grip tightens and he groans in my ear. He keeps one hand on my waist and slips the other around my front to hold me closer. "You wear this for me?" he whispers huskily in my ear.

"No. I wore it for me." I'm so fucking proud of myself, my voice is strong and doesn't waiver. I expect him to shove me away and storm off like he normally does, the fact he is here dancing with me out in the open where Corvin can spot us, tells me he either doesn't care if we're caught or he's stupid.

"I want you," he says, his words have need coiling inside me. If my suit wasn't wet from my swim earlier, it would be damp with my arousal now. I want him so bad but I also can't deal with his hot and cold behavior. I turn in his hold. His eyes shine with need, need for me. He reaches around me and grips my ass covering it with his hands, I gasp. "No one gets to see this but me." My jaw slackens, his words and his nearness have my rationale short circuiting. He doesn't give me a chance to pull myself together or formulate a rational thought, his mouth is on mine in the next second. The feeling of his soft lips meshed against mine has an involuntary moan slipping from me. He uses that to his advantage and slips his tongue inside my mouth. The taste of him has me, reevaluating my plan. The second he tries to deepen the kiss a throat clearing from beside us has me pulling back and out of his hold. He shoots me a pissed off look, fuck it's so easy to give into him.

"I think you dropped this." Garrett holds out my sarong. I grab it from him and smile my thanks before quickly securing it around my waist. The tension between Darius and Garrett is so thick it's suffocating.

"There you are." I dart my gaze to the side of Darius to see Chelsea making her way toward him. She shoots me a scathing look as she stands beside him. Garrett moves to my side, I refuse to allow my judgment to slip and ruin my night. I suck in my pride, smile at Darius and shrug my shoulders. He's grinding his teeth so hard I think he may actually break them.

"See you around," I say as I turn to leave, but he snakes his arm out, grips my wrist and yanks me to him. Garrett steps forward ready to protest but Darius beats him to speak first.

"I'll break your fucking jaw before you can utter a word. Learn your place asshole, because it isn't beside her."

"Babe," Chelsea says in a sickly sweet voice. I narrow my eyes at Darius as I yank my arm free much to his dismay.

"Your girlfriend is calling you," I grit out before walking off, leaving him and that tramp alone. Anger simmers inside me at the thought of that bitch with her hands all over him. So, I do the only thing I can think of and find Beck. One look at me and he hands me the hip flask he had in the side of his board shorts. I take it, unscrew the cap and skull. It burns my throat but in the best possible way. It's stupid to drink away my issues but fuck it, YOLO.

CHAPTER EIGHTEEN

Darius

I have watched her all night. She's drunk that hip flask herself and is going to have the worst fucking hangover tomorrow. Beckett has remained by her side all night while she dances. Cody appeared about three minutes after Corvin did, with messy hair and sand caked to the back of her head, it doesn't take a genius to figure out what they were doing. Since Cody and Katie have been back she has been dancing. It pisses me off to see all the guys with their eyes on her. Everyone went nuts before when she jumped onto that guy Nathan and started grinding on him while he held her. The only reason that fucker isn't picking his teeth up off the floor is because he bats for the other team and I know he isn't interested in her.

She starts to sway on her feet. I lurch forward but Beckett is there to catch her and swing her into his arms bride style. I'm angry, frustrated and horny as fuck, those three things mixed together isn't a good cocktail. I stalk over to Beck to find Leah passed out in his arms, she looks so beautiful it hurts.

"I'm gonna take her back to her dorm." I cut my gaze to him and shake my head.

"No. She comes home with us," I say in a matter of fact tone.

"Nuh uh, she made me promise not to let any of you take her

back to your house," Katie says as she steps up beside Beck, Cody and Nathan stand next to her nodding.

"And where the fuck are you staying?" I snap at Nathan, the bastard bats his lashes.

"Well, under you of course." I choke on my spit. Beckett shakes with silent laughter and the girls find humor in my horrified face as they begin to laugh. "I'm staying with them. Trust me, gorgeous, your girl does not get my cock hard." I shudder at the thought of what does get him hard.

"Right, well I'm taking her home," Beck announces. I turn to follow after him but the sound of my name being shouted has the five of us pausing, Beck turns his head toward me and says in a stern tone. "Deal with that shit now." I grit my teeth and nod. Turning around, I spy Chelsea rushing toward me. She stops a foot away and smiles suggestively at me, but before she can utter a word I decide to lay it out.

"Take the fucking hint, you and me are never going to happen. The thought of you has my cock shriveling up, you were nothing but a hole to get me off. Jesus, I couldn't even get hard to use said hole." We have garnered the attention of the bystanders but I don't care, I've tried to get her to take a hint but she won't.

"You asshole, go waste your time on that washed up slut then!" Anger soars inside me, but before I can do anything or say something, a blur of brown hair whizzes past me, then punches Chelsea right in the nose. She drops to the sand like a sack of shit, screaming as she cups her bleeding nose.

"Call my friend a slut again, you washed up twat, and next time I'll make sure I break your fucking nose!" I stare at the back of Cody's head, stunned and proud as fuck. I didn't think the girl had it in her. Everyone around us erupts into cheers at the catfight. Cody turns on her heal and marches away, grabbing me by the arm and pulling me along with her.

"Well, baby girl, I did not see that coming," Nathan says proudly as he wraps an arm around Cody's shoulders.

"Neither did I. I'm sick of all of them calling her a slut when they don't know the fucking truth. They think because she was hooking up with Darius and a video of her being raped got aired that it somehow makes her a slut." I tune them out, unable to hear anymore. As we reach the road, Leah stirs in Beck's hold, a drunken smile breaks free as she stares up at him.

"I love you, Becky." *Becky?* Beckett snorts and shakes his head.

"Love you too." It amazes me how easily they can say those words to each other.

"You're so pretty, Becky." I keep my gaze forward and watch as Nathan and the girls stumble ahead of us, out of the three of them, Cody is the least drunk.

"That's those beer goggles talking, babe," he answers.

"Why can't you be *him*," she says sadly. I see Beck tense out of the corner of my eye. "He doesn't love me." Pain erupts inside me.

"Yeah, he does, babe. I told you before, you need to talk to him." She snorts and closes her eyes.

"No, he doesn't. He just wants to fuck me, then throw me away like last time." I dart in front of Beck making him slam to a stop. I don't ask his permission as I pull her to me and carry her back to her dorm. She lazily blinks her eyes opens. When a small frown mars her beautiful face she says, "You're not my Becky." Beckett snorts beside me.

"Nah, I'm not," I say. I hold her closer against my chest and she snuggles into me.

"You're prettier than Becky." That has a laugh tearing out of me and earning myself a whack on the back of the head from *Becky*.

"Yeah, I am way hotter than him, Goldie."

"I'm horny." Beckett and I both slam to a stop, I look to the heavens praying for strength.

"She's drunk."

"I'm aware, captain fucking obvious," I say as I force my feet to move. Within a second she is fast asleep in my arms. We reach her dorm way quicker than I would have liked. I follow Katie in as Cody holds the door open for us. I glare at her futon on the floor. "When the fuck is your dorm opening again?" I ask as I lay her gently on the mattress.

"After the break," Cody says, I can hear the annoyance in her voice. I pull the cover over her and brush her hair from her face, she smiles in her sleep.

"Darius?" she mumbles, I see Katie and Cody jumping into one of the beds and Nathan hops in the other.

"Yeah?" I answer.

"I love you." My breath gets caught in my throat, I know they all heard that, I can feel their eyes on me, waiting to see what I'll do next. I lean down and place a soft kiss to her forehead.

"I love you too," I whisper.

I wake the next morning feeling lighter than I have in weeks. The sun is out and the weather isn't too cold. I decide to cook breakfast for the guys. I've been a dick lately and need to make it up to them, and the quickest way to do that is through their stomachs. An hour goes by, while I slave away in the kitchen, when the four of them finally start to trickle in.

"Oh my heart, he cooks too."

"Ha ha, asshole," I say to Saint's stupid ass comment.

"Something smells good," Beck says before he yawns, then makes his way over to the coffee pot that I just finished making.

"Pour me one!" Crue calls to Beck as he takes the seat next to Saint. Corvin is the last to walk in, his hair is a mess and he looks like a dogs ass.

"I'm never drinking again." The four of us laugh at his dumb ass statement.

"Yeah and I'll never eat another pussy," Saint mocks. Too hungover to even reply, he flips Saint off over his shoulder.

"What's the plan for the day?" Beck asks as he hands everyone a cup of coffee. I thank him before answering.

"I invited the girls and Nathan over to hang out for the day." I focus back on cooking the eggs avoiding their stares.

"Huh, which girls exactly?" I turn and pin Crue with a dry stare.

"You might know one of them, yeah I think you do actually. She was the one grinding on both your cocks last night?" Saint grins proudly, while Crue ducks his gaze to look at the table.

"Well, if I recall Katie wasn't the only girl getting some action," Saint quips. Corvin pins me with a dark look.

"Dude, Leah was fucking wasted," he admonishes. I quirk a brow and shake my head.

"My cock was in my pants all night and they weren't talking about *my* girl, they were talking about *yours!*" Corvin's eyes widen for a second before he schools his features. He can't fool me, he's trying to act like he doesn't care about Cody but I saw him last night watching her every move—he couldn't keep his eyes off her. Which leaves me to wonder, why isn't he making shit official?

"After breakfast I'll head out and get some shit. We'll have a cookout today and chill out in the pool." We all agree with Beck, that actually sounds like a great idea.

"So, will anyone be using the *spare* room tonight?" Crue taunts. I look to the heavens praying for strength not to beat his ass.

"Shut the fuck up. I don't want to hear, see or know anything, at least that way I can pretend my sister is still a virgin." I snort and Beck coughs to masks his laughter. "I fucking hate you both," Corv moans as he moves to join the other two at the table.

"He is going to cockblock you bad," Beck says, low enough for only me to hear.

"I know and I already have blue balls," I whine.

Just before lunch time, a knock sounds at the door. Before any of the others get off their asses, I'm already halfway across the room shouting that I'll get it. I ignore their mocking laughter as I swing the door open, the smile drops off my face when I only see Cody, Katie and Nathan standing there.

"Well clearly we only got invited because of a certain blonde," Nathan taunts.

"Where's Leah?" I ask.

Cody rolls her eyes and pushes past me. "She'll be here soon," she calls over her shoulder. I look back to Katie for an explanation, she sighs and takes pity on me.

"She went to Garrett's to get her phone, I forgot to grab it off him last night for her." I nod, my good mood has slipped as I step aside and let them in. Nathan pauses in front of me, he says nothing as he waits for Katie to be out of ear shot.

The normal carefree look in his eyes is gone, a serious look overshadows his face. "You may not like me or my relationship with Leah but you need to know, I care about her and won't let a little dick like you hurt her." My brows raise to my hairline surprised he had the balls to man up to me. "Word of advice, whatever is holding you back, let it go before she lets *you* go." I stand here staring at his retreating form for a solid minute before I snap myself out of it.

An hour passes by and Leah is still nowhere to be seen, worry begins to churn inside me, I can't explain it but something doesn't feel right. I sit here on the edge of the pool while the others swim and laugh, without Leah here I have nothing to smile about. When the sound of Ella Mai's "Watchamacallit" pierces the air, I jump to my feet and rush over to the lounger. I set her ringtone to our song the night she gave me a lap dance. I hit answer and place it on speaker as I dry myself with my towel.

"Hey, Godlie."

"Darius!" I turn to stone, my blood freezes in my veins at the sound of fear in her voice. I drop the towel and pick the phone up. I feel the guys closing in around me.

"Baby, what's wrong?" I try to remain calm so I don't scare her.

"Darius, I need you!" she screams, I hear glass shatter in the background, she screams in fright.

"Leah, where are you?" I shout.

"Stop, please no—" she screams then the line goes dead. I hit redial immediately but it goes to voicemail. I try again, only to get the same thing. I throw my phone across the yard growling.

"Where the fuck is my sister?" Corvin yells, I turn to the pool where the girls lean against the edge looking horrified.

"I don't know, she said she was just going to get her phone and then come straight here," Cody says, her voice thick with worry. Nathan leaps out of the pool with a murderous look on his face, I rush over to him, wrap my hand around his throat and slam him against the banister of the deck getting right in his face.

"You have three seconds to tell me where the fuck my girl is or I'll start breaking your bones." He doesn't cower or flinch.

"I have a feeling Garrett finally snapped. I think she's with him."

"He's fucking dead!" I snarl.

CHAPTER NINETEEN

I skip up the path that will lead me to Garrett's frat house, guys sit on the porch laughing. I walk through the open door and look side to side for Garrett but can't spot him anywhere.

"You looking for Garrett?" a boy calls from the living room.

"Yeah," I answer.

"Upstairs, last door at the end of the hall," he calls out.

"Thanks," I mutter as I head up the stairs. I don't like the idea of going to his bedroom but I need my phone. The quicker I get it, the quicker I can get the hell out of here, I tell myself. My head is pounding, no amount of painkillers or water is getting rid of this bad boy and I have no one to blame but myself for being an idiot and thinking I could handle Jack. I follow the guy's directions and head toward the end of the hall. I stop outside the door, take a deep breath and square my shoulders as I reach up and knock.

"It's open," Garrett calls out. I turn the handle and open the door. Garrett sits at the desk in the corner of his room, shirtless. When he spots me in the doorway he lurches out of his seat clearly surprised to see me. "Leah."

"Hey," I say awkwardly.

"What are you doing here?"

"Uh, I forgot to get my phone off you last night." The smile on his face falters slightly.

"Yeah, of course." He sounds annoyed and I feel like an ass. He moves across his room to his dresser where my phone sits. He grabs it, instead of handing it over he holds it hostage in his hand. "Leah, can we talk?"

A resigned sigh escapes me as I nod. I like Garrett, he's a nice guy. Even while I was away he would send me his calculus notes, which was sweet of him. Except, he had no idea I switched majors and no longer take that class, thank God! He waves his arm toward the bed to have a seat, I act like I didn't see where he was pointing and sit on the chair he just vacated. His lips pinch in annoyance. I brush it off, not able to deal with his mood and my headache. He kicks the door closed before he drops on the edge of the bed with his arms resting on the tops of his thighs.

"I really don't have long, I'm meeting my brother–" I clamp my mouth closed when his upper lip pulls back and his eyes darken. Fear begins to swirl in my belly.

"Where did you sleep last night?" He tries to mask the anger in his tone but fails.

"In my own bed," I answer hesitantly. Garrett leans forward and I push back further into the chair wanting to put as much distance between us as I can.

"Huh, Chelsea said she saw you leave with Darius." I frown.

"And if I did, why would that bother you?" His eyes narrow.

"How many times does he have to treat you like shit before you realize that he is no good for you?" Fear works its way up my throat. I dart my gaze toward the closed door wondering if I would be able to make a break for it before he catches me.

"Garrett," I say softly, trying to ease his anger. "I'm not with Darius."

"But you want to be!" I recoil at the sound of his booming voice.

"I think I should leave," I say as I attempt to climb to my feet. He shoves me back into the chair. I snap my gaze to his in fright, this was a bad idea, I should have listened to my gut. Nathan's warning from last night springs to mind. I'm such a fool! Garrett leans into me, his nose brushes mine, he drops my phone into my lap as he cups my face. Before I can shove him back he smashes his lips against mine. Immediately my mind screams at me to push him back, I try but his grip on my face tightens. I feel his tongue prod at my lips trying to gain entry, and a thought hits me. I open my mouth and fight not to gag when his tongue slips inside. He moans, then I bite down on his tongue as hard as I can. He tries to yank free but I won't let go. When he slaps me across the face I release his tongue as I tumble off the chair and hit the floor. He stumbles away from me, covering his bleeding mouth. I spy my phone and grab it, I quickly unlock it and don't even hesitate to dial his number.

"Hey, Goldie."

"Darius!" I scream, Garrett darts his gaze to me and I panic.

"Baby, what's wrong?"

"Darius, I need you!" I shout as Garrett storms toward me. I shuffle back on my ass as fast as I can along the floor.

"Leah, where are you?" I hear Darius shout, Garrett cocks his arm back.

"Stop, no please—" I scream as he hits me again. My phone goes flying out of my hand, my ear ringing from the force of his hit. He stomps on my phone, smashing the screen before he turns back to me. He grips a handful of my hair and yanks me to my feet. I cry out in pain. He uses his grip on my hair to throw me across the room. I smack into his shelf before hitting the ground, the contents from his shelf lands on me, drawing a pained whimper from me.

"You like whoring around, do you?" he screams as he grips my hair and drags me along the floor. Tears cascade down my face as I try to free myself. He pulls me to my feet by my hair, I cry out when I feel strands of my hair ripped from my head. The look in his eyes is one I've never seen before, he's unhinged and clearly lost the plot.

"Garrett," I whimper. He bares his teeth at me before spitting right in my face.

"I tried to be nice, I gave you time and now I'm gonna take what I'm owed." He shoves me backward and I flop onto the bed. Before I can move he's on top of me pinning my arms above my head.

"Get the fuck off me!" I scream hysterically as fear chokes me, I can't go through this again. He holds my wrists in one of his hands and uses his free hand to tear my shirt down, exposing my bra. "Darius is going to fucking kill you!" I scream right in his face. He doesn't use words, he silences me by punching me. Pain explodes in jaw, black spots dance in the corner of my eyes, and I pray that I pass out. I would rather be unconscious while he rapes me.

"You fucking cunt. I'm gonna destroy you. When I'm done fucking you, he won't take a second look." A sob tears out of me as he reaches between our bodies and pops the button on my cut-offs. Uncontrollable sobs continue to fall from me as he forces my shorts down my legs. I close my eyes, not wanting to witness him defile my body. Bile rises up my throat and I'm powerless to stop the vomit that forces it way out of me. I manage to turn my head at the last second as the contents of my breakfast messily lands on his bed. "Fucking bitch!" he snarls, grips the thin strap of my thong and rips it. A switch inside me flicks, I begin to scream and claw and fight with everything I have.

"Fuck you! Darius!" I scream over and over again. He manages to land a few more hits to my face and body but I don't feel a thing. I continue to try to maim him anyway I can even when I hear the door kicked open. Everything happens within a second. I'm clawing at his face while he's punching me, then he's gone and I'm yanked off the bed. I see nothing but Garrett's face.

I kick, scream and hit trying to break free. "Darius!" I scream so fucking loud my throat feels numb.

"Open your eyes, Goldie, I'm right here!" I trick myself into thinking I can hear his voice. "I'm here, baby, open your eyes. I'm right here!" I slowly blink my eyes open, the sight of his coffee-colored eyes is the first thing I see before I scream and throw myself at him. He arms band around me and hold me tightly against his chest. "I got you, Goldie." I can barely hear him over my own screams.

"Get her the fuck out of here," I hear my brother shout. I attempt to turn my head but Darius pushes my face into his chest.

"Beckett, give me your shirt," Darius grits out. I feel him shift a moment later. He tries to push me back but I won't let him. "Baby, I need to put this on you to… cover you." When he gently pushes me back a step, I allow an inch of space between us but no more, and my body begins to shake uncontrollably. Darius has a murderous look in his eyes. He gently pulls the shirt over my head. I hiss when the material scrapes my cheek. He curses beneath his breath as I push my arms through the holes, Beckett's shirt reaches past my knees. "I'm gonna carry–" Before he can finish, I launch myself at him, locking my arms and legs around him then bury my face in his neck. He pulls the shirt down over my ass and keeps one hand there while the other grips the back of my neck.

I can hear grunts and sounds of a struggle but I don't dare look. Darius walks us out of the room. I tighten my hold on him when we descend the stairs, even when I feel the sun on me I don't look up. I hear a car door open, but still I refuse to leave my hiding spot.

"You need to get in there. Crue and Beck are trying to pull him off that cunt," Darius growls.

"On it," I hear Saint say before the sound of his footfalls meet my ears.

"Goldie?" he says softly, when I don't move he sighs. "You

gonna sit on my lap the whole way home?" I nod, a small chuckle escapes him as he maneuvers us in the car. "Baby, can you unlock your legs, we can't fit this way." I do as he says and shift so I'm sitting across his lap. I rest my sore face against his pec and stay silent. Neither of us say a word when the others return. Beckett slips into the driver's seat beside us, flicking his gaze to me and glowers.

"Let's go!" Corvin shouts from the back. Beck pulls his gaze from me and slams the car into gear before he drives away. Everyone is silent the whole way back to the guys' house. Beck kills the engine and no one makes a move to exit the car. I can't stop the tears from falling, quiet sobs continue to work their way out of me as I cling to Darius.

"If we don't get out, they're coming in." I flick my gaze up to see my friends standing at the bottom of the porch steps. Crue's right, the looks on their faces tell me we have mere seconds to decide before this car becomes overcrowded. I sit forward on Darius's lap and swivel around so I can see out the windscreen. A small hiss escapes me, my side is burning and it hurts to breathe. I think he may have fractured one of my ribs.

"Beckett, take Darius and Leah inside." I spy Beck nodding his agreement to Corv's order out of the corner of my eye. Darius shifts behind me and reaches over to open the door. I attempt to get out of the car but a whimper escapes me.

"Fuck!" Darius curses as he gently grips my arms and holds me in place. "Beck, get your ass over here and help her." Beckett rushes around to our side and offers me a hand with a warm smile, I take it. He and Darius help me out of the car. The second I stand on my own two feet, I feel like I am able to take a breath easier.

"Want me to carry you?" Beck asks. I shake my head and cringe when pain erupts in the side of my face. "Let's get you inside," he says as he wraps an arm around my waist leading me toward the house. I peer over my shoulder to see Corvin and Darius standing by the car staring at me. At the look of fury and pain on their faces I turn away. Cody and Katie stand there with tears trailing down their cheeks at the sight of me. Nathan rushes up to me, forcing us to a stop.

His eyes search mine for a second then he rushes past me toward the others. "I'm coming with you," he says. I don't have the energy to digest what they are up to. I smile at the girls, both of them stand there holding each other with heartache clear as day on their faces.

"You should see the other guy," I rasp out, trying to lighten the mood. It doesn't work, they both sob. Beck ushers me forward and up the porch steps, helps me inside and pauses in the living room.

"What do you need, babe?" he asks gently.

"A shower," I answer instantly. I need to scrub his touch from my skin. A shiver of disgust rolls through me.

"Okay, come on," he says quietly as he leads me to the stairs, helping me the whole way to the bathroom I shared with Darius. He releases his hold on me as he reaches into the stall and turns the shower on. I try to pull the shirt off but the pain in my side flares to life every time I move to lift my left arm. Beck steps in front of me and the distraught look on his face kills me. I don't even have the guts to look at the mirror. If I hurt this much I can only imagine what I must look like to them.

"Can you help me?" I ask, a whoosh of air escapes him as he nods. He grips the hem of his shirt and slowly pulls it over my head, when a growl escapes him I peer down at my body and flinch. My left side is bruised already, my thong is torn, hanging to one side exposing the top of my pussy. My shirt is hanging on by one thin piece, the strap on my bra is torn and scratch marks cover my body. Beck reaches out and tears my shirt. I shrug the material off and stand here before him in my ruined underwear.

"I'm so sorry, babe." The pain in his voice has me feeling the need to comfort him, I don't get the chance.

"I got it from here," Darius says as he comes to stand beside Beck. He runs his gaze over me, making me feel like I need to shield myself. I try to cover myself with my arms, but he isn't having that. He darts forward, and I flinch involuntarily when he reaches out to me. A horrified look crosses his face. "Goldie…" he breathes out my name brokenly.

"I'm sorry," I choke out, shaking my head. He slowly lifts his hands again to gently cup my face, careful not to apply too much pressure and cause me any more pain. He leans down resting his forehead against mine, I breathe him in trying to draw on what little strength I have inside me.

"Do you want me to help you get her in the shower?" Darius takes a shuddering breath as he slowly draws back but keeps his eyes on me.

"It's up to her." Darius answers quietly.

CHAPTER TWENTY

When she doesn't answer I try asking again. "Do you want Beck in here to help?" I can hear the strain in my own voice. I hated having to ask that but right now, I would give her anything she wanted. The fear in her eyes when I reached for her will haunt me for the rest of my life. She darts her tongue out to moisten her lips before flicking her eyes over my shoulder to Beckett. My heart drops, she would rather he help her than me.

"Becky, can you get me some water and painkillers, please?" I try to keep the surprise from my face.

"You got it, babe. I'll leave them on the side table in D's room," he says before he rushes off to do as she asks.

"Can you close the doors, please?" she asks quietly. I nod and do as she asked, closing and locking both doors before stepping in front of her again. I'm unsure of what the hell to do next. I fear with how angry I am, that if I touch her, I may cause her more harm. As if she can read my thoughts she speaks again. "Can you unhook my bra?" I nod and reach around her. She rests her forehead against my chest as I slowly push the straps down her arms, then kneel in front of her and slowly pull her ruined thong down her legs. I run my gaze along the inside of her thighs trying to spot any sign of bruising or… blood. "He never got the chance. I fought him, Darius," she cries. I stand in front of her, hating the broken look in her eyes. "I fucking fought him… I didn't… I wouldn't let…" Sobs wrack her tiny frame and I curse before throwing caution to wind.

I strip off and gently wrap my arm around her trembling form and usher her into the shower. I gently angle her under the spray and have to take several calming breaths when blood begins to cover the tiled floor. Her cheek is split, her eyebrow is cut. Her nose has crusted blood but it's not broken. Her bottom lip is covered in blood but no sign of a split. I gently run my hand through her hair, trying to get rid of the chunks in it. She reaches out and holds my waist letting me just comb my fingers through her hair.

"You're the strongest person I know, Goldie." She rests her head against my naked chest.

"I don't feel very strong." I gently lift her chin until her eyes are on mine, making sure she can see the seriousness in my eyes.

"You are, Leah. You have been through some fucked up shit and still you stand before me, unbroken and smiling. What Gary did to you…" I take a deep breath knowing this is overdue and needs to be said. "I should never have walked out on you that night. I allowed my trust issues from my past to bleed into what we shared. You needed me and I wasn't there. The things I did and said to you when you got here was fucked up." Fresh tears roll down her cheeks. "That night when that cunt played that tape, I should have been the one you came to, it should have been me that held you and helped you, not Beck. I'll never forgive myself for that, Goldie. I've fucked up a lot but I'm standing here before you asking you to give me one more chance, allow me to prove to you that I am worth it. Let me love you like I should have years ago."

"I want to believe you, I really do," she breathes out.

"Today, when shit went down you didn't call Beck or your brother, you called me. Why?" Her mouth opens but no words come so I push on. "You were screaming for *me*. You called my name, not Corvin's or Beckett's. Want to know why?" I don't give her a chance to answer. "Because deep down you know that no matter what I said or did to you, when you need me, I'll always be there. I'll always come when you call." It breaks me to say this but I know I have to. "If I've blown this and lost my chance, just tell me. I know Beck and you are close, it will flay me open to see you with him but—"

"I love, Becky," she cuts in, and my heart shatters inside my chest. I drop my gaze to the floor, unable to move or speak through the pain. "But not like you think." I snap my gaze back to hers. "Beck is like a… I don't know how to explain it but he's my Becky."

"And what am I?" I push.

"My everything," she whispers. My eyes search hers trying to see if she is lying but I see no sign of deceit.

"What does that mean, Goldie?" Her shoulders deflate.

"It means that I hate what you did to me and how you treated me but no matter how hard I tried, I couldn't hate you. I wanted so badly to just to stop the hurt I was feeling but I couldn't. I can never hate you because I love you too fucking much."

"You love me?"

"I've loved you since I was fourteen, Darius. I won't be your secret anymore, I can't." I brush my thumb along her bottom lip.

"I'll never hide you again. I swear just tell me you're mine."

"Only if you tell me the truth about everything?"

"Deal, now say it." She smiles then flinches, and I growl, "Fuck, let's get you cleaned up and out of here, then into bed."

"I need to scrub his touch from my skin, can you help me?" I nod unable to speak for fear of losing the tiny grip I have on my temper. A part of me wishes I had gone with Corvin to finish the job, but I knew she needed me. Knowing that it was me she called and me she was screaming for had me turning down the offer and racing inside to be there for my girl. I'll never be able to unhear her screams. As I ran up the stairs of that frat house, hearing her screaming my name, I didn't think as I followed her screams, then kicked the door open. I froze for one second, then I was throwing that cunt off her. I didn't care about him, I just knew she needed me. Corvin and Crue beat the cunt and kept going even after he passed the fuck out. They gagged him and tied his ass up in his closet before they left. The three of them and Nathan have gone back to *dispose* of the evidence. Garrett will never be a problem again.

After making me scrub her twice and washing her hair she finally let me get her out of the shower. I dried her gently before dressing her in one of my shirts and putting her in my bed. She took the painkillers Beck left for her and five minutes later she was asleep. I sit here in the dark just watching her sleep. I'm unable to take my eyes off her for more than a second, guilt eats away at me for how I've treated her. I don't know what I would have done if that motherfucker raped her. I scrub my hands down my face trying to rid myself of those thoughts.

"I'm such a fuck up," I mutter to myself.

"Nah, man." I snap my gaze to the doorway to see Corvin standing there, the soft glow of the hall light casting him in a dark light. I look him over and slowly climb to my feet at the sight of blood on his shirt. He meets my stare as I step in front of him. His eyes are haunted and have a look in them I have never seen.

"What happened, Corv?" I ask softly.

"I did what I had to do." The conviction in which he says this has a pang of dread shooting down my spine. "Your brother's next." I furrow my brow.

"What?" His eyes harden, he reaches out and clutches my shirt in his hands.

"Gary told Garrett that my sister was fair game. That mother-fucker thought he had a right to touch my sister because your brother told him she was *easy*." My eyes widen and my jaw slackens.

"When?" I ask.

"Garrett was the fucking witness, Darius! He was the one who caught Vic and Gary talking about what he did to Leah. Needless to say with that bastard suing you, that video of him admitting to what he did is long gone now!" I shake my head trying to deny what he is saying, that video was the key piece of evidence that we had to drop this case against us. I know this case against us is a big deal but the merger is complete, we have the money to back us. There isn't a thing Victor can do about that.

"I get it, Corvin, I do, but that shit has to wait. Right now, the only thing I care about is your sister and making sure she's okay." His face pulls taut, he uses his grip on my shirt to pull me closer leaving only a sliver of space between us.

"She comes first before everything in your life." I nod. "She didn't call me, Darius, she screamed for *you*, not me." The anguish I hear in his voice has me reaching out to grip the back of his neck and pushing my forehead against his.

"She called me because she knew no matter what happens between us, that I'll always come running. I put her through some fucked up shit and I have a lot to make up for."

"Yeah, you do." Comes from behind us. I tear out of Corv's hold as I rush toward her. He flicks the light on before he joins us and sits on the opposite side of the bed. I perch on the edge of the bed and reach out to grip her hand in mine. Her face is busted up and bruised. I hate the pained look I see in her eyes, her vibrant green eyes have dulled.

"How you feeling?" Corv asks softly. She tries to smile reassuringly but it doesn't reach her eyes.

"Sore, but also glad to see you two not fighting." Corv and I both chuckle.

"He's a dick but... seeing what he went through to get to you today showed me, I have to get over my hang up on you two...

being together." Leah's face is a picture of surprise. "You two are together, right?" he asks as he looks between me and her.

"Yes."

"No," we answer in unison. I narrow my eyes at her.

"The fuck do you mean *no*?" I grit out. I ignore Corvin as he whistles between his teeth. Leah's face is blank as she stares at me. "We talked this shit out in the shower!" I growl.

"Fuck me!" Corvin grounds out but we ignore him.

"I told you, I want the truth and until I get that, no, we're not together." I take some deep breaths through my nose to try calm my anger.

"It's not just his story to tell," Corvin answers for me. "You want answers about why we started our business then you need to hear it from all of us, but only when you're better." She nods. "Do you really want to know?"

"About your business or about the blood that is covering your hands and clothes?" she retorts, causing Corv to flinch. "Look, if it's something you guys don't want to share then that's fine, I get it."

Fuck this. "Everyone has their own reasons for wanting to start this, mine is a lot more petty than the others," I answer. She searches my gaze trying to find any sign of deceit, which she won't.

"Okay." I frown.

"What does that mean, Goldie." She shrugs.

"It means, I'll wait for you to tell me when you're ready." I nod, I may be reading between the lines here but I feel like there is a double meaning to what she's saying.

"Thank you?" It comes out more like a question than I want it to.

"So, now that we have that sorted, can I pee and go to the spare room?" My eyes snap wide.

"What?" I cringe at how loud I say that, the little devil just smiles at me.

"Well, we're not together and it would be wrong for me to

share your bed." Corvin's laughter just pisses me off, the fucker isn't going to be laughing in a second.

"We weren't together while Corvin was away at camp and you sure as shit didn't fucking mind staying in *my* bed then." Corvin leaps off the bed like it burnt him, laughter tears from me at the disgusted look on his face.

"Fuck you! Get the fuck out. My sister doesn't like you and needs to pee." I lull my head toward him and smirk as I say.

"So, you gonna help her out of her thong so she can pee…" I let my sentence trail off, and the glare he shoots my way has me shaking with silent laughter.

"Millions of people in the world and she chooses you!" He looks back to Leah with a hopeful look in his eyes. "I'll find you someone else, anyone else, just not this prick." Laughter bursts from Leah before she hisses and grips her left side in pain. Corvin and I are on her in a second.

"Call the doc," I snap.

"On it," he says as he races from the room to do as I asked. I reach out and brush her hair back from her face, hating that I can't take her pain away.

CHAPTER TWENTY-ONE

Darius insisted he be the one to help me pee. I have never been more mortified in my life than having him help me. He never commented once, even though shame burned through me. He stayed by my side the whole time as the doctor checked me out. I have bruised ribs which should heal in a couple weeks, nothing broken in my face, just badly bruised. I nearly died of shame when the doctor told me I would need to wait at least a week before resuming sexual activities.

"I'm so sorry I wasn't there, we should have come with you." I clasp Katie's hand in mine and smile. Her, Cody and Nathan barged in the second the doctor, Corvin and Darius went into the hall to *talk*.

"This isn't your fault," I tell her.

"I fucking hate that dog shit bastard." My eyes widen at Cody's outburst.

"He won't be hurting you or anyone else ever again." I turn to look at Nathan who is leaning against the wall across from me. He doesn't have his usual... spunk on display, he looks weighed down.

"What does that mean?" I ask hesitantly. He sighs before running a hand through his blonde hair, his green eyes are hollow and plagued. I hate seeing that look on him. He tears his gaze from me to stare out the window, ignoring my question. I decide to let it go, I don't need more shit to deal with on top of everything else.

"So, you and Darius, huh?" Cody teases. I shake my head causing a frown to mar her beautiful face.

"We're just… friends," I answer. A snort comes from Nathan, drawing our attention to him.

"Baby, no *friends* look at each other the way you two do and trust me, that man stares at you with hunger." His words have a fire stirring in my belly. "From what I heard, Mr. tall dark and handsome sure as fuck doesn't want to be friends."

"Who told you that?" He shoots me a dry stare.

"He told Beckett that if he ever touched you again he would break his arms and make it look like an accident." I gasp, what the fuck! "Want my advice?"

"Uh, sure?" I answer warily.

"Get out of your own way and stop denying what is inevitable. You two are cosmic. That type of love happens once in a lifetime, don't blow it." His words hit me hard as I hear the truth in them. I know he's right but I just need time.

The pain in my side rouses me awake, I cringe when I shift slightly then freeze when I feel something pressed against my back. I peer over my shoulder and roll my eyes at the sight of Darius asleep behind me. I kept my word and slept in the spare room, the girls and Nathan said they would stay with me. Darius was pissed but didn't argue, now I get why he didn't. He never planned to sleep in his own bed. I slowly edge myself out of the bed and sit up slowly so I don't aggravate the pain in my side. Swinging my legs over the side of the bed, I stifle my gasp.

My heart burst inside my chest, laying there on the floor beside me on a mattress is a sleeping Beck. I carefully stand and make sure not to step on him as I try to make my way out of the room. I freeze when I reach the end of the bed, my friends did sleep in here just not alone. Katie is sandwiched between Crue and Saint, Corvin is wrapped around Cody as they sleep. I spy Nathan's feet peeking out from the other side of the bed, and a smile breaks free. I am so fucking lucky to have these amazing people in my life. I am honestly so blessed. I slowly make my way through to the bathroom and out Darius's open bedroom so I don't wake anyone using my bedroom door.

It takes me an age to get down the stairs, but I manage. As soon as I enter the kitchen, I flick the coffee pot on before grabbing some of the pain pills from the drawer. I down two with a glass of water, praying they will kick in soon. My face is tender and achy today, the doctor said that was to be expected. Getting punched in the face from Gary was a walk in the park compared to this. I pour myself a cup of coffee once it's ready and decide to head out the back and enjoy the crisp morning air. It's going to be too cold soon to be out here, so I want to enjoy it while I can.

I slowly lower myself into one of the loungers, I snag the throw blanket off the other chair and wrap it around my legs before reclining back and sipping my coffee. I sit here silently reflecting on the events of yesterday. They were horrific and will take me time to get over, but if those events didn't occur would Darius have had the balls to tell me how he really feels?

"I planned to tell you yesterday." I startle at the sound of his voice. I lean forward and shoot him a dirty look for scaring me.

"Tell me what?" He pins me with a *really* look before coming over. He doesn't ask or even see if I mind, he just hops in behind me and settles me between his legs, caging my own between his.

"You were thinking out loud again, now lean back and share that blanket." I sigh but do as he says. I'll admit this is much more comfy leaning on him than the plastic of the chair. He absentmindedly runs his fingers up and down my arms as I sip my coffee. "Why are you up so early?"

"You wouldn't know I was up this early if you were in your

own bed," I sassily reply. He laughs lightly, leans down and places a kiss to my cheek, before whispering in my ear.

"Get used to it, because you're moving in with me." The feeling of his lips scraping against the shell of my ear almost has me distracted enough to not comprehend his words—almost.

"I'm not moving in with you," I say firmly.

"Fine, you want the truth, Leah? I'll give it to you but once I do tell you, you better give up this whole bullshit."

"What bullshit?" I snap.

"The next time you tell someone we are just *friends*, I'll fuck you right there in front of them just so they know how *friendly* we really are!" His words should piss me off, but all they do is turn me the fuck on. Something is seriously wrong with me.

"You heard that, huh?" I ask, trying my hardest to not laugh.

"I mean it, you're mine, Leah, and I'm tired of lying to myself and everyone else about it. I let you go once and I won't be dumb enough to do it a second time." His words have my heart soaring.

"What about Corvin?"

"He knows how I feel about you and even if he isn't good with it, I made my choice, Goldie."

I dart my tongue out to moisten my lips. "What did you choose?" I ask quietly. He wraps his arms around me gently and buries his face into the crook of my neck, where he places an open-mouthed kiss.

"I picked the right sibling this time." Tears prick the backs of my eyes. "I'll never make you doubt your importance to me again. You'll always be my first choice, Leah."

"Tell me the truth and I'll give you my answer." He snorts.

"I'll just fuck a yes out of you but whatever helps you feel like you're in control, for now." I balk at his boldness. "Here we go. Once upon a time." I can't stop the laugh that breaks free and immediately regret it when the pain in my side flares to life. "No laughing or I stop." I nod. "Okay, so you know about my mom and me moving in with you guys." I nod. "Okay, well I lied to you. I found out who my dad was when I was twelve. My mom let it slip in one of her episodes about him and how he took the good twin. I didn't believe her at first until I did some digging."

"Did Corvin know?" I feel him nod behind me.

"Yeah, he knew. He helped me get the records of my birth. I hadn't planned to do anything at that time, it wasn't until we met Saint, Crue and Beckett that we came up with a plan."

"Why?" I ask still unable to piece all the dots together myself.

"Saint would go on about how he hated his father and what he did. He didn't tell us why until one night we all got drunk. I spilled about who my father was, and that was when Saint came clean. Honestly, the only ones with a vendetta are me and Saint. Crue, Beck and Corvin are doing this to help their families and support us as well, but also set themselves up with a great future."

"What did Saint say?"

"He said that his dad knew Victor and that they did shady dealings together. He went on to tell us about his dad's tech company and how he made an app. This app wasn't like any of the others he had ever made before. To get this app you had to pay a hundred grand."

"For what exactly?" I can feel this story is about to take a dark turn.

"This app is used to distribute any information. You can post videos that can't be traced, download illegal content of children." I gasp, horrified at what he is saying. "You see, Victor is a sick fuck and he used his hotels and resorts to film children. Devon sold the content on his app. This made them both millions. We decided there and then that we would do whatever it took to take down mine and Saint's father. We worked our asses off, studied the stock market and learned how to invest. We didn't have the money, so we started out small and truthfully, we got a lucky break that made us the money we needed to expand. We kept expanding until we had enough money to buy Victor's company that has been in his family for generations–still is, I guess. He has a gambling problem and was in debt up to his eyeballs. He had to either sell or go bankrupt, needless to say when we put in the offer he jumped at it."

"I don't know what to say, I had no idea." I feel so disgusted and heartbroken for those poor children that were used.

"There isn't anything to say. With Katie helping us now, we are so much closer to being able to take Devon down. Saint is planning a hostile takeover with the board of Devon's company as soon as he has the proof."

"Then what?"

"Then Saint is selling the company. He wants nothing to do with his father's empire. His dad has tried to blackmail him for years and get him to give up his dream of being drafted and go work for him." I sit here silently for a long moment trying to digest what he's told me.

"What about Gary suing you?" I ask.

"He can try. We have the money this time and he doesn't. His daddy is broke. We'll hold him up in legal paperwork until he runs out of money. This is his last ditched effort to try and one up me. He'll never get the upper hand, we made sure of that." A shiver runs through me at his words, they sound so final.

CHAPTER TWENTY-TWO

Darius

I start to get worried when she says nothing for a long time. I know I just laid shit out for her but if telling her the truth means I get my girl, then I have no regrets.

"Gary used me to get to you, didn't he?"

"Yeah, Goldie."

"Did Gary know about you being his twin?" I shake my head even though she can't see me.

"No, he hated me and Corvin because of football. He had no idea that we were even related at that time. Gary is fucked up, Goldie." She snorts.

"Yeah, I'm well aware of that fact."

"Gary knew my mom sold her body for drugs. After what he did to you, he tried to *buy* my mom." She gasps and slowly turns sideways so she can face me, her face a picture of disgust.

"He tried to sleep with his own mother?" I roll my lips over my teeth and nod. "Oh, that is just gross."

"Yeah, it is," I admit.

"Did he... do it?"

"No."

"Thank God—"

"It wasn't from his lack of trying. But, apparently even Jenny Lockhart has a moral compass and draws the line at fucking her own son," I say with an edge to my voice.

"Wait, so your mom knew who Gary was the whole time?" I grit my teeth and nod, her eyes soften. "How?"

I take a deep breath before giving her the story she eagerly wants. "When Gary and I turned one, Victor turned up at the trailer park demanding one of us."

"Why?" I hear tinges of pain in her voice, but it isn't for herself, it's for me.

"Victor's father told him that he wouldn't hand over the company to him unless he had an heir that he could pass the company onto." Anger flares to life in her eyes.

"Victor never wanted Gary, he just wanted to inherit his fortune." I nod. "How did he know your mom?"

"Jenny said she met him at a bar she used to sing at, some swanky joint in the city. He would screw her every time he was in town. She got knocked up and Victor fled, leaving her alone and pregnant. She lost her job and had no choice but to move out of the city into a trailer park where she raised us for a year, until Victor came and stole Gary." Her eyes widen and her mouth pinches to the side. I can see the cogs of her mind turning over. "Just say it."

"When did your mom start doing drugs and... prostituting herself?" I frown.

"Why?" She reaches out and cups my face between her hands, sadness clouds her features.

"Just answer, please." I try to think back to when I first remember her starting to dabble in narcotics.

"Maybe around the time I turned two. She didn't shoot up at first, she just started to drink. Then, when that didn't give her a buzz, she started on the hard shit and well, you know the rest."

"Oh, Darius," she says brokenly. I lean forward and gently grip her waist as I place a soft kiss to her lips.

"Don't pity me, baby. Look at me now," I say in a light tone, trying to ease some of the tension. She shakes her head.

"Darius, you don't get it, do you?"

I furrow my brow, not picking up what she is putting down. "Get what, Goldie?" I ask, slightly exasperated and over this whole conversation. Dragging up the past does nothing. All it ever does is make me hate Jenny and Victor more for not loving me like the Williams's love their children.

"Darius, your mom turned to drinking and drugs because she was broken hearted."

"What?" I practically shout.

"Did she willingly hand Gary over?" I scrunch my face up as I try to remember that day. I can't, all I know is what she told me.

"She said she hated Victor because he took her purpose away. I… I don't think she gave him up, I think Victor just… took him."

"Your mom was trying to dull her pain through alcohol and drugs, Darius." I cock my head to the side and stare at her, trying to process her words. "The day you moved in with us, what did your mom say?" I scoff.

"The bitch packed my shit for me," I bite out.

"So, she said nothing else to you?" I roll my eyes and try to think back to that day. I remember the Williams's calling her and her agreeing to let me live with them. When we drove to the trailer park, I went and grabbed my bags and then—my eyes widen.

"She told me… that your parents could give me a better life. She said sorry and… cried." My stomach drops and a lump forms in my throat. Holy fuck. Is Leah right? Did my mom actually love me?

"Darius?" she whispers my name, trying to draw my gaze back to her. When I take too long, she grips my chin and lifts my face to hers. Her eyes are filled with pity and it causes me to flinch.

"I don't need your pity," I snarl. She doesn't pull away or reprimand me for my harsh tone.

"I don't pity you, babe. I pity Jenny for what she went through." Is it wrong that the only thing I heard out of what she just said was *babe*?

I smirk. "Babe, huh?" She rolls her eyes.

"I'm serious," she says sternly.

"What do you want me to say? It's too late now. I'm not a little kid anymore, Goldie. I gave up hope a long time ago."

"It's never too late. If you want to find her, I'll help you and be there with you every step of the way. I promise!" I mull over her words. What if she's right and Jenny really was just fucked up and trying to ease the pain of losing a child? She didn't have the money to fight Victor and she was dumb enough to put his name on our birth certificates, so it's not like he was kidnapping in a way and knowing Victor, he would have threatened her to not go to the cops.

"I'll… think about it." Before we can discuss this any further, the back door opens and a pale looking Crue stands there. "What's wrong?"

"We have a problem." The solemn tone of his voice has us both climbing to our feet. I help Leah and then lead her inside where we find the others sitting in the living room with news playing on the TV.

'The remains of college student Garrett Jones has been found near the local park. It appears that this wasn't from natural causes and the police are treating this as a homicide. Anyone with information is urged to come forward–

Corvin turns the TV off before the rest can be heard. No one says a word. We all stand around, reeling over what we just heard. My first thought is thank fuck the cunt is dead and the second, what the fuck did Corvin and the others do?

"What did you do?" Leah breathes out as she looks at her brother. Corvin doesn't look broken up or even worried. He cuts his gaze to Cody and Katie, both the girls look to be in shock. His gaze hardens as he continues to stare at Cody, daring her to say something. She swallows audibly before standing on shaky legs, she squares her shoulders and lifts her chin as she meets Corvin's harsh stare.

"We know nothing. We came over yesterday to continue the celebrations from the Thanksgiving party and everyone was here the *whole* night." Corvin pulls his gaze from Cody to look at Katie. Unlike Cody, her gaze is fixated on the two guys standing beside Corvin. Crue and Saint have a mask of indifference in place, keeping their emotions locked down. She pushes to her feet and ignores Corvin as she stands before the duo. Those two boys would die for each other, there is nothing and no one in this world that could ever come between them. If Katie has any hope of making it a trio, her answer better be the same as Cody's.

"Whatever you need me to say, I'll say it. I won't lie, I'm not sad that asshole is dead and if that makes me a shitty person, so be it." The tension drains from Saint's shoulders. Crue grips Katie's face and plasterers his mouth to hers. Well, clearly that was the right answer after all. I look to Corvin to find his gaze already on me, I see it. I can read him better than anyone, they did it. They killed Garrett.

🏈

After setting Leah up in the living room with Cody and Katie, the five of us and Nathan make our way to the basement. Once we're inside, Crue closes the door while Saint sets his phone up to the Bluetooth speaker, no one speaks until the music begins to play.

"What happened last night?" I ask as I look between Nathan, Crue, Saint and Corvin. I'll admit I'm shocked as fuck that Nathan was a part of this, we never do any dodgy shit with someone else around only each other.

"It's not what you think," Crue begins but Corvin cuts him off.

"We got back there, the fucker was dead in the closet. What the fuck were we supposed to do?"

"He was breathing when we left," Beck interjects. Corvin just shrugs his shoulders.

"Well, he wasn't when we got back." Corvin forgets I can read him, I know he's lying but the thing I don't get is why? "We disposed of the body and made sure nothing would link back to us."

"The whole fucking house saw us running through there to get to Leah!" I rebuke.

"They're taken care of," Saint answers.

"How?" Saint's mask falters, I stare at him for a second as I try to piece this all together. How the hell would they have got a whole fucking house to remain silent and not snitch about a murder?

"Look, we did what we had to," Crue says in a matter of fact tone.

"And what about him?" I ask as I nod my head toward Nathan, he glares at me.

"Well I won't be saying shit, will I?" he snaps.

"We're just supposed to believe that?" Beck asks.

"Asshole over there snapped a pic of me carrying the body, so I'd say I'm good at keeping my mouth shut." Corvin nods his agreement, this shit is too much to deal with.

"All of you get your clothes from last night and burn them now, all the bedding you slept in needs to be burned. Whatever car you took needs to be detailed stat. You need Katie to hack into any cameras around the area that you went to and scrub the footage. We all need to get our story about yesterday straight and come up with a damn good lie about Leah's face."

"Since when did you become a pro on covering up a murder?" Saint jokes.

"Since this isn't my first cover up," Beckett answers in a flat tone, he marches out of the room as the rest of us stare at his retreating form, stunned.

"He wasn't joking, was he?" Crue whispers. I shake my head.

"I think there is still a shit load we don't know about Beck and something tells me, he was telling the truth just then," I utter.

We come up with a plan that the girls and Nathan will stay with us for the rest of the break, that way if the cops come knocking, we'll all be together. Saint and Crue left an hour ago with Katie to go back to the dorms to pack them some shit. Nathan left not long after them to go grab some shit for himself.

"This is so not how I envisioned my homecoming to be," Leah mumbles. I wrap my arm around her shoulders, she rests her head on my chest. Corv and Cody sit on the sofa opposite us while Beck sits on the bean bag near the fireplace stoking it, burning the clothes and bedding.

"Me either," Cody answers, shooting her friend a rueful smile.

"How did you picture it?" I ask.

"I can't answer that with my brother in the same room." I splutter as Corvin shoots Leah a scathing look.

"That shit isn't funny," Corv snaps. He's been in a salty mood since Cody said she would be staying in the spare room. Beck offered up his room to Nathan, so of course Leah had to then offer him to crash with us in *my bed*.

"It was a little funny," she teases. I shake my head at the pair of them. "Becky?" she calls. Beckett slowly turns to face her, he smiles but it's forced. "You okay?"

"Yeah, babe, just thinking." I hate that he fucking calls her stupid ass pet names, it works on my nerves. The front door opens to reveal Crue, Saint and Katie. I narrow my eyes. Katie's cheeks are flushed, her hair is a mess and Crue's shirt is on backwards.

"So, campus is like a five minute drive and by my calcula-tions, you guys have been gone over an hour?" Katie shoots

Cody a dirty look before dropping the bag in her hand to the floor.

"Whoops," she hisses as she stares at Cody.

"Bitch, you better not have broken my GHD," Cody mumbles as she slouches back into the couch. Fuck me, I can tell I'm already going to regret having them all stay with us.

CHAPTER TWENTY-THREE

Leah

One week…

It's been a week since *that* day. None of us have left the house and I'm starting to go stir crazy! Darius is constantly hovering making sure I'm okay, Nathan and Saint are always bickering. Cody and Corvin fight nonstop all day which means we all have to listen to them fuck nightly. That's not the worst part, once Cody starts screaming, Crue and Saint make it their life mission to make Katie scream louder! Beck kicked Nathan out of his room and put him in the room next to Darius and me since Cody never sleeps in it. I'm glad my girls are getting–well I'm glad Katie is but it grosses me out to think about Cody and my brother. My ribs are fine now and my face doesn't ache, the bruising makes it look worse than it is. I've tried for the past two nights to get Darius to touch me but he won't, and it's fucking killing me!

I need something to help ease the stress. I'm walking around a house with five hot as fuck guys, Cody says it's six guys but eww, the sixth doesn't count because he's my brother! These guys barely wear clothes, they prance around shirtless all day. Some days they don't even wear shorts and just walk around in their boxers. I can't help it, no matter how hard I try my eyes always seem to stray to their cocks and fuck me, I already know Darius and Beck are *huge*, but I can't miss the bulges in the other two's pants.

"Goldie!" Darius snaps. I dart my gaze to him to find him pinning me with a murderous glare. "I'm sitting right fucking here!" I throw my hands up as I push back from the table. I place my hands on it and lean over slightly, narrowing my eyes.

"Maybe I wouldn't be caught staring at their dicks daily if you actually let me see *yours*!" I yell. I can feel the others staring at us but I don't care, there is no such thing as privacy in this house anyway.

"Leah!" Corvin shouts behind me. I ignore him as I watch Darius slowly stand from his chair opposite me and mimic my stance. His eyes burn with lust, that look has heat spreading throughout my body.

"You want me to fuck you?" he asks huskily.

"Yes!" I shout.

"No!" Corvin and I both answer in unison. I grit my teeth as I spin around to find Corvin being blocked in the kitchen by Katie, Beck and Crue. I spy Nathan and Cody out of the corner of my eye watching us from over the back of the sofa. Saint still sits next to Darius eating his sandwich.

"So, you get to fuck every night while we all have to listen but I can't?" I grind out.

"Yes," Corvin answers, which just pisses me off.

"Uh, no, that does not work for me!" My brother narrows his eyes in warning.

"I don't care. That shit is not happening while I'm in the house–"

"Then get a fucking hotel!" I shout. I hear Darius and Saint laugh behind me, I even see Crue and Beck shake with silent laughter. Corvin's face turns red, he looks like he is about to blow a blood vessel in his forehead.

"You know they have slept together before, right?" Saint quips.

"Not while I've been around!" he answers cockily. I smirk and tilt my chin up as I say,

"Are you sure?" Darius chokes on something behind me as Corvin's mouth drops open. He darts his gaze over my head to Darius.

"She's full of shit...right?" The pleading in Corvin's voice nearly has me curling over and laughing.

"Y-yeah?" Darius stutters.

"Why the fuck did that sound like a lie?" Corvin shouts.

I throw my hands in the air. "Because it was. I gave him a blow job on the couch at home while you were passed out on the other chair. He also snuck into my room most nights, oh and we also fucked in your shower at home." He turns pale and hunches over gripping the edge of the counter. Darius is cursing beneath his breath behind me. I turn around and pin him with a stern look that has him standing up straight. "Just in case you didn't get the point, you either start putting out or I'm moving in with–"

"Swear to fucking God, if you say Beckett..." Darius warns. I scrunch my face up.

"I was gonna say Nathan," I answer. The tension eases from his shoulders.

"Why would it matter if she stayed with Beck?" Nathan fails at whispering to Cody. I roll my lips over my teeth to stop from smiling which earns me a scornful look from Darius.

"I need a fucking drink," Corvin grumbles behind me. An idea hits me as Darius eyes me warily.

"Why are you looking at me like that?" he asks suspiciously.

"We're about to play a drinking game that guarantees I get laid!" I say nodding, pleased with myself.

"You don't even care about me!" I whine as he holds my hair while I wash my face in the bathroom sink.

"Goldie, I have held your hair back while you threw up, helped shower and change you, brushed your teeth and here I am currently still holding your freaking hair back. How the hell is that me not caring about you?" I ponder that for a second, my mind is fuzzy from the alcohol I consumed. I thought it would be a great idea to challenge the guys to a drinking game hoping to get Darius drunk enough that I could seduce him. Turns out all the guys and Nathan are pros at beer pong. I thought us three girls playing in swimsuits would throw them off their game. What a stupid idea that was.

"You haven't even asked me if I'm okay." I pout as I meet his gaze in the mirror. He rolls his eyes heavenward and takes a deep breath, almost like he is praying for patience.

He flicks his eyes back to mine and asks, "Are you okay?"

"No!" I practically shout and stomp my foot like a child.

"For the love of fucking Christ, what's wrong now?" he asks. I spin around and lean against the sink as I try my hardest to look sexy.

"I hurt," I say in the best sad voice I can muster.

"Where?" I keep the smirk off my face as I reach out, grab his hand and place it flat against my pussy.

"Right, here." His eyes darken, a small groan slips from his lips as he closes his eyes.

"We can't." His voice is pained. I can see from how stiff his shoulders are and the way his breathing has picked up that he's close to giving in.

"Why? You said you would do *anything* to make me feel better." He slowly lifts his eyes to meet mine. I can see a war inside them, he wants me but he's holding back. I don't want to give him too much time to think, so I release my hold on his hand–which he leaves against my pussy—grab the hem of my shirt and slowly pull it over my head. Chucking it to the side, his eyes drop to my exposed tits. I grip the waistband of my booty shorts and push them down, forcing his hand away as I do. I stand here naked and ready for him to take me, but he still won't make a move.

The buzz from the alcohol is still there so I decide to embrace it and allow my inner temptress out. I push up onto the counter and scoot back until my back is against the mirror. His gaze runs over me sending a trail of heat through my body. The hunger in his eyes is what gives me the courage to make my next move. I open my legs, bending them at the knee to balance on the edge of the counter. His eyes drop to my exposed pussy. I bite my bottom lip as I slowly trail my hand down my chest and stop when I reach the apex of my thighs. Darius clenches his hands into fists at his sides, he's shaking, trying so hard to not give into his need. That's fine, I'm no quitter and I plan to have him inside me tonight no matter what it takes. I slip a finger through my folds and gasp.

"Stop…that's, you—fuck!" I smirk at his inability to form a coherent sentence. I push a finger inside my tight, wet hole, moaning his name as I do it. "Ah fuck," he grits out. I continue to pump that finger in and out of myself a couple times before switching to circling my clit.

"Oh my God," I breathe out as I arch my back off the mirror. "Yes!" I moan.

"Fuck it!" he growls before my hand is smacked out of the way. I smirk when he scowls at me.

"If you won't make me come then I have no choice but to take care of my own needs." He pushes forward until he stands between my legs, he bends his head down and ghosts his lips over mine as he says,

"I'm the only one who will be taking care of your needs, baby, no one else." He smashes his lips against mine. I open for him like always. I try to deepen the kiss but he jerks back like I just burned him.

"What the fuck?" I shout. He shoots me a pleading look, urging me to understand but I don't. "Why won't you fucking touch me?" I gasp as it begins to dawn on me. "Oh my God…" I push off the counter and quickly grab my clothes before racing into our room and trying to find my bag to pack my stuff and leave.

"What the hell are you doing?" he asks as I start toward the closet to grab my things. He blocks my path but I can't meet his stare.

"Let me go," I snap as he grips my arms holding me still.

"Not until you tell me what the fuck is going on?" I drop my chin to my chest.

"You should have told me." I hear the watery tone of my own voice.

"Told you what?" I shove him against his chest, causing him to stumble back a step. Not giving a shit that I'm standing here butt naked, I place my hands on my hips and hold his angry gaze.

"If knowing about Gary and what happened with Garrett has… put you off me, then you should have said something!" I latch onto my anger so I don't cry, his face drops.

"The fuck, Leah?" I flinch at the anger in his voice. He eliminates the space between us, gripping the back of my neck in a punishing grip as he pulls me toward him. I try to shake free but he uses his other arm to wind around my waist and hold me flush against him.

"Let. Me. Go," I snarl. He pushes his face against mine, not trying to mask the fury in his gaze.

"Shut the fuck up!" I keep the surprise off my face at how angry he is. "You think that the sight of you turns me off?" He thrusts his hips forward forcing me to feel his hard cock against my stomach. "Does that feel like the sight of you disgusts me?" he grits out.

"Then…why?" I ask.

"Because I didn't want you think I was fucking pressuring you after everything you have been through. I wouldn't blame you if the idea of sex put you off. But you couldn't let me be the nice guy, could you?" I open my mouth to answer but no words come out. "Close your fucking mouth or I'm putting my cock in it and I'll show you just how much the thought of fucking you disgusts me." I'm a wanton mess. I can feel the slickness between my thighs, my nipples hard and begging for his touch.

"Do it," I taunt. A sinister look enters his eyes before he darts his tongue out to lick my lips.

"You tempt me, but not tonight." My face falls. "I'll shove my cock down your throat tomorrow. Tonight, I'm gonna fuck you and show you just how much the sight of you makes me crazy and forces me to lose control. There is nothing about you that I don't love." I can't even process his words before his mouth is on mine, he doesn't hold back this time. This kiss isn't rushed or forced, it's him pouring all his feelings into it and showing me without words that he loves me. I wrap my arms around his neck, needing him closer. He moves his hands down my body leaving goosebumps in his wake as he grips the backs of my legs and lifts me. I break the kiss as I stare down at him, I see nothing but love and raw need for me in his eyes. "I love you, Leah, don't ever doubt that."

My brows draw in at his words, my heart takes flight inside my chest. "I love you too, now show me how much you want me," I taunt. A dark smirk crosses his face, forcing me to quirk a brow in question.

"I plan to make you scream all night long. You ready for the silent treatment from your brother tomorrow?" I cringe and screw my face up in disgust.

"Don't ever, and I mean ever, mention my brother when I'm naked and begging you to fuck me." He laughs as he walks us back toward the bed and lowers me down gently. He stands there between my legs, looking down at me for a minute before he trails his fingers up the top of my thighs and along my stomach. The closer he gets to my tits makes me fight the shivers that want to break free. At the last second, he skims his hands around the sides missing my nipples and drawing a pained whimper from me.

"What's wrong, baby?" he asks, teasingly, as he skates his hands down the same path. He may have said everything right but I can tell from the way his touch is unsure that he still thinks I'm not ready for this.

"Darius?" His eyes slowly lift to mine. "I'm not made of glass, you won't break me." He cocks his head to the side, frowning. "I want this, I want *you* to wipe away the bad and replace it with the good. Can you do that?" He searches my face for a sign of me being unsure, he won't find that. This isn't just about sex, this is about me needing to feel close to him again and reconnecting us in the most intimate way.

CHAPTER TWENTY-FOUR

Darius

I push my shorts down my legs, allowing my cock to spring free. Immediately her eyes zero in on it. It's been driving me crazy watching her check out the guys all week, jealousy reared its ugly head when I would find her staring at Beck. I've held myself back from touching her because I was scared that I would scare her or cause her to have a flashback. She didn't make it fucking easy! Tonight, the little show she put on nearly had me going crazy watching her prance around in that little yellow two-piece that barely covered anything.

I move forward and slowly lower myself on top of her, placing my hands on either side of her head before slowly lowering to my elbows. We've had sex plenty of times but the last time wasn't good between us. I need to make up for that. She rakes her nails down my back sending a shiver trailing down my spine and has a proud smile gracing her beautiful face. I kiss her, loving the way one kiss from me has her melting. I grind my cock into her, forcing a gasp from her. I refuse to allow her to break the kiss, swallowing her moan when I do it again. I can feel her arousal all over my cock as I slide it through her folds. She whimpers into my mouth and digs her nails into my sides. I relish in the pain.

I allow her to break the kiss. "Please." The way she says that one word with so much necessity has me caving and abandoning my plans on drawing this out and making her beg. I grip her face between my hands and splay my fingers wide, brushing the tops of my thumbs over her lips, then I slowly ease inside her. The second the head of my cock breaches her entrance her eyes begin to glaze over. I keep pushing inside her slowly, wanting to savor this moment and the feeling of being inside her. It's a feeling I'll never take for granted again.

I thrust in and out of her slowly while maintaining eye contact the entire time. I've never wanted to look at anyone but her while having sex. I love the way her mouth parts as a small moan slips free or the way her eyes turn glassy when I hit that sweet spot inside her. I just love looking at her, knowing that I'm the one bringing her this pleasure. I'm the only one who gets to bring her to this apex of a high that has her breaking apart beneath me, yet trusting me enough to allow me to do it.

"Darius, just like that." Her voice is raspy, her face slightly scrunched as I continue to push in and out of her, loving the way her pussy grips my cock, trying to keep me inside her. "I need more," she cries. I release my hold on her face as I grip her under her arms and pull her up as I rest back on my haunches. She lowers slowly down on my cock moaning. She runs her fingers through my hair before kissing me. I run my hands down her back, gripping the globes of her ass in my hands. She moans into my mouth and I pull my hand back and spank her ass. She jolts in my hold. Her eyes are wide with shock, but before she can think too much, I do it again but this time she cries out in plea-sure. Fuck.

I grip her ass and hold her in place as I fuck her. I tried to give her slow and passionate but that's just not us. Leah and I love to fuck. She loves it hard, rough and dirty, just like me. The harder I slam inside her the louder her cries grow. She locks her arms around my neck as she throws her head back, screaming. I lean forward and bite down on the soft flesh between her neck and shoulder, sucking it into my mouth making sure to leave my mark on her.

"Oh my God, don't stop!" she screams. I know without a doubt everyone in the house can hear her and I fucking love them knowing that she's mine and it's my cock she's about to come on.

"Come for me, Goldie," I grit out. My command is her undoing.

"Darius!" she cries out as her pussy walls clamp down on my cock, and shudders roll through her. I'm too far gone to bring her down gently. I slam inside her harder than before, chasing my own release. I continue to pound in and out of her, loving the screams that tear out of her. She slams her mouth against mine, swallowing my moans and as I come inside her, a tremor races through my body the moment I stop moving. She breaks the kiss, resting her forehead against mine. We're both breathing fast and coated in a sheen of sweat. "We are so back together, just in case that wasn't clear."

I laugh then plant a quick peck to her lips before turning us and lying flat on my back with her on top and my cock still inside her. "We were always back together." She leans forward and crosses her arms over my chest before resting her chin atop them and staring down at me. I wrap my arms around her back and hold her here.

"You chased my buzz away," she says, then giggles. I'll never tire of hearing the sound of her laughter.

"You gave me a buzz." She rolls her eyes.

"Bet you say that to all the girls," she jokes.

"Nah, baby, only you. There was never anyone else for me but you." Her face softens.

"So, does that mean I can officially call you my boyfriend?"

I smile, we've never officially had a title before. "Yeah, Goldie, shits real this time." She smirks, and then places a chaste kiss to my lips before leaning back and forcing a groan from me when she shifts causing my cock to move inside her.

"Well, as my boyfriend, I order you to make your girlfriend a grilled cheese, put a movie on in the lounge and then eat me out under the blanket." I choke on fucking air. She shoots me a wink as she slides off me and walks her naked ass into the bathroom.

Her wish was my command. I sit on one end of the sofa with her feet on my lap while she lays back watching *Wednesday* and eats her grilled cheese. I never thought I would ever see my weekend spent like this, not with her and especially not with Corvin in the same house. I hear someone coming down the stairs and lean my head back to see Katie and her duo. She's wearing one of their shirts, her blonde hair is a fucking mess.

"Well fucked?" I ask the moment they spot us on the couch. Saint and Crue laugh, high fiving each other over Katie's head. Katie just turns a bright shade of red and ducks her head. Leah sits up and peers over the back of the sofa.

"Bitch, get your ass over here and spill the deets." I squeeze the shit out of her ankle.

"Ouch!" she yelps as she shoots me a dirty look.

"Sitting right fucking here!" I growl. She rolls her eyes.

"And you guys don't sit around talking about our asses and tits?" she sass's.

"No."

"Fuck no!"

"Nope," Saint, Crue and I all reply in unison, her jaw slackens as she looks from me to them.

"Seriously?" Katie asks.

Crue nods. "No guy wants another guy to know what his girl looks like naked. Would you want another girl knowing what mine and Saint's dicks looked like?"

"Oh shit," Leah breathes out, garnering the three of their attention. She smiles at her friend who looks distraught which confuses the fuck out of me.

"Not a freaking word!" Katie warns. Leah laughs and pretends to zip her lips and throw away the key.

"What the fuck was that?" Saint asks. I shrug as I look to Leah who looks like she is about to burst if she doesn't spit whatever it is out.

"Don't do it," Katie says in a stern voice, now I have to know. I run my hand up my girl's legs suggestively.

"I'll make you come." Four little words and she spills the beans just like I knew she would.

"Fine! That was the first time one of them has admitted that they're *all* sleeping together," she says it all so fast she's breathless and gasping for air.

"Uh, babe, everyone knew they were," I say.

She rolls her eyes. "Men, it's not official until it's said aloud, duh." The sound of a door opening upstairs draws all our attention to Corvin and Cody making their way downstairs. Corv is wearing a pair of shorts and Cody is in one of his shirts, red faced and smirking. They just fucked for sure. "That's nasty," Leah says the second she spots her brother. He shoots her a glare.

"I can't even look at you," he says in disgust, forcing me to turn away so he can't see my smile.

"Uh, why?" she asks, genuinely confused.

"Seriously?" Corvin snaps as he makes his way toward the other sofa with the rest of the crew following him. Cody drops down beside him while Saint, Crue and Katie take the bean bags. Leah looks to me. I take pity on my girl and lean over toward her to whisper.

"You were screaming my name loud enough for the neighbors to hear." I expect her to blush, cover her face or run from the room but what I don't expect is for her to laugh and point at her brother.

"Payback, fucker," she says through her laughter, which just causes everyone but Corvin to laugh along with her.

"Next ball I throw is aimed right at your dick, asshole," he spits at me, causing us all to laugh harder. Fuck, this feels good to be able to laugh with him and have no secrets between us. We all settle into comfortable silence as we watch the stupid show the girls all seem to enjoy. Beck comes ambling into the room halfway through the first episode. Leah sits up and pats the spot beside her. He drops down, smiling at her. She switches around so her feet are on his lap and her head rests on mine.

Good call, baby, I think to myself. If her head had of been on his lap, I would have smacked her ass right here in front of everyone. By the time the third episode rolls around, Leah is fast asleep and Cody is crashed out, snuggled into Corvin's side. I look down at the three on the floor and see Katie sleeping in Saint's arms while holding Crue's hand.

"I kind of feel bad," Corvin says to no one in particular.

"About what?" Crue asks.

"Beck's the only one not getting any action." I snort out a laugh and try to mask it by coughing. "I mean, Nathan is asleep upstairs," Corvin tacks on, earning a dry stare from Beck.

"Don't worry about me. I'm still sated from my recent action with Darius and a certain someone." The smile drops straight off Corvin's face, I'll admit I have to fight to keep from laughing because Beck just bummed Corvin right the fuck out.

"Dick move, asshole," Corv mutters. Saint grabs the remote and switches the channel. The rest of us mutter our thanks. The only reason I watch that shit is because of Leah. Saint pauses his channel surfing when we spot a picture of Garrett being displayed on the news.

"Turn it up," Beck orders.

'Local homicide case has now been closed. Police have arrested the culprit who will be remanded in custody awaiting trial early next week. Garrett Jones family have said they don't understand how this could have happened, their son was loved and adored amongst his peers.' All of us mutter about how full of shit they are. Garrett wasn't liked by anyone. *'It's shocked the entire community to find out–'* The reporter stops speaking and presses on the earpiece in her ear,

her eyes widen a second before she faces the camera again. *'I've just been notified of the identity of the alleged suspect.'* My eyes pop open so wide that they begin to water when a picture of Victor is plastered on the screen. *'Business mogul, Victor Hayes is now in police custody. Casey is live outside the station, over to you Casey.'*

Another woman appears on camera out in front of the local police station where we can see Victor in handcuffs being led inside by four officers. *'Yes, Maddie. I'm here as officers lead Victor Hayes inside to process him. We have been informed that an eyewitness came forward with video evidence of Mr. Hayes at the site where Garrett Jones's remains were located. Police also found other evidence linking Mr. Hayes to the murder–'*

Saint puts the TV on mute, cutting off whatever else the reporter had to say. I sit here staring at the TV but not really seeing anything as my mind reels with what I just learned. Victor is going to jail for Garrett's murder. Victor was nowhere near that frat house last week.

"Darius!" I shake my head and turn to Corvin who looks slightly concerned. "You good?" I don't know how the hell I'm supposed to answer that. Do I care that he's in jail? I think about that for a second… No, I don't care what happens to that piece of shit but how the hell did he get convicted?

"Say something," Saint urges me.

"I don't know what to say," I utter quietly. I can feel all their gazes on me and something inside me says there is one person responsible for this. Slowly I turn to face Beckett, who has a blank stare plastered on his face. "How?"

"This would be the part where I tell you that you have plausible deniability and would recommend that you are better off not knowing the details. All you need to know is he won't be getting out, nothing leads back to us and we're all in the clear to carry on living our lives." I see Beckett in a whole new light. We may not know everything about him or his past but he's proven time and time again that he's got all our backs. I nod before turning back to Corvin. I know the truth but I just need to hear him say it.

"He wasn't dead when you got back there, was he?" Corv cuts a glance to Saint and Crue before looking back to me.

"It makes no difference. Leah's safe and we have nothing to worry about, like Beck said. We never mention it again or ever speak about it. We leave it in the past and move on."

CHAPTER TWENTY-FIVE

Leah

Three weeks later…

It's the last day of school before Christmas break. I'm so ready to get the hell out of here and spend the next two weeks at the cabin with my *boyfriend*–I don't think I'll ever get tired of saying that word. Corv and the others are coming too, even Nathan and my girls. I managed to convince Val and Dawson to come along as well. We met up the day I started back to school and stopped doing online classes. She is fucking awesome and so is her son. Dawson is the sweetest little boy you will ever meet. When I went over to their apartment that's off campus, my heart broke. It's a tiny one-bedroom apartment, not in the best area but she wasn't granted a twin suite in the dorm and couldn't afford to pay to live on campus whilst being a mom and student. I girl tutors and cleans just to make enough money to cover their living expenses. When I found out they would be alone for Christmas, I practically forced her to come with us. Her and Dawson are riding up with me, Cody and Katie.

"Ready, bitches?" Cody shouts as I finish packing the last of my stuff. I zip up my duffle and shoot her a toothy grin as I nod.

"Let's go!" I squeal as I make my way out of mine and

Darius's room. Yeah, so, he got his way and I moved in here with him. The girls moved back into our old dorm room. Corvin had paid for my dorm for the year, so Katie jumped at the chance to share with Cody instead of going back to her old room. Honestly, I'm happy for them because I love coming home every day and getting to cuddle up with my *boyfriend*. Fuck, it's only been like six hours and I miss him already.

"Come on, bitches," Katie shouts the moment we come out the front door. I lock it before running over to Cody's car. I dump my bag in the trunk before calling shotgun and slipping in next to Cody, forcing Katie to sit in the back. I rattle off the directions to Val's place and Cody plugs it into her GPS. Fifteen minutes later we pull up out the front of Val's place. She's standing on the sidewalk with Dawson beside her. Cody parks and I jump out to help load her bags as she straps Dawson's car seat into the car. She makes it look easy as hell putting that thing in. She buckles Dawson into his seat, then she rounds the car and hops in the middle seat.

"Let's roll!" I shout excitedly, it's an eight hour drive to the cabin so we won't get there until late tonight but none of us care, we all just want to get the hell out of here. My phone rings, the girls groan knowing who it is since he decided to change his ringtone to *our* song. I pull it out of my pocket and hit answer.

"Hey, you." I ignore Cody fake gagging beside me.

"Hey, baby, have you left yet?" God just the sound of his voice has me practically panting.

"Yeah, we're just hitting the interstate now." The guys left last night to get everything set up and to do the food shopping for us. The girls and I couldn't leave until today because the three of us and even Val had papers due and we couldn't miss it.

"Thank fuck, we are never fighting again." I frown.

"Uh, we're not fighting," I tell him.

"Well if we do fight, we are never sleeping apart again. I fucking hated rolling over and not having you next to me." My heart fucking bursts inside my chest.

"Agreed. I hated not waking up next to you," I whine like a petulant toddler.

"I make ew better, Lee," Dawson calls out from the back. I peer around my seat and shoot the little guy a wink.

"Shit, I forgot about the kid. No screaming for you then," Darius quips. I laugh, unable to keep it in.

"There will be none of that!" I hear Corvin shouting in the background.

"I better go before he starts getting big mad," I tease.

"Okay, baby, drive safe and I'll see you tonight, beautiful."

"Love you."

"Love you too, Goldie." I'll never tire of hearing him say those words to me. I end the call smiling, while excitement thrums through me. I never thought Darius and I would ever find our way back to each other. We have gone through some tough shit but I believe it has made us stronger. He continues to tell me daily how much he loves me and promises to never hurt me again. I believe him and tell him that, except each night he says he has to show my body he means it. If this is what I get for the rest of my life, I won't be mad about it. I'll drop to my knees and thank G.O.D himself.

"You two are so cute it makes me sick," Cody mocks.

"And seeing you and my brother together doesn't make me ill?" I jibe, causing her to shake her head and shrug.

"We're just... hanging out." The longing in her voice has me feeling sorry for her. Corvin won't commit to her and I have no idea why. Cody is amazing and I can tell she really does care about my brother, but she is constantly getting hurt by him. She won't tell me what he does to make her cry, but the girl also can't seem to stay away from him.

"Are you sure everyone doesn't mind spending the holidays with a random girl and her kid?" Val asks shyly.

"Of course not," Katie reprimands.

"They'll love it. Nathan is excited to finally get to meet you and Dawson," I say. "Plus, it will finally stop Darius from thinking I made you up."

"Why would he think you made me up?" Val asks, confused.

"Darius is jealous of the toilet paper for touching her hoo-ha," Cody mocks, earning an eye roll from me.

"What's hoo-ha, Mommy?" Dawson asks. I cringe and shoot Val and apologetic look that she just waves off.

"Nothing, sweetie," she says as she places a kiss to his head. We spend the next few hours listening to music and singing along until Dawson falls asleep. Not wanting to wake the wee man, we cut the music and fill the car with conversation. Val asks about me and Darius. I tell her our story which has her swooning and claiming that we have an epic love story. Katie and Cody fill her in on their friendly relationships with Crue, Saint and Corvin.

"What about you?" I ask Val. She sighs and looks over at her son with a sad smile on her face.

"There isn't much to tell. I was sixteen and thought I was in love. He left, I found out eight weeks later I was pregnant. I tried to find him, even went to his house only to find it vacant. He disappeared from my life and broke my heart."

"I'm so sorry," I say quietly, feeling sorry for her. Darius ghosting me hurt but I can't imagine how hard that would have been if I was pregnant like Val.

"It's okay. I mean, he may have vanished but he left me behind the best gift I could have ever asked for. Dawson makes all the heartache worth it. I wouldn't change a thing." How she can be so upbeat and positive given her circumstances is admirable. I don't think I would be as strong as her if our roles were reversed. Being a single parent must be so tough, that thought has me thinking about Jenny Lockhart. Darius refuses to seek her out. He says he isn't ready and I respect that. I just hope one day he changes his mind and actually speaks to her so he can get the closure he needs from her.

He's had so much on his plate lately. He's busting his ass to train for football, studying, and learning the role of CFO of Saint Hart Holdings. He has now refused to go to Chicago, saying that he wants to go with Beck to Alaska. He's done that for me. He knows that I loved it there and said he would run shit from there and he and Beck would both learn the ropes of the resort and the daily running of the company. He and Beck both have been up late most nights working, their dedication awe inspiring. Darius leaves with Beck after the New Year—he's been asking me every day to go with him. I haven't decided what I want to do yet. After spending one night without him, I know there is no way I can go six months without seeing him every day. I grab my phone from the cup holder and text him.

> You win! Book me on that flight, baby, I'm coming with you Xx

I cringe when I think of having to switch back to online classes, again. I think if the guys weren't on the board I would have been kicked out already for fucking the administration around so much. My phone pings with his reply almost immediately.

BIG D

> Don't play with me, Goldie.

> I'm not. Last night made me realize I can't be without you. I know you have to do this for your business.

BIG D

> Our business, baby. Are you sure?

> I've never been surer in my life.

BIG D

> I fucking love you. I'll show you just how much this means to me when you get here.

I clench my thighs together to try to dull the ache that is beginning to form. I'm so far gone where he is concerned.

> I expect you to show me all night long <3

We finally pull into the drive of the cabin just before eleven. We're all tired and sore from sitting in the car for so long. We only stopped once to use the restrooms and get food, refusing to stop again, too eager to get here. I spot Beck, Saint and Corv's cars parked in front of the garage and smile when I see Darius's bike there as well. Why they all didn't just come in two cars I have no idea. Nathan came with Saint. I love that he has slotted into our crazy family, he hangs with the guys just as much as us now.

"Oh my God," Val breathes from the backseat.

"Right? It's so beautiful here. Just wait till the morning when you get to see the view, it is gorgeous," Katie says. Cody parks the car and the four of us all jump out to stretch. God my ass is numb. I hear the front door open and squeal as I take off. I race down the pathway, smiling at the sight of my man running at me. I launch myself at him, clinging to him like a monkey and kiss the shit out of him. He grips my ass to keep me from slipping.

"Fuck, stop that!" I pull away and look over his shoulder to see my brother standing there with a sour look on his face. Darius places a quick kiss to the side of my neck before putting me back on my feet.

"Come on, let's grab your things." He grabs my hand and walks me back to the car. I introduce him and Corvin to Val. He seems at ease seeing for himself that she is actually a girl. He and Corvin carry Val's belongings while we grab the rest so she only has to worry about carrying a sleeping Dawson inside.

"Where's the guys?' Cody asks as we follow the guys inside.

"They tried to wait up but they crashed. Katie your boys said to tell you to lock the basement door after yourself." Katie rolls her lips over her teeth and nods. I freaking love how shy she gets, like the girl can take two dicks but as soon as you mention it out loud, she blushes. "Nathan took the fold out bed in the theater room, so, Val, you and your boy can have the spare room next to Darius's." I dart in front of the guys and open the door for them, the only light that is on is in the entryway. Truthfully, I'm beat and I think the others are as well, so Val will just have to wait till morning to get a tour of the cabin. Corvin pauses in the entryway and hands Katie her things. She's blushing so hard as she shoots us a quick wave and scurries off toward the basement. I attempt to move around Corvin and head upstairs, but he blocks my path. I look up at him and frown.

"What's up?" I ask. He smiles proudly and it throws me for a loop.

"I know shit has been hard for you but I just wanted to say I am so fucking proud of you for finishing you English paper and not quitting." I melt. "Also, Darius told me about Alaska." My shoulders tense thinking he's about to fight me on my decision. "I spoke with Mom and Dad and told them about it. They agree with me that this would be good for you."

"W-what?" I mumble, stunned as hell that he is being so... good about this.

He smiles down at me. "I may not enjoy the sight of you and dickhead together." Darius snorts beside me but Corv carries on. "But I also know he is a lot of the reason why you are doing so well. I expect your ass on a plane back to CHU to visit me every two months." I squeal and jump at him. He drops the bags to catch me. I hold him tight and love that my big brother is happy for me.

"I love you, Corv," I whisper, feeling him soften against me.

"I love you to, Lee."

CHAPTER TWENTY-SIX

Darius

I place Val and her kid's bag in the spare room while Leah helps her settle in and tells her where the bathroom is. Val thanks her and tells her that she'll see her in the morning. Leah promises to give her a tour and introduce her to everyone then. I'm beginning to grow impatient as I wait for her. My cock is rock fucking hard and dying to be buried balls deep inside my girl. I mean, I did promise to show her how much I loved her *all* night long. I never break a promise.

"Leah, go, I swear we will be fine." Leah nibbles on her bottom lip and nods.

"Okay, if you need me I'm right next door," she says before heading my way. I close Val's door after Leah, place my hand on the small of her back and practically push her into our room. She stumbles forward a step and spins to face me as I close our bedroom door. "What the heck?" she whisper-shouts.

"Strip." Her eyes widen at my demand.

"What?" I quirk a brow, daring her to defy me again as I say,

"Either you strip willingly or I rip them off, but either way, Goldie, I'm getting inside that pussy." Her eyes flare to life with lust, a small smirk breaking free as she unzips her jacket and lets it drop to the floor. Her top is next to go, then lastly is her jeans.

She stands there in nothing but a purple bra and thong that has my mouth watering, needing to taste her.

"Come get me," she says in a sultry tone that has my cock twitching in my sweats. I eliminate the space between us, grip the back of her neck and haul her up toward my face, forcing her to stand on her tiptoes. She grips my shirt in her dainty little hands, her breaths coming in quick pants.

"You wet for me, Goldie?" I ask as I brush my cheek along hers, loving how a shiver shoots through her at the feeling of my stubble against her skin. I nibble on her lobe, loving the small whimper that escapes her. I dart my tongue out and lick her ear relishing in the shudder that overcomes her. Fuck, I love how reactive she is to my touch. "It's been over twenty-four hours since I've been inside this pussy, baby, I think I need to remedy that." I grip her waist and lift her, like always she locks her legs around my waist. She peers down at me with raw hunger in her gaze as I walk us back toward the bed. "I never got to fuck you last time in here, so we need to ruin every surface of this room with your cum."

"Fuck, yes," she breathes out. I fall forward crushing her beneath my weight against the mattress. I grind my cock into her and crash my lips against hers, at the same time swallowing her moan of pleasure. I continue to do that until she is a writhing mess of need beneath me, only then do I pull back and slip off the bed. I look down at her, red faced and panting. Her eyes beg me to fuck her until she is nothing but putty in my arms. I run my gaze down her flushed body. A satisfied smirk makes its way onto my face when I see the wet patch in the middle of her thong.

"You dirty little girl." She squirms as I reach down and peel the scrap of lace down her toned legs, bring it to my nose and inhale her heady scent. Her mouth drops open in surprise, and before she can utter a word I ball up the lace and shove it inside her mouth, causing her eyes to widen. "Can't have you screaming and waking up your friend's kid now, can we?" She shakes her head and tries to clench her thighs together. I grip her knees and push them wider. "You close these again and I'll make sure you don't come for hours." Her eyes widen to the size of dinner plates. I grip the back of my shirt and pull it over my head, her greedy gaze roams over my exposed skin and slowly lowers to my sweats, expecting them to go next.

Silly girl, I plan to draw this out and make her fucking beg for my cock before finally giving it to her. I yank the cups of her bra down and suck her nipple into my mouth. She arches her back off the bed, the thong in her mouth muffles her cries. I glide my teeth along her hardened peak before swiping my tongue over it. I pay the other side the same amount of attention before I lick a trail down her body, stopping at her belly button and hiding my smile when she begins to groan out her annoyance. I slip off the edge of the bed, drop to my knees, grip her legs and yank her down until her pussy is directly in front of me.

I reach out and part her folds with my fingers, stifling my own groan when I see the slickness dripping out of her. I lean down and run my nose along the inside of her thigh, loving the whimpers that come from her. I keep doing this until she is shaking and only then do I take pity on her and swipe my tongue through her wet cunt. The second the taste of her arousal hits my tongue I moan, a need so strong and dominant overcomes me, forcing the need for me to make her come my soul purpose in this moment. I push my tongue inside her tight wet hole. She bucks her hips. I place my hand flat against her stomach holding her in place as I eat what is mine. I push my tongue in out of her before replacing my tongue with two fingers and sucking her clit into my mouth.

"Hmmmm," she cries out, writhing beneath me. I pump in and out of her, keeping a steady pace as I alternate between sucking and licking her clit. I can feel her tense and know she won't last much longer so I slow my pace—orgasm denial is torture but when I do eventually allow her to come, it will be the most intense orgasm of her life. I do this three more times, bringing her right to the cusp of climax before stopping. She grips a handful of my hair and yanks it hard, telling me she's about to go crazy. I peek up at her reddened face and smile.

"Want to come, baby?" She lifts her head, narrows her eyes at me and tries to hurl what I'm sure are a few choice words, but thanks to the lace in her mouth, I don't hear shit. It's the look in her green eyes that tells me if I deny her again she is going to rip my cock off. That's all it takes for me to stand and finally push my sweats and boxers down my legs, exposing my cock. It's angry and hard as stone from being teased by the taste of her. I push her legs wider to accommodate me, lifting them and resting her ankles against my shoulders, then pushing on the backs of her thighs to push her knees against her chest. Lining my cock up, I slowly slide inside her. The feeling of being inside her is like none other. Her eyes roll back as her mouth opens but her thong masks the sounds. When I'm halfway inside her, I pause for a second before slamming all the way, loving the muffled scream that tears from her throat.

I push forward until her ankles are either side of her head and shift up into an almost standing position. She reaches out and grips the sides of my arms, needing something to hold onto. I pull almost all the way out before slamming inside her, keeping a quick and steady pace, knowing how she loves to be fucked hard. Leah may look like a goody two shoes in the street but my girl is a freak in the sheets! Her nails dig into the sides of my arms, her body becomes taut, ready for her impending orgasm to rip through her. The sounds coming from her grow in pitch the closer she gets to her release. I place my hand over her mouth to keep her quiet. I slam inside her harder and deeper making sure to hit that sweet spot. Leah's eyes roll back, her back arches off the bed.

"Come for me, Goldie." As if my words are her undoing she comes all over my cock, her screams muted by my hand. I can't bring her down slowly, the need to mark her and make sure everyone knows who she belongs to consumes me. I lurch back pulling out of her. Gripping my cock in my hand, I pump it three times watching as jets of my cum spurt all over her stomach and tits, her name tearing from deep inside me. My chest rises and falls in rapid succession as I stare down at her all flushed and eyes dazed. I reach down and smear my cum all over her. Call me possessive or whatever the fuck you like, but knowing that my cum is all over her, marking her as mine, has me wanting to beat my fists against my chest.

I slowly blink my eyes and yawn. Leah was insatiable last night. We barely slept, needing to be connected and reminding the other who we belong to. I flick my gaze around the room and bite my lip to stop my laugh from breaking free. We fucked everywhere and the destruction all over my room shows that. I roll over and bury my face in the crook of her neck. She moans as I wrap my arm around her waist and pull her naked body flush against my chest.

"Hmmm, I need more sleep," she mutters with sleep thick in her tone. I smile into her neck.

"I'm hungry," I whisper huskily, a shiver rolls through her at my double meaning.

"Is everyone awake?"

"Hell if I know, why?" She rolls over and smiles at me. Fuck she looks so beautiful. Leah's beauty is something I can't even put into words, the sight of her steals my breath away. I reach out and cup her cheek as I lean in and kiss her. Touching her, kissing her or even fucking her isn't a want, it's a *need*. I can't be without her. When I ghosted her for two years, I was half a man, lost and spiraling. I didn't know why I couldn't find happiness or a reason to be grateful for what I had achieved in life until she came back. The world seemed better, colors looked brighter and food tasted richer. Leah is my reason, my purpose for everything in life and I'll never lose sight of that again.

She pulls back, smiling at me with love in her eyes. "I would love to stay here with you all day but I need to be there for Val and introduce her to everyone." I sigh in annoyance.

"Did you have to bring her?" I grumble.

She swats me on the chest. "Babe, she would have been alone for Christmas. I couldn't do that to her and Dawson." As much I hate to admit it, I love that she cares about everyone and always goes above and beyond for those she loves. Just sometimes I wished she was selfish like me, so she wouldn't feel guilty about spending the day in bed, fucking me.

"Doesn't she have family?" Leah's brows draw in as she shakes her head.

"I don't think so. She hasn't said anything but she did say she's been on her own since she was pregnant with Dawson." Sadness is thick in her tone.

"Where's the kid's dad?"

"He took off before Val could tell him she was pregnant." What a fucking drop kick. Who the fuck does that? Man, I could never turn my back on Leah if she was pregnant. I don't want kids anytime soon because I can't stand the thought of sharing her with anyone, even our own kid.

"Fine. You have an hour to eat and hang out with your friend, then we're hitting the hot tub so I can fuck your ass while your pussy is being destroyed by the jets." The sadness in her eyes for her friend is gone, replaced by raw hunger for *me*. Fuck, I'll never tire of seeing that look in her eyes.

"I love you." I smile triumphantly knowing I'll be the only man in this world to ever hear those words come from her sinful lips.

"I love you too, Goldie. Now, get the fuck outta the bed or I'll be balls deep inside you in a second flat and your friend can face the crew by herself."

CHAPTER TWENTY-SEVEN

You best believe I leapt out of that bed like it was on fire, Darius would have kept his word and pinned me down until I was screaming his name. I managed to snag the shower before Val. Of course, I only managed to have mere minutes alone before Darius stormed in, demanding that I help him deal with a situation. The situation of course was me helping get rid of his boner, which did lead to me plastered against the shower, biting down on his shoulder so my screams didn't wake the whole house. When we finally exited the shower after using all the hot water, I quickly brushed my teeth and combed my hair before changing.

I'm sitting on the end of our bed pulling on my Ugg boots when a knock sounds at the door. Darius pulls his hoodie on before going to open it. The bedroom door opens to reveal a sleepy Val with a smiling Dawson in her arms. I pull my boot on and stand, making way over to them to pluck Dawson from her hold and kissing his gorgeous face until he is laughing and begging me to stop.

"Could I ask a favor?" I see Darius stiffen next to me but I ignore as I look at my friend.

"Of course, Val. What do you need?" She seems nervous.

"Could you please watch him while I take a quick shower. I

swear I won't be long. I'm just worried about the stairs if he came out of the room while I was in there and—" I cut her off, feeling so sad for her that she feels like asking to watch her son for five minutes is a huge burden.

"Val!" She clamps her mouth closed and pales slightly. I try to smile reassuringly to help ease some of her nerves. "Go shower, wash your hair, do whatever you want and take your time. Darius and I will take Dawson down and get him breakfast. Crue and Saint will love having the little guy to play with." Her eyes widen.

"Are you sure?" I shift Dawson to one side and use my free hand to rest against Val's shoulder in a comforting gesture.

"Yes! Go shower, take your time. When you're done, break-fast will be ready and waiting for you downstairs." Her eyes grow misty.

"Thank you, Leah." Her tone is watery and that fucking hurts me.

"Val, we're all here for you. Once you get to know the guys, you will understand that we are family and we take care of our own. You and Dawson are ours now. Whatever you need, we got you." She swallows loudly as her eyes fill with tears. Before they can fall, she nods and scurries back to her room. I turn to Darius to find him staring at the spot Val just vacated with a look of pain etched into his beautiful face. "Are you okay?" He shakes his head and nods.

"Yeah. Come on, let's go eat." I hate that I know he is lying, it's hard for him to see a mom care for her child. I hope one day my man can find it within himself to find his mom and speak with her because I hate that there is this hurt inside him that I can't take away.

I smile as I look around the table at everyone. Dawson sits on my lap eating the pancakes Beck made him. Beck and Darius sit on either side of us. Nathan, Corv, Crue, Cody, Katie and Saint all shout and laugh as they fight over who can beat who at Mario Kart. I shake my head and hide my smile as I place a kiss to the top of Dawson's head.

"I go Becky?" Silent laughter shakes my shoulder as I hear Beck grunt beside me. When we came down this morning to see everyone and get some food, I introduced Dawson to the others and I may have forgotten to introduce Beck as *Beck* and not Becky. Dawson instantly took a shine to Beck and demanded to stay with him and help make pancakes. I was stunned when Beck plucked him from my arms and set him up on the counter to help. Dawson reaches out for Beck, the big man's eyes soften as he grabs Dawson from me and sits him on his lap, wrapping his arms around him protectively. Darius drapes his arm around my shoulder as I stare at the duo beside me. He leans in and whispers, low enough for only me to hear.

"Stop looking at my best friend like that." There's heat in his tone that has me turning to face him, we're so close that our noses brush against each other.

"Huh?" His eyes narrow but he can't hide the lust that sparks to life in those beautiful eyes.

"Keep looking at him like that and I may have to make a mini me just so you'll look at me like that." My eyes snap wide, he laughs before pecking me on the lips and leaning back in his chair while I stare at him.

"Get the hell away from my son!" I snap my gaze to the dinning entry way to see Val standing there with an angry look on her face. The room is doused in silence from her outburst.

"Valance…" Beck whispers beside me. I flick my gaze between her and him as he slowly stands from his chair with Dawson still in his hold. The moment he steps away from the table she rushes toward them stopping a foot away from Beck.

"Give him to me now!" she grits out, her tone is hard but I can hear the hurt that she tries to mask. They know each other, how? Beck looks down at the boy in his arms before turning back to Val—Valance. I thought Val was short for Valerie or something, I never thought to ask her.

"He's your… son?" Beck clips out. Val's eyes widen for a split second. I slowly stand from my chair and move to stand beside Beck.

"Yes," she grits out, her features pull taut. She darts her gaze to me, pleading for my help silently.

"Becky, pass me Dawson," I say but Beck ignores me as he keeps his gaze on Val.

"How old is he, Valance?" His tone is laced with anger. Val's shoulders bunch, her hands clench into fists at her sides as she holds his angry stare.

"He's… four." Beckett's brows jump to his hairline as his eyes widen, Dawson reaches for his mother. Val lurches forward and yanks him from Beckett's hold, clutching her son against her chest as she peppers kisses on his head. She darts her gaze to me, this time all I see in her eyes is regret and pain. "I need to go home." Those five words seem to have Beck snapping out of whatever trance he was in, he closes the space between him and Val, glaring down at her.

"You aren't taking *my* son anywhere!" he snarls, and gasps break out around the table. My jaw unhinges as I stare at the couple in front of me. Dawson is Beck's kid, how? Val's blue eyes burn with hatred as she scowls up at Beck.

"Fuck you, Beckett. He isn't yours!" A humorless laugh leaves Beck, the sound of it has me tensing knowing something bad is coming.

"He isn't mine?" Val nods stiffly. "Right, so, Valance, why the fuck did you name *your* son after me?" I frown unsure what he means. Val shakes her head.

"Oh shit." I snap my gaze to Darius as he stares at Beck's back. "Beckett Dawson." Oh fuck!

"Please, don't," Val chokes out, drawing my attention back to them.

"You gave *my* son my last name as his first name," Beck

shouts. Dawson cries in fright, Val tries to soothe him but he continues to cry. "You're not taking him anywhere!"

"Screw you, Beckett. You'll never get near him again," Val says with so much conviction I actually believe her.

"I'll take your ass to court. I have the money and you don't, so say your goodbyes now." Val's face pales, panic fills her features for a second before she hardens her gaze before taking a deep breath.

"Take me to court and I'll tell them how you are a murderer. You and I both know I have the proof of your crime." The icy tone of her voice fills me with dread. I feel Darius behind me as he wraps his arms around my waist and pulls me flush against his chest. The guys stand from their seats with angry glares pointed directly at Val, who looks like a deer caught in the headlights.

"You can try, but heed my warning, *Valance*," Darius spits her name like it burns his tongue. "You run your mouth to anyone and I promise you that we will bury you six feet fucking deep and take that kid from you without remorse." Tears flow down her cheeks, she darts her gaze to me for help but I'm stuck. She's my friend but Beck is... my Becky. He's one of my ride or dies and I can't turn my back on him. Which is why, when Beck yanks Dawson from her arms I don't intervene, not even when Crue and Corvin grip her arms pulling her from the room.

BONUS
CONTENT

Bonus chapters will contain spoilers for the other three books in the series.

The bonus content will lead you into the Dirty Temptation series where all unanswered questions will be resolved...

Part One

Darius

13 years later…

Leah Lockhart.

My wife, my perfect fucking woman. She changed the entire game for me, I miss her when she isn't in the same room. Being together for as long as we have, I thought the need to have her in my eyesight, or just wanting to feel the heat of her body against mine would lessen but—.

"Darius Cameron Lockhart!"

Well, she is perfect, that is until she full fucking names me!

I debate making a run for it, maybe hiding out at Corvin's next door until she calms the fuck down. I have no damn idea what I did this time to get the full-name treatment, but I don't want to stick around and find out. I creep out of my office and look both ways when I realize she must be upstairs. I make a break for the front door. I'm almost within reach of it when she suddenly appears out of thin fucking air. I slide along the wooden floors and screech to a stop, right before colliding with her.

Her eyes narrow as she looks up at me, then to make her point further, she places her hands on her hips, and I know without a doubt I'm in some fucking deep shit!

"Goldie—." I try to plead, but then she scrunches her face and I snap my mouth closed, bracing for impact.

"Who the fuck is Vivian Tempest?" I reel back as if she sucker punched me, and instantly raise my hands, surrendering to my wife, knowing it's always best not to aggravate her further when she's in this type of mood.

"Goldie, I have no idea who that woman is, I swear—."

"Oh save your bullshit ass excuses, Lockhart." I cringe and smile sheepishly.

"Baby, that is our last name, and you know how I feel about you using it in that tone." Her face slackens and I step back. My wife has always been hot-headed and quick to pop off, but ever since my sperm landed in her egg, she has been a ticking time bomb. My brothers avoid me, refusing to come over because they don't know if she is going to cry, or rage at me. Well, she rages at everyone, aside from fucking Beckett. That mother-fucker seems to be the only male exempt from her rage, which pisses me the fuck off.

When tears start welling in her eyes, all my defenses fall, the urge to protect my girl overwhelming me and I reach for her, pulling her body into mine. She begins sobbing as I wrap my arms around her and hold her close. I may be a heartless piece of shit to every other motherfucker, but never her. She is my haven, my home, my fucking everything, and I'll never admit it but I'm terrified to become a father. I'm scared I won't be able to love our baby as much as I love her. I'm terrified that I'll end up being a fucked up parent, just like mine were.

"Baby, you have to stop crying or I'm gonna be forced to find this Vivian bitch and hurt her for making you sad." That gets a watery chuckle from her and I sigh in relief. She pulls back, looking up at me with that doe-eyed look she always gives me, and I'm done for. She could ask me for the world and I'd find a way to give it to her. Twelve years ago I made her my wife. At thirty-seven, I never thought I would become a father, but I know becoming a mother has always been a dream of Leah's, and we've been trying for years. We were on the brink of giving up and exploring the possibility of adopting, and then suddenly, our little miracle happened.

"Who is she, halfback?" She whispers brokenly, anger soars through me and I instantly want to hunt this bitch down, and destroy her world for upsetting my girl.

I cup her face and brush away her tears with my thumbs. "Baby, I swear on my life I have no idea who the fuck you are talking about." She opens her mouth to argue, so I push on. "The only woman I have eyes for is you! You are still the only girl I have ever loved, you were my first kiss and you will be my last. Never doubt that."

"We have to go to Becky's." I grit my teeth and try to calm myself. Even after all these years I still get jealous when I know I have no reason to. Beck is married to Val, and they are happy with each other and their kids. I know Leah and Beck don't love each other like that. The bond they share is one I will never understand but will always support because Beckett loves my wife, and he would lay his life down for her. Their love is more of a siblings, and best friend type of love.

"Why?"

She rolls her eyes and pushes me back. "Because this bitch has been looking into Becky, my brother, Crue, and Saint as well." Instantly my hackles rise, it's been over a decade since we have had someone sniffing around our shit. The last person brave enough to was Saint's father. I reach around and pull her coat off the hanger, helping her pull it on before reaching for my own. I interlock our fingers as we walk out the front door, and see Corv and Alexa heading to Beck and Val's too.

"Jailbait, I didn't do shit!" I smirk at the sound of my best friend going through the same fucking thing I just did with his own wife.

"Shut the fuck up, Reaper, I'll deal with you after I sort this bitch out." Alexa snaps as she storms ahead of him. I wipe the smirk from my face when Leah looks up at me.

"How did you find out about this Vivian chick, Goldie?" I ask, walking along the sidewalk.

"Katie found her trying to hack into her server or something., She was trying to find information about all of you."

"Why?"

"I don't know. We have no idea who she is, but Katie called and told us girls to get our guys and head to Beck's." I mull over what she said as we make our way into Beck's head into the living room, and I can't help but frown at the sight of all the guys standing on one side of the room, and the girls on the other. Leah tries to let go of my hand but I tighten my hold, drawing her gaze to me.

"I can feel the tension and see the divide already, we aren't them." Her brows furrow. "You and me, we are fucking united. You stay by my side." She softens instantly and leans up on her tiptoes, pressing a kiss to my lips.

"You're mine, halfback, and I'll cut a bitch if she thinks she can try and take you from me." She says quietly.

I grip the back of her neck and rest my forehead against hers. I stare into her green eyes. "My heart is yours, Goldie. You own me, no one will ever come between us. After we sort this, I have a surprise for you this Christmas." Her eyes widen and a broad smile stretches across her face.

"What is it?" She breathes out excitedly.

I pull back and shoot her a wink. "It wouldn't be a surprise if I told ya now would it?" She purses her lips and tries to look angry but fails.

"I have it!" Katie shouts enthusiastically. When the guys rush toward the girls, the four of them skid to a halt when Alexa shoots them a look filled with scorn.

"Seriously?" Crue snaps, Katie shoots her man a timid smile, and I scoff, drawing all their attention to me.

"Got something to say, Lockhart?" I wrap my arm around my wife's shoulders and pull her into my side.

"Yeah, I do actually, Val." I bite out, earning a scoff from the fiery redhead. "You are all pissed off at us for something we have no fucking clue about. Katie isn't angry at her husband's so that should show the rest of you heathens that we didn't do shit."

"Exactly!" Corvin adds.

"I have no fucking clue who the fuck this woman is, and I've been trying to tell you that, Valance!" Beck shouts.

"Why the fuck is she looking into all of you then?" Alexa exclaims.

"I can answer that!" Katie says in a victorious tone.

"Well, can you share with the rest of us because I need to pee again, for the hundredth time today!" I wince. Leah hasn't had the easiest pregnancy, and she really does have to pee all the time.

"Vivian Tempest has a twin brother, Vox Hatchett," Katie says.

"And who the fuck is he?" Saint snaps.

Katie rolls her eyes. "Calm down, babe. Vox has applied to attend CHU, and after doing some digging into him, it looks like his girlfriend, Nova Quinlin, has applied here as well."

"And we give a fuck because?" Corvin is clearly about to run out of patience soon.

"Because he plays just as good as you did, if not better," Katie says with a smug smile. Corvin's face blanks, and then he marches across the room and snatches the laptop from Katie's lap. He pushes play on a video and we all stand here watching his face morph into shock, disbelief, and then…he smiles fucking wide.

"This kid is good, like really fucking good." He sounds

almost proud, and Corvin isn't the type to ever dish out compliments.

"From what I gathered, his best friends, Archer Malik, Hayze Draven, and Ezekiel Tempest applied here as well. They are also football stars and fucking good, too."

My brows slam together. "Wait, you said Ezekiel Tempest?"

Katie nods and smiles at me. "I did indeed. Darius."

"How old is she?" I push.

"She's nineteen and married to Ezekiel." She answers.

"See," Corvin shouts, looking at his wife. "She's young enough to be my fucking kid."

Alex snorts. "Age didn't seem to be a factor when you were trying to screw me." Everyone tries really hard to bite their tongue and not laugh at Corv's expense, but of course, Crue and Saint are the first to lose it and we all join in, unable to control our laughter.

"Ya'll are a bunch of fucking assholes, you know that right?" Corv grits out.

"Okay, so what does she want?" My girl asks.

"From what I can gather, she just wants a meeting with the guys," Katie answers.

"Why would she want to meet with us?" Crue hedges.

"I have no idea but I must say, I love her persistence and the fact she was able to hack my system shows how good she is." Katie sounds almost proud.

"But you're better aren't you, Katie baby?" Saint coos, earning an eye roll from his wife.

"Of course. Which is why I have accepted the guys and Nova's applications and set a date for you all to meet with her."

Part Two

Leah

Darius has been acting weird for a couple of weeks now. I've tried asking him what's wrong but he just keeps brushing me off and now I'm scared. I know this pregnancy has been rough on us both, but I'm starting to worry that he's resenting me for wanting this little miracle so badly. I know my halfback would do anything for me, but I just hope this baby wasn't something he gave me to keep me happy at the expense of his own happiness.

"Lee?" I smile at the sound of Beck's voice.

"In the kitchen!" I call back, and my best friend saunters in and smiles at me. I try to hide my emotions, but the instant the smile falls from his face, I know I failed, and tears begin to fall on their own accord. Beck rushes toward me and wraps me in his embrace. I break down and start sobbing.

"Baby girl, what's wrong?" His tone is laced with worry.

"I think…Darius…doesn't want our baby." Beck gasps and

pushes me back, resting his hands on the tops of my shoulders, then bends down until we are at eye level.

"Why the fuck would you think that?"

My bottom lip trembles. "He won't even touch me, he leaves the room every time I walk in, and he's been avoiding me at all costs."

Beck's eyes darken, and his features pull taut. "I'll kill the spineless fuck." He growls.

"Becky, I can't lose him." I choke out.

He sighs, cups my face between his hands, and brushes away my tears with his thumbs. "Lee, he is a fucking idiot but everyone can see how crazy in love with you he is. Darius is a cold fuck, and the only person I have ever seen him be tender towards is you. Do you really think your brother would have agreed to let him marry you if he thought Darius was gonna break your heart?"

"No," I whisper.

Becky smiles lovingly. "Exactly. Whatever is going on with him will pass. You just need to let him deal with his shit. Becoming a parent isn't easy for him considering everything he went through as a kid." Guilt churns inside me at the reminder of what my husband had to endure as a child.

"He isn't his parents, and I know he'll love our baby—."

"Exactly. You just said it yourself. He may be a hardhead and act a fool most of the time, but he will burn the world to the ground for you, Leah. Never doubt how much he loves you, D will come around. Just give him time."

"Maybe…I just need to get out of here for a while and give him some space."

Becky jerks back and shakes his head. "No. If you leave, he will destroy everything in this house, Lee."

"Becky, please, I just need…time."

Beck groans and spins away from me as he starts pacing my kitchen. I can tell he is torn between being my best friend and a loyal brother to my husband. "Fuck." He snaps as he turns to me and tugs on the strands of his head.

"Please," I beg.

His eyes soften and a groan of frustration escapes him. "You have eight hours, after that I'm telling him you left."

"I love you, Becky."

He rolls his eyes. "Yeah, you better love me after your husband breaks my fucking nose for not stopping you." He mutters.

***

I sit outside on the loveseat and watch the snowfall. This cabin has many happy and bitter memories, this cabin has become the place we all escape to so we can forget our daily lives and live in the moment with the people we love most.

When I feel my baby kick, I gasp and cover my bump, smiling. "I love you, bug," I whisper. It tears me apart inside to think about Darius not wanting this baby. I love that man with everything I have, but if it becomes a choice between him and our baby, I will choose my little bug. I pull the blanket tighter around me to ward off the chill. I should be inside in front of the fire, but I can't find the strength to stand and face the empty cabin. "God, I wish he was here," I mumble.

"Then next time, invite me along for the ride, Goldie." I close my eyes at the sound of his voice, and I don't bother turning around in my chair because I know he'll come to me. He always does. I blink my eyes open when I feel the chair dip. Darius sits there looking at me with so much uncertainty and fear in his eyes that it robs me of air. "Why'd you leave me, baby?" He whispers.

Tears gather in my eyes, and I'm powerless to stop them from falling. "I don't want to choose between you both." I sob, his brows furrow in confusion.

"Between who?"

"You and the baby!" I snap.

Darius reels back like I slapped him. "Why the fuck are you choosing between us? That baby is half mine Goldie, and I'm not giving up on my kid without a fucking fight!" He roars, shocking me.

"Then why won't you look at me? For weeks you have been avoiding me—."

"Because every time I'm around, all I seem to do is make you cry and I fucking hate it. I never want to cause you pain, Leah but it seems that's all I do lately." His response stuns me to my core.

"You don't make me sad. I love having you around," I admit.

"Then why do you cry every time I touch your belly or talk to the baby? You always cry when you see me doing things in the nursery or talking to the guys about the baby?"

Tears trail down my cheeks and I bat them away. "Every time you touch my belly or speak to my belly, I cry because I never thought this would be my future."

He gasps. "You don't want our baby?" He asks in disbelief. I dart forward and grip his face between my frozen hands, but he doesn't seem to notice how cold they are.

"I want this baby more than anything. I cry because I never thought I would ever get you back, halfback. Knowing I will be the mother to your child means everything to me. The tears I cry are happy tears and because I love you so fucking much, and it makes me emotional every time I see you doing things in the nursery for our baby. The pride I hear in your voice when you talk to my brother and the guys about our baby means every-thing to me. I just don't want you to hate me for wanting this baby, and I know kids aren't something you ever wanted, but —." He silences me by pressing his mouth to mine. I melt into him instantly, but he pulls back before I can explore his mouth.

He rests his forehead against mine and smiles. I see nothing but love in those beautiful eyes as he stares at me. "I never wanted kids unless it was with you. I never wanted anything aside from you but now, I get two of you, and I couldn't be happier, Goldie. You have given my life purpose, and I am so sorry for making you think I didn't."

"I love you too, so fucking much. Don't ever leave me, Darius, because I won't survive losing you." I plead.

He places a chaste kiss on my lips. "Even in death, I would never leave you Leah. You're my soul, the very fucking essence that makes me, me. Without you, I'm a shell baby. I was fucking petrified when I got home from picking Cody up from kindergarten for Corvin and Alexa and couldn't find you. When you weren't with your brother, I knew there was only one person you would have told." I smile sheepishly, which just causes him to narrow his eyes. "That motherfucker took a lot of persuading, but in the end, Beckett gave up your location."

"Darius, tell me you didn't hurt him?" I chide. He scoffs and pulls back, puffing his chest a little.

"I didn't do shit. Your brother broke his nose for letting you drive alone a month out from your due date."

I balk at him. "What the fuck?" I snap.

Darius waves away my concern. "Now that I know you aren't leaving me, you better be prepared to make it up to me."

"What?" I rasp out in outrage.

His face slackens. "Goldie, you took our fucking Mustang, which has my car keys on it so I had to ride my bike all the way up here in the fucking snow! My balls are frozen." I bite my bottom lip to keep from smiling, which just has him glaring at me. "Get your ass up now. We're going inside so you can give my dick mouth-to-mouth to revive it." Laughter bursts out of me, and he grabs my hand, gently tugging me to my feet. The devilish glint in his eyes has me clenching my thighs. He stands in front of me with a lustful look in his eyes that has butterflies erupting inside me. "I love you, Leah Lockhart. Never fucking doubt that again. Because my world is nothing without you in it."

I press up on my tiptoes and kiss him. His hands drop to my

ass, and I gasp into his mouth, giving him the access he needs to tongue fuck my mouth.

"Fuck." He growls as he breaks the kiss and drags me inside the house. He may want inside me more than his next breath, but he manages to find some restraint as he slows his pace and helps me up the stairs to our bedroom. He doesn't bother closing the door behind us before he pounces on me. The second his tongue brushes mine, I'm done for. It's been so long since I have felt him inside me. Our hands are manic as we tear each other's clothes off. I step back to admire him, and instantly, I feel self-conscious. "Stop."

"Huh?" He rolls his eyes, then turns and races out of the room. I stand here gaping at the sight of his naked ass running out of the room and wondering if the sight of me big and round is that much of a turn off. Before tears can gather, he rushes into the room a second later and my jaw unhinges at the sight.

"Still want to ride my face?" He asks, then winks.

Laughter bursts out of me. "Why are you wearing a Santa hat and elf ears?" I ask between fits of laughter.

He shrugs. "I saw it in your eyes, baby, never doubt your beauty because to me, you are still a 50/10, and I'll live the rest of my life like a cocky fucker knowing I'm punching above the belt because I got the fucking grand prize of women." My heart swells.

"You can keep the hat but lose the ears." He shrugs and rids himself of the ears, then comes at me. The kiss consumes me and robs me of air. Feeling his bare skin against mine is euphoric and has more liquid heat gathering between my thighs. He gently lays me down on our bed and hovers above me, smiling. "What?"

"Nothing, I just can't believe my life sometimes." His words have tears pricking the backs of my eyes, but I fight to keep them back when he slowly trails kisses down my neck. When he moves to my nipples and blows his hot breath over them, I cry out. They are so sensitive lately and he loves it. When he sucks one into his hot wet mouth, I arch off the bed, pressing my belly against him. He switches sides and does the same, making me scream and squirm until he finally takes pity on me and moves lower. He pushes my legs open wider. My belly is so big I can't even see over it to watch him. But I can feel it. The first of his tongue has me bucking my hips and withering with need.

"Darius." I whimper. It's been too long since I have come, and I know with every stroke of his tongue, I won't be able to last.

"Give me what I want, baby." He growls. I'm a puppet trying to defy its master, and I know it's a fight I won't win. Even after all these years, he is still the only person who can make me bend to his will with just one look. He pushes a finger inside me and hooks it to stroke that fucking sweet spot inside me, and I'm done for. He sucks my clit into his mouth, and I shatter with his name tearing from me. Stars dance in my eyes as he throws me over the cliff, but I know he'll catch me.

"Halfback." I rasp out as he shifts up my body, and I can see the residue of my orgasm on his chin and fuck, it makes me feel powerful knowing it's me that is covering his skin, and I still get to wake up next to this bad boy every day for the rest of my life.

His eyes stay locked on mine as he lines himself up with my entry. I suck in a sharp inhale when he pushes inside me. Fuck, he feels amazing.

"Jesus, Goldie, I've missed this perfect pussy baby." I arch my back and gasp when he slams inside me. "I can feel you clenching my cock." He grits out.

"Darius, I need you to move." I pant, and he smirks cockily, loving that he can still get these reactions out of me. He places his hands on either side of my head, careful to keep his weight off my stomach, and then he moves, and I see nothing but him. All I feel is him. Every inch of him is mine, and I relish that thought. I can tell it's hard for him to go slow, and as much as I love how soft he is being, I need him to fuck me! "I need more." I snap.

He pulls out of me and helps me to roll onto my hands and knees, and heat spreads through me when he lines himself up behind me. He slams inside me, and I jolt forward, screaming. He grips my shoulder in one hand and my hair in the other to hold me in place.

"You want me to fuck you like this?" He growls as he slams inside me again, pulling another hoarse scream from me.

"Yes, just like that." I push back, needing him to fuck me like a savage and dominate my body. I want him to rip my next orgasm from me, not build me up and slowly push me over the cliff.

"Tell me how much you love this cock, Goldie."

"I fucking love it. I want to feel the ghost of you inside me for days."

He growls his approval, then tugs me back against his chest by my hair and smashes his lips to mine as he thrusts inside me ruthlessly. He swallows my cries, his hands cup my tits and tweak my nipples, sending sparks of need through my body, my pussy clamps down on his cock.

"This is my pussy, and no one ever gets this but me." He snarls. I nod, trying to fight off my orgasm so I can drag this out, but he sees what I'm doing. He wraps his hand around my throat and applies enough pressure to make me gasp. "Come on this cock, show me how you own it." I moan and obey. I bounce up and down on him meeting his thrusts. Within a minute, we're both roaring out our release.

Our bodies are slick with sweat. All that can be heard is our labored breaths. "Fuck, I love you baby."

I melt into him. "I love you, halfback." He places a kiss on my forehead.

"Come on, let's clean up." He says, slowly easing out of me, but then we both freeze. "Uh, did you just squirt? Please tell me you squirted, and my dick didn't just break your placenta." The panic is clear in his tone. I turn and peer over my shoulder at him.

"Halfback, we need to go now. My water just broke."

Nine and a half hours of hard labor later, I'm standing here holding the most perfect little girl I have ever seen in my life. She's four weeks premature, but the doctors and nurses say she is perfectly healthy, but I don't believe those fuckers, they don't know shit. She should be inside her mother still, but… I'm selfish, and I'm fucking happy that she's here with me and not still hiding inside Leah.

She has a head full of black hair like me but the eyes, she has her mother's eyes. God, she is beautiful, and I'm…in love for the second time in my life. I never thought I would ever be able to love another person like I love my Goldie, but…I do, and I'm not ashamed to admit it. I now know what it means to feel my heart beating on the outside of my body. When she finally came out screaming, the doctor placed her on Leah's chest, and my heart blew the fuck up. It literally jumped out of my chest and nestled itself inside my daughter. That artery is no longer my own. It belongs to my little queen.

"Knock knock." I dart my eyes up to see my brothers. Corvin doesn't wait for Leah or me to respond when he sees his niece in my arms. He barrels straight over to me, with Becky, Crue, and Saint following after him. "Man, I get it, I do, but you have to share her for just a minute. I need to see my niece." I fight the urge to punch my best friend in the face when he takes my daughter from me. He turns his back and the guys begin to hover around him, blocking my baby from view so I have no choice but to peer through the gaps of their heads to make sure they hold her neck and head right. When I see her swaddle loosen, I try to reach over and tuck it in, but Saint smacks my hand away.

"Hey, asshole, that's my kid!" I bite out, and those fucking cocksuckers ignore me as they continue to talk to my daughter.

"Halfback?" I turn to Leah and frown. Katie, Val, and Alexa all stand there fighting back smiles, which earns them a glare from me. Leah pats the space beside her and quirks a brow. I look from her to my baby, who is being cooed at by those dicks, and I'm suddenly torn. Do I go to my wife or stay with my daughter in case she needs me? "Darius Cameron Lockhart, she is fine!" I grit my teeth and ignore the girls snickering at me as I drag my feet across the room to my wife and drop them down beside her. She smiles and places her hand on my leg. "She's fine." She tries to reassure me.

"You don't know that." I snap.

Leah narrows her eyes. "I just pushed a seven-pound baby out of my vagina, lose the attitude." I cringe and smile at her sheepishly.

"Yuck, never mention that again." Corvin scolds her as he hands my baby girl to Crue. A devilish smirk crosses my face, and then suddenly, Corvin doesn't look so smug. "Darius I am warning—."

"Santa emptying his sack into your sister gave us all an early Christmas present." Corvin shoots me a scathing look while the girls all giggle behind me.

"You're fucking lucky my niece is in the room, or I would break your fucking nose." Beckett snaps his head toward Corvin and glares.

"No one needs another broken bone, thank you, dick." Beck snaps, earning a laugh from all of us except Leah.

"I'm sorry, Becky." She mutters. He shoots her a wink and shrugs.

"I'm not. Now we have this beautiful angel because of it." He answers. I turn to my wife and nod, encouraging her to tell them.

"Becky?" She says just as Crue passes my baby to him. He turns to Leah and smiles proudly. You can see the love this big fucker has not only for her but my baby in his eyes, and I just know my girl made the right call.

"What's up, Lee?" He asks.

A whoosh of air escapes her, and she flicks her eyes to me. I smile at my girl and nod. She's too choked up to tell them so I do it for her. I stand and face my brothers four of them look at me with frowns. "Would you like to know her name?" The four of them share a look and then nod, but I can see the apprehension on each of their faces. "Beck." His face blanks as he stares at me. I can see he is waiting for me to say something stupid, but not this time.

"Yeah?" He answers.

"Meet your namesake, Becca." Tears gather in the big fuckers eyes as he stares at me, then he cuts a glance to Leah, who is crying. Val and the other two are all standing there with their hands covering their mouths with tears in their own eyes.

"You named her after...me?" He whispers, and Leah nods.

"You're my best friend, Becky. I love you and couldn't think of anyone better to name my baby after." Leah chokes out. Becks eats the space up between them in four strides, and he holds Becca close to his chest as he bends down and hugs Leah.

"I love you, Lee, and I promise I'll love her like she's my own." My heart fucking thumps inside my chest whens she pitched the idea to me a couple of hours ago. I didn't argue because I know how much Beck loves my wife and there is no one I would trust more with my daughter than him.

"What about us?" Crue whines with a pout. Saint throws his arm around his shoulders and pulls him in close.

"Clearly, we aren't the favorites," Saint mutters with fake sadness.

Crue bats his lashes at Saint, and I groan. "But I'm your favorite, right?"

Katie rolls her eyes at her husbands. "Excuse those idiots." She mutters.

I fight back my smile when I see Corv deflate. "Corvin?" He cuts his gaze to me and I smirk.

"He may be her best friend, but you're mine." His brows furrow. "Her full name is Becca Corvina True Lockhart. She is named after all of you, so don't fucking make me regret naming my daughter after you idiots."

I sit beside my wife and watch our family pass our daughter around, and I can't help but smile. I'm one lucky motherfucker.

"Hey, it's midnight," Alex announces.

"So?" Saint adds. She rolls her eyes, leans down, and places a kiss on Becca's head.

"Merry Christmas, beautiful girl." I balk at her. In the frenzy of everything and going after my wife and then her going into labor, I forgot all about it being Christmas. I turn to my Goldie and kiss her. She melts into me like she always does.

"Merry Christmas." She whispers against my lips.

"Thank you for giving me the best gift I've ever received, Goldie. Merry Christmas, baby." She smiles at me. "How long before I can slide inside your chimney and put another baby in you?" Laughter erupts from her, and I can't help but join her. "Merry fucking Christmas, you ugly fuckers. Now give me my baby and piss off home to your own kids."

Sitting here with my wife and daughter in my arms is the ending I never thought I would get. I never knew what love was until I met Leah, and now I can finally say I know what love at first sight feels like because I felt that tonight when I saw Becca. These are the most important people in my life.

I may be the halfback, but I scored the fucking touchdown and won the girls.

Thank you!

Holy shit, honest to G.O.D I never expected these books to go the way they did but fuck I'm not even mad about it! Darius and Leah are the best fucking thing since sliced bread, I can't even tell you how much I love these two!

Well, obviously thanks to that ending you know Becky is getting a book, duh! After that scene with him and Darius fucking Leah and how close he got to her I just knew he needed a book. I freaking hope you loved Darius and Leah as much as I do because I just may cry if you don't! I love how much of a bad bitch Leah is and refuses to cower away from Darius even when he is dick.

Thank you for taking a chance and reading *Offside* and *Touchdown*, these books hold a special place in my heart. I never thought I could ever pull off writing a sports romance let alone make it a bully but voila! Here we are and I couldn't be more grateful.

If you could leave a review on Amazon, Bookbub or Goodreads that would be freaking amazing!

SPORTS ROMANCE

Playing For Keeps

Duet

Offside

Touchdown

End Game

Hail Mary

MAFIA ROMANCE

Murdoch Mafia Series

Played By The Bishop

Tormented By The King

Tortured By The Knight

Tempted By The Queen

Turned By The Pawn

Ruined By The Rook

Fairytales With A Twist

Condemned Beast

RH SPORTS

Hate Us Like You Mean It

Love Me Like You Mean It

PARANORMAL ROMANCE

The Dream Series

The Dream Trilogy.

A Beautiful Dream

A Twisted Fate

A Beautiful Nightmare

Redemption

Anarchy

Brutal Savages

Savage Lies

Brutal Truth

Savage Beast

Brutal Beauty

Acknowledgments

Marcus, obviously had to put you in here because I need to thank you for allowing me to use your juicy dick as inspo for the sex scenes in these books! I'm still fucking salty you wouldn't let me bring another guy into the room to try out the three-way you party pooper, you're lucky you have an amazing dick or I would be rioting for you declining me about a threesome!

Leah, these books wouldn't be here without you babe so I can't thank you enough for allowing me to share your story! I'm so glad you never shot your shot or I wouldn't have been able to write these books xxx

Tash, Clare, and Sarah, my Beta/Alpha girls. I couldn't do this without you ladies so thank you from the bottom of my heart for pushing to always write daily and telling me when a bit in the book is shit lol I love you!

My ARC team, fuck you ladies are the light of my life man, I can't even put into words what you ladies mean to me. I never thought I would find a group that I could fit in with and yet here we are, you ladies are fucking amazing, and thank you for loving each of these and the characters as much as I do.

Lizz, oh my God, thank you so fucking much for everything you have done on these books! You make them all perfect and pretty and I can't thank you enough, I freaking love you.

My babies, thank you for being you and allowing me to hide away and work nonstop so I can get these books out. You are

both my driving force and I love you more than words can
express. Xxx
Last but not least, my amazing readers,
Thank you from the bottom of my cold dead-ass heart for loving
all these books and taking a chance on me. Your support and
love is the reason why I get to live out my dream of being an
author, I appreciate each and every one of you.
I love you.

Sam
Xxxx

About the Author

Samantha Barrett is a dark romance, PNR author who loves to write out-of-the-box stories. She is originally from the land of the long white cloud, New Zealand. She is totally fluking her way through this whole author gig, if she isn't writing you can find her kicking back with her kids and husband with a bag of chips and a glass of wine in her hand.
Sam loves Twilight and is a TWIHARD proudly.